Also by J. H. Sanderson

The Roadhouse Sons Series

Dangerous Gambles
Renegade
Cold Front

Other Titles

Shadows Present, Shadows Past: A Ghost Story

CODE NAME: WANDERER

J. H. SANDERSON

ISBN: 978-1-4834-5535-8 (sc)
ISBN: 978-1-4834-5534-1 (e)

Library of Congress Control Number: 2016912346

Lulu Publishing Services rev. date: 07/26/2016

To

Klaus Renft, dissident musician and bane of the Stasi;

Percival A. "Al" Friend, the epitome of wrestling managers;

Plasse Dennis Bradford Conway, a.k.a. Tiger Conway Sr.,

a true gentleman and a Worker; and

Bob Leonard, preeminent wrestling photographer

and dean of Canadian wrestling history.

Music Foreword

While I was still at school, all I really wanted to be was a musician, so imagine my surprise when I left school and three months later I was off on the road with my first professional band. Over the next few decades, I played pretty much every size and type of venue (I forget how many), ranging from the very smallest pubs to large arenas and everything in between.

Throughout these halcyon years, I'd been signed to major labels, indie labels, and no labels at all, playing sessions on albums ranging from black metal to new age to cover bands like the Roadhouse Sons, and generally having a great time doing it.

More recently, a huge highlight for me was being invited to narrate *Dangerous Gambles* by J. H. Sanderson. When I first read the book, I suspected that J. H. must have been secretly following me around, as he had so perfectly captured the essence and camaraderie of the touring bands I've been involved with. The highs and lows—yep, they were all there—along with the arguments and disputes with management (yep!). But perhaps most important was the way J. H. flawlessly captured the heart and soul and unspoken loyalty that dominate life on the road. By the time I had finished the book, I had picked up traits from nearly all the characters, and my own observational skills had considerably improved.

The process of narrating a book brings you ever closer to the story, so this was a dream job for me, as I instantly identified with the characters as if I'd known them for years. I could sense their empathy, anger, frustration, and elation through every chapter and every twist and turn in the fascinating story lines. When you share the same proximity 24-7 with four musicians over extended periods of time, you get to know one another pretty well, and J. H. Sanderson really understands this. Narrating *Dangerous Gambles* was, at times, almost like a trip down memory lane, as it evoked many of the same emotions I had felt so long ago. They were great times, and although on occasion it may have felt like it was the band against the world, I wouldn't have swapped it for anything. This was a fantastic opportunity for me to relive my youth through the vehicle of the Roadhouse Sons, and (note to J. H.) if Cameron is ever looking for another band member, please tell him to call me and I'll be there.

As the series continues with *Renegade* and the Roadhouse Sons' confrontations with punk band Boney Jack, then through *Cold Front* as the Roadhouse Sons' work in espionage threatens them even further in J. H.'s edge-of-your-seat fashion, I don't want to spoil your journey by revealing too much. I will tell you that J. H.'s fourth installment, *Code Name: Wanderer*, is stunning and thrilling.

I would like to take this opportunity to thank J. H. Sanderson for writing such great books! I can't tell you how chuffed (stoked) I am to be a part of it all.

—Trevor Sewell

Described by Stuart Epps (Led Zeppelin, Elton John) as a brilliant musician with a fresh approach to the blues, Trevor Sewell is a Hollywood Music in Media, IBBA, and IMP Award–winning guitarist He has garnered a prestigious British Blues Award, fresh nominations in Hollywood, and two number-one albums on the UK and American blues charts.

Espionage Foreword

by "Cowboy" Bill White, US Army (ret.)

I would like to recognize, acknowledge and thank all the people from all parts of Berlin, Germany that made the missions that were tried and resulted in saving so many of the friends and family of those in East Berlin and transporting them to safety. You can also thank all of the men and women who lost lives trying.

There were American, British and French soldiers involved along with a lot of Berliners that this book takes notice of. This book is inspired by true stories as told to the author and as researched by him.

By the time you finish this book, you will read and have some good insight about what went on in Berlin as the Wall went up and in the years after. Please note that there are many important and vital concepts that you are about to read in this book. This is done so that people will see and read and understand how hard life was 110 miles behind the Iron Curtain with only square miles of freedom available and how hard it was to obtain this freedom. I hope you will come away with feelings of the men and women who attempted these things deserved that freedom.

I promise that you will not look at Berlin, Germany the same way again.

[Author's Note: While in the Army, Bill White was stationed in Berlin, serving there during the early days of the Berlin Wall. His account of being on a reconnaissance mission in the Eastern sector while the East German NVA were constructing it helped provide inspiration for some of the adventures of the Roadhouse Sons in this book. Bill was also in one of the armored personnel carriers involved in the standoff with Soviet tanks at Checkpoint Charlie. Following his tour of duty in the Army, Bill became a professional wrestler and embarked upon a career that took him to every wrestling 'territory' in the United States, and saw him work with such talent as Chief Jay Strongbow, Jimmy Valiant, Mr. Fuji, "Dr. Death" Steve Williams and Greg Gagne, just to name a few. Bill White retired from wrestling in 1987. He was honored by the Cauliflower Alley Club in 2006.]

Preface

The title of this novel, *Code Name: Wanderer*, comes from the name given to the operation by the East German secret police to monitor the rock-and-roll counterculture. While this had been going on for many years, it became especially prevalent in the 1980s. This was to be expected for the same reason the Nazi regime hated the swing movement; any totalitarian system is diametrically opposed to anything that speaks to the essence of the human spirit, which music is designed to do.

Rock and roll gives voice to the angst and frustrations that disenfranchised people feel, and it is only too easy for this release to turn into political statements. This was made clear by the East German Ministry of Culture, which told the Klaus Renft Combo that it "no longer existed." While this might have satisfied the East German bureaucratic mentality, it was ultimately futile. Though suppressed for many years, in 1990, long after East Germany and its bureaucracy had ceased to exist, the Klaus Renft Combo returned to the enjoyment of their many fans, who were waiting for the Berlin Wall to come down.

It is the unspoken theme of this book to demonstrate how the human spirit can persevere against monoliths like totalitarianism, prejudice, and suspicion. In this book, the character Doug Courtland overcomes the prejudices he has faced because of his lack of education by participating in a program then known as Jobs for Delaware's Graduates. This was a real program and is now known as Jobs for America's Graduates. It was designed to assist at-risk students to not only stay in school but also learn the leadership skills they need to succeed both academically and personally. It does not simply tell students that they have an inherent dignity and value; it helps them to discover this reality for themselves and take ownership of it. Initially started as a program in one high school in Delaware, limited to high school seniors, it is now found in thirty-two states with more than one thousand program affiliates. It is no longer limited to high school grades; it also works in some middle schools and serves the needs of adult education as well.

Another unspoken theme in this book is the means by which the human spirit is able to persevere, and that is by the bond it forms with others. The Roadhouse Sons had a bond that years of traveling and performing together can give. They may not have seen one another in years, but once they pick up their instruments and start playing, it all comes back. Doug and his wrestling background demonstrate a similar bond. Like musicians, professional wrestlers find themselves in a world that separates them from other people but forges a fellowship with those who belong to that unique reality. This fellowship is what Stoughton plays to with Doug Courtland, and it is by virtue of this fellowship that Doug is able to assist the Roadhouse Sons in their mission. The organization that Stoughton makes reference to, the Cauliflower Alley Club, is a real organization.

Founded in 1965 by "Iron Mike" Mazurki, a professional wrestler and actor, the Cauliflower Alley Club is a fellowship of professional wrestlers, boxers, stuntmen, martial artists, and actors. I have the distinct honor of being a life member of the CAC, as well as having served on its board of directors. But mostly I have the pleasure of having made so many friends through this organization, including Tiger Conway Sr., whose smile was always the first thing you saw; his son, Tiger Conway Jr.; and the legendary Vachon family of Montreal, Maurice "Mad Dog" Vachon, Paul "Butcher" Vachon, and Luna Vachon, all of whom I can list among my dearest and closest friends.

These wrestling friends, whose company I have always so enjoyed, and a few historic persons are the only actual people mentioned in this book. All the characters featured here are entirely fictional, and any resemblance to people, living or dead, is purely coincidental.

Acknowledgments

I would like to thank all who made this book possible. All of you who uttered words of encouragement were a sounding board for ideas and scenarios and were the unintended inspiration for characters and plotlines.

I would also like to thank all those who got me into the crazy world of professional wrestling, where things were wildly crazy for the eleven years I was in the ring—and have been almost as crazy since I got out of it! I had initially wanted to have these protagonists be professional wrestlers; however, I am of the old school and could not bring myself to break "kayfabe," as we call it. Therefore, the spandexes were passed to an '80s rock band, and I hope my fellow workers agree that "they" have worn them proudly. And yet, despite the similarities between cover bands and the world of independent wrestling, I could not bring myself to totally ignore the contributions I have received from wrestling, especially when one of my wrestling brothers, Cowboy Bill White, so graciously shared stories of Cold War Berlin with me, helping inspire some of the Roadhouse Sons' latest escapades.

I would like to thank Greg Oliver and Pat Laprade for allowing me access to their vast knowledge of Canadian wrestling history and providing me with the small details that help uncover the double agent.

I would also like to thank my long-suffering editor and publicist, Mia Moravis, for motivating me to take off the training wheels and take more control of my writing.

Last, but not least, I would like to thank two authors I have never met for their help in fleshing out characters and situations that appear in this book. The first is Anna Funder, whose book *Stasiland* provided me with a fascinating understanding of the daily life of the average East German dealing with such an authoritarian system, as well as the aftereffects of trying to integrate into the West, and what is required to survive in each. The other author is Markus Wolf, former head of East Germany's Hauptverwaltung Aufklärung, or Main Directorate for Reconnaissance, which was the foreign intelligence division of the Stasi. His mildly self-serving autobiography, *Man Without a Face*, gave a detailed insight into the procedures and mind-set of the Stasi and its agents that helped me realize some of my story lines might not be as far-fetched as I had thought.

Chapter 1

"Sunglasses at Night"

Cameron Walsh could not believe what he had just heard, least of all from the person who'd said it. "You want me to do *what*?"

"I'm suggesting putting the band back together," replied Special Agent Barbara McIntyre.

"Come on, Barbara. Admit it," he coaxed. "You've been watching *The Blues Brothers* again, haven't you? Well then, I think you'd better stick to the movie, because this is real life, and it simply does not work that way."

Despite his veneer of confidence, Cameron doubted that she would agree. Barbara McIntyre was a woman who had risen to her position through hard work and serious dedication. She not only would never take no for an answer but also did not waste time and energy on idle speculations or frivolous concepts. Her ideas were always clearly thought out before she ever voiced them to anyone. Cameron instinctively knew that this time would be no exception.

What he did not take into account, however, was the fact that she was also a sharp realist and knew that her proposal would not be without its challenges, least of all from the very ones she would be approaching. That was why she proceeded cautiously; she realized that she would be dealing with not only a fellow agent but also one with an artistic temperament.

Special Agent Cameron Walsh was not the stereotypical FBI

agent. He was found most often wearing a T-shirt, blue jeans, and a pair of battered but comfortable sneakers. His unruly hairstyle and facial hair were often just ever so slightly longer than regulations permitted. Being his only visible expression of rebellion, it was tolerated by his superiors, of whom McIntyre was one. This was because when the situation demanded it, Cameron would transition into the required suit and tie, with carefully styled hair, trimmed mustache, and no voiced protests.

Cameron Walsh had come a long way since being recruited as an asset six years ago. At the time, he had been the lead vocalist, guitarist, and front man for the Roadhouse Sons, a rock-and-roll cover band that traveled the Northeast region of the United States. By providing covers for the more famous and, therefore, more expensive bands of the day, the Roadhouse Sons had gained regional popularity in the early years of the Third World War. This popularity was why the bureau recruited them to monitor the burgeoning bootlegging and war-profiteering rackets on the club circuit. Inadvertently, the Roadhouse Sons had shown themselves to be more valuable than mere informants. They proved their skills in a variety of situations, finally resulting in Cameron, along with Evan Dixon, the band's former drummer, formally joining the bureau.

After the breakup of the Roadhouse Sons four years ago, Cameron's previous involvement as an asset facilitated his acceptance by the law enforcement agency into its ranks. However, despite that experience, there were still many areas in which he was required to become proficient. As a result, in counterbalance to his truncated enrollment, an intensive field-training program was developed for him with a variety of departments. On completion of this program, he was assigned to establish a light and sound company. This company was a front that provided the FBI with opportunities for both counterintelligence and surveillance monitoring of illegal activities by affording them access to a variety of situations without arousing suspicion.

This aspect of his work kept Cameron quite busy. Therefore, any musical pursuits he might have engaged in were limited to simple jams with friends or being asked to sit in with local musicians and visiting notables at local venues, all of which significantly decreased over time. Now all that seemed about to change.

"Okay, I will admit that I can't help but think of you guys whenever I watch that movie," McIntyre conceded, holding up her hands in mock surrender. "But it was only when I was asked to sit in on a developing situation that I began thinking seriously about this and wondered if life couldn't possibly imitate art. I even discovered some information that I think you might be interested in."

"I should hope so. You show up here with Evan on my first day off in weeks, and you want me to do something I haven't done in four years? Whatever it is, it had better be pretty damned interesting."

"Have I ever steered you wrong … yet?" She smiled.

Sipping his drink, Cameron held up his right hand and wiggled it, the unspoken reminder of traumatic injuries sustained in an investigation that spelled the end of his career as a musician and the beginning of his career as an agent.

"I am reminded of you every time it rains," he said quietly.

McIntyre shook her head, the jovial expression now long gone. "I didn't mean to sound callous. I'm … I'm sorry."

Cameron shrugged as he thought back to that night four years ago. In a dank basement near Seattle, there was the crashing blow of a large, greasy monkey wrench wielded during interrogation by a Russian spy. That night had vastly altered the course of his life.

"I wouldn't worry about it too much if I were you," he sighed. "It did heal … eventually. And I can play again, even if not quite as good as before, so I guess it all works out, doesn't it?"

"One can only hope." McIntyre smiled.

Her awkward tone indicated that she was still embarrassed, and Cameron felt bad for a moment. In an effort to reverse the gloomy atmosphere that was now forming among them, Cameron turned his attention to his former drummer. "You've been pretty quiet, Evan, old man. Don't tell me you've been let in on this before I have."

"Not one bit of it," Evan replied. "But just between you and me, it would be a bad idea to play poker with her. She keeps things way too close to her vest and can have the ultimate poker face when she wants to. Apparently, she wanted to with this."

Though he laughed, Cameron was aware of the tension in his voice and body language. *He's as edgy as I am*, he thought. With an exaggerated sigh, Cameron leaned back in his easy chair and gave an expansive wave of his arms. "Very well then, my dear," he said with a wry smile. "You now have a completely captive audience. Do, please, proceed."

"All right then," McIntyre began. "What would you say if I suggested that you not only get the band back together but also go on tour?"

Cameron sipped his drink and studied her over the rim of his glass. McIntyre could tell by his expression that he was intrigued but also guarded. Finally, he nodded.

"I'd say I'd be interested to hear your reason for that. But I want it understood that my interest in no way implies acceptance of any proposal or section thereof."

"Ditto," echoed Evan.

"Agreed." McIntyre nodded. "But I think you guys might change your minds once you hear it."

Cameron cast a glance at Evan, who shrugged. "Don't look at me. I already told you I'm as much in the dark as you are. She's already said more to both of us together than she's said to me alone."

"Really? Then things *are* getting a bit interesting. I can't wait to hear the rest of it. Please proceed. I'm aquiver with anticipation."

"You'll never hear it if you don't stop interrupting," McIntyre warned. "Now then, I suppose I don't need to remind you that even though the UN cease-fire has been in effect since the end of last year, things are still quite tenuous between the US and the USSR."

Cameron nodded. The United States currently enjoyed a hard-won, though possibly temporary, respite. The war, which began in 1978 with the Soviet invasion of Alaska, had seemed to turn against the allies with the death of Marshall Tito in the spring of 1980. Yugoslavia, though still officially nonaligned, had been an anchor for NATO in applying pressure to the Warsaw Pact in the Balkans by being the constant potential for a new front for NATO. Tito's refusal to come out on any side kept a large number of Warsaw Pact forces on alert in that region, preventing them from shoring up stalled advances elsewhere or suppressing unrest in Communist countries.

However, with the Yugoslav leader's death, there was no clear indication that the country would survive the ethnic divisions and tensions Tito's force of will had contained. Despite this concern, American and NATO forces launched a massive counteroffensive, and events had begun to turn in favor of the United States and her NATO allies shortly before the presidential election in 1980. The Carter administration had hoped to build on these successes as well as the traditional reluctance of the American public to change administrations during wartime to ensure reelection. Not surprisingly, the American people chose the bold and defiant image of Ronald Reagan on a horse, leading the charge of modern-day Rough Riders against the forces of Communism, over the cautious and dedicated Jimmy Carter.

As inspiring as this change was, many feared that changing not only an administration but also an entire party in the middle of a war would be a recipe for disaster. Indeed, some turmoil within the NATO alliance did occur. In response to these global concerns, Reagan was enthusiastically supported by the recently elected prime minister of Great Britain, Margaret Thatcher. Between these two decisive leaders, the momentum of the counteroffensive continued, and by 1981, NATO had driven the Soviets out of North America, recaptured Vienna, and halted Soviet efforts to open a new front in the Middle East.

The Soviets, now forced to contend with supporting their Warsaw Pact allies against internal resistance movements, as well as becoming increasingly bogged down in Afghanistan, were unable to capitalize on the forces now freed by Yugoslavia's turmoil. These commitments meant the Soviets had no reserves to commit to recapturing the Alaskan front, and no serious counteroffensive was launched. The confidence of the American people was buoyed by these events, a confidence shaken by the attempted assassination of Reagan in 1981.

Immediately following this, forces on both sides of the conflict went on high alert. Tensions relaxed only slightly in the days that followed when it was determined that a lone gunman, motivated by personal reasons rather than as an agent of a foreign government, was behind the shooting.

Ironically, the event that gave the American and European public the most hope for peace gave their military and political leaders the most cause for concern and kept the unspoken reality of a nuclear strike alive. That event was the death of Soviet leader Leonid Brezhnev in 1982.

The average person saw this as a hopeful opportunity for new leadership and a chance for peace. However, military and intelligence sources knew that for the past two years—and possibly longer—Brezhnev had been essentially a Kremlin figurehead, with directions to the Politburo and military coming from KGB director Yuri Andropov.

When Andropov succeeded Brezhnev, it was assumed that the man who so fearful of any challenge to the Soviet system that he had insisted on the invasion of Hungary in 1958 and the crushing of the Prague uprising ten years later would not demonstrate any restraint in facing Russia's archenemy. These fears seemed to be confirmed when the Soviets downed Korean Air Flight KAL-007, carrying noted anti-Communist representative Larry McDonald, and walked away from the peace talks the following month. Military forces around the world braced for the worst. Yet they were in for a surprise.

Western intelligence agencies were never aware of the full extent of Andropov's failing health or the degree of his obsessive paranoia regarding the potential collapse of Communist governments. These factors prevented him from prosecuting the war as NATO had anticipated. Instead of launching counteroffensives or opening new fronts, resources were pulled from active military efforts to help support troubled regimes. As a result, all previous gains the Soviets had acquired were now sacrificed, with no clear indication they would ever be recovered. Andropov's failing health became rapidly worse, and he died a mere fifteen months after coming to power.

In a strange twist of fate, it was Andropov's rival and successor, the known hard-liner Konstantin Chernenko, who provided the respite for the world. Originally considered the successor to Brezhnev, it was initially feared that Chernenko would return the USSR to the hard-line Brezhnev-era policies. When the world witnessed his near inability to deliver the eulogy at Andropov's funeral, many feared this display of dotage would lead to a power struggle before he was even dead, with control of the Kremlin and military to be fought over by the ossifying members of the Soviet leadership. Yet, it was soon apparent that while Chernenko was, publicly, the leader of the Communist world, behind the scenes a more moderate hand was controlling things.

Hard-line Russian negotiators in Geneva were replaced by ones more receptive to a UN-brokered cease-fire, and the Kremlin confirmed East Germany's previous declaration of West Berlin as an "open city" and ordered captured military personnel and political leaders paroled back to the West. East German NVA forces were withdrawn to prewar East German territory. Warsaw Pact forces remained within the confines of Eastern Europe, though still stationed on the western borders of member countries. Everyone knew that even the slightest misstep anywhere could alter this delicate balance.

"Tenuous is a very cautious description," Cameron noted.

"Cautious but accurate," McIntyre replied. "I assume you are also aware of the UN's cultural exchange program."

Evan nodded enthusiastically. "I certainly am," he enthused. "My wife and I watched one of the dance troupes on TV a few weeks ago. They were quite impressive."

"Well, there are many who think it would be nice to include a little more American culture in this exchange," McIntyre continued.

Cameron eyed her suspiciously. "I thought there were American and allied programs involved in all of that," he said.

"There are," she assured him. "However, it has been discussed that perhaps including something a bit more contemporary would be nice."

"Why do I not like where this conversation is heading?" Cameron grumbled.

"Now, Cameron, you should at least wait for me to tell you what I was thinking before you get all upset about it." She smiled innocently.

He gave her a dirty look. "I don't think I need to wait."

McIntyre ignored him and continued. "Did you know that American bands from the seventies are having quite a surge in popularity in Europe? This is especially true in Eastern Europe where they are only just now getting heard."

"Congratulations to them." Cameron closed his eyes.

"Congratulations to *you*, you mean. The Roadhouse Sons are quite popular in East Germany from what I understand."

"I am thrilled. Perhaps we can talk with Herr Honecker about artist's royalties then?"

"You're probably better off not. If you got paid at all, you'd be paid in East German marks, which are absolutely worthless outside of East Germany and worth precious little inside it. No, I am thinking of something a bit more *tangible*, shall we say."

"No, we shall not say because some things are better left unsaid," Cameron replied.

"Why not?" McIntyre, as usual, was not about to take no for an answer.

Cameron opened one eye and saw what he had expected to see: McIntyre watching him with a look of pure innocence.

Now I know she's up to something. "Because I'm beginning to think you are proposing an adventure," Cameron muttered.

"And what, may I ask, is wrong with an adventure?" McIntyre demanded.

"To quote one Mr. B. Baggins, 'Adventures are nasty, bothersome affairs that make one late for dinner,' and I require regular and wholesome nutrition. Therefore, no adventures."

"I'm certain that if I opened that refrigerator, I would not find a single bit of solid food," McIntyre countered. Cameron shook his head.

"Liquid diets are perfectly acceptable for one of my delicate constitution."

"Old Mother Hubbard would feel lucky if she looked in your cupboards," McIntyre replied, not surrendering her position.

Cameron shrugged. "Well, what can I do about that? The mice are fussy and the cockroaches are on a complete vegetable diet, so there's no point in stocking the shelves."

"Besides, while they still put celery, olives, and cocktail onions in the drinks, Cameron will never starve," Evan chimed in.

"And don't forget all of the protein from the peanuts and the starch from the popcorn. See, I do just fine. A well-balanced diet."

"How do you figure that?" McIntyre was becoming irritable again.

"He most likely means he has a drink in both hands," replied Evan.

McIntyre, now losing patience, stared at them icily.

Cameron, realizing he had carried the joke almost too far, smiled and repositioned himself in the chair. "Okay then, let's hear it. What new intrigue have you got planned?"

"I thought it would be a good career move for you if you got the band back together and went on tour."

Cameron raised an eyebrow. "You said that before. However, I think you've forgotten that both Evan and I have different careers now," he reminded her.

"That's why you folks were the first ones we thought of." Her sweet smile confirmed Cameron's suspicions.

"Who, exactly, is *we*?" he asked.

"I don't think you really want me to go into that just yet," McIntyre confirmed coyly. "And, even if you *did*, there isn't any way that I *could*."

"That was what I was afraid of," Cameron replied. "Can you at least tell me, exactly, what it is you have proposed?"

"No, not entirely, I'm afraid."

"That was also what I was afraid of," he sighed. "Very well then, carry on. As best you can at least."

"As I was saying, American music and styles are becoming quite sought after in Eastern Europe with the relaxing of restrictions. Things no longer in demand here are having a unique renaissance there. That includes the Roadhouse Sons."

Cameron held up a finger to indicate a pause. "Okay, that is one thing I want to know," he said suspiciously. "Exactly how did we even become *known* there? We were barely known here, even with our work with the USO."

"Are you forgetting your albums?" she asked with a smile.

Evan emerged from his silence again to interrupt. "You can't expect us to believe that had anything to do with it," he declared. "I mean let's face it, they weren't exactly chart toppers here!"

"And, ironically, I believe that has everything to do with it." McIntyre smiled. "You were a cover band; people hired you in place of the bigger, headlining bands because of wartime expenses. True?"

"True," Evan agreed.

"Well, that was also the reason you got recorded and people wanted your records ... because they were cheaper."

Cameron eyed her suspiciously. "To the best of my knowledge, we only have a handful of records," he declared.

"Correct," said McIntyre. "About seven, I believe."

"None of which have been produced since 1981," Cameron continued.

"That, too, is correct," she answered.

"None of which were sold outside of the US," he informed her.

"None of which were sold outside of the US with your *consent*," she corrected him. "However, some of your records did make it over there, and you do have a bit of a following, especially behind the Berlin Wall."

"But we were just a *cover band*," Cameron insisted impatiently.

"That's the reason you're so popular. To their way of thinking, you are resisting the bigger bands and labels by doing things smaller and on your own. People see you as a type of protest against authority, in a sense, while the government sees you as a stand against capitalism."

"But each song we ever played was always properly licensed," Cameron exclaimed.

"That doesn't matter ..." McIntyre began before Cameron interrupted her.

"That, my dear Barbara, was the wrong thing to say, and I was the wrong person to say it to," he snapped. "I might carry a gun and shield now, but I am still a musician and still respect my peers and will not be accused of condoning any pirating or bootlegging of their intellectual property!"

"No one is accusing you of that," she assured him. "The fact that your fans in Eastern Europe don't understand that whole principle isn't your fault."

"True," Cameron conceded reluctantly.

"And should anyone say anything, we can point out that we are in the same boat the bigger bands we covered are in," said Evan, laughing.

"Just what do you mean by that?" Cameron scowled, not appreciative of his colleague's abstract way of thinking.

"*We're* not getting royalties either!" The thought caused Evan to laugh even harder.

"Hardly a consolation," grumbled Cameron. "Okay, let's have it. You've been dancing around what you've been wanting to say, so let's hear it."

"Like I said," McIntyre explained once again, "I think it would be a good career move for you to put the band back together and go on tour. Specifically, a European tour."

"Like *I* said, I already have a career and it *isn't* behind a mic anymore."

McIntyre was not so easily put off. "This might be a way to enjoy both." She smiled.

"In which case, I will likely enjoy neither," he countered. "Now, you've talked about the music part enough. What I need you to tell me is why that would be considered."

"Obviously, going into any full disclosure is not going to be possible outside of a more secure location and without other elements to be involved with the planning present. However, I can tell you this much. There is someone behind the Iron Curtain who would like very much to come to the West."

"You have described everyone but Mr. and Mrs. Chernenko. And I think that, given the opportunity, even she might leave! What does any of this have to do with us?"

"The individual in question is a big fan of American rock bands and apparently you in particular."

"Exactly why is he a fan of ours, may I ask?"

"You certainly may." McIntyre smiled. "That is, once you've helped him escape to the West."

Cameron sat upright. "Okay, I knew I wouldn't like this conversation," he shouted. "You want us to smuggle someone out of Eastern Europe while on tour there? Barbara, for God's sake, if you hate me that much, demote me or fire me or, better yet, shoot me yourself! There are a lot less complicated ways of getting rid of me than that."

"No one wants to get rid of you, I assure you of that. You are very good at what you do, and it just so happens that *that* is the reason you were even considered in the first place. You do your job well, and you've performed well under similar circumstances."

"Similar circumstances? In the first place, I have no recollection whatsoever of helping someone through the Iron Curtain, and secondly, if I really do perform my duties well, I'd like to keep doing them. Which I can't if I am in a Russian gulag, or worse."

Then he turned his attention to Evan.

"Did you know anything about this before you came over?"

The former drummer shook his head. "Like I told you already, this is the first I've heard of it."

"Very well then, do you have any opinion on it?" Cameron asked.

Evan nodded. "Oh yes, I certainly do. I have a lot of opinions on this. However, I'm going to keep them to myself until I've heard a bit more."

Cameron glared at the two of them and leaned back in his chair, staring at the ceiling. He said nothing, but they discerned from the way his foot bounced slightly, as well as how he swirled the remainder of his drink, that he was thinking about what they had said.

"Okay then, please tell me what you can," he muttered.

"I'm afraid that isn't a lot just yet as I'm sure you'll appreciate," McIntyre explained. "However, the gist of it is this: there is a highly positioned person in the Soviet government who wishes to defect. This person can offer intelligence insights that would be invaluable to us."

"Sounds too good to be true," Cameron mumbled. "And I don't need to remind you what they say about that, do I? If it sounds too good to be true, it usually is!"

"Do you think we're new at this? That is the first thing that everyone thought of," McIntyre assured him. "That was the first thing I said, the director said, and all of our friends in the agency said."

"And?" asked Evan.

"And we have all examined it very closely and have every reason to believe the offer is genuine. Apparently, he was someone who, at one point at least, was a KGB golden boy but has now suffered severe damage to his image and reputation and has every reason to fear for his life."

"It still sounds like a potential setup to me," Cameron replied.

"I've got to agree with Cameron on that," Evan concurred. "That whole thing could be a highly tempting dangle."

Cameron nodded enthusiastically.

"I'm not going to lie to you; that idea is not far removed from anyone's mind," McIntyre assured them. "I don't suppose either of you are familiar with the name Yury Nosenko, are you?" They both shook their heads.

"Nosenko was a KGB defector from their office in Geneva back in 1962. He, likewise, seemed too good to be true, and they treated him accordingly."

"How, exactly?" Cameron asked.

McIntyre shook her head. "It was pretty rough. I'm not sure of all of it, but I know he had been kept in solitary confinement by the CIA from around 1964 to 1967 while they tried to determine if he was genuine or not."

"That long," Cameron exclaimed. "I don't expect he was in the penthouse suite all that time?"

"Like I said, I'm not one hundred percent certain on all of the details. I do know that the CIA counterintelligence director got called on the carpet for it."

"To put it mildly, I can imagine," Cameron said. "All right then, let me ask you this. That Nosenko fellow, was he genuine?"

"Between you and me, the jury is still out on that."

"And they want to run the risk of that again," exclaimed Evan.

"The circumstances are a bit different this time," McIntyre replied.

"Different enough that they want us to take the potential wrap for it," Cameron grumbled.

"Different enough that we think he might be the keys to the kingdom," McIntyre corrected.

"Or he might be the Trojan horse," grumbled Cameron.

"If it is any consolation, every argument that you have brought up with me has been brought up already," she said. "I even raised some of those arguments."

"And that didn't faze anyone?" Cameron demanded.

"It fazed everyone," she explained calmly. "However, the potential reward is equal to the risk."

Cameron shook his head, unconvinced. A quick glance over to Evan showed that he, too, had serious doubts.

"Guys, I don't need to tell you what is at stake here," she sighed. "In the last year or so, there has been a shift in Soviet policy, a drastic shift, and we are trying to find out exactly why. You don't simply go from attempting to conquer the free world to accepting a brokered cease-fire almost overnight without a reason."

"Maybe they didn't have the stomach for it," Cameron replied derisively.

"You are talking about a country that took the brunt of Hitler's military actions during the Second World War and managed to grab half of Europe when they fought back. The Russians haven't experienced anywhere near that devastation this time around."

"So what are you suggesting?" interjected Evan, hoping to keep things from escalating.

"One possibility is that this is a genuine desire for peace," she explained.

"And the other possibility?" Cameron asked. He felt his stomach tighten as he did so.

"The other possibility is that this is all just a ploy and they're framing a plan for regrouping, or worse," she replied.

Cameron knew what she was referring to. It was the one unplayed card in the entire game: nuclear weapons. Thus far they had not been used by either side. However, the whole world knew that they were available.

"One nuclear bomb can mess up your whole day," murmured Cameron.

No one laughed. No one said anything. Thoughts and images that no one dared have began to fill his mind. Cameron felt the tension build as the silence grew longer. He needed sound to break that grip of fear—a noise, any noise would do. He waited, but no one spoke. At last he could bear it no longer and broke the silence himself.

"Okay, what is it that we are expected to do?" Even though it was his own voice, the sudden sound made him flinch.

"The first step is to get the band back together," McIntyre explained. "Once you do that, we brief you further."

Inwardly, Cameron lamented the fact that dialogue in no way dispelled the anxiety he felt. Instead it increased it.

"And, let me guess, we're not allowed to say anything about this to any of the guys when we talk to them. Is that correct?" Cameron sighed.

"Do I really need to answer that?"

"I hate you; you know that, don't you?" he muttered. Then he turned to Evan. "So I guess that means we need to decide a couple of things."

"Are we going to do it, you mean?" the former drummer asked.

"That's one thing," Cameron agreed. "Are we in?"

"I think an awful lot is riding on our decision," Evan observed.

Cameron nodded. "I was thinking the same thing, but I don't see how refusing is going to make that much difference."

"No positive difference," Evan agreed. "They'll try to put together another team."

"Made out of whole cloth," Cameron added. "And a team that does not have either reputation or credibility, at least not musically."

"And would probably raise enough suspicions with their target demographic that someone would point that out, potentially risking the entire operation," Evan observed.

"And make an extremely delicate operation a potential incident," Cameron pointed out.

The silence that followed provided the unspoken fear that everyone shared.

"I don't think I need to point out that every concern you just mentioned about an alternative effort is equally as applicable to you as well," McIntyre explained quietly.

"No, you don't," Evan said calmly.

"So we could either help score a major coup or finally push the button," Cameron said, finishing his drink.

"That is an accurate summation," McIntyre agreed.

"Then that just leaves Evan and me to determine one last detail."

"What the hell could that be?" Evan demanded.

"Which one of us is going to be Jake, and which one of us is going to be Elwood?"

Chapter 2

"Hello, Again"

Cameron parked his car across the street from the apartment building and scanned it to get an idea of which one was Rich Webster's.

Downstairs, first building, a corner apartment, he observed, double-checking the address on the last letter he had received from his friend.

The apartment complex was small by Mesa, Arizona, standards, and the neighborhood was a quiet one. Pioneer Park, with its shady palms, was located directly across the street to the east, and the Mormon Temple and its manicured grounds were directly across the street to the south. Cameron surveyed the cars parked immediately in front of that section of apartments, but nothing appeared to be any kind of a vehicle Rich would drive.

Maybe he's not driving anything.

Cameron gave a rap on the door, which was quickly opened by a very angry young woman.

"What do you want? I told you, you'd get the rent payment as soon as I had it, didn't I?"

"I think you've got ..." Cameron began, but was loudly interrupted.

"You've got a lot of nerve coming here like this! This is harassment, I'll have you know, and don't think I won't report you because I will!"

"Uh, is Rich here?" Cameron blurted out. He had hoped that by mentioning his friend's name, he might have the chance to explain to her that he was not there as a bill collector, but it was to no avail.

"Oh, you can't get anywhere with a dumb woman, so you've got to talk to the man of the house, is that it?"

Cameron sighed and tried to keep his patience. "No, that's not it," he insisted. "I'm here to see Rich Webster. Is he here or isn't he?"

"What if he is; what if he isn't?"

"This was the last address I had for him, and I was hoping to look him up. Now is he here or isn't he?"

"Does he owe you money, too?"

"No," Cameron replied. He tried to keep his answers calm but was getting increasingly irritated.

"Okay then, I suppose that you owe *him* money."

"If I do or not, that is none of your business," Cameron snapped. "Now answer my question. Is Rich Webster here or not?"

"Yes, I'm here" came an irritated voice from the back of the apartment. Cameron looked past the woman to see someone shuffling down the small hallway to the living room. Judging from his tousled hair and dull expression, Cameron assumed that Rich had been sleeping.

Or maybe trying to?

"What the hell is going on out here?" Rich rubbed his eyes as he stumbled into the living room, oblivious to who was at the door.

Rich Webster had been Cameron's closest friend in college. Together, they had formed the band El Dorado and, when that broke up, the Roadhouse Sons. Back then, Rich was known for having a darker, more exotic look, consisting of long, black hair and a Fu Manchu mustache. With his stoic personality, combined with dark denims, dark shirts, and motorcycle boots, he had given the perception of a rock star back when they were touring. Now his appearance was somewhat altered.

The long, black hair was shaped into a mullet, and the Fu Manchu had, at some point, been traded in for a goatee. A once dark T-shirt, now faded to gray, still boasted the remnants of a Lynyrd Skynyrd logo but was a bit tight around the belly. However, those were the only perceptible changes that Cameron could discern at the moment.

"This guy is looking for money," the woman snapped.

Through bleary eyes, Rich studied the man standing in the doorway and recognition grew along with the smile on his face.

"Well, if he is, he only wants to search the couch cushions for it." Rich laughed, grabbing Cameron in a warm embrace.

"Wait, you *know* this guy?" she demanded.

Rich nodded. "Yeah, I've told you about him, remember?"

From the disgusted look on her face, Cameron could tell she was unimpressed. "If you did, I don't remember it!" With a snort, she turned away.

"And who was that charming creature?" Cameron asked quietly as she stormed into the kitchen.

"That is Gretchen." Rich yawned. "You'll have to excuse her. She doesn't take well to strangers and is an acquired taste, I guess."

I'll pass.

Rich ushered Cameron into the living room, punching shape back into a cushion on the couch for him.

"So what brings you here? I thought you were back East and working for …"

"I've got a light and sound company now" Cameron spoke over Rich, giving a wide smile, accentuated by raised eyebrows.

Drawing from his time with Cameron as a former asset, Rich instinctively knew that the subject of Cameron's current employment was a sensitive one and not to be discussed around Gretchen. Nodding, Rich segued into more musician-related topics.

"Have you got a gig out here, then?" he asked.

Cameron shrugged. "I'm not sure just yet. I'm looking at some possibilities right now, to be honest."

Rich nodded but said nothing, and Cameron realized that his former bass player was suddenly suspicious about his motives.

"Well, tell me all about it," Rich said, smiling broadly.

Before Cameron could respond, there was an outburst from the kitchen.

"Wait just one minute! This is my apartment and I don't want anyone in here!"

Rich gave a weary sigh and rolled his eyes. "This is our apartment, darling. We split all the expenses, remember? So that makes it *our* apartment."

"My name is on the lease and the bills! So that makes it *my* apartment, and I say I don't want him in here!"

"What are you going to do about it?" Rich asked, calmly putting his feet on the coffee table.

The young lady started, aghast at this unexpected display of defiance. Cameron winced inwardly, hating the awkwardness of being caught in the middle of an argument. He began formulating ways to get himself out of there when Gretchen stormed back to the kitchen.

"Maybe now isn't such a great time ..." Cameron began, but Rich waved his hand.

"It won't make any difference, trust me."

The light hearted camaraderie they had shared a moment ago was gone, its absence as gaping as a raw wound. However, the two men had the benefit of many years' acquaintance and many shared experiences, so it was not far from being recaptured. In its recovery, Cameron took the lead.

"So what have you been doing lately?" Cameron asked.

Before Rich could reply, Gretchen rushed back into the room. "Nothing," she shouted. "He hasn't been doing a thing!"

Rich rolled his eyes in response. Cameron simply sat there and hoped the storm would blow over without involving him. Then he wondered how he could get rid of her without antagonizing his closest friend.

"He quit his job, did you know that?" Gretchen smiled with satisfaction as she leveled the accusation against Rich, relishing the chance to demean him in the eyes of someone he liked.

Cameron clenched his teeth as he replied. "Um, this is the first time I've seen him in four years, so, no, I obviously didn't know that. And I really don't care."

Gretchen failed to notice the sarcasm, or his angry tone. "He'll tell you he got laid off, but he quit! Even if he won't admit it, he quit!"

"I can't collect unemployment if I quit, dear," Rich sweetly reminded her.

Gretchen simply shook her head. "I don't believe you are collecting it! When are you supposed to be getting it then, eh? I haven't seen a check yet."

"I only applied for it yesterday, sweetheart."

Cameron noticed Rich's mirthless smile and entertained the hope that Rich might just be willing to accept Cameron's offer—if he ever got the chance to present it.

"Oh, and this is after not working for how long?"

Rich closed his eyes and rubbed his temples as he composed himself before responding to her challenge. "As I already told you, I applied yesterday on my way home after being laid off."

Rich's words were carefully spoken, but there was no overlooking the tension in his voice. Cameron realized that he needed to remove his friend from this situation because this was not going to end well.

"Well, I might have a solution," Cameron offered enthusiastically as he slapped Rich on the knee. "I've been thinking about getting the band back together! What do you think about that?"

Rich looked at him curiously. "I thought you said you had some other stuff going on?"

"Well, you know what they say: all work and no play makes Jack a dull boy!"

Rich smiled, giving Cameron a knowing wink.

"Oh, now you think you're going to be a musician," Gretchen sneered.

"Yes, as a matter of fact, I do. In fact, I think this proposal came at just the right time. And could provide me with some excellent opportunities!"

"Oh, and just what would those be?" Gretchen demanded, crossing her arms.

Rich smiled as he rose from the couch. Suspecting something, Cameron rose as well.

"Ah, that would just bore you if I went into that now," Rich replied. "But I've got to get something in the bedroom. Could you get Cameron something to eat? He looks a bit hungry."

"Oh, and just what do you think I am now, the maid?"

Rich hurried back to the bedroom while Gretchen glared at Cameron.

"Well, what do you want? I haven't got all day!"

"Oh, just some toast, please," he said after a moment's hesitation.

"What?"

"I'd just like some plain white toast." He smiled.

Gretchen gave him a look that left no doubt as to how stupid she thought he was. However, she went back into the kitchen. Cameron stood in the living room, listening to the two of them, in their respective rooms, making noises pertinent to their tasks at hand. After a few minutes, Rich returned. As Cameron had expected, Rich was carrying a large duffel bag with articles of clothing protruding from it in one hand and his bass guitar in another. He had a backpack over his shoulder and a smile on his face.

"Okay, let's go!" Rich said, beaming.

Without waiting for an explanation, Cameron followed Rich to the door, hurrying out just as Gretchen came into the living room.

"Where are you going?" she demanded. Her grating tone of voice suggested much more outrage than concern.

Cameron continued across the parking lot, wondering if she would attempt to follow. He heard Rich reply, "I'm going out," and caught the note of relief in his voice.

"When are you coming back?" Gretchen snapped.

"I'm not," said Rich.

Cameron could tell, even without looking, that the calmness of Rich's voice suggested that he was smiling broadly.

"What the hell do you want me to do with this toast then?" she shouted.

Rich paused for a moment on the sidewalk, then returned to the doorway, and said something in response. He had said it too softly for Cameron to hear, but judging from the loud shriek, followed by a stream of profanity and the two pieces of toast that came flying out of the doorway, Cameron guessed it wasn't nice.

But it was probably still nicer than if I said it.

"Let's go." Rich smiled, motioning for Cameron to lead the way.

Behind him, Cameron heard the slamming of a door and could still hear yelling from inside the apartment, even as they hurried away.

"Was it always like that?" Cameron asked as he helped Rich store his belongings in the trunk.

Rich shook his head. "You mean like what you just saw? Oh, hell no, I can assure you."

"You mean it was worse?" Cameron asked, teasingly.

As Cameron pulled out of the side street and began driving east, connecting with Route 60, Rich switched on the radio, adjusting the dial until he found a station he liked. Then he turned up the volume slightly before turning his attention to Cameron.

"So, now that we can talk, tell me about this sudden decision to put the band back together."

Cameron looked at him out of the corner of his eye and smiled. *Old lessons are not soon forgotten, it seems.* "Do you mean we can talk now because we won't be interrupted, or because we can't be heard?"

Rich grinned.

"Both, I guess. It drove her crazy when I would turn on the radio before talking."

"Old habits die hard," Cameron assured him.

"More than I thought they would," Rich admitted. "Now, out with it. What's the angle for this reprisal?"

"Like I said, I want to get the band back together."

Rich chuckled. "Are you on a mission from God?"

"Well, maybe not quite that high up, but, yeah, sort of."

"That's what I suspected. Details?"

"None that I can say, really."

"That's also what I suspected."

"It's not that I don't want to," Cameron insisted.

"I know, it's because you really can't," Rich assured him. "Top secret, special clearance, and all that shit. I remember the drill."

"Well, not just that," Cameron replied. "The fact is, I really *don't* know any more than that. They haven't divulged a great deal of information at this point."

"No shit! Your mission, should you choose to accept it, is classified. That sort of thing?"

"Well, since you put it that way, yeah, I guess."

Rich drew a pack of cigarettes out of his shirt pocket and took one, offering one to his friend, and then pushed in the car's cigarette lighter. A few moments later, they heard the familiar click, indicating it was hot. Withdrawing it, Rich lit his cigarette with a smile.

"I see you got the lighter fixed," he said.

Cameron took it from him and lit his own cigarette. "This is a rental," Cameron warned. "If you even *think* of tossing it out the window, you'll be following after it!"

They continued on through the Arizona desert, watching Superstition Mountain grow ever closer as they approached it and catching up on each other's news and any information concerning their old friends.

"I know that you and Evan decided to go all the way in," Rich said.

Cameron appreciated that he did not make direct mention of his new career. "Yes, but we don't work together. I've got a light and sound company that I run. He's working in analysis."

"Do you still see McIntyre at all?"

"Who do you think was the one that came up with this idea?"

"Is she your boss now?"

Cameron nodded.

"What about Chuck? Have you seen or heard from him at all?"

Cameron shook his head. Out of all his past associations, that was something he truly regretted. He had not heard from their former case officer and erstwhile band manager, ever since the night that the band broke up. Nor had Cameron attempted to contact him, another fact he also regretted.

"Not since we left Seattle. I know they pulled him from things the night that everything went down, but that was it. I've thought about him, too, but never asked anyone about him."

"What the hell happened out there that night anyway? No one said much about it when everything was done."

Cameron considered his response carefully. There were so many other things that occurred that night other than just the breakup of the band. Each circumstance contributed to the other, and all were responsible for how events had arrived at this exact moment, with him sitting with his closest friend in a car driving through the desert. Yet Cameron could not tell him half of what occurred.

"A lot got said, actually. But there was so much fallout, it doesn't surprise me that you didn't hear the full extent of everything."

"Well, you got that right," Rich sighed. "But, to be honest, I just wanted to get the hell out of there and took off at the first chance I got. And after I left, there was no one to ask about it later. But I have to admit that I've always wondered about what details I missed."

"Okay, here goes with the *Reader's Digest* version."

Cameron reminded Rich of the alleged kidnapping of Cameron's then girlfriend. "Well, McIntyre and I discovered that they really *didn't* have Doreen. But, because that was the only lead Chuck and McIntyre had for the KGB guy they were hunting, we had to proceed with things as if we still believed them, so they wouldn't know that we'd discovered the truth and spook them off."

"I think I remember that, but go on."

"Well, when we got to where we were supposed to make contact, I got grabbed by their agents, and while McIntyre was trying to follow, they involved her in a staged car accident."

"Holy shit." He whistled.

"Well, I was kind of out of the loop for the rest of it," Cameron sighed. Once again, he found himself at the subject he hated discussing, the one that would sometimes keep him awake at night.

He had some help in getting past it, but still, something would trigger a memory.   *Nothing like facing it head on, I guess.*

"They put a hood over my head, tied me up, and drove me around awhile. They took me to some place out on Bainbridge Island and kept me in a small room."

"Were you hoodwinked the whole time?" asked Rich.

Cameron shook his head. "No, after they tied me in a chair, they removed the hood and that was when I saw him."

"Who?"

"The KGB agent everyone had been looking for. Then the interrogation began."

"What the hell did they want to know?"

"About the code I found and how much I knew about it. They found that out from your buddy Ralston."

Now it was Rich's turn to be uncomfortable. Due to his role as the bass player, their case officers had used him in an attempt to form a friendship with Jack Ralston, the bass player of the popular punk band Boney Jack. The FBI had evidence suggesting that Boney Jack had links with a Soviet network, and the agents were desperate to find out what it was. What no one knew was that Jack Ralston was the link, and by encouraging Rich to form a friendship with him, the FBI had opened up its entire operation to enemy surveillance and, on the night in question, nearly got Rich killed.

"Thanks for bringing that up," Rich winced.

"That's right," Cameron recalled. "You had your own adventure that night, didn't you?"

"Yeah, I had quite the adventure, and with Ralston. He came back looking for that wireless transmitter he had given me."

"Which, it turns out, had been transmitting more than music, wasn't it?"

Rich nodded. Once again the camaraderie deserted them. This time, however, its recovery was hindered by mutual recollections of individual trauma. Recollections that nearly overpowered the filial bond they had shared for so long.

Finally, Rich resumed his account. "Ralston found Clyde and

me at the apartment, where Chuck had us covering the phone. You know about the fight, about us getting the gun away from him and what happened with Clyde, right?"

Cameron remembered what little he had been briefed on, how Ralston had tried taking them captive at gunpoint and Clyde Poulin, the band's other guitarist, had gotten the gun away from Ralston. In the ensuing struggle, Clyde shot him when Ralston tried attacking with a concealed knife. It was ruled a clear case of self-defense, but the effect on Clyde was still traumatic. Never one to be aggressive, even in his conversations, the fact that he had acted in such a way as to kill another human being left Clyde devastated. He refused to talk to anyone in the band after that night, or for years afterward. He never returned Cameron's letters or phone calls.

No doubt Clyde is going to be the one who will be the hardest to get to return. "Yeah, I heard it hit him pretty bad," Cameron sighed. "Have you heard anything from Clyde since then?"

"Not lately," Rich replied. "I got a letter a while back. I guess he was staying with his folks at the time. But, aside from a card at Christmas once, I haven't heard from him at all.

"What happened to you that night? They had me debriefing on all the shit that went down with me, so I never heard everything that happened to you."

"Well, that Russian agent got impatient with that Kalbe character ..."

"Wait," interjected Rich. "Who?"

"Oh, that's something you didn't know about, I take it. The KGB even had someone impersonate Doug's old buddy, the one who worked on the *Mustang.*"

"No shit! Then why didn't they contact Doug instead of you?"

Cameron cocked his eyebrow and studied his friend carefully. "Just how well do you think that would have worked? Let's face it, even they aren't that stupid!"

"Or that brave!" Rich laughed.

Cameron had to agree. Doug Courtland had been the roadie for the band for many years and was known for his hard exterior and grumpy disposition. However, that was a persona reserved for people he either did not know or did not like. The image was reinforced by a quick temper and a former career as a professional wrestler. For those few he considered his friends, Doug was devoted and loyal. Often possessed of more courage than brains, he was the last one to run from danger and in fact was often the first to run into it. As such, he had served as security for the band on many occasions. After the band's recruitment, Doug extended that duty into their roles as assets, which twice nearly resulted in his death.

Doug Courtland was not one to permit himself to be encumbered with abstract concepts. He saw the world purely in primary colors; his emotions were always intense, and his loyalty toward his friends was absolute. One such friendship had been a scientist aboard the ill-fated USS *Mustang*, an experimental submarine developed for use in the Arctic. When Don D'Lorenzo was assigned to them, it was revealed that he had been responsible for convincing Doug's friend Gus Kalbe to reenlist in the navy to be part of that project. Kalbe, along with everyone else on board, was killed when the *Mustang* was destroyed. To Doug, Special Agent D'Lorenzo was a murderer, pure and simple, and he treated D'Lorenzo accordingly. The animosity became so volatile that it resulted in D'Lorenzo's removal from the case and was a constant black mark against Doug with the FBI.

"Anyhow, they were trying to find out what knowledge Doug may, or may not, have had about things and worked me over pretty good to find out what I knew," continued Cameron.

"Is that how your hand got messed up?"

"Yeah, you could say everything got smashed that night." *I'm not living in this gloom, anymore.*

Cameron cleared his throat and tried to change the mood. "So, enough about the night the shit hit the fan; tell me what happened with you after all that?"

"Well, that won't take too long." Rich laughed. "You know all about the mess with Ralston, so I don't need to go over that. But I hung around Seattle for a little bit, mostly to keep an eye on Clyde, but also because Chuck's bosses were still trying to find out about what might have been transmitted from the studio with the listening devices that Ralston had installed. Eventually they were pretty satisfied that nothing of any importance had been mentioned, mostly music-related stuff and personal details. I guess Chuck had also given them the scoop on all that, and they were just confirming everything with me. Anyhow, about three weeks after all this went down, they told me I was free to go, and I decided to get as far away from the rain as I could and headed down here."

"Well, that was quite the change, I bet!"

"Oh, hell yeah! But I didn't mind it. I had my money from the band and was able to get a place—not that one, by the way—and took some time just to soak in the sun. I did some pickup work with people looking for a bass player and just kind of drifted around. I worked for a year or so with a tribute band for The Animals, but that didn't last."

"What did you finally do then?"

"I lived off of what I had saved, and when that started to run out, I looked for work where I could and ended up working in a music store."

"No shit! I can't picture you behind a counter."

"It wasn't so bad. I kind of liked it, actually. I got to meet a lot of local talent and got to work with some other bands, which was fun. Even if nothing eventually came of it."

"You mentioned back there you got laid off. Was that the truth, or did you really quit?"

"I got fired."

"You're kidding me! What the hell happened?"

"After about two years of listening to snot-nosed kids come into the store and butcher 'Stairway to Heaven' and 'Free Bird,' pretending they were the next Robert Plant, I couldn't take it anymore." Rich moaned, leaning back in the seat. "Yesterday some brat came in to look at a guitar and wanted to show his buddies what he could do, and it was just awful. I grabbed the guitar out of his hand, went through both songs, and handed it back to him. 'That's what the thing sounds like, kid,' I told him."

Cameron burst out laughing. "Man, I would probably have done the same thing! So, what? Your boss didn't like it or something?"

"Turns out, the little shit was the boss's stepson trying to impress his friends on his ability to score playtime in Daddy's store. He got brought down a peg or two, and that didn't go over too well."

Cameron regarded his friend with a sideways glance. "Let me ask you something else then. Did you really apply for unemployment on your way home?"

"Fuck no! I stopped by a roadhouse in Chandler and got a part-time gig with another band."

"Is that going to turn into anything?"

"Most definitely not, I suspect. They were supposed to have called last night."

"So you really don't have anything keeping you here then?"

"Everything I own is now resting securely in the trunk of this car. My only entanglement at the moment is you."

"Then you're free to do whatever you want, is that right?"

"I'm as free as the wind."

"So, are you in?"

"Why not? It's not like I haven't done this sort of thing before. Probably just like riding a bike, I bet."

I seriously have no fucking idea.

The two men drove on, listening to the Talking Heads singing about life during wartime:

"This ain't no party, this ain't no disco, this ain't no fooling around. No time for dancing, or lovey dovey, I ain't got time for that now ..."

Life imitating art?

Chapter 3

"I'll Just Stay Here and Drink"

"**I**t was a complete waste of time," Evan snapped, throwing his coat in the chair. "He wouldn't even let me discuss it, for crying out loud!"

It was quite out of character for Evan Dixon to ever be this upset, a fact not lost on McIntyre. Evan had a reputation for being levelheaded and calm in nearly any situation, a factor often cited by his superiors.

Evan had been with the Roadhouse Sons since the band's formation in 1971. Prior to that, he had been the drummer for a band that billed itself as Murphy's Law until the day when he, along with several other musicians, found themselves in a strange predicament. They had all arrived for a well-publicized Battle of the Bands at a roadhouse in upstate New York. Other members of these same bands, however, had not. Among the lost souls in search of a band were Cameron Walsh and Rich Webster. Being driven by a need for the potential prize money, Evan, Rich, and Cameron formed an impromptu band, which Cameron quickly christened the Roadhouse Sons.

While the band did not win the competition, it did well enough to receive bookings in another area club, which helped to make up for it. From that moment their musical careers became a serious pursuit and continued for another decade. Eventually, they added Clyde Poulin as a guitarist and occasional keyboard player. In all that time, Evan had been the voice of reason and the island of calm in the occasionally stormy seas of their career. Now McIntyre was shocked to see he was the very antithesis of his previous self.

"Let me ask you a question. Did you, or any of the others, ever try contacting Clyde prior to your arrival?" McIntyre asked.

"Of course I did!" he shouted. "I even called and told him I would be in town and wanted to get together with him. I kept everything low key, talking about going out for lunch, not anything mysterious."

"That's not exactly what I meant. And don't yell at me. I meant, in all these years, have you stayed in contact with him or attempted any contact?"

Her concern was not purely idle curiosity. Clyde Poulin was not only a talented musician, but his resemblance to Robert Plant also was an image that the band had exploited, and it was that image that young female fans of the Roadhouse Sons were enjoying behind the Iron Curtain. For him not to be a part of this would have serious consequences for their plans, if not terminate the entire operation.

"We went out to lunch," Evan began, slowly regaining his composure. "Everything was fine. We talked about old times. We laughed; we had a few drinks. I brought him up to date on as much as I knew about how everyone was doing and caught up with him."

"How *is* he doing exactly?" She hoped that his response might provide a clue for her to determine how to proceed.

"He seemed to be doing fine. He's not living with his parents anymore; he's on his own. He's settled down with a nice girl, and he's found a job working in a record store that he seems to enjoy very much. He was fine; it was all fine up until then. It was when I mentioned that some of us had talked about getting the band back together that he started to become agitated and reluctant to talk."

"How exactly did you phrase it?" she pressed.

"*Exactly* like you and I had rehearsed. I told him that Cameron and I were thinking about putting the band back together and trying some new stuff. I didn't even mention you or Chuck or anything related to counterintelligence, surveillance, or anything. It was all strictly band-oriented conversation."

"All right then, what did he say exactly?"

"He said he had decided to take time off from playing."

"Well, you have to admit, that is a plausible response."

"If you're going to take some time off, it is a few months, maybe a year, maybe two at the most," Evan protested. "His time off has been four years. He's not taking time off; he's quit playing."

McIntyre digested Evan's report. The carefully conceived plan was unraveling even before they had started anything. As she contemplated that, she ran various scenarios that had been considered as possible contingency plans. However, in light of this development, each one of them seemed to be wholly inadequate.

"I just wish he'd mentioned something about that decision before I drove all the way out to Pennsylvania," Evan continued to grumble. "I had indicated that was why I was going to be talking to him anyhow!"

"Would you have gone otherwise?"

"What?"

"I said, would you have bothered to go see him if he'd said no?"

"Well, yes, of course I would have. I might not have done it right now, but I'm sure I would have …"

"Eventually?"

"Well, yes. He is my friend after all."

"After all," McIntyre sighed. "Then, once again, how many times before now have you been in touch with him?"

"I don't know, a few times I guess. Why?"

"Long phone calls or detailed letters?"

"Well, maybe a few phone calls and a letter or two, but none of us are that much into writing, and besides, you can't say I've exactly been idle since I last saw him!"

"No, I can't say that. Neither can I deny that none of you are letter writers, as you put it. But that doesn't mean he might not have missed a friend and wanted to have some connection with his past, I guess."

"Just not enough to be drawn back into it?"

McIntyre sank into a chair and sat thoughtfully for a long time. "Have you ever killed a person," she finally asked.

"No, I haven't. What does that have to do with anything?"

"Then you don't know what it feels like," she replied. Evan was slightly unnerved by the distant tone in her voice. "It is an awful thing, knowing you are now responsible for someone's death. Even if you know it is a reality and a possibility in your line of work, when it happens, it still hits you hard. Chuck and I were trained to use deadly force. We know that is an unpleasant fact of our professional lives and had accepted that fact long before we ever met you. And that was a fact that, for some of us, has been proven. However, Clyde didn't have that training and preparation. Neither he, nor any of you, had any reason to ever expect to be in that situation. You were musicians. You were supposed to play music. You made people happy. You made them want to dance. You made them forget their troubles for a little bit. No one was ever meant to be hurt and certainly not meant to be killed."

"Except it didn't exactly work out that way, did it?" Evan's voice was distant as he began to realize the trauma that had been inflicted on his friend.

"No, it didn't," she agreed. "Chuck and I, and everyone, were all aware that it did a lot of damage to him, and we tried to get him all the help we could. I think that help did enable him to deal with the trauma, to an extent, and go on with his life. But now I think that he has no intention of ever giving it a chance to happen again."

"Then why did he agree to see me?"

"Because I doubt he wants to forget about all the years he was a musician. Just the issues that he can't deal with."

"So, it wouldn't do any good to pursue it further?"

"Not a bit," she admitted, her voice tinged with dejection.

The two of them were silent, each contemplating the possible consequences of this development, and trying to find an alternative rather than consider the failure that seemed so inevitable. Suddenly, Evan snapped his finger.

"Rufus!" He laughed.

"And who, may I ask, is Rufus?" McIntyre was in no mood for games and realized her response was perhaps unnecessarily sharp, but if Evan had noticed, he did not indicate it.

"When I was in high school, there was a band called Rufus," he explained. "They were incredibly popular and always did a sellout whenever they played. Long story short, they suddenly broke up during the height of their popularity, and a lot of people were pretty disappointed. Some people were even devastated by it."

"What, exactly, does that have to do with anything?"

"I'm getting to that," Evan assured her. "Well, like I said, their breakup was not well received by their fans. So you can imagine everyone's surprise when posters started appearing, advertising them being at a local fair that summer. I was one of the first ones to get a ticket to see them because I knew it would be a sellout, and it was! When I showed up, I was surprised to see that the only original member of Rufus was the rhythm guitar player and everyone else was a replacement. A couple of them *looked* like the old members, the lead vocalist *sounded* like him, but they were all different."

"I bet the fans were fit to be tied when they found that out."

"Well, yes, some were. But almost everyone was just glad to be at one of their shows and have a good time, and it was easy to get lost in everything and pretend it was like old times."

"How did they get away with fooling everyone, if you don't mind my asking?"

"That was the beauty of it." Evan laughed. "They really hadn't! I went back to look at the poster later and saw that they had, in fact, been totally honest in the advertising, just no one bothered to notice. They had the name of the band in big, bold type like they typically did. But underneath it, very small, were the words 'one original member.' So, you see, no one had really been deceptive."

"And do you seriously think that might work with us?"

"Well, we either do that or we just do a three-piece band. That is doable as well. We could say that Clyde was ill or had a scheduling conflict. Then we'd have to eliminate some of the songs from our set that Clyde usually sang, that's all."

"But what if those songs are the ones people want to hear? I hate to sound like a concert promoter, but I honestly think that the band's dynamic is what would make the mission a success. To not have all of you guys would be a serious risk."

"I can certainly appreciate that, but don't you think that is something we could at least pursue?"

"What, you mean just using three of you?"

"Well, if that wouldn't work, then what about auditioning someone for his part?"

"Absolutely not! Haven't you paid attention to *anything* I've said? This is part of a highly sensitive mission, an intrinsic part! It has been a hard enough sell with three agents and two experienced assets, but to substitute one of them for a complete stranger would kill the idea from the beginning."

"Who are the three agents?"

"You, Cameron, and me, of course. I've got some reputation as your business manager, and we were hoping to play on that to explain why I was associated with it. It is also essential that I be involved and be present as the mission unfolds."

Evan nodded thoughtfully and then smiled.

"So if we consisted of four agents, then this might be a little more agreeable to the powers that be, wouldn't you say?"

"Where are you getting four agents?"

"I can't believe in the entire intelligence community there isn't someone who looks half decent and can play a guitar and sing!"

"There is no way that we can search for someone for an operation like this! There is too much risk of exposure involved."

"Oh, for crying out loud, I'm not suggesting that you post a notice on the bulletin board in the break room," Evan explained, rolling his eyes. "However, I'm certain that there are individuals directly connected with undercover operations, who are fully vetted and have some proficiency with music. It is mathematically inconceivable that there aren't!"

McIntyre made no immediate response, but Evan could tell that he had made enough of an impression for her to consider the possibility.

"I'll admit that it does have some merits. However, I'll have to talk to some other people about it, and there is no guarantee that they will be any more convinced by it than I am. The ideal solution would be to get Clyde back on board to work with us."

"You know that as well as I do, but there is no way Clyde will be a part of this, and no amount of coercion will make it happen. And, even if it did, he would be too unreliable to use safely, and you know that as well as I do. So we might as well forget that option. Clyde Poulin is no longer a part of the Roadhouse Sons, *period*."

"Has Cameron said anything about this?"

"I haven't told him yet," Evan informed her. "You are the first one I've reported to."

"Where is Cameron anyway?" McIntyre wondered.

Evan shrugged. "He said he had something to take care of in Baltimore before we went any further on this; that's all I know."

"What could be so pressing up there? We're pressed for time here!"

"That was all he said after he got back here with Rich."

"And you have no idea what he could be doing?"

"None at all, though I do have a suspicion."

"And that is?"

Evan hesitated before answering. "You might not like what I'm thinking."

Chapter 4

"A Country Boy Can Survive"

Cameron maneuvered deftly through the crowded aisles of the department store, past the mannequins dressed in the latest fashions, which loomed over the shoppers like idols in the newly restored temple of capitalism. Relaxed rationing on purchase items saw a surge in spending and enthusiasm in a population that had borne restrictions for a long time. Cameron was reminded of the maenads, the frenzied followers of Dionysus, as people pushed and shoved one another in an attempt to find the latest deals that, while available, were hardly numerous. He was elbowed, shoved, and jostled, cursed at and smiled upon. Cameron apologized when he was bumped and smiled when someone stepped on his foot or pushed him, conscious of the fact that he was now a special agent and not a rock star. Thus his response could not be what it once was.

I'd better remember to stay the hell away from here at Christmas.

Finally he reached the back of the store and the entrance to the area marked Employees Only, where he was accosted by a man in white bell bottoms and a green polyester shirt. The man's hair was freshly permed, and his mouth was drawn into a tight bow, giving an aura of annoyance and disapproval. At first, Cameron assumed he was a customer, until he saw a name tag on the man's chest.

"I'm sorry, sir, this is a restricted area," the man said, holding up his hand. His tone was at once authoritative and condescending, and Cameron realized that this man was used to talking down to others.

"You're the manager," Cameron stated.

The man gave a weary sigh and was about to respond when Cameron withdrew his badge.

"I'm Special Agent Cameron Walsh," he said, cutting off the man's response. "I understand you have one Douglas Courtland in your employ?"

"Uh, why, yes, yes we do," the man stammered. "Why? What has he done?"

"I would just like to ask him a few questions," Cameron said. He did not snap or speak rudely, but he did speak firmly enough to let the man know that he was also used to giving orders—and that he was not going to waste time.

Yes, my dog is bigger than your dog.

"Well, what is this in regard to, if I may ask?"

"You may not ask." Cameron replaced the badge, never removing his gaze from the now nervous manager. "My business is with him, not with you. Now, is he here?"

"Well, I'm, I'm not sure. I'll have to check with his supervisor, and I don't know where she is at the moment. What is this in regard to, if I may ask?"

"I already told you, you may not. Now if I need to speak to his supervisor, please have her paged," Cameron instructed.

The man hesitated a moment, and Cameron deduced by his confusion that this man was more accustomed to issuing orders than receiving them. Now, with the roles reversed and on his own turf, the man was having difficulty accepting such a situation. After a few moments of internal debate, the manager finally hurried off to the office to track down his associate. Soon the same syrupy voice that had announced the latest specials came over the loudspeaker once more, this time requesting the presence of one of his employees.

Cameron noted how both this request and the mercantile announcements had the same quasi-cheerful tone, lacking in any genuine sincerity or personal connection, beautifully masking an unspoken contempt for everyone but himself. A motion out of the corner of his eye interrupted Cameron's musings, and he noticed a woman moving briskly toward him. She was roughly five feet eight, slightly past middle age, and in nondescript but obviously new clothing. In possession of neither handbag nor shopping cart, she wore a look of general suspicion and disdain.

You could not be more clearly identified as store security if you had a gun and a badge.

"I believe this area is closed to customers." She spoke to him in a pleasant but encouraging tone, the same one that teachers used when working with an underachieving student. It was a tone designed to inform and educate people she felt did not have the capacity to navigate their way through life without her watchfulness, yet without the open implication of making one feel insulted. Cameron, however, did feel insulted but said nothing. He showed her his credentials and allowed them to do the talking. To his surprise, the woman did not become flustered. Calmly, she returned his shield and motioned for him to follow her. Cameron did, however, notice a marked difference in her tone and demeanor.

"My name is Ofelia Rodriquez," she said, once they were away from the store. "I assume you are aware that I am head of store security. How can I help you, Special Agent Walsh?"

"I'm here to talk to one of your employees, but the manager wasn't certain if he were here or not. Do you know if Doug Courtland is in today?"

"May I ask what he's done?"

"You many not," Cameron explained. "I want to know if he is here and if I can speak with him."

"Art knew perfectly well that Doug was here," she muttered. "He was only trying to make Doug look bad, again. Yes, you can speak to him. He's in the control room upstairs, monitoring our surveillance cameras. Would you like me to take you to him?"

"If you would, please. That would be most helpful. And may I ask you a question?"

"Certainly, what is it?"

"Are you former law enforcement or military?"

"Both," she replied with a smile. "A tour of duty as a nurse in the US Army and some time in a nice, small-town police force."

"Why did you move to this then?"

"My husband and I started a family, and it made more sense to have a job that I would come home from every night, rather than one where I might not."

The woman led him through the manager's office to a steel door indicating that only authorized personnel were permitted past.

"Doug is not permitted on the floor by Art's orders," the woman explained. "Art feels that it might subject us to potential liability to have Doug in contact with customers. It's rather hard to explain, but let's just say Doug is somewhat less refined in his approach than most people. That is why he is required to stay up here, monitoring, and his duties are limited to surveillance and merchandise retrieval. Unlike me and our other store security, Doug isn't in plain clothes. He's required to wear a store uniform clearly indicating his function."

I can just imagine how well that goes over.

"Ordinarily, we wouldn't have even considered him for the position," she said. "But you need to understand that there is a labor shortage and we simply had no choice. Hopefully, with the world situation improving, that can be corrected before much longer. We can talk with him in my office."

"I would like to speak to him alone," Cameron told her.

She gave him a disapproving look. "I'm afraid that I must protest. If there's to be any type of criminal investigation being conducted in this store, I need to be aware of it. There is the store liability to consider."

"Your protest is duly noted," Cameron assured her. "However, my presence here in no way involves you or your store. My business is with Mr. Courtland and is confidential."

"Very well then. The monitoring room is the last door on the left. Be sure to knock before you go in."

"Why's that?"

"Let's just say it puts him in a more sociable mood," she explained.

"Really?" Despite his training, Cameron was unable to contain his surprise. Of all the adjectives that had ever been used to describe Doug Courtland, Cameron could not recall *sociable* ever being among them.

"If you knock first, he doesn't throw things at you when you come through the door," she sighed.

Ah, now things are back to normal.

Cameron stood in front of the door and considered his idea once more. He could see nothing but confrontation resulting from it and knew that he would have tremendous difficulty in convincing anyone else of the merits of his idea. Cameron knew that the first person he would have to convince would be the one he was about to talk to, and that would also be the hardest challenge.

Nothing ventured, nothing gained.

Taking a deep breath, he gave a quick, rhythmic rap and then waited. Silence. Cameron wondered if anyone had heard him, and as he was about to knock again, a voice answered.

"Are you going to get your ass in here or not?" the voice demanded.

Cameron smiled, realizing he was in familiar territory once again.

The room was dark, save for the white glare from the screens. There was a table in front of the monitors and a desk off to the side. The chair in front of the monitors was occupied by a familiar figure in a most unfamiliar outfit.

Doug Courtland was a muscular, though wiry, individual. As Cameron recalled, Doug was roughly six feet tall with raven-black hair that fell in waves past his shoulders, and a black beard and mustache to match. His customary mode of dress consisted of a black trucker's cap, a T-shirt, blue denim jeans, and work boots. The appearance of the figure before him challenged that recollection.

There was no longer a cap, and the once-long black hair was now barely shoulder length. The beard and mustache were neatly trimmed. Gone were the T-shirt and denims; in their place were white polyester slacks, a green shirt with a butterfly collar, and a teal polyester jacket. Where once there were work boots, now there were white loafers. The only parts that were familiar to Cameron were the arms crossed in defiance and the glowering expression on his friend's face.

Cameron had known Doug Courtland for almost a decade. In that time Doug had mostly served as a technician, or roadie, for the Roadhouse Sons, but he had also been the driver for the band's trucks and served as security at shows. Despite his coarse manners and dislike of authority, Doug's natural intuition and life experiences had been lifesavers for the band.

A couple of times, literally.

"Look at you, all suited up," Cameron said with a smile.

Doug sneered, still staring at the monitors. "Pot, kettle, black."

"Yeah, but at least I look suave in mine."

"I swear that jack-wagon manager gave me hand-me-downs out of his own closet. I've never seen anyone else here wear this monkey suit!"

There was no mistaking the bitter tone in Doug's voice. Cameron knew it wasn't just about having to wear only authorized clothes. It was about being confined to a room, being judged and second-guessed by people who never bothered to look past their own prejudices, and not allowing him to put his innate talents to use. It was the voice of someone being stifled.

"I do admit that jacket doesn't bring out your eyes." Cameron laughed.

"The hell it doesn't! It makes them bug right out of my head."

Cameron stopped laughing when Doug turned to face him.

"All right, let's cut the crap. I've barely heard from you in three years. The last time was when you started the job that makes you dress like that. And, just so you know, you don't blend into a crowd at all. I spotted you the minute you came through the front door and had no trouble following you through ladies' apparel and the shoe section. You made straight for here, so you obviously have something on your mind, and it isn't making stupid jokes about my wardrobe. Out with it!"

Cameron was actually pleased to see that Doug had not changed in the intervening years. He had always been known as no nonsense and direct, but with a sharp eye.

Everything is still in place. That might make more sense than I thought.

"I'm working on getting the band back together," Cameron declared.

"What? No shit! You mean you're finally quitting the feds?"

"No, not at all; in fact, they're the ones who want me to do it."

"You've got to be kidding."

"I know, right? Can you believe it?"

"No, frankly I can't," Doug replied.

"I'm serious, man! McIntyre was the one that suggested it."

"I might have known. Well, have fun with it then. Let me know where your first gig is. I'll try to come by and see it."

"I was actually hoping you would come back and work for us again."

"What? And leave all this? Where else can I dress like a booger, watch television, and smoke cigarettes for a living?"

Just then the phone rang. Doug made a face and answered it. "Value Mart Department Store, Baltimore, how may I direct your call? One moment, please. Mr. Shirley, pick up line two. Mr. Shirley, pick up line two."

Cameron waited for Doug to hang up the phone. He used the blinking light that indicated a phone call on hold to count the time as he waited for Doug's response, but none was forthcoming.

"So what do you say?" Cameron asked, becoming concerned over his friend's lack of response.

Before Doug could answer, there was a beep from the phone, indicating that the hold call had not been answered. Doug once more issued another page for Mr. Shirley.

"I don't wonder Diaper Man isn't answering," Doug grumbled. "That's his wife, and she's even more of a pain in the ass than he is."

"Who's Diaper Man?" Cameron laughed.

"That would be Art Shirley, the store manager. I call him that because he's always full of crap and always on my ass."

"I can get you away from all this," Cameron offered.

"And into something just as bad," Doug replied. "You forget, your experiences with them haven't been the same as mine, so your opinion of them is a little higher!"

Cameron knew that he could not argue Doug's point. From the moment the Roadhouse Sons had been recruited, the transition had been difficult for Doug. Mostly because his personality conflicted with the requirements of their situations and often resulted in his being subjected to disciplinary action and mistrust by his superiors. And yet, Doug would manage to redeem himself and often be vindicated, but Cameron often felt that his friend simply made things more difficult than they needed to be.

"This time will be different," Cameron assured him as the phone beeped again.

"Yeah, sure it will," Doug grumbled, once more issuing his page. "Mr. Shirley, pick up line two."

"Yes, it will," Cameron insisted. "Look, I'm an *agent* now; *I'd* be the case officer. I'd be one of the ones in charge, not just a source like last time. I could keep some of the heat off of you. It won't be like it was."

"I'm not that stupid! It is still for the same group, so it won't be all that different."

"Hey, just because I'm a suit now doesn't mean I don't know what you've got to offer! It's not like I'd forget you or ignore your talents or doubt your abilities. It's because I recognized them that I'm here in the first place!"

"Well, you're not J. Edgar Hoover, and you're not a big shot, so it isn't like you'd be able to make things too different from the way they used to be."

The phone beeped once more and Doug issued another page. Cameron noticed that while his friend's voice was still professional, it was beginning to show a slight strain.

"Look, I might not be one of the big wheels, but there is something that has changed, if you want to know the truth."

"And just what would that be?" Doug sneered.

"I think I finally figured out what you went through all this time."

"Oh, this shit should be good!"

Cameron ignored his friend's sarcasm and continued talking. "About a year ago I was working an undercover case. I can't go into details obviously, but it was serious, *really* serious. We had been up all night and arrested the people we were after shortly before dawn. I had to stay behind to help wrap things up at the scene, and by the time it was time to go, I was exhausted. We headed for the car that came to get us, and I bumped into a guy on the sidewalk. He turned and called me a bum and told me to watch where I was going."

"What does that have to do with me?"

"You were the first thing that popped into my head at that moment. Here I was, just having risked my life helping keep him safe, and he didn't give a damn. He didn't even bother to look past the end of his nose to see what I had done. He just wrote me off. You were the first thing that popped into my mind, and I finally understood how you felt all those times you lost it."

Doug nodded silently for a moment and once more issued the page for his manager.

"Man, I *need* you," Cameron pleaded as Doug hung up the phone.

"What about Snapper?" demanded Doug. "Have you asked him? He's as good as I was, even better, because he was a light *and* sound man as well. I was just the roadie. He's two for the price of one!"

Snapper had been the other half of the Roadhouse Sons' road crew. Christened Phillip S. Napier at birth, he became known as Snapper by his colleagues in the music business. Small in size, he more than made up for it in ability and talent. His skills with soundboards and lighting made each performance a true experience for both the band and the audience. During Doug's absence, Snapper had been duly recruited into the team and trained in the additional protocols required of him. He had performed his duties admirably. However, he, too, had been a victim of the Wagnerian tragedy that played out at the close of their assignment in Seattle. After discovering evidence of sabotage and Soviet monitoring of the band's activities, Snapper was nearly murdered.

"You weren't *just* the roadie," Cameron protested. "You were also security, don't forget. I don't just want someone who can lug things. I can get any idiot for that! I want someone that I know for a fact is looking out for me."

"Any idiot? Wow, that makes me feel so special now. Keep going, the offer is becoming irresistible!"

"That is not what I meant and you know it!"

"In other words, Snapper said no."

Still not one to waste time, are you? "Okay, yes, I asked him as well and you're right. He said no."

"Did he tell you why?"

Why beat around the bush? Yet Cameron hesitated to speak.

"You and I know perfectly well why he said no," Doug answered for him.

Yes, we do, don't we? "You're right," Cameron conceded. "He thought that he had paid enough skin for this line of work. Like he said, he never signed up to be an agent, just a source."

"I can say the same thing," Doug reminded him bitterly. "Only *I* never had much of a choice and *he* did. Plus, he walked away with all of his parts; I didn't. Or did you forget that? Speaking of which, I don't recall too many visits from *any* of you guys when I was in the hospital, except from Chuck."

Doug's stinging rebuke recalled the jumbled collection of chaotic images and searing pain that Cameron had reconstructed as best he could from what he had been able to discover on his own. In short, Doug, in his typical manner, would not abandon the team even after being ordered to by Chuck. Following the others, Doug intercepted a Soviet agent attempting to kill one of the FBI agents on the scene. In his efforts to prevent that from happening, Doug received the bullet intended for the agent. While ultimately not fatal, the bullet damaged one of Doug's kidneys sufficiently enough to require its removal in order to save his life. Cameron, recovering from his own injuries, did not have a chance to follow up with his friend before they were sent on their separate ways to recuperate.

"Man, you know I was messed up as well, and so was everyone else! We were all in shock and just wanted to get away. Don't play the pity game with me. I deserve better than that!"

"You're right," Doug said, his tone sorrowful and quiet. "You do. But so did I. Though I have to admit that Chuck did right by me when all was said and done."

"What do you mean?"

Before Doug could reply, the beep of the phone once again interrupted them.

"Mr. Shirley, pick up on line two!" Doug repeated into the phone, making little effort to disguise his agitation. He did not turn back to face Cameron when he hung up. His shoulders sagged and his head was lowered.

"I know you don't owe any of us anything," Cameron pressed. "I'm not claiming that you do. To be honest, I agree it is probably the other way round. But, man, I *need* you! I can't do this without knowing there is someone who has my back."

Doug turned and faced Cameron, who felt the pointed gaze of Doug's dark eyes study him closely. Involuntarily, he shuddered.

"What, exactly, are we talking about then?"

Cameron did not reply, as much as he wanted to. The knowing nod from his friend confirmed that the other man understood.

"That's what I thought. You can't tell me, can you?"

"Not yet, no," Cameron sighed. "But that is kind of the reason I'm here. I don't know exactly what is going on, but I know it isn't insignificant, and I need to know there is something involved with it that I can count on. So, please, say you'll come back."

"It's not that easy," Doug muttered. "You probably aren't aware of it, but some things have changed with me ..."

Before he could continue, the phone beeped once again. In utter exasperation, Doug reached for the intercom to make yet another request for the manager and then paused. Looking over his friend's shoulder, Cameron saw what caught Doug's attention.

On one of the monitors, apparently displaying a storage room, the camera image revealed Art Shirley involved in a passionate embrace with a young woman who was in a partial state of undress.

"You son of a bitch," Doug growled. He then picked up the phone for another storewide page.

"Art, get your damn hands out of Ruby's pants and answer your wife's phone call, you asshole!"

Cameron stared in stunned disbelief as the monitor showed the manager and his paramour hastily rushing out of view of the camera while the other monitors revealed scenes of customers erupting into laughter. They also displayed Ofelia Rodriguez hurrying through the store. Cameron could only assume she was headed for the monitoring room, and he knew this would not be good.

"Doug, you really shouldn't have done that!"

Ignoring his friend, Doug picked up the phone once more to issue yet another storewide page. "Oh, and in case any of you geniuses haven't figured it out yet, I quit!"

Doug slammed down the receiver and stood up, facing Cameron. "I hope you were serious about that job offer, man. Because it looks like I'm going to need one."

"Oh my God, Doug! What have you *done*?"

"I think that is what they call 'giving notice.' Let's go."

Doug stormed past Cameron. As they entered the hallway, Cameron heard loud voices engaged in an angry confrontation. Doug laughed.

"Ruby was one of Ophelia's floor walkers," he informed Cameron, who shook his head in stunned disbelief.

"Doug, you can't behave like that! I cannot afford to be involved in a confrontation with anyone. I can't bring attention to why I'm here!"

"Relax," Doug assured him. "I guarantee no one will bother us. Ophelia has it in for Art anyway, so she's going to be tied up dealing with him. You just wait here while I change."

"We have got to get out of here, *now*!"

"Man, I don't care if they've dropped The Bomb in the parking lot and the Russians are storming men's wear; I refuse to be seen in public looking like Lenny the Lounge Lizard! Either wait for me or leave. I'll only be a second."

Cameron stayed behind in the doorway, hoping no one would notice him. He could hear loud and angry voices, though he could not understand what was being said. Cameron began to consider possible scenarios that would enable them to leave the store without being detained or confronted by anyone.

Maybe this wasn't such a good idea, after all.

His thoughts were interrupted by another storewide page. This time, however, it was not one of Doug's angry outbursts but was similar to the treacly tones of earlier pages announcing specials in various departments.

"Attention, Value Mart shoppers! To show our appreciation for you, our customers, for the next thirty seconds, whatever you can make it out of the store with, you can *keep*!"

Horrified, Cameron listened to the sounds of the department store erupting into absolute chaos. It was then that he decided, mission or not, he needed to get out of that store. Before he could act, Doug came running up behind him.

"I told you I'd only be a minute." His friend smiled.

Despite his anger, Cameron felt an odd sense of relief when he saw Doug. Gone were the outlandish clothes of a few moments ago. In their place were the more familiar denims and T-shirt Cameron was accustomed to seeing him in, along with a black baseball cap that was more of a relief to Cameron than he thought it would be. Doug held the other garments in a bundle under his arm. Grabbing Doug by the shoulder, Cameron pulled him close.

"Listen, bright eyes, I'm a federal agent now. You can't be pulling shit like this! This could have serious consequences, and I can't be implicated in them."

"What are you talking about?" Doug protested innocently. "I only quit my job. What trouble could you get in over that?"

"Oh, you mean to tell me that you didn't have anything to do with that announcement just now?"

"Did it sound like me?"

It was then that Cameron realized it had sounded quite similar to the manager's voice. Yet there was no way he could picture the manager making such an announcement.

"Well, no. But you can't expect me to believe that Art or whoever it was decided to do something like that!"

"Wasn't I changing out of their clothes and into mine?"

"Well, yes, that's true. But you could have done it from there."

"Oh, really? Do you know if there's a phone in there or not?"

"Well, no I don't, but what has that got to do with anything?"

"It means, Mr. Federal Agent, that you don't have any evidence to prove I made that page. So quit getting your undies in a bunch and let's go!"

The two men headed out onto the floor and were assaulted by the sounds of arguments and shouts. Doug guided them through the aisles away from areas such as electronics and housewares where people were most likely to be trying to grab items. Suddenly, Cameron saw Art Shirley emerge from the crowd and attempt to block Doug's path. Without hesitating, Doug threw the bundle of clothes at the manager and continued toward the front of the store.

"Make sure you wash those pants good, Arty-boy," Doug shouted. "I go commando!"

Cameron winced at the horrified expression on the man's face and hurried to the front entrance. There he found Doug holding his denim jacket open for several harried clerks to inspect, indicating that he had no merchandise concealed. Cameron did the same, as well as holding out his badge. The two men were quickly waved through, and Cameron and Doug emerged into an eerily silent parking lot.

"Do you have any idea how much trouble you could get into for that?" Cameron hissed, turning on Doug. "You always need to make things more difficult than they have to be!"

"Again, you have no proof that I did anything," Doug replied calmly.

Cameron was surprised to notice that Doug was not defensive or angry, which were historically his typical response to situations where he was challenged or accused of something. Instead the former roadie was composed and rational.

"Besides," Doug continued, "I think everything worked out pretty well. We were able to leave without being bothered by anyone, and you got me to agree to go along with whatever scheme you've cooked up, which you can't tell me anything about. You got everything you wanted and with a minimum of fuss, so stop complaining!"

"A minimum … of fuss …" Cameron choked.

Doug flashed him a toothy grin.

Cameron eyed him suspiciously as Doug waited for him to unlock the car. "You know you're going to hell for that, right?" Cameron stated as he pulled the car into traffic.

"*If* I had done it, it would have been entirely worth it," Doug replied with a smile, to which Cameron merely shook his head.

"So can you please tell me more about what it is you want me to do," Doug asked before his friend could go off on another lecture.

"No, not really," Cameron sighed. "To be totally honest, I didn't expect you to be free quite this suddenly. I was actually just trying to see if you would even be interested in considering it. I haven't even pitched this idea to McIntyre or anyone else."

"I thought you said she was the one who suggested it?"

"She suggested getting the band together again, yes. Getting *you* back? I'm afraid that was my own idea."

"Why does she want you to start this up again, anyhow, if you don't mind my asking?"

"All right, that much I can say. It seems the band is pretty popular after all and has garnered a bit of a following, so she thought it would be a good idea to go on tour again to capitalize on that."

"Popular where, exactly?" Doug asked, casting a suspicious glance at his friend.

"Europe."

"No shit." Doug laughed. "Well, I think I've just solved your problems then."

"How so?"

"I don't have a passport, and with my record, I doubt I would get one. So that lets me out of the whole scene. I wish you had told me that sooner. Might have saved us a lot of trouble and kept me in polyester a bit longer."

"Hey, you can kiss my ass," Cameron snapped. "Even if I had spelled it all out, your actions back there were your typical overreaction, and things would still have ended up the way they did, and you know it!"

"You're probably half right." Doug yawned. "I've been getting sick of that place for quite some time. But if I hadn't thought there'd be an alternative, I'd never have chucked. Well, not just yet, anyhow. But it is what it is, I guess."

"Yeah, you can say that again. But can I ask you a question?"

"Shoot."

"Back there you mentioned that Chuck had done right by you. What exactly did he do?"

"Oh boy, where do I begin? Well, for one, he helped me get back into school."

"You mean you finally got your GED? That's great!"

"More or less, yeah. He helped me with that, and he helped me with something else. That something is the reason I've got to figure out what I'm going to do for work, and pretty darn soon."

"What's that?"

"He helped me locate my son," Doug blurted out. His words came out quickly, as if he wanted to rush them past Cameron before they could be heard too closely.

"Your *what*?"

"I thought that would be your reaction," Doug sighed. "Okay, back before I ever started working for you guys, I was going with a girl and she got pregnant. Not long after the baby was born, I got laid off from my job, and because I was a dropout and had a record, I had a hard time finding another one that paid enough to support us. She discovered she could get more money from state aid if I wasn't around and broke up with me. She wouldn't even let me hang around to see him and told me to get away from there, which I did. Then I found you guys at that summer concert, and the rest, as they say, is history."

"No, shit …" Cameron whistled. "You with a little Dougie, that's cool! How old is he?"

"He just turned ten a month ago. He lives with his mom in Wilmington, and I get him every other weekend. But that is probably about to change."

"Why?"

"Let me do the math for you. No job equals no money, which equals no rent or support, which equals no place to stay, which all adds up to no Eli."

"Eli? Is that his name?"

Doug nodded. It was impossible for Cameron to miss the anxiety in his friend's eyes.

"Well, let's not write things off too quickly," Cameron assured him. "We can probably work something out. I mean, you can always stay with me till you find something. I'm usually not home half the time, and you can keep an eye on my place for me. In fact, that gives me an idea."

"I don't know if I want to ask what it is, but what is it?"

"I can hire you to take care of things for me and help me out. You know, sort of like how Pluto helps out the Green Arrow or whoever it is."

"That would be Kato and the Green Hornet, and you've got to be kidding. You want me to add valet to my resume now?"

"I'm totally serious," Cameron assured him enthusiastically. "You can take care of the place for me and be around if anyone is trying to get ahold of me. You've been with us long enough to know protocol, and I won't have to worry about not saying something in front of you. Besides, I live in Edmonton, Virginia, which is only about two hours or so from Wilmington if you still want to bring your boy down to spend weekends with you. I'd have to be careful about what I said around your son, but other agents have kids and manage that, so I guess it can't be that big an issue. He might have to sleep on the couch, but that's no big deal. Hey, you could take the train into DC and hit the museums and stuff like that. He'd love it, I bet!"

"You figured out a solution awful fast for someone not sure of what they were doing," Doug said suspiciously. "Okay, I'll admit that sounds like it could work. But I am not, repeat *not*, doing your laundry! I'll keep an eye on the place and help you out, but you can wash your own damn leopard-print underwear."

"Keep my underwear out of this, if you don't mind. Look, we can work out the details later. Keeping an eye on the place and watching my back will be enough for me for now, trust me. Do you still have your license?"

"Yeah, why?"

"Running errands for me, stuff like that. I just want to make certain you can do that. You weren't a half bad cook either."

Doug continued to eye him suspiciously. "Exactly how far is this valet thing supposed to go?" he asked. "If you're expecting me to bring you coffee in the morning, I can guarantee you that I will."

"Really?"

"Yeah, and then I'll dump it on you."

"I'm not sure, but I don't think Kato would do that. Would he?"

"Listen, you get me a black 1965 Chrysler Imperial Crown to drive around in like he did, and maybe, just maybe, I'll act like Kato. Until then, you're stuck with good old Doug."

"You won't be getting a car like that on an agent's salary; I can promise you that!"

"Really?"

"Man, I can't even afford the leopard-print underwear anymore!"

"I liked your suggestion about leaving your underwear out of this," Doug muttered. "How much will this deal pay, anyhow?"

"Not enough to retire on, but you get room and board and a little money in your pocket. I don't need to inform you that you're not going to get rich, but it can help you maintain access to your son until you find something better."

"So maybe picking up another job would be a good idea?"

"That would be a very good idea."

"So you tempt me away from a major department store with the offer of warm beer, cold pizza, and the opportunity to crash on your couch. I guess you really aren't that far removed from the band after all, are you?"

"Look," pressed Cameron, "all joking aside, will you accept my offer?"

"Well, I'll be honest. It's the best offer I've had all day," Doug sighed. "But I need to ask you something first."

"What is it?"

"Were you leveling with me back there?" asked Doug. "I mean, about understanding how I felt all this time?"

"Yes, I was. Why?"

"I was just curious, that's all. Well then, old buddy, it looks like you've got yourself a Kato."

Chapter 5

"Boys of Summer"

Col. Adalrich Fuchs was not a happy man. He had not been happy for quite some time, and he doubted that he would ever be happy again. The cause for his anxiety, however, was one he could not readily complain about. To do so would risk making his situation worse than it currently was, much worse.

Fuchs reread the memo for whatever number of times it might have been. He had lost count. Fuchs looked at the date once more to be certain that this memo was, in fact, the most recent one. They had all begun to seem the same to him. Despite being issued by the office of Stasi Director Erich Mielke, Fuchs was well aware of the unspoken reality that, like all of the preceding ones, it had originated from the desk of Vladimir Kryuchkov, head of the First Chief Directorate of the KGB. And, like all of the preceding ones, the message was the same.

"It is of the highest priority that young Mikhail Nikolaevich Sechenov be monitored closely, at all times. Isolation from others cannot be permitted. However, prolonged fraternization with the students of Schwerin is prohibited. Sechenov has been encouraged to write to approved students residing in areas outside of Soviet jurisdiction. This shall be permitted to continue. However, all communications must continue to be monitored. All incoming packages are to be examined closely. All outgoing packages must be through venues approved by the State. Only previously approved materials are permitted to be in his possession."

Fuchs was about to crumple the memo in frustration but stopped. Too many people would be likely to notice and be even more likely to comment. However, the comments would not be directed to him but rather to his superiors, which would complicate his situation a great deal further. Folding the memo out smoothly, he once more searched the contents in hopes of discovering a clearer directive. A clearer directive other than the obvious: that he was to deal with a problem that no one else wanted to deal with and to keep something everyone else wished would go away.

The proverbial fly in Fuchs's ointment was Mikhail Sechenov. Sechenov was the privileged only child of privileged parents working within the KGB's First Chief Directorate. They were responsible for espionage efforts against the West. Zoya Alexeyevna Sechenov, the boy's mother, had been something of a Soviet celebrity. A vibrant and beautiful woman, Zoya was touted as an equal to any of the glamorous beauties in Western magazines and was promoted as such by Soviet propaganda machines. Her charm and personality matched her beauty, and she was sought after by Soviet businessmen to appear at trade delegations and meetings with Western industrialists. This adulation was encouraged because in reality she was a KGB agent who easily gained access to the confidences of smitten industrialists and military contractors, who competed with one another in an effort to impress her.

When Zoya bore a son, the image of motherhood served to advance, not detract, from the carefully cultivated image of the ideal Soviet woman, and young Mikhail became the darling of Soviet media as well. Of her husband, there was never any mention, leading to rumors of estrangement or widowhood. Since her superiors in the KGB felt this added to her aura of mystery, Zoya would neither publicly confirm nor deny any of the rumors.

Her activities had long ago attracted the attention of American counterintelligence agencies, and her death in 1977, under tragic and mysterious circumstances, caused her to be regarded as the Soviet

Marilyn Monroe, a young beauty taken much too soon. It also made young Mikhail a de facto heir to the focus of Soviet obsession.

However, Mikhail Sechenov was proving to be an uncontrollable heir apparent. Typically, such individuals would usually grow up to find themselves stationed in some obscure agency or low-ranking position where they could be quietly marginalized and ignored. In this particular case, unfortunately, such a solution would not be so easy. The complication was that the child was considered valuable.

Both of Mikhail's parents had been orphans. All of Mikhail's grandparents, aunts, and uncles had perished in either the Great War or the purges in the years leading up to it. Mikhail had been the younger of two children, the eldest of whom died of meningitis, thus leaving Mikhail to be the sole focus of his parents' attention. This was a beneficial position for a child whose mother was highly favored by the Soviet government. The father, however, was a different matter altogether.

Much of the identity surrounding Mikhail's father was deliberately shrouded in mystery. The man's reputation had, at one point, eclipsed that of his late wife. Rumors of his death or their separation had been encouraged during the ascendancy of his career in an effort to keep his identity and activities a closely guarded secret. The Soviets could not afford to have someone as valuable as he was meet the same fate as his wife. Unfortunately, in a society that was never far removed from Stalin's purges, it was still possible to fall out of favor and for such a fall to be as fast as one's rise. To fall out of favor with the Kremlin and the KGB bosses would place him in a precarious position.

This was a fact that Mikhail's father was reminded of each time he was reposted to a less prestigious position. His superiors certainly knew it, and so these old rumors of his death were kept alive in order for them to avoid having to face any public inconvenience in the event of his disappearance.

Ironically, it was his father's disfavor with Moscow Central that kept Mikhail in the style to which he had long ago become accustomed. As the last living relative of an object of concern, the boy proved useful as leverage to keep his father in line. The fact that

Mikhail despised his father was something that the KGB officials delighted in, even permitting the youth to adopt the maiden name of his mother as his surname. Such an action served as a reminder to his father that he could cease to exist and no questions would ever be asked.

Since the young Mikhail was acutely aware that his every action was in some manner a reflection on his father, he seemed determined that any such reflection would be as unfavorable as possible. Relaxed restrictions on items from the West provided the perfect outlet for Mikhail to be a constant embarrassment to his father by openly flaunting American styles. This was not only encouraged in an effort to annoy his father but also to provide the Soviets with the public relations benefit of allowing their citizens to fondle the trappings of capitalism, so long as they did not accept them.

While Mikhail's obsession with all things capitalist might be a source of embarrassment to his father, it was certainly an embarrassment to the more hard-line KGB officials. By saying young Mikhail was being enrolled in the exclusive Schwerin school in East Germany, he was shipped off to be dealt with under Stasi supervision, far from the eyes of the Kremlin. However, that did not prevent him from being a source of obsession for the more conservative KGB leaders and their love-hate relationship with this family. That was how Fuchs managed to acquire a sizable dossier on the need to deal with a problem the KGB did not want to deal with, but could not get rid of.

"Why must I be punished?" Fuchs muttered as he replaced the file in his cabinet. Fuchs was to deal with the boy but not punish him. He was to allow him to be a thorn in his father's side but not in anyone else's. He was to allow him to acquire as much Western items as he wished but not enjoy them. Fuchs was to keep the boy out of sight but make certain he was clearly visible.

"Allow him to chew his food but not to taste it," Fuchs sighed, slamming the cabinet closed. A sudden knock at his door made him apprehensive. How loudly had he talked to himself or slammed the cabinet?

"Come in," he called.

The door opened to reveal the fresh, smiling face of one of his assistants—a face that did nothing to allay Fuchs's disquiet.

Lieutenant Rudolph Hertz had recently been assigned to Fuchs's office and had proven himself to be quite competent and dedicated to his work. He was enthusiastic and ambitious, which, in Fuchs's eyes, made him both an excellent assistant and a potential rival. However, in a moment of sudden insight, Fuchs realized that Hertz's ambition could make him the solution to Fuchs's own dilemma.

"Good morning, comrade," Hertz enthused with a smile. Fuchs absently acknowledged the greeting and then motioned for him to be seated.

"I have an assignment for you," Fuchs began. "Our young Russian friend needs some special attention, it seems."

"Are you referring to Sechenov by any chance?"

Fuchs rankled at Hertz's implied familiarity. "You mean Mikhail Nikolaevich Sechenov. Yes, that is who I am referring to," he stated. "Apparently, our young comrade is becoming an object of concern to those in high places."

"Do you mean an object of concern or an object of embarrassment?" said Hertz with a laugh.

"Need I remind you that an object of embarrassment to the Russians is an object of concern for us?"

Fuchs did not shout, or raise his voice. His demeanor did not change in any noticeable way. However, the statement was a sudden slap, and with the realization of his misplaced humor, Hertz's smile vanished. Fuchs watched with satisfaction as the young man shifted uncomfortably under Fuchs's steady gaze.

"As I was saying, young Mr. Sechenov needs special attention. Those responsible for him wish that he continues to enjoy the taste of the West's forbidden fruits. However, there seems to be a concern that he sees them as his right, not his privilege. Our impressionable young charge needs to be reminded of the proper way to view things."

"I see," replied Hertz. "And I am to be the one who helps him to see the error of his ways, I take it?"

"I believe you are most suited to be the one who helps prevent him from falling into excess, yes."

"Why don't they simply eliminate his privileges if they are going to become such an object of concern?" Hertz remarked bitterly.

"Because to do so is not convenient at this time," Fuchs explained patiently. "As long as he is permitted these little enjoyments, the Western media believe that conditions in the Eastern Bloc are relaxed and the West is winning."

"Is it that important to have them think that way?"

"Would you prefer the alternative?" asked Fuchs. "I believe that would place you back at the front, would it not?"

Rudolph Hertz became very quiet. He had been recruited by the Nationale Volksarmee (NVA) at the outbreak of the war and had been involved with the invasion and occupation of Austria. Through the political connections of his family, Hertz had been transferred from the active duty army to the Felix Dzerzhinsky Guards Regiment. This enabled him to serve as part of the security for the Stasi without the dangers of serving directly on the front. Hertz had been assigned to protect the former embassies of various Western diplomatic missions. His abilities in helping Stasi agents classify and secure captured security and intelligence information attracted the attention of Stasi officials. Hertz was then recruited into the less public workings of the agency and saw rapid promotion to the rank of lieutenant colonel. Here Hertz was secure from both the dangers of life on the front and the public hostility toward the Guards Regiment, the only visible face of the Stasi.

"Of course I don't want to see that," Hertz replied.

Fuchs did not miss the anger in his colleague's reply, nor the anxiety, but saw no point in pressing it. Both men were aware that Fuchs had scored sufficient advantage.

"Then you realize the importance of allowing the illusion."

"What is it that you wish me to do?" Hertz's voice reflected his resignation to the situation.

"You are to go and stay with comrade Sechenov, for the time being at least. Help him to have a more, shall we say, balanced view of his situation. That would be beneficial to everyone concerned."

"In other words, you want me to be a babysitter, is that it?" demanded Hertz.

Fuchs shrugged. "If you choose to adopt that perspective, that is your prerogative. However, I should think that would only encumber your efforts, not facilitate them."

"Why do you want me to do this, may I ask?"

"It's really quite simple. If I were to go, I would simply be viewed as another old man out of touch with modern times and tastes," Fuchs explained patiently. "You, however, are close enough to his age to appreciate the things he does and possibly relate to him. I would be viewed as a meddlesome uncle, but you? You have the opportunity to become a big brother, if you will, a possible confidant. Someone he could consider a coconspirator as it were. You might even consider initiating some mischief, subject to approval of course. I think you would be in an excellent position to allow him to enjoy his little playthings, while at the same time guiding him away from his usual embarrassing excesses."

"That is hardly a task I envisioned myself working on when I began here."

"Perhaps you can have your uniform let out then? I suspect your recent, soft lifestyle has no doubt made it a bit tight, hasn't it?"

Fuchs's reply was like a splash of cold water. The younger man accepted the rebuke.

"When do I begin?" Hertz asked quietly.

"My secretary will contact you with all the necessary arrangements. Until then, if I were you, I would be making my preparations for a prolonged stay."

The younger man rose and bade farewell to the older man, who watched as he left the office. Fuchs smiled as the door closed. He had every reason to smile. He had potentially killed two birds with one stone.

Chapter 6

"(Just Like) Starting Over"

S pecial Agent Barbara McIntyre was livid. Cameron was hardly surprised.

"What on earth possessed you to bring him here?" she demanded.

"I have already explained it to you," Cameron calmly repeated. "I just thought the guys would have wanted a chance to say hello to him once more. You know, like a reunion. I had no idea ..."

"You knew perfectly well that this was going to be a highly classified meeting and that no one not directly connected to this was going to be allowed into it!" she reminded him.

Doug and the other band members watched the exchange between McIntyre and Cameron with unease, the same way they would have watched their parents fight. At Cameron's suggestion, Doug had accompanied him to the house in the Washington suburb. Evan had brought Rich, who was supposed to be there.

Initially, the reuniting of the band was supposed to be coordinated with the meeting to discuss the undisclosed mission. This was agreed upon to prevent anyone from inadvertently revealing the motive behind the band's activities. While Evan was delayed in attempting to recruit Clyde, Cameron had decided to find Doug.

Cameron realized that there was no way Doug would be part of the mission and that things would be moving too rapidly once it got started for all of them to be together. So, in a moment of nostalgia, he orchestrated a small get-together well before the time scheduled for the meeting. To his dismay, McIntyre was already there.

"I had no idea that anyone other than us would be here this soon," Cameron protested. "I thought we would have a chance to be human before we had to get back into this! Besides, it's not like I'm the only one who has ever used these places for something personal."

"You have been an agent too long to revert to your petulant routine, so don't even try playing that game with me. In case you haven't noticed, I am far less tolerant than either Chuck or Dwyer were. You are a professional, and I will expect you to act like it. At *all* times!"

"Okay then, you win. I'm sorry," Cameron conceded. "But the last time we were all together we deserted one another, and I thought it would be good to have a chance to reconnect and patch things up. I honestly thought that if I got everyone here early, we would have a chance to relax a bit before we had to get back into all this. Yes, I'm an agent now and so is Evan, but you need to remember that the others aren't."

"One of whom shouldn't even *be* here!"

Cameron glanced at Doug, expecting the roadie's characteristic defensive outburst. To Cameron's relief, and surprise, the roadie maintained a placid expression. Doug did not display any trace of annoyance at being talked about, something that in the past would throw him into a rage. Hoping to take advantage of Doug's lack of irritation, Cameron tossed him his car keys.

"Do you remember how to get home?" Cameron asked.

Doug nodded, catching them in midair. "Will you be wanting a ride home later, Mr. Reid?" he asked. His tone was calm and polite.

Ha! Just like a real valet.

"Oh, you're the Green Hornet now." Evan laughed.

Before Cameron could answer, they heard a car door close.

"Shit," muttered McIntyre.

Moments later, the door from the garage opened and two agents entered the kitchen. They gave what appeared to be a casual glance around the room. To the more practiced and experienced, however, it was obvious they had taken in every pertinent detail—a suspicion confirmed when their attention focused on Doug.

"I didn't see his photo in the dossier," one of the agents said.

"Gentlemen, permit me to introduce Doug Courtland," McIntyre sighed. "Mr. Courtland is a former associate of the band and was just leaving."

"I'm afraid he isn't," the agent replied. "As of now all systems are go, and no one leaves here until things are finished and the coast is clear."

"Shit," repeated McIntyre. "Very well then, there is nothing left to do but make introductions, I suppose. Gentlemen, permit me to introduce Special Agent Eric Colby and Special Agent William Dietrich. They are in charge of the security details for this meeting. Incidentally, as you have probably noticed by the expressions on their faces, they don't like surprises any more than I do."

Colby had been the agent who addressed McIntyre. He stood roughly five feet eight inches tall. He had a tanned complexion, closely cropped hair, and a square jaw. Cameron wondered if the man had not previously been in the military. The other agent, Dietrich, was taller and more heavyset. His hair was longer than Colby's and slicked back. His face was fuller, and Cameron suspected that he spent more time behind a desk than in the field. The second agent did not linger in the room long but disappeared once McIntyre had made her introductions. The sound of more cars pulling into the carport attached to the side of the house could be heard, and Dietrich reappeared and whispered something to Colby.

"Okay, it looks like our guests are arriving," Colby announced. "Special Agent McIntyre, please take your people for their security check while we secure things down here."

"Cameron, will you and the others follow me?" McIntyre said, motioning toward the door. "Doug, I'm afraid you're going to have to stay down here with these agents."

The roadie made no reply but held his arms up as another agent patted him down and checked him for listening devices. Once the security check had concluded, Doug sat down again. Agent Dietrich continued to watch Doug but did not attempt to address him.

Cameron followed McIntyre up a flight of stairs to the second-floor hallway. There, they were all given a similar security clearance. Cameron thought back to a wintery night six years before when the band was recruited. They were taken to a place that they initially believed was a hotel but were surprised to discover that it was actually a safe house and surveillance station. This house, by contrast, resembled a regular colonial-style residence from the outside, but once inside he saw that it had been adapted for more secure uses.

The windows were all fashioned with upper and lower sections, each consisting of six small panes of glass. Each pane of glass was created to make it appear that one was looking underwater without a scuba mask. To the casual observer, this would resemble the typical colonial manufacture of windowpanes, which could be seen in many of the historic houses in Williamsburg and elsewhere around the area. However, their design provided the added benefit that anyone looking in from the outside would be able to read the lips of any of the occupants. Each window also possessed interior shutters, common in houses built in the seventeenth and eighteenth centuries. Cameron suspected these twentieth-century counterparts had the added benefit of being bulletproof.

No telling what else they've rigged up in here.

"Evan, you'll stay here with Rich," McIntyre explained, stopping at a small room. "Cameron and I have to be in the other meeting. You will each be interviewed by some of the others who are directing this operation."

"Is that when we finally find out what this operation is?" asked Evan.

"No, you find that out if they decide to go ahead with it or not," she replied.

"And if they don't decide to do it, what happens to us?" asked Rich.

"Then you're free to go," McIntyre explained.

"And if they do decide to do it …" he asked once more.

"We'll cross that bridge when we come to it," she said.

Before anyone could ask anything more, she turned and left. Cameron followed but not before casting a glance back at his friends. The anxiety that shone on their faces matched his own feelings. For a brief moment, the thought of being back with them had brought with it the euphoric sense of freedom that characterized so much of their time together. A freedom represented by a period in his life when his wardrobe consisted of torn jeans, worn T-shirts, and motorcycle boots and his only concerns were about playing shows, getting paid, and not going home alone. Cameron knew that the moment he turned away from them, reality would face him once again, and with reality came danger.

He followed his colleague down the hallway to a room that faced the sunken garden in the back of the house. Cameron supposed that at one point the room must have been a spacious master bedroom, but it had since been gutted to create a soundproof conference room. In the center was a large conference table surrounded by chairs, with stations for drinking water and cups evenly spaced on its surface. In the far wall was a small opening that Cameron recognized as part of a projector room and suspected that on the opposite wall was a screen. The room was devoid of artwork, lamps, and statuary.

No place to plant a listening device.

Cameron noticed that McIntyre was as composed as ever, at least outwardly. Her attention to nearly every detail on this was indicative of her anxiety about the acceptance of her proposal and any possible consequences. To Cameron, this offered a possible explanation for her displeasure at discovering Doug at the meeting place. It was something totally unscripted. He wanted to remind her that such variables would almost certainly be a part of any operation, but he knew that wasn't necessary. Besides, that would be a bad idea. Just then Special Agent Colby, who had remained outside, opened the door to admit three other people, two men and a woman.

The two men were in military uniforms, one from the US Navy and the other from the US Army. From the insignias on their uniforms, Cameron noted that the sailor was a lieutenant and the soldier was a major. The woman, however, was the one who attracted his attention. She was McIntyre's size but of slighter build, with auburn hair and an alabaster complexion, adorned with light freckles. She was dressed in a smart skirt and jacket and had a pleasant expression on her face, though she did not speak. Before anyone could introduce themselves, Agent Colby opened the door once more and admitted three other men.

The first was an older man, with worry lines on his face and gray hair. The other two were perhaps the same age, and all three were dressed in dark suits.

"Has he arrived yet?" the first man asked no one in particular.

"No, he hasn't," McIntyre replied. "He prefers to wait until everyone is here before arriving."

"Is everyone here, then?" the man asked.

McIntyre looked at everyone and nodded. "Yes, I believe so."

"Well, then I guess we wait," he grumbled. "They wouldn't by any chance have something to drink in here, would they?"

"Just water, I'm afraid," McIntyre explained. "His request. All participants in this meeting are to be clear and focused."

"Typical of him," the man protested.

McIntyre introduced Cameron to the other people in the room. He learned the names of the two servicemen; the man from the navy was Lt. Bailey Franks and the man from the army was Maj. John Kendall. The three older men were more intimidating once Cameron discovered who they were. The first was Eugene Parker, while the other two introduced themselves as Lewis Alderman and Vernon Gray. As they moved off, McIntyre whispered to him that the first man was from the National Security Agency and the other two were from the Central Intelligence Agency. It was only then that the full weight and measure of McIntyre's earlier implications concerning the risks of this operation truly took hold.

Cameron thought about his friends in the other room, sequestered from him. The familiar bravado of their relationship, which previously had been such a source of confidence to him, now seemed tinny and artificial when measured against the ominous enormity of the matter that had yet to be revealed.

No, I mustn't go there. To overanalyze is to paralyze, and I sure as hell can't afford any paralysis now.

Special Agent Dwyer, Cameron's first mentor, taught him the familiar axiom. Dwyer, the cool and methodical agent who always seemed to be focused and alert. Dwyer, the agent found murdered in an abandoned warehouse in Burlington, Vermont. The knot in Cameron's stomach grew tighter, and he cast about for anything that might provide him with solace and security. It was then that his eyes lit on the one person he had not been introduced to yet.

While McIntyre had been making the introductions, the other woman had been getting a cup of water at the opposite end of the room. Cameron nudged McIntyre.

"Let's not be rude now," he whispered. "There's someone I haven't said hello to yet."

"Will you behave, for God's sake?" McIntyre whispered back. "You were the rock star downstairs; you're the agent up here."

"And it would reflect badly on us if I were rude to a guest, wouldn't it? So then, permit me to be introduced."

McIntyre flashed a warm smile as she took him by the elbow and directed him toward the other end of the room, but judging from her grip, Cameron knew that she was not pleased with him. At that moment, fate seemed to intervene as the door opened once more. Two men in dark suits entered, and he could see two other men take up positions outside the door. Agent Colby closed the shutters on the windows, causing the room to fall into a half-light. McIntyre released her grip on his elbow.

I wish you hadn't done that.

The occupants of the room all focused their attention on the doorway as another man entered the room. There was no jovial greeting or friendly smile on any of their faces, and Cameron was aware of a slight stiffening of some of them, as if they were standing at attention. The man was imposing but not so much due to his size as to the aura around him. He stood six feet, two inches tall. He was broad shouldered and heavyset, though his frame suggested a trace of an athletic build that would have defined him in his youth. He was African-American, with skin that shone like polished ebony. His hair was gray and cut close. His visage was stern like a thundercloud, and Cameron did not doubt for a moment that any fury unleashed by this man would have the same devastating effects.

This must be the one we were waiting for.

McIntyre nudged him toward a seat as the other occupants of the room sat down, with the newly arrived gentleman at the head of the table. The two men who had entered the room with him were positioned on either side of the now-closed door.

I guess there's no turning back now, is there.

"Well, I think everyone is here," began Vernon Gray. "Shall we begin?"

Out of the corner of his eye, Cameron noticed the slight twitch of McIntyre's eyebrow, which she always did when she was irritated. This time, however, he shared her irritation at the presumptive attitude of their CIA counterpart.

Well, this is our safe house; we should have had the prerogative of beginning!

"My name is Vernon Gray and this is my associate, Lewis Alderman," he continued. He gestured toward the man sitting across from him, who made the obligatory nod of recognition. "Mr. Alderman and I are representing William Casey, the director of the Central Intelligence Agency."

Gray paused and motioned toward Cameron and McIntyre.

"Here we have Special Agents Cameron Walsh and Barbara McIntyre, who are representing FBI Director William Webster. I also should like to add that the bureau has graciously offered to host this highly classified meeting, and I would like to thank them for their hospitality."

Cameron noticed yet another twitch of McIntyre's eyebrow and saw her neck muscle tighten. He knew that as soon as she had the chance, she would be going for a jog and the Washington pavement would be paying the price, not only for Gray's arrogance but also for his misogynistic disregard for her seniority in introducing them.

"Here we have Eugene Parker, representing Lieutenant General Faurer of the National Security Agency," Gray continued. "To his right are Major John Kendall and Lieutenant Sidney Franks, representing the intelligence branches of the United States Army and Navy, respectively. To my right is Miss Siobhan Fagan of Interpol. This meeting will be chaired by the esteemed Evander Stoughton. Due to the pressing nature of the subject of this meeting, Mr. Stoughton has been authorized by the president to be the final voice in deciding if the operation is to be accepted or rejected, and his authority to do so has been confirmed by Congress by way of Senator Barry Goldwater, chairman of the Senate Select Committee on Intelligence, and House Speaker O'Neil. I do not think I need to remind you all of the seriousness of this matter, or of the implications to national security should we decide to proceed."

My God, you are a pompous ass. Why not just say none of the principals will be here so that if the shit hits the fan, they can say they didn't know about it?

"Ladies and gentlemen, we have a highly unique opportunity presented to us," Alderman stated in a campy, dramatic tone. "Our agents in West Germany have received an offer from a person highly placed in the Kremlin who wishes to defect to the West."

"Why in the world should we be bothered with all of this secrecy if that is all it is?" demanded Parker. "How many of these offers do you people get in a day? Are you going to shut down the entire intelligence community over all of them?"

"This particular offer carries with it both unique opportunities and unique challenges," Alderman explained. "When I say that he is highly placed, I am not exaggerating."

"Who is it then, Chernenko or Chebrikov?" snorted Parker to polite titters from some of the others, except for Stoughton whose stoic expression remained unchanged and silenced the reactions of the other participants.

"Obviously not that highly placed," Alderman insisted. "But if our intelligence is correct, they are not too far removed from that gravitational pull."

"Exactly how close to the top?" Parker demanded.

"Close enough to be the proverbial keys to the kingdom," Alderman replied.

"Then they're also just as likely to be the proverbial Trojan horse," Parker countered.

"We realize that," Gray assured them. "This has been checked out by not only us but also the British and the West Germans. We are all convinced this offer is genuine."

"Exactly who is it then?" asked Franks.

Alderman's expression reflected his annoyance at being questioned by someone several years his junior in both age and experience. "For obvious reasons, even in this secure environment, the actual name of the subject cannot be used," he responded.

Cameron noted the slight scolding conveyed in the man's tone and wondered how Franks was receiving it. The young lieutenant's body language provided no indication.

"The KGB refers to our subject only as Alexi," Alderman continued, addressing the room once again. "From the intelligence that we've received, he has been key to the Soviet war effort from the very beginning. There is adequate proof that he was directly involved in the implementation of the Soviet invasion of the United States, if not the actual planning of it."

Cameron could not believe what he had heard. Was Alderman actually talking about the individual responsible for the death and destruction that the country had been enduring for the past six years? Could one person even *be* responsible for something of this magnitude?

"Do you honestly believe the Soviets would let someone of that caliber out of their sights for a minute?" demanded Parker. "I don't care what the British or the Germans say; that is simply too good to be true!"

"Our sources have uncovered information regarding Alexi from the beginning of the Alaskan Offensive and the effort to push the

Soviets out of North America. It seems that while Alexi was a rising star prior to that, his fortunes went into a rapid decline with every mile we recaptured. With the recent shake-ups in the Kremlin following the deaths of Brezhnev and Andropov, some of his patrons are no longer around and he is not the golden boy he once was."

"So we're going through all of this nonsense for a knockoff," sneered Parker. "Are you folks over at Langley that bored?"

"No, we're that astute," Gray replied coolly. "Someone on that level will know the name of every Soviet operative remaining here in the West, as well as details of Soviet war plans and capabilities that would take us years to discover if we were to attempt it on our own."

"Is that what he has offered?" asked Kendall.

"That has been one of the things, yes," confirmed Alderman.

"How do you know that he's telling the truth?" demanded Parker. "We all know that potential defectors promise the moon and you're lucky if you get the lid of a bean can!"

"We can assure you that intelligence he has passed on to us thus far has, in fact, been tested and proven to be quite accurate," Alderman explained.

"Are you at liberty to share that information?" asked McIntyre.

Alderman hesitated a moment and then continued. "Not entirely," he explained. "However, let us just say that the person that Alexi revealed to MI6 would have made Kim Philby very jealous."

The reference to the infamous British spy and defector to the Soviet Union was not lost on Cameron. Philby was a highly placed Soviet agent with access to both British and American intelligence, whose discovery sent shock waves throughout the intelligence community, some of which were still being felt.

"My God," whispered Parker, all traces of his previous arrogance gone.

Alderman resumed his presentation. "Neither we, nor the British, believe that the Soviets would sacrifice one of their most valuable assets for a ruse. Therefore, we are convinced of the legitimacy of this offer and the need to act upon it, and act fast."

"Why the urgency?" Parker asked. "We need time to analyze

this and decide how to proceed. If this is as hot as you say, then we need to be very careful how we handle it."

"I'm afraid that the urgency is very real," explained Gray. "As we mentioned, Alexi is not currently in a position of favor, and as such, his situation is quite precarious and could be terminated at any moment. The fact that it hasn't at this point indicates that he still has some value for the Soviets, but we don't know when that capital will be used up. I'm afraid the only briefing and analysis that can be done has to be done right here, in this room."

"That is ridiculous," protested Parker. "You can't expect us to make a decision like that based on an afternoon session around a conference table!"

"That is precisely what we must do and precisely why I am here," explained Stoughton. The man's deep, baritone voice rumbled like thunder in the room and caught Cameron by surprise.

"I have the authorization to say if this is to be undertaken or rejected, and I am the only one who has this authorization. This was given to me by the heads of your agency, as well as the CIA and FBI, not to mention the president and Congress. The fact that this is unusual, in every respect, is not lost on anyone. Neither is the fact that this is potentially the greatest opportunity and greatest risk in American intelligence. Success means that we have gained access to the Soviet play book."

"With all due respect, sir, what then does failure mean?" asked Parker, his insistence not in the least reduced by his deference.

"Failure means we have played the final card," Stoughton said.

Chapter 7

"Rock Me Tonight"

Yakov Petrovsky placed the report on his desk with a cool, deliberative motion. What he had read fueled his suspicions, which had been eating at him for a long time.

"Alexi," as the report referred to its subject, reported for work at his post with the Soviet embassy in Warsaw each day at his appointed time. He performed the duties required of him without complaint, and both his supervisor and the Soviet ambassador spoke highly of his commitment to his work. Alexi's reports and observations of the mercurial situations of post-martial-law Poland were flawless and accurate. He was not observed doing anything out of the ordinary, and phone taps in both his residence and workplace revealed nothing. The report indicated there was nothing at all suspicious about his behavior or any reason for them to be concerned about him. However, as Petrovsky knew perfectly well, that meant they had every reason to be concerned about him.

With the report were stacks of surveillance photos, which Petrovsky once more examined. Taking each one, he envisioned a grid over each photo and methodically studied each invisible square, looking for any indication of a dead drop, a transfer, a brush pass, a signal, or any evidence of Alexi's communication with a foreign agency. He found nothing. Petrovsky was hardly surprised.

Alexi had been one of Petrovsky's own protégés, and one of his better ones. He had learned everything that the older man was able to teach him, sopping it up like a sponge and employing it with such skill that the Kremlin noticed it, to Petrovsky's credit. So much so, in fact, that Alexi and five others were assigned to develop a series of sleeper cells to work in North America, Western Europe, and the Middle East. At the outbreak of the war, the efforts of these cells had been instrumental in aiding the advance of Soviet and Warsaw Pact forces and not only aided occupation forces but also severely weakened the efforts of the enemy to respond. Their efforts had helped to bring victory so close, the Kremlin could almost taste it. There was even speculation that Brezhnev was planning a celebratory meal to be served on his first night in the White House. But opportunity unraveled with almost the same speed with which it had begun.

Alexi bore the brunt of the Kremlin's anger for the simple reason that he was the only one who still alive. The other five had all perished valiantly in the struggle against capitalist imperialism, or so read the Soviet account of such things. However, Petrovsky, along with a few others, knew the truth. They had all taken their lives, knowing perfectly well the fate that would await them.

Yet Alexi had chosen not to. Why? That question haunted many people but not Petrovsky He knew perfectly well why Alexi had chosen to live. Alexi was now valuable—and not just to the Americans.

Time spent deep undercover had provided him with access to information, and informants, that the KGB realized could provide the Soviet Union with the opportunity to reverse their losses. Alexi represented the belief that they could still win the war. The current truce was providing the Soviet military with the breathing space needed to regroup. The current cultural exchange was providing the KGB the opportunity to seduce the West by giving the appearance of Soviet concessions. When the time was right, Alexi could provide the means by which the West, drunk with imagined victory, could be brought down by a dormant Fifth Column.

Petrovsky's eye fell on the emblem of the KGB that hung on his wall: the sword and shield. A two-edged sword. Petrovsky realized

Alexi was just such a sword. The same benefit that he could provide the Soviets, he could also provide to the Americans. Alexi's knowledge of military and intelligence secrets made it impossible to gauge the extent of any damage that could result from his possible defection to the West. Conventional wisdom would suggest getting rid of him now, before giving him the opportunity to betray them. With annoyance, Petrovsky reminded himself that such an action would be impossible. No matter what danger Alexi posed, the potential reward was equal, if not greater.

Alexi was bait to be dangled before the big fish of the West. He was expensive bait, used for catching a big trophy. However, it was just as likely that the trophy could snatch the bait and get away, leaving you with nothing. Such a scenario would spell the end of everything.

"Which is why you must be watched," Petrovsky muttered, studying the photos again.

Chapter 8

"Distant Early Warning"

"I'm afraid I am confused as to Ms. Fagan's presence here," Parker stated. "Interpol does not involve itself with political policy whatsoever. Or has that position changed, Ms. Fagan?"

"I assure you, Mr. Parker, Interpol's objectives have not changed in any way, nor are we proposing an involvement in this operation whatsoever," she replied. Cameron suppressed a sigh at the sound of her Irish brogue. "Yet, while our organization does not plan on participating in this, owing to the sensitivity of the actions proposed, we need to be satisfied that this is not, in fact, a kidnapping."

"That brings us to our next item," Alderman declared. "I realize that the details of this proposed operation have been limited to only a few of us—me, Special Agent McIntyre, Ms. Fagan, and of course, Mr. Stoughton. I cannot impress enough the extreme sensitivity of this operation and the need for utmost secrecy and confidentiality. Any disclosure of this discussion will be considered a threat to national security and will be dealt with accordingly. I would also remind you all that, despite the current truce that is in effect, the United States is still at war. Under such conditions, failure to keep these proceedings confidential will be regarded as treason."

Jesus. Cameron felt a chill as the enormity of the situation became even clearer. He wondered briefly if it would be possible to ask to be released. *I haven't heard any details yet,* he reasoned. *No one told me anything; even under torture there is nothing I could reveal. Would it be possible to just get up and leave?* But he knew, deep inside, that wouldn't be possible. He would see this through. *I have to.*

"Very well," Alderman continued. "As I have revealed, we do have a highly placed individual who wishes to defect. A highly placed individual that the president wants us to assist in any way possible to achieve that desire. However, this will come with a price, and that is why we are all here."

"Then I take it the price is steep," muttered Parker.

Alderman glared at him briefly before regaining his composure. "The price could very well cost us everything," he stated.

Cameron felt his mouth go dry but did not dare reach for the pitcher of water in front of him. There was a charge in the atmosphere, a charge that held everyone in its grip, and he feared what would transpire if the spell they were all under was suddenly broken. Alderman paused, looking about the room. As a showman, Cameron could appreciate the need to ensure that his words were having the desired effect. That did not assuage the panic he was feeling in any way, however.

"The individual in question is under no illusions as to the magnitude of his defection on the Soviet Union and realizes that they will do anything in their power to retaliate," Alderman said. "He obviously has many concerns about his decision, and his chief concern is any consequences to be borne by his family."

"Obviously, the Russians will not let someone that valuable go quietly," reiterated Gray. "There is an established precedent of the Soviets retaliating against family and colleagues of defectors, and I shudder to think what would be done in this case."

"So what are you suggesting?" demanded Parker. "An operation designed around evacuating this Alexi person's entire family? That's insane and you know it."

"Fortunately, that is not going to be necessary," Alderman assured him. "This individual only has one living relative, a son. He has assured us that if we can get him safely to the West, his defection is assured."

"You mean to tell us that he isn't here yet?" asked Franks.

"No, he isn't," confirmed Alderman. "Currently, he is on his regular assignment with the KGB. Our decision to proceed with this operation will mean that his defection will have to be coordinated to take place in conjunction with that of his son. Any delay, in either operation, will be catastrophic."

"Is his son posted with him?" asked Kendall.

Alderman shook his head. "The subject has indicated that his son is at an exclusive boarding school in East Germany, reserved for upper-level members of the government."

"Humph," snorted Parks. "So much for a classless society, I guess."

His remark brought light laughter, which noticeably lightened the tension of the room.

If you weren't so damn ugly, I'd kiss you.

"What is the timetable for this to take place?" Franks asked. His tone revealed that he, too, appreciated the levity.

"As soon as possible," Alderman explained. His tone retained its gravity, but gone was the ominous undercurrent of before. "We can't run the risk of anything happening to him, or to his son."

"Good God, man, you do realize that the logistics of planning, not to mention coordinating, dual operations such as this require time! There is no way that this can be done at the spur of the moment," cried Parker.

"That is why we are not suggesting two operations," interjected Stoughton. "If the decision is made to proceed, we will decide which of the operations we will be concerned with."

"But that will still leave the other one to be done," insisted Parker. "It isn't going to take care of itself."

"I understand that," Stoughton replied calmly. The finality of his tone made it clear that there would be no further discussion on that point.

A tense silence fell over the conference table, with nervous glances directed among colleagues.

"So, what is left to be done?" Kendall asked. His voice was quiet, barely disturbing the solemnity of the room. Cameron could not help but be reminded of people speaking at a funeral.

"You have all heard what Mr. Alderman has presented," Stoughton explained. "You are all aware of the risk involved. I want to hear, from each of you, arguments as to why we should or should not proceed. When I have heard what you all have to say, I will make my decision."

"If you don't mind my asking, sir, when will you present your decision?" asked Parker.

"We will not leave here without the issue being decided," Stoughton replied.

I was afraid of that.

Beginning with Alderman, each intelligence agency presented their arguments. Stoughton listened carefully, asking questions of each person with the finesse of a trial lawyer. Weaknesses in arguments were revealed, with demands to clarify, explain, consider, and reconsider. Strong points were expanded upon. Due to the absence of any clock, and his own reluctance to look at his watch, Cameron had no idea how long they had been there. Even watching the light through the windows was not an option, due to the shutters. He tried following the arguments and discussions, but it was becoming impossible for him to keep track of what was said. With the tendency to discuss and dissect each aspect independently of the context as a whole, it was maddening trying to determine who was for or against what decision. Mercifully, McIntyre was the one to speak on their behalf, which she did ably. After what had seemed an eternity, everyone finally concluded their presentations, and the table fell silent once again.

"Ladies and gentlemen, I thank you for the benefit of your experience and your wisdom," Stoughton said, his deep voice taking on a contemplative tone that underscored the enormity of their discussions. "Our government has placed an awesome responsibility upon my shoulders to make a decision affecting not only our nation's future but, potentially, that of the world. Such a responsibility cannot be undertaken lightly. I appreciate the faith that the president and the leaders of Congress have placed in me to make such a decision, and I appreciate the cooperation of your respective agencies assisting me in performing this duty. You have all presented valid concerns and considerations regarding this, for which I am also grateful."

The man fell silent, a distant look in his eyes, as he considered what he was about to say. Cameron held his breath in anticipation.

"Nevertheless," Stoughton continued, "a decision must be made, and it is up to me to make it. The risks regarding this are tremendous, almost too tremendous to consider. However, the rewards are no less tremendous, too tremendous to ignore. Therefore, it is my decision to proceed with this operation."

I was afraid of that, too.

Resigned and nervous glances were exchanged around the room, but no one spoke. Words were inadequate to express the enormity of what they had just decided to do. Cameron felt his mouth go dry once again. This time he didn't care if it broke a mood or not. He needed something to calm his nerves, and the pitcher of water in front of him would suffice for the moment. As he reached for the glass, he heard an audible sigh. Relief? Resignation? Concern? He could be no more certain of that than he could be of who uttered it. Alderman, predictably, took advantage of the distraction provided by Cameron's movements and leaned forward, addressing the room in a grave tone.

"Very well then," he said. "We are, therefore, committed to see this enterprise through. Now it remains for us to decide how we wish to proceed with the operation."

I find your pomposity oddly comforting, you officious pain in the ass.

"Excuse me, sir," said Franks, "but exactly which operation? We discussed two separate needs that had to be addressed."

"Clarification, if you don't mind, Lieutenant." Alderman's tone was harsh, and Cameron noticed the disapproving look on the man's face.

What? Pissed that the kid blew your moment? Shit. Possible nuclear annihilation and petty egos are not going to make this any fun at all.

"With all due respect, sir," the naval officer continued, "you had mentioned previously assisting with the defection of the highly placed Soviet operative. However, you also mentioned the need to relocate his son. Since it was decided that we would not, in fact, be coordinating two operations, which one will we be discussing at this time?"

I like this guy, Cameron thought. He watched Alderman flush as Franks revealed that in his desire for self-importance, Alderman had completely forgotten his previous statement.

"That is what we are going to decide now," interjected Gray, saving his colleague from further embarrassment. "When this was initially considered, I recalled a meeting that had involved Special Agent McIntyre, in which we discussed a possible plan to help make contact with some of our operatives in East Germany's counterculture movement. She had shared with us her role in the FBI's recruitment of a band of musicians, among them Special Agent Walsh. They had been able to work unobserved, yet in plain sight, and were beneficial in not only uncovering various black market operations and profiteers but also assisting in the breakup of a Soviet spy ring that threatened our efforts on the Alaskan front."

"I'm afraid I don't understand how musicians can be of any use to us," interrupted Parker. "This is a serious and delicate matter that can't be left haphazardly in amateur hands. While I don't doubt that these men performed admirably in their duties, the fact remains that they were not trained agents, and Special Agent Walsh does not have any experience in these areas. This is far more complicated and has to be handled by agents specially trained in these matters."

"That is understood, sir," McIntyre assured him. "While I acknowledge that Special Agent Walsh and Special Agent Evan Dixon have not been part of any work of this type, I can assure you that any efforts on our behalf would be in conjunction with the Central Intelligence Agency and their operatives in situ. However, as requested by Mr. Gray, I did form a proposal for your consideration."

Briefly, McIntyre outlined the same proposal she had made to Cameron. As she did so, Cameron studied the faces of the other people in the room. Most listened with polite interest, while Parker was clearly unimpressed. Stoughton maintained the same somber expression that he had shown throughout the entire meeting.

How is this shit going down with them?

"How exactly do you feel about this, Special Agent Walsh?" asked Alderman. The man leaned back in his chair and crossed his legs, resting his chin in his hand while studying Cameron.

Just like a job interview. Okay, you want to play it that way? Fine. Here goes nothing!   "Well, ladies and gentlemen," Cameron began, nervously clearing his throat, "I do confess to obvious feelings of trepidation. An operation such as this, as has been mentioned, is extremely sensitive and indeed difficult. However, as has also been mentioned, we would be working in conjunction with an agency that has handled situations like this many times, and I would be working with people more skilled than I am. I am confident that, under those circumstances, we would be successful."

"While we thank you for the compliment, Special Agent Walsh, I'm afraid I need to point out that this is neither the time nor the place for on-the-job training," Alderman replied. "I'm also afraid that trepidation has no place in an operation such as this. He who hesitates is lost, as the saying goes."

Patronizing prick. "I can appreciate that, sir," Cameron replied with a smile. "However, I'm sure if you surveyed members of the 101st Airborne, you'd find that even they tighten their sphincters before jumping. Yet they still jump. I might have trepidation about this, sir, but I will still jump, and I will work closely with those placed in charge, who are experienced in this, to ensure it is a successful jump."

Alderman nodded his appreciation at Cameron's remarks. "Special Agent Walsh," he replied, "if you had made any other response, this meeting would have been over."

Is that a good thing or a bad thing?

"Special Agent McIntyre, I have a question for you," said Gray. "You indicated in your proposal to me that the band in question had four members. However, only half of them will be agents. Don't you feel that, under the circumstances, this would be a major breech in security?"

As McIntyre was about to speak, Cameron leaned forward.

"I would like to answer that if I may," he said, casting a glance at McIntyre. "I realize that you are probably aware of Special Agent McIntyre's record of service and her credentials. It would simply be gilding the lily to have her explain further when I realize that the unknown variables are my band members and me. While the drummer and I are both special agents, one of our guitar players, Rich Webster, is not. However, he has proven himself capable of working under stressful situations and is aware of the risks and the need for respecting protocols, and he will be committed to whatever requirement is demanded of him."

"I appreciate your evaluation, Special Agent Walsh," Gray replied. "But let's face it; everyone thinks highly of their friends."

"I'm not basing my assumption solely on my person relationship with him," Cameron assured him. "I am basing it on my evaluation of his responses on our last mission, where he was almost killed by a Soviet agent, and further evaluation of his acceptance of my offer to reform the band in order to perform another mission, even though I was not able to divulge to him at that time."

"So he was buying into this thing sight unseen, is that what you're telling me?" Gray pressed.

"Yes sir," Cameron replied. "He might not be a special agent, but at least he won't try to play one on TV either. He will follow orders and follow them to the letter."

"I would like to reiterate everything that Special Agent Walsh has said," McIntyre added. "I have worked closely with Mr. Webster and have known him to be a man of courage, dedication, and responsibility. I would not have made this proposal if I did not have complete faith in their ability to cooperate fully."

"Your proposal referred to four members of the band, Special Agent McIntyre," Gray reminded her. "You have only accounted for three. What about the remaining one?"

"Clyde Poulin did not express any interest in rejoining the

Roadhouse Sons," McIntyre admitted. "Therefore, we have conducted a search of members of the intelligence community that we feel might be a suitable replacement. The criteria were based upon musical ability, appearance, and of course, security clearance."

"Has your search been successful?" asked Alderman.

"Obviously, sir, I have only been able to do a preliminary search and not a full audition," McIntyre explained. "However, I have narrowed it down to a handful of potential candidates, one of which is Major Kendall here."

Alderman turned his attention to the soldier. "How do you feel about this, Major?"

"Well, sir, I was not aware of the full implications of my superior's request for a tape of my performances. However, under the circumstances, I am certainly willing to participate if it will assist this mission."

"And you are confident that he will work, Special Agent McIntyre?" asked Gray.

"Yes sir, I am," she replied. "However, I have left the musical evaluation to Special Agent Walsh's discretion."

"And what is your opinion, Special Agent Walsh?" Gray asked.

"I have to admit that I was pretty impressed with the tapes I heard," Cameron replied. "I'm sure we can work with him and pull it off. He doesn't hit all of the high notes that my former guitar player did, but we can adjust the songs we will perform to accommodate that."

"So you're willing to proceed then?" Alderman asked.

Oh shit. This will make it real, won't it? "Yes sir, I am," Cameron said, feeling the words catch in his mouth.

Once again, the room fell silent and Cameron felt crushed beneath its weight.

Suck it up, cupcake. There's no backing out now.

"Then I suppose it's all over but the screaming," said Alderman. "Or, in this case, the singing."

Cameron appreciated the man's attempt at levity, as possibly misplaced as it was. It was, for Cameron, a hint of normalcy in a frightening situation.

Music, I can relate to. Music, I can understand. There are no wars on a fretboard.

"Our next task is to decide exactly how this is going to happen," said Gray. "We need to have the details worked out before we leave here. Ms. Fagan needs to be able to report back to her superiors on our decision, and we need to begin coordinating our efforts with both the MI6 and the West Germans immediately."

"What exactly is the target date for this operation?" asked Parker.

"We will have to do this as soon as possible," Alderman insisted. "We can't be certain of the safety of Alexi for the foreseeable future, so time is clearly of the essence. Special Agent McIntyre, did you have a date in mind?"

"Initially, I was aware of a concert series planned for the summer in various cities in West Germany, concluding in West Berlin in August. However, I agree with Mr. Alderman that such a time frame is too far out for us to rely on. I have been looking into the possibility of working with cultural exchanges to get the Roadhouse Sons booked for a single tour."

"Wouldn't a private tour be suspicious?" wondered Alderman.

McIntyre shook her head. "No sir, I don't believe so. Several American bands have already done that, and not necessarily the larger, more famous ones. The Roadhouse Sons are enjoying a certain popularity in West Germany right now, due to the availability of bootleg recordings, and these are also being distributed in Eastern Europe with the recent relaxation of restrictions. For us to capitalize on that popularity would seem perfectly normal under those circumstances."

"Yes, but would that get us access to either subject?" wondered Kendall.

"I'm afraid I don't follow," McIntyre said.

"We've decided that we are going through with this," Kendall pointed out. "Now we're talking about the means that will be getting us a team in place over there. However, we have not determined who will be the target for our operation. Is it Alexi, or is it the son?"

"There will need to be two phases to this operation. The plan that I have formulated and presented for consideration assists the defection of the son," McIntyre explained.

Could that be what Siobhan meant, that she was here to ensure that this is not a kidnapping? Cameron realized that would be impossible. *No one would have released this to a foreign organization before this discussion.* He concluded that Interpol's concerns must be involved with defections in general.

"What proof do we have that the son is even willing to defect?" Kendall asked.

From his glance at the Interpol agent, Cameron realized the major had come to the same conclusion.

"In concrete terms, we don't have any," Alderman said. "We only have the request from his father to ensure his son's safe transmission to the West."

"Will that be enough to stop the shit storm that will follow?" Kendall demanded. "Excuse my language, sir, but let's face it. That course of action is going to give a lot of ammunition to any critics, and I mean that both literally and figuratively. Can you honestly be basing any of this on the request of a highly placed KGB agent?"

"I assure you, Major, we are well aware of that," Stoughton replied. The sudden rumble of his deep voice startled Cameron, who had almost forgotten the man was there. "Initially I, too, considered it too fantastic to be conceived. However, closer analysis of military and political intelligence has left us with more questions than answers, and answers are vitally needed at this juncture. The Russians are making an almost one-hundred-and-eighty-degree turn in their foreign policy. Why? Are they in more serious trouble than we realize, or are they preparing for a major offensive, or worse?"

"Then, if I may ask, sir, what is our justification, or our defense, for proceeding with this course of action?" Kendall pressed.

"Only our communications with Alexi," Stoughton replied.

"That's it?" the major cried. "We're basing everything on that one roll of the dice?"

Stoughton merely nodded. The solemn expression of his ebony features carried with it a trace of concern and sadness. He, too, was aware of the dangers of their decision. Slowly, Stoughton rose from his chair.

"Ladies and gentlemen, if you will excuse me," he said in a voice as stately as he was, "I have something that I need to attend to. I will be back shortly."

Cameron watched the older man head to the door, his movements slower than when he had arrived, as though weighted down by the decision that had been made. At the door, Stoughton motioned for the agents who had accompanied him to remain at their positions in the room.

Chapter 9

"That Is All"

The young man lay on his bed, staring at the ceiling. His mind played out various scenarios over and over, where he exacted his revenge on the headmaster and the teachers. Sometimes he imagined doing it collectively; other times he would focus on each of them one by one.

"I'll report them for unpatriotic activities," he muttered. "That should be an easy charge to make." Providing, of course, he remembered what he would charge them with. Then he realized that they would not be in their positions if they had not demonstrated impeccable party and ideological loyalty.

He considered charging them with disobeying directives to allow him to enjoy his privileges, but he knew his privileges had been restricted due to his abuse of them. Wherever he looked, Mikhail's mind could not find a way out of his situation. They had the upper hand; he did not, and he would never get it. In frustration over this realization, he tried harder to find a solution. His rage returned when he looked to where his stereo had been. They had taken it away that night.

"You are not allowed to play it after eight o'clock," the staff member had told him. "We've warned you repeatedly! If you can't resist the temptation to listen to it, then we will have to remove the temptation from you."

"You can't do this to me," Mikhail raged. "Do you know who I am? I will have your job for this!"

"You're welcome to it then," the staff member sneered. "Let's see how you like dealing with all the little shits pretending to be big shots! Until then I'm taking this, and you can have it back when they decide you've rehabilitated yourself."

In defiance, Mikhail tried to grab it out of the man's hands, but the staff member was too strong for him. The realization that he could neither bluff nor intimidate this man into obedience shocked Mikhail. In desperation, he gripped the stereo tighter. The man was amused at this futile attempt and laughed, giving it a quick tug, to which Mikhail responded by trying to twist it out of the man's grip. In the struggle, the stereo had nearly slipped and fallen on the floor. Mikhail screamed when he thought it would be smashed to pieces because he knew that there was no guarantee it would be replaced. The staff member caught it as soon as Mikhail released his hold and held it out of reach as he laughed even harder. It was then that the youth realized he had exposed his weakness. It was then that he realized this man had known his weakness all along, and that was why it had been targeted. It was then that he realized there was nothing he could ever hope to do about it. This total humiliation was too much, and he burst into tears. The staff member made no effort to hide his pleasure at this result and continued to laugh as he left the room.

Mikhail, wiping his nose on his sleeve, stared at the now-closed door overcome by the reality of defeat. He realized he must look like a child, wailing as his favorite toy was taken away. The carefully constructed image of the tough, worldly teenager crumbled into dust as he sniffled and sobbed once more. Perhaps that staff member had initiated his humiliation, but Mikhail realized that he had finalized it himself. They had won again. With a howl, he threw his pillow against the wall, striking a poster and tearing its corner, causing it to droop downward in imitation of his own dejection. Mikhail stared at the now-exposed wall, transfixed by the sudden gap in the covering of posters and photos placed in an effort to conceal every exposed surface of his dorm room wall. He knew as soon as he saw the damage that they would not give him any tape to fix it. The exposed portion taunted him, ridiculing his efforts to forget that he was a student, a privileged prisoner in a gilded cage, and that his every movement was curtailed and every aspect of his life was regulated, despite appearances to the contrary.

The bitter irony was that these images made it harder for Mikhail to accept his situation because they kept everyone from believing what he tried to say; that he was in reality a prisoner, with less freedom than any of them had.

"You expect us to believe all that bullshit, Misha," they always said, laughing. "Look around you; anything you want is at your fingertips! Which one of us enjoys any of that, eh?"

Despite his protests and insistence, he could never convince anyone that all of the benefits they saw were merely illusions. The more playthings he was given, the less freedom he had to enjoy them. The boy's frustrations boiled over, and he buried his face into his remaining pillow, stifling the sounds of his impotent rage. He would not give them any more satisfaction of knowing how deeply they had gotten to him. He could deny them that much, and he would.

Later, his anger spent and his tears dried, he stared at the ceiling once more. He no longer plotted his revenge. Now he plotted his escape.

Chapter 10

"Are We Ourselves?"

Doug sighed wearily and leaned back in the chair. The agent at the door had barely moved and did not respond to anything Doug asked.

"Can I at least go to the bathroom, for crying out loud?" he pleaded.

The agent shook his head. Doug grumbled but said nothing. There were no magazines or books in the room, nor a radio or television. There was only a cabinet displaying various decanters of what he assumed to be alcohol. Realizing there was no chance he'd be permitted to have any of it, he didn't ask. So Doug hummed songs softly to pass the time but stopped when the expression on the agent's face became irritated. Periodically, another agent would come in to confer with him in a hushed voice, but no one addressed Doug. That was just fine with him. He pulled his hat down over his eyes and tried to go to sleep, hoping a nap would help the time go faster. The roadie heard some muffled sounds at the other end of the room and expected the agent to kick his feet to keep him from falling asleep. Peering out from under his visor, Doug discovered that the agent was nowhere to be seen. Someone else now stood where the agent had been. It was an older man in an expensive suit with a stern expression on his face.

"Don't let me disturb you, young man," the older man said in a rumbling voice.

Doug rose from his chair. "You weren't, sir," he replied.

Doug had no idea who this person was, but judging from his bearing and the absence of any other agent, Doug assumed he must be important. "I'm afraid I was an unexpected guest and was just waiting for them to tell me when I could leave. I'm sorry for intruding if this is your house. If you say the word, I'll be on my way."

"I can say many words, young man," the man responded. "However, I would prefer to know who I am saying them to. What's your name?"

"My name is Doug Courtland, sir," he said, nervously removing his hat. "I work for Cameron now. I used to work for his band."

"Cameron? I assume you're referring to Special Agent Walsh," the older man said.

Doug nodded. "Yes sir, I am."

"Then you should refer to him as such. They go through a great deal of trouble to become agents and should be afforded that respect. Courtland, you say? I believe I've heard that name before."

"You probably have, sir. It's also a variety of apple." To Doug's dismay, his joke produced neither a smile nor a laugh.

"No, that's not where I heard it," the older man replied sternly. "I seem to recall coming across it in various reports I was reviewing recently."

Doug felt his face flush, realizing that he was speaking to a federal agent and that the man was no doubt quite familiar with his past involvement with the Roadhouse Sons and their exploits, both good and bad.

"Permit me to introduce myself, Mr. Courtland," the man said, extending his hand. "My name is Mr. Stoughton. We need not concern ourselves with first names for the moment. I came down here for a drink. Would you like to join me?"

Doug was not certain how to respond. Previous interactions with agents and government officials typically involved a great deal of shouting and profanity, usually by him, as well as a great deal of intimidation tactics, usually by them, which did nothing to produce an atmosphere of congeniality. Now he was being asked to join one of them in a drink and had no idea how to proceed.

"Sure," he murmured. "I'd like that a lot."

"Would you be so kind as to pour me a glass?" Stoughton asked. "I'd like a bourbon, if you would, please."

With a smile, Doug went to the cabinet and opened a decanter of dark liquid. Giving it a sniff, he made a face.

"What's the matter?" asked Stoughton. "Isn't that bourbon?"

"Yes, it is," Doug explained. "But you strike me as a top-shelf kind of guy, and this sure isn't top shelf."

Without a word, he opened the doors of the lower portion of the cabinet and began moving bottles until one happened to catch his eye.

"Aha," the roadie declared in triumph. "I thought there had to be some good stuff tucked away." With a smile, he withdrew a bottle of Rebel Yell and poured some in two glasses.

"Would you like me to get you some ice, sir?" Doug asked, handing Stoughton a glass. "Though I don't think you'll need it. You don't use ice with the good stuff, and this is pretty smooth, if I do say so myself."

The old man raised his glass in a small toast to Doug before taking a sip. "How did you know to look there?" Stoughton asked.

Doug shrugged. "Well, this place doesn't look like just the average guys use it; I'm pretty sure you big shots do, too. I've been in enough places to know that the bosses don't leave the good stuff out for just anyone to enjoy. One sniff told me the cheap stuff was what was in the decanter. So I figured there had to be something better hidden away."

"Very good observations." Stoughton smiled. "I can see why Special Agent Lamont wrote so highly of you."

Doug said nothing. He did not like to speak of Chuck Lamont, the former band manager and case officer. His relationship with the man had not always been pleasant, and the memories were not always comfortable. However, once Doug had left the Roadhouse Sons and Chuck had left the bureau, their relationship had become more cordial. Chuck had been a great assistance to Doug in his efforts to rebuild his life.

"Chuck is a good guy," he muttered, hurriedly sipping his drink.

"Yes, he is," Stoughton agreed. "You know, it was largely through his advocacy that you were not charged with interfering with a federal investigation. There were plenty of people who wanted your head on a platter, influential people."

"What are you talking about?" Doug demanded. "I never interfered with any federal investigation! I worked for him, for crying out loud. I never did anything I wasn't supposed to."

"I am referring to an evening in Seattle about four years ago involving a ring of Soviet saboteurs. I assume you remember the event to which I am referring?"

"Yeah, I remember," Doug replied bitterly. "Do you want to see the scar?"

Stoughton shook his head. "No, that will not be necessary. I seem to recall Agent Lamont's report indicating that you prevented a Soviet agent from shooting one or more of our agents, is that correct?"

Doug nodded but said nothing.

"You nearly died for your efforts, I believe?"

Doug nodded again but still said nothing.

"Were you told to assist them?"

"No," Doug sighed. "Chuck had told me to stay behind. I decided to follow on my own."

"Why? Didn't you realize that it was a high-risk situation and should have been left in the hands of trained federal agents? Any actions on your part could only be perceived as reckless and interfering in a federal investigation."

Doug nodded. "Yeah, I realized that. But, in spite of that, that was why I went," he explained. "Chuck was in the car with only a couple other guys. There was no way to say what they were up against, or if they were outnumbered. So I followed. Mostly to see if there was any backup or if they were on their own."

"And? What qualified you to make that assessment, and what would you have done if you felt they had adequate assistance?"

"I know when something feels right and when it doesn't. I've been around them long enough to know that is what they base things on as well. If I thought everything was fine, I'd have turned around and gone home. I'm not a hero, and I'm not a vigilante."

"Yet, you *did* stay and *did* involve yourself in a federal investigation," Stoughton pressed. "Even if you had your reservations about the situation, that was reckless and irresponsible and could have jeopardized their entire operation. That is something that can't be dismissed."

"No, I suppose it can't."

"I'm glad we agree on that point, at least. What exactly were your intentions once you decided to stay?"

"Like I said, to make certain things were okay."

"As we've already established, Special Agent Lamont and the others were trained federal agents performing their lawful duties. In addition, Special Agent Lamont had years of military training and experience. You were a technician for a rock band. You must assume that no matter what, they were sufficient to the task they were facing and you were not."

"That is entirely true, sir. But the agents weren't the ones I was worried about." Doug looked Stoughton in the eye when he said that, and the older man noticed the resolve in the younger man's deportment.

"Would you mind elucidating that point for me?" Stoughton demanded.

"My friends were there," Doug explained. "I'm talking about Cameron and, yeah, probably McIntyre, too. I needed to make certain they were safe."

"Special Agent McIntyre was a trained professional acting in the line of duty."

Doug shook his head forcefully. "Chuck had said they lost contact with her, and no one knew if she was even alive or not, and that meant that Cameron was on his own," Doug countered.

"It is the responsibility of the agents on the scene to ascertain the safety of all parties involved, not yours!"

"With all due respect, sir, it's been my experience that you folks sometimes are pretty quick to forget about the little people," Doug hissed through his clenched teeth. "If you didn't, then I wouldn't have had to find my way across the country working for handouts because you folks declared me dead and I couldn't get a ration book!"

To Doug's surprise, the older man did not get angry. Instead, a smile crossed his face and he began to chuckle. "Somehow, I don't believe the Crimson Mask worked for mere handouts, Mr. Courtland. I understand that you wrestled in front of decent-sized audiences, didn't you? Your payoffs might not have been princely sums, but you hardly went hungry, correct?"

Doug's jaw dropped as he realized what he had just been asked. "You mean, you heard …"

"Special Agent Lamont's reports were very thorough." Stoughton smiled. "And so were my questions to him and to others."

"You've been talking with Chuck?"

"Yes," Stoughton replied. "When we were first contacted about the Roadhouse Sons, I decided to do some homework. In reading the reports, your name kept showing up—sometimes in a good context, but most often in not so pleasant terms. I don't think I need to go into detail, do I?"

"No sir, you don't," Doug muttered.

Stoughton sipped his drink, studying Doug over the rim of his glass. "Let me ask you a question, totally unrelated to anything we've been discussing," the older man said. "Have you ever heard of a wrestler by the name of Tiger Conway, by any chance?"

"Senior or junior?" Doug asked, eyeing the man suspiciously.

"Either one." Stoughton shrugged. "But senior is the one I am concerned with."

"Yes, I have," Doug responded. "I've never met him, but I have heard of him. I think he started wrestling in Texas, but I'm not sure. What does that have to do with anything?"

"Then if you've heard of him, I suppose you've heard of a wrestler named Danny McShane?"

Doug nodded. "Yeah, anyone who knows Tiger knows that McShane was the guy who talked Tiger into wrestling."

"Correction," Stoughton replied with a smile. "He was the one who talked Tiger and *another* fellow into wrestling. You've probably never heard of the Brown Sheik, have you?"

"No, I can't say as I have."

"That is hardly surprising," Stoughton replied with a shrug. "I only wrestled for a few months that summer before joining the army. McShane had found us both working at that hotel in Houston and persuaded Tiger to get into the business, as they put it. Tiger showed the most potential and was the one McShane was most serious about, but I was encouraged to get in as well so there would be a better chance for him to have someone to work with. You see, in those days, it wasn't just busses and lunch counters that were segregated."

Doug nodded in recognition. "Right. I remember hearing that he used to wrestle on what they called the 'chitterling circuit' because whites and blacks couldn't wrestle together back then."

Suddenly, the implication of what Stoughton had just revealed dawned on Doug, and once again he stared in disbelief. "You mean, you're …"

"Yes," said Stoughton, smiling. "I'm one of the boys, as they say. It has been nearly thirty years since I last laced up my boots, I'm afraid. However, by virtue of membership in the Cauliflower Alley Club, I have stayed in touch with some of the people I was involved with and still follow it to an extent. That is why I am not unfamiliar with your ring name."

"Holy shit," muttered Doug. Then, with a smile, he muttered a phrase and waited for Stoughton's response. To his surprise, Stoughton responded with a smile and a similar phrase.

"You speak carney, too." Doug laughed. "I guess you really *are* one of the boys!"

Stoughton gave a slight bow. "I learned my art well." He smiled. Then, just as quickly, the smile vanished. "Now, since we've established that you and I belong to a rather exclusive fraternity, I trust we can speak frankly and honestly. I also trust you will believe me when I dispute your charge that your friends were going to be ignored. So I want an answer as to your motive for involving yourself in that investigation, and I want it now!"

Doug clenched his jaw in anger and then relaxed.

"I give you my word, sir, that *was* my only motive. I wanted to know if my friends were all right, nothing more. I was only getting as close as I did because I saw them standing there and wanted to make certain they were unharmed. I didn't even intend to speak with them, or even let them see me; I was going to turn around and leave once my question was answered. Finding the guy with the gun was pure chance. So was catching that bullet."

Stoughton regarded him silently and then nodded. "I accept that answer."

"Thank you," Doug sighed.

"Incidentally, that was the same thing Agent Lamont told me."

"Good old Chuck, I guess."

Stoughton said nothing, and Doug wondered if he had been too flippant and caused offense. Stoughton sipped his drink, letting Doug wonder.

"Now, can I ask you a question?" Doug said.

"That seems only fair, I suppose."

"Why were they going to charge me with interfering in an investigation? Everything was done, and everyone was standing around in handcuffs. There was nothing to interfere with."

"That night, someone very important managed to escape," Stoughton explained. "Someone we had been after for a long time. It was also realized that someone very highly placed in the bureau's office had been a traitor. Emotions were extremely high, and they wanted someone to focus their emotions on. You, possessing no legitimate reason for being there, would have been the perfect target."

"But, I told you, I did have a legitimate reason," Doug protested.

"The reasonings and motivations you provided are not acceptable within the context of an investigation," Stoughton said. "There is no room for sentimental reactions in something of that nature, and your actions were based entirely upon sentiment."

Doug reflected on Stoughton's words and an uneasy silence descended on the room, finally broken by the older man.

"Since we are being honest and open with one another, it should come as no surprise that, as I have already stated, I am familiar with your file and that I am also familiar with the various other details it contains."

"You're talking about Gus and the *Mustang*, aren't you?" Doug demanded. The roadie struggled to keep the anger out of his voice, but the familiar feelings of judgment, condemnation, and disregard he had experienced from the various federal agents he had worked with in the past prevented him from doing so.

In the years before the war began, Doug had been close friends with a man named Gus Kalbe, a man the government had encouraged to reenlist in the US Navy to assist with developing a top-secret submarine prototype. Unfortunately, the Soviets had also targeted Kalbe for recruitment and hoped to use Doug as an influence on his friend. Kalbe did reenlist, and the *Mustang* was destroyed under suspicious circumstances, sparking the Soviet invasion of North America. Rumors of Soviet infiltration and sabotage had been rampant ever since.

As fate would have it, one of the agents who recruited the Roadhouse Sons had been one of the agents who helped to reenlist Kalbe, a fact that Doug refused to overlook and a fact that had been a constant source of conflict in his relationship with the bureau ever since. When it was later discovered that the Soviets had considered Doug a possible asset, the situation became worse, leading to mistrust on their part and increased animosity on his.

"You would be extremely naive to think I wouldn't know of that," Stoughton replied.

"Yes, I suppose you're right," Doug grumbled.

"I don't mean to give offense …" Stoughton began.

"Then you'd be the first one who didn't," Doug snapped, cutting him off.

Stoughton gave him a stern glare, which softened into understanding. "By reading between the lines of all the reports, I could tell you were not handled with a great deal of finesse," he agreed.

"That is putting it mildly," Doug muttered.

"Would you permit me another go at it?" Stoughton asked.

"What have I got to lose?" Doug replied, with a shrug. "You're going to do it anyway."

Stoughton gave a smile and a polite nod.

"Very well then," the older man began. "Let me start by explaining it came as no surprise that the Soviets would have targeted you for recruitment. That is not meant as an insult, but intelligence agents try to pick an average person that no one would be suspicious of, who could move about undetected."

Doug listened in silence as the man continued.

"The fact that you were Kalbe's roommate and close friend made you an irresistible target. You would have been in an ideal position to reveal anything incriminating that they could use on him or to assist them in influencing him to work with them. That is standard procedure with any intelligence agency, including ours. What surprised everyone, however, is how quickly they abandoned that plan and how adamant they were that it would not be wise to pursue it further."

"Would you mind elucidating that point for me, sir?" Doug asked.

"According to our examination of that agent, you had a dedication and loyalty to your friends that terrified them, if you want to know the plain facts," Stoughton continued. "Their agent feared more for his safety if you uncovered him than if we did. Judging from what I gathered reading your subsequent performance reports, that suspicion was probably justified."

"Was that the only reason they suggested not pursuing me?"

"I'm afraid I don't follow you."

"Chuck shared with me that someone we thought was just a regular neighbor was in fact a Russian spy," Doug explained. "He said some things about me and Chuck wanted to discover if they were true. So Chuck forced me to read a book aloud in front of everyone, or rather, *try* to. Or didn't *that* part make it to your desk?"

"Yes, as a matter of fact, I did read that," Stoughton confirmed. His tone was softer now, more understanding. "There was a question as to your education level, or lack thereof. However, I assure you I am not the elitist that others might have been, in that regard."

"Why not?" demanded Doug.

Stoughton sipped his drink before continuing.

"I am not usually one to discuss my own personal history. However, I think in this case it might be justified. You see, my grandfather was born a slave and freed after the Civil War. He was renowned in the area where I grew up as an experienced vet and animal husbandman. He could diagnose an animal's illness almost by mere observation. He could identify aspects of an animal's anatomy and organ structure by pointing to the areas where they were located and describe in precise detail their processes and functions. There were many summers when veterinary students would stay at my grandparents' farm for the opportunity to study with him. However, despite living to almost one hundred, in all that time he never learned to write his own name or read a newspaper. So you see, unlike most, I do not discount a native intelligence."

"Thank you, sir," Doug replied softly. "I appreciate that."

Stoughton nodded. "Now, I want to ask you a question."

"Shoot."

"What have you done since moving here?"

Doug hesitated once more before answering. "Well, mostly tried to find work and reconnect with my son," he muttered, draining his glass.

"Is that all?"

"Yeah, that's all there is," Doug said, giving a disinterested shrug.

"I don't believe that for a moment," Stoughton declared. "You see, I know that in addition to the close proximity of your son, the other reason you were in Delaware was because of a special program you were enrolled in through the assistance of former Special Agent Lamont, isn't that correct?"

"I don't know what you're talking about," Doug said, blushing.

"Come now," Stoughton insisted. "There's nothing to be ashamed of! Bettering yourself is a commendable pursuit. From what I've revealed, you should know I am well aware of some tremendous obstacles you've overcome in your life. You were involved with Jobs for Delaware Graduates, were you not?"

"Yeah," Doug muttered. "Chuck knew some guy who worked for Governor DuPont and was able to get me hooked up through that program he started, and I was able to get my diploma, finally."

"You mean your GED, don't you?"

"No," Doug insisted, shaking his head. "They got me signed up with a high school in Delaware, the one where the governor got the program started. A real tough place at one point, from what I understand, and I did some classes through them. I've got a real, honest-to-goodness high school diploma. Only about ten years late, but that's okay, I guess."

"You realize that employers value a diploma over a GED, don't you?" Stoughton asked.

"No sir, I didn't realize that," Doug replied with amazement.

Stoughton wondered if the roadie realized the full implication of the benefit he had earned and suspected he was becoming aware.

"Do you have any other ambitions?" Stoughton asked.

Doug shook his head. "No, getting a diploma was enough," he replied quietly. "I don't want to get above myself."

"There is a vast difference between improving yourself and getting above yourself, young man!" Stoughton admonished. "Never forget that. Because, if you do, you have wasted a valuable opportunity. Now, if you had your chance, what would you be doing?"

"Law enforcement," Doug replied, without hesitation.

"Indeed!" Stoughton exclaimed, genuinely surprised.

Doug nodded. "Don't misunderstand me; I'm not talking about the cops-and-robbers part of it. I mean the whole thing about examining a crime scene, examining the evidence, analyzing what it all means, and following that lead. It fascinated me when Chuck and McIntyre were working on that stuff!"

"What you are referring to, my boy, is referred to as the field of forensic science. Yes, that is quite a fascinating area of law enforcement, and also essential. A case can be made, or broken, on an item as obscure as a cigarette butt. I'm of the conviction that they are as essential as the detectives and other officers involved in a case. But, tell me, why not pursue that if you are so interested in it?"

Doug paused. Gone was the openness that he had previously shown the older man; in its place was his typical defensiveness and distrust.

"If you are as familiar with my background as you said you were, you realize there are a few things that make that impossible." Doug flushed.

"You are referring to your criminal background, I assume?" Stoughton asked.

Doug nodded in reply.

"The incidents that transpired during your tenure as an asset have all been removed," Stoughton assured him.

"I didn't know that, but thanks." Doug nodded. "But those weren't the only things I was talking about."

"Yes, I am aware of the previous charges against you," Stoughton replied. "I am also aware that it was dropped from a felony assault to that of simple assault, a misdemeanor, with credit for time served. You spent a weekend in the Caledonia County Jail and were released, without probation. That was quite unusual, if I may say so."

Doug made no reply.

"Unusual enough for me to look into, in fact," Stoughton continued. "You were charged with assault and battery on your mother's boyfriend. According to the police report, you beat him so severely that the man was found unconscious."

Doug clenched his jaw as he recalled the situation, but nodded in acknowledgment of everything Stoughton had said.

"That was not the end of the situation, though, was it?" Stoughton asked.

Doug shook his head.

"There was an investigation, wasn't there?" Stoughton pressed.

Doug nodded once more in affirmation.

"The investigation uncovered evidence that you attacked him when you discovered him in the act of sexually assaulting his deaf daughter, didn't it?" Stoughton asked.

"She also had Down syndrome," Doug replied, his voice small and weak. "The bastard thought she could never tell on him. Did your report mention that she considered me her big brother? It probably didn't. It probably didn't say that she'd hold my hand when I walked with her to and from school. We had our own sign language. She said I protected her from the monsters. I thought she meant other kids who picked on her."

"Apparently, she felt the monster you were protecting her from was her own father."

"Didn't do a very good job, did I?" Doug replied, choking back tears. "He had been doing it for years, we found out!"

"They found that out as a result of your intervention, extreme though it was, and such abuse was brought to an end and she got the help she needed. She was put into a home and removed from there."

"Yeah, well, so was I!" Doug said, hurriedly downing his drink. "My mom threw me out of the house for breaking up her home, and I never saw any of them again. No matter what they reduced the charges to, they're still on my record and I can't get away from that."

"What if I told you I could make them go away?" Stoughton said.

"How?" demanded Doug. "A presidential pardon?"

"Now, young man, that would be overkill." Stoughton smiled. "However, it would be along those lines. You see, your friends are upstairs discussing a possible reactivation of the Roadhouse Sons. I will not be going into detail, but as you know from past experiences, such duties are not confined solely to musical pursuits. They could find themselves in a highly dangerous situation. Your name has been referenced as a valuable asset to their assignments in the past. I had considered if you might not be valuable to them once more, despite your history. Not as an active agent, mind you, but as someone to help watch their backs, shall we say. I had been wondering how I would get someone to evaluate that opinion. As luck would have it, I have had the opportunity myself. Now, tell me. Will you take my offer?"

"Deal or no deal," Doug replied. "I'd do anything to help my friends. You should have realized that about me." Then, with a wink, he added, "And I'd certainly be willing to help one of the boys."

"Then that calls for another toast." Stoughton smiled. "Would you pour, please?"

"Do you mind if I only stick with club soda?" Doug asked, patting his side. "I'm trying to take it easy now."

Stoughton stared quizzically.

"I'm down one kidney," Doug explained. "I'm trying to make wiser choices these days."

"You learn your lessons well, brother. By the way, would you mind pouring a third glass?" Stoughton said. "I'll be right back."

Doug watched as the older man left the room, and he soon heard voices in the hallway.

"There is someone I want you to meet." Stoughton smiled upon his return and sat down in one of the chairs, sipping his drink and saying nothing. A few moments later, a soldier entered the room.

"They said you wished to speak to me, sir," the soldier explained.

Stoughton gestured toward Doug as the older man rose from his chair.

"Major Kendall, I would like you to meet Mr. Douglas Courtland. Mr. Courtland does not like being addressed by the formal expression of his name, but I trust that he will excuse my doing so now, as I feel it adds an air of formality and solemnity. Mr. Courtland, I would like you to meet Major John Kendall, US Army Intelligence and graduate of Ohio State University with a varsity letter in both football and wrestling."

Kendall gave Doug a quizzical look but politely offered his hand.

"Nice to meet you," the soldier muttered.

"Likewise." Doug smiled.

"Mr. Courtland is a wrestler as well," Stoughton informed the new arrival. "You have something in common."

"Though, I have to admit, I don't have an amateur background like you do," Doug explained.

"You wrestle?" Kendall asked politely.

"He's being rather modest, Major." Stoughton smiled. "Mr. Courtland, let's not be inhospitable; give our guest his drink. Major Kendall, you'll be pleased to know that young Mr. Courtland was trained by the Vachon brothers of Montreal, and I assume you realize that they would have given him a solid basis in the fundamentals of Greco-Roman wrestling."

"Yes, wasn't Maurice an Olympian?" asked the major, now warming to the topic. "He won a gold medal, I believe. No, wait, that was in the Empire Games. Yes, I bet they did make sure you knew what you were doing!"

Doug smiled with satisfaction as he handed the third glass to the major.

"So, if you were trained by the Vachons, that means you worked for Grand Prix Promotions in Montreal," Kendall said. "At least, I think that was what it was called."

"Yes, it was, but the Vachons were no longer running it by then," Doug explained. "But they did persuade Yves Robert's son to give me a shot. They also helped me get some work in Minneapolis. Verne Gagne expected you to know how to wrestle, not just perform. Since Mad Dog had been the one who worked with me the most and had worked with Verne a lot, Verne also expected a lot more out of me than some others."

"So did Bob Geigle," said Kendall, laughing. "I take it you learned what it felt like to be a pretzel then?"

"You were a pro, too? If you worked for Geigle, that means you worked in Kansas City for Heart of America Promotions, didn't you?" Doug smiled. "I tried getting in there, too, but it didn't work out."

"I hate to sound like one of those girls who pose for the scandal rags, but I did it to help pay for college," Kendall replied.

"We could go on with this all day and well into the night," Stoughton interrupted. "However, I think our other guests are growing increasingly concerned with our absence. Major, we had best be getting back. Mr. Courtland, I'd like you to remain here for the present. Make yourself at home, please. I will see that no one bothers you."

Doug smiled at the offer and, to Stoughton's surprise, turned back to the liquor cabinet and replaced the bottle of whiskey where he had found it and began gathering the glasses.

"I'd rather make myself useful, sir," Doug replied. "That is, if you don't mind."

"We have people that come in to clean and restock the house," Stoughton insisted. "You don't need to concern yourself with that."

"Maybe not, sir," Doug said with a smile, "but you see, just sitting makes me stir crazy."

"Suit yourself," Stoughton replied with a shake of his head. "Major, if you'll follow me, please."

The two men left the room, and Doug heard Stoughton speaking to someone in the hallway, assuming it was one of the agents. He didn't hear what they said, but he noticed that no one came back into the room to monitor him.

Taking the glasses into the kitchen, Doug turned on the water in the sink and let it warm up. Standing in the kitchen, with its frosted windows, he began to feel the familiar isolation that he had experienced that night when he had first been recruited. Until this moment, he hadn't realized how grateful he had been to be free of it. Now he felt it gripping him with icy fingers once more. Doug saw the dishwasher but decided to wash the glasses by hand. Doing so gave him a sense of familiarity and security and held off the fear. He had no idea how long either the relief or the fear would last. He would be damned if he'd rush into finding out.

Chapter 11

"Run to You"

He stubbed out his cigarette in the ashtray and gave a last look around his office. Everything was in place. All folders were carefully filed away. Notepads were stripped of the upper sheets, preventing anyone from studying the impressions of previous notes. Not that there would have been anything incriminating on them. In this office, he was the liaison for an engineering firm, nothing more. The only phone calls or conversations here related to supplying the Polish firms that contracted with them for the needed parts and equipment for their own operations. Such conversations were boring, monotonous, and tedious, but safe all the same.

As he left his office, his secretary was still working at her desk in the anteroom. With a pleasant smile, he told her where he could be reached that evening in case anyone needed to get ahold of him. She, in turn, smiled and nodded but said nothing in reply.

The evening air was cool, with a breeze blowing in from the Gulf of Gdansk. Despite the chill, he did not wish to put on his overcoat, and it remained draped over his arm. He carried no briefcase, and by not wearing a coat, he deflected any suspicions that he was concealing anything. To further allay suspicions, he kept only a slight routine. He would usually take the same route home, either by foot or by public transportation, but never consistently. Perhaps for a few days he'd walk, then ride, or vice versa. Sometimes he would alternate each day. Never enough to form a concrete habit, but never enough to draw attention. Tonight he took a casual pace home. Randomly, he would sometimes eat at a restaurant along the way, but never the same one twice in a row or in any pattern. Tonight he didn't feel like eating. He wanted to go home and be alone.

Upon arriving at his flat, he turned on the lamp by his window, a subtle announcement that he had arrived home. He did not turn on the television or the radio, instead enjoying the silence that complemented the fading light of the evening. The days were growing longer, and the lingering light remained in the room more and more each evening. Once or twice he thought it would be interesting to time exactly how long it would take for the light to fade to a certain point, but he thought better of it. Such an action was a pattern, and patterns can be observed, patterns draw attention, and patterns raise questions. He didn't like any of that.

The ringing of the phone broke the silence; however, he didn't jump nor was he startled. He smiled because he knew that other people were not as free of patterns as he was. The phone always rang exactly ninety seconds from the time he turned on his light.

"Good evening, comrade" came the cheerful greeting. Tonight it was a man's voice. To their credit, they did make some attempts to vary their routines. The two spoke for a few moments in a superficial conversation before bidding one another a pleasant good night and hanging up.

Alexi poured himself a drink and sat back in his chair in the half-light. He did not bother going to the window. He knew that he was being watched. If he had felt so inclined, he could have gone to the window and spotted the observation posts they occupied; the car on the corner, the third-floor window of the building across the street, and the man in the doorway of the building next to it. However, by now he no longer felt so inclined. He knew that he had been followed home from the office and that his secretary had dutifully reported his departure as soon as he had left her sight. He knew that just as assuredly as he knew she reported his arrival each morning and his luncheon appointments each noon.

Alexi knew that eyes were upon him, even without checking.

He also knew that all of his actions designed to allay suspicions were raising suspicions and would keep all eyes firmly fixed on his every move. He should know that. After all, he had trained the eyes that were watching him now. He taught the watchers everything they knew, and that knowledge brought a smile to his face. Yes, he had taught them everything that they knew, but he hadn't taught them everything that he knew.

Chapter 12

"No Way Out"

Cameron was relieved when the meeting broke up. It had seemed to go on interminably, with everyone talking in circles.

Damn it, we've decided to do this already. Why does everyone need to keep explaining how important this is?

The answer, he suspected, was that if this mission was successful, each agency would be able to somehow claim credit for its success.

If it fails, none of us will be around for the finger-pointing anyway.

Cameron's interest in the proceedings were renewed when Stoughton had Kendall summoned from the room, due entirely to seeing the consternation on everyone else's face and listening to the muttered considerations of possible motives. However, Cameron did not need to be a mind reader to know what the unspoken concern was; someone other than themselves had attracted the attention of the group's Alpha. The fact that no one knew for certain if it were for positive or negative reasons was of no consequence. Someone was getting attention that the rest of them weren't.

The atmosphere in the room did not change much upon Kendall's return. Despite the neutral expression on the major's face, his body language suggested that he was in a good mood. As he passed Cameron, the agent thought that he detected the odor of alcohol.

If anyone else smells that, I imagine there'll be hell to pay.

The major took his seat, muttering apologies for interrupting the proceedings. Alderman gave him a stern look as he accepted the man's apology and was about to say something when Stoughton returned to the room.

"Ladies and gentlemen, please accept my apologies for my absence," Stoughton declared. "However, I was conferring with a colleague of mine. I would like to say that this meeting is now adjourned."

"You can't do that," exclaimed Gray. "We're still formulating our objectives."

"Mr. Gray, I assure you that I most certainly can do that and, in fact, I have," replied Stoughton. "Our objectives have been defined. All details pertaining to their execution are properly discussed in even more secure surroundings than provided here and with a smaller circle of participants. Each unit will confer only with the principals involved with their objective until such time as efforts need to be coordinated. I do not have to remind you of the highly sensitive nature of what we have discussed here. Therefore, to minimize the security risk, each part will be worked out independently. The only phase of this operation to be jointly discussed shall be in the final coordination of its execution and under my direct observation."

Alderman began to say something, but Stoughton ignored him.

"Ladies and gentlemen, I thank you for your attendance," Stoughton continued. "Your drivers await you downstairs. You may use the back stairs, the same ones you came up. Special Agent McIntyre and Special Agent Walsh, I would like you and Major Kendall to confer with me downstairs in the den, please."

Before anyone could say anything else, Stoughton left the room. Alderman glared at McIntyre. "I will expect a full briefing of that meeting," he warned.

"I'm confident that if Mr. Stoughton or Director Webster deems that necessary or appropriate, it will be provided, sir," she replied calmly.

"Need I remind you that your office possesses no mandate for operating on foreign soil? Only we do. So, for the duration of this operation, you will be working under our auspices," Alderman explained. "If you wish to make this joint effort a successful one, it would be advisable to learn how to be a team player."

"You needn't worry about that, Mr. Alderman," McIntyre replied. Cameron noticed that her tone, while respectful and calm, was cool and hard. "However, I play for my team and by their rules and have no intention of going behind anyone's back. Any information provided to you will come through the proper chain of command and issued by an authority greater than me. Now, if you gentlemen will excuse me."

Before either man could respond, McIntyre turned and walked away. Cameron hesitated a moment before following her. He heard the two men mutter to one another as he passed, but he could not make out what they said.

"Was that really wise?" Cameron whispered to her on the stairs. "Antagonizing them like that might come back to haunt you."

"So would caving in to them," she whispered back. "I'll take my chances."

Downstairs they found Stoughton relaxing in the den, and McIntyre was surprised to see him in deep conversation with Doug and even more surprised to find them smiling and laughing. Stoughton gave them all a smile as they entered the room and quietly asked Doug if he would get them some refreshments.

"Remember, get them the good stuff," Stoughton said with a wink.

With a smile and nod, Doug did as he was directed, removing several bottles from under the cabinet and mixing. McIntyre began to speak, but Stoughton held up a finger, urging silence.

"Not yet," he softly admonished.

Doug ignored everyone as he poured the contents of various bottles into a mixer and gave it a vigorous shake before filling a martini glass and handing it to McIntyre.

"I hope that's the way you like it." He smiled. "I'm not too good at mixing those!"

"It's not bad," McIntyre said, sipping it. "A little lighter on the vermouth next time, maybe?"

"Major Kendall and your other two friends will be joining us momentarily," Stoughton said. "You might want to have something ready for them, as well."

Doug nodded obediently and set up three more glasses.

"Uh, you might also want to consider your boss, as well," Cameron coughed.

"Oops." Doug chuckled, not turning to face him, but he quickly rectified the situation.

"Mr. Stoughton, I see you've met Doug Courtland," began McIntyre, but Stoughton interrupted her.

"Yes, Mr. Courtland and I have been getting acquainted," Stoughton said, smiling. "You might be surprised to learn that he and I have some common acquaintances, and we were sharing reminisces."

"I must admit that I am quite surprised," she said, sipping her martini. "I could not imagine what you two would have in common."

Cameron glanced at Doug, wondering how he would react to her remark. His friend had a long history of responding to slights, real or imagined, in a manner out of all proportion to the alleged insult. For him to react like that now could have serious implications. To Cameron's relief, Doug mixed the drinks with a slight chuckle.

With a smile, Stoughton informed the others of his more colorful past and the common experiences he shared with Doug.

"And I should add, with Major Kendall as well," Stoughton said, with a gesture to the army intelligence officer. "Major, I was just sharing with them the more exciting but lesser-known elements to my curriculum vitae."

The arrival of Evan and Rich interrupted Stoughton's explanations. McIntyre assumed the responsibility of making introductions, and when she was finished, Doug passed around the tray of drinks.

"Gentlemen, and lady," Stoughton began, "I seriously doubt that I will have any further opportunity to meet with you. My involvement with this project from this point on will be primarily as administrator and coordinator of the various elements that will constitute it. However, I realize that the six of you are about to find yourselves in a serious position. A position that I do not envy you in the least. My sense of decency required that I at least see your faces and speak to you, in person, before turning you over to your assignment."

"Excuse me, Mr. Stoughton, but I do not believe that this is the proper situation to be discussing this," cautioned McIntyre.

Stoughton smiled. "Your concerns are noted, Agent McIntyre. However, all parties present have been informed of the essence of the assignment, if not the details. I should like to inform you that I have taken it upon myself to add Mr. Courtland to this company."

"Sir, I'm afraid I must protest," she began, but Stoughton held up his hand.

"I anticipated your objections, Agent McIntyre," he assured her. "I can guarantee that I have vetted him more thoroughly than anyone else in this room, including you. I am aware of his past situations but also of his past performance and his potential. Of your group, four of you are active intelligence officers, but only three of you have had field experience. Mr. Dixon, while the recipient of numerous citations from his supervisors for his capabilities, is an analyst, and Mr. Walsh, while experienced with undercover work, is still a novice when it comes to intelligence. You are all about to find yourselves in circumstances where there will need to be eyes everywhere. You and Major Kendall will be the senior operatives as you have the most experience with this type of thing. Mr. Walsh, Mr. Dixon, and Mr. Webster will be able to surveil any involvement with the band. However, that leaves a dangerous breach in security and that is the behind-the-scenes theater of operations. For that, I feel that Mr. Courtland's expertise will be invaluable."

"Mr. Stoughton, I assure you that we can find the best personnel to maintain security backstage and with the equipment and personnel who will not be potential liabilities themselves," McIntyre protested once more.

"Then have them work with Mr. Courtland," Stoughton replied firmly. "I want him there. I am aware of the challenges he has presented in the past. However, I am not totally convinced that these challenges were entirely his fault. The method and manner in which he was dealt with left a great deal to be desired as well. And I refer not only to his initial handling but to everything else, as well. Further, I am convinced that he is not the same person you once dealt with, anymore than you are the same person he dealt with. You, and everyone else, will need to trust me that I would not ask any unknown quotient to be part of something so vital as this."

Cameron could see that McIntyre was not entirely convinced. *To be honest, neither am I.*

As if reading their minds, Stoughton asked, "Do you realize that you were one of the reasons he followed Special Agent Lamont in Seattle?"

All eyes were on the roadie, who made no response but stood with a detached expression on his face, though Cameron thought he detected a slight flush to his friend's cheeks.

Are you blushing?

Stoughton went on to explain the results of the investigation into Doug's conduct that night and the conclusions that were arrived at, even by those who wanted him to bear the full brunt of their frustrations for that event.

"Further, there is a noticeable maturity in Mr. Courtland since those days," Stoughton pointed out. "I believe you will be relieved and surprised at what you will have to work with this time. Previous situations will not be repeated, will they, Mr. Courtland?"

"No sir, they won't," Doug assured them, with a smile. "I look forward to working with my friends again, as well as Agent Kendall."

"That's Major Kendall," the soldier corrected.

Doug smiled apologetically.

"I'm going to get some water," the roadie said, breaking the tension. "Would anyone else like some?"

"What, you're a teetotaler now?" Rich laughed.

"Not a chance." Doug smiled, patting his side. "You might not remember, but I'm not firing on all cylinders anymore. I try to take it easy. I had a drink with you guys and one with him earlier, but that's all I want to do. There are only a couple bottles of soda for mixers, so I've been drinking water."

When no one else accepted his offer, Doug went out to the kitchen.

"What was he talking about?" Evan whispered.

"That night, on the island that we were on, he got shot," Cameron explained. "He lost a kidney, almost died."

"Holy Jesus, I didn't know that." Rich whistled.

"Yeah, things were worse than ever really mentioned," Cameron sighed. He then turned his attention to Stoughton. "So, do you really think that has had an effect on him?"

"I most certainly do," Stoughton assured him. "He has had a mouthful of mortality and will not be so quick to fly off the handle or play cowboy in the future. Fortunately, that has not diminished his sense of loyalty or commitment to any of you. I think you will find him most agreeable to work with from now on."

"Except when it comes to managing the equipment," Doug remarked as he entered the room. "That will never change. No one messes with anything they're not supposed to; I don't care if it's the president himself."

"Our fixed point in an ever-changing universe." Cameron laughed.

McIntyre said nothing.

Chapter 13

"Middle of the Road"

"**Y**ou know, you don't need to keep using that stuff," Cameron explained. "They've relaxed the dairy rationing."

Doug added another spoonful of the nondairy creamer to his coffee and shrugged.

"Yeah, I know. But I got used to it during all the rationing and don't feel like changing back."

"Suit yourself," Cameron replied. "That just means more of the good stuff for me. Listen, I might be keeping odd hours for the next few days. If any of the sound company clients call, just say I'm off at a jobsite and you don't know when I'll be back. If anyone else calls, just say I'm not here."

"Same as usual, in other words." Doug laughed.

"Well, sort of." Cameron smiled. "Only now you're not dealing with so many groupies to keep separated."

"Now that you mention it, I had noticed their voices were a bit deeper than usual."

"That's very funny. Seriously, though, I'm going to be at the office planning the next event, and it might be some odd hours because we've got a lot of subcontractors to deal with on this one." He cocked an eyebrow at his roadie, who nodded in acknowledgment.

Cameron felt relief with his decision to get his friend to stay there. They could easily use a "double-speak" when referencing any of his more covert activities. Cameron regularly checked for any listening devices in his apartment, more out of habit than anything else. He had never found any.

But you never know.

By referring to the sound company that Cameron operated as a front for his undercover work, he could easily keep Doug informed of his activities and, as much as possible, of his whereabouts in case anything should happen. A simple facial gesture would inform Doug if it was the sound company he was talking about or something else. If Cameron hadn't checked in at a specified point, Doug had a number he was to call and inform someone that Cameron was out of contact.

Like having a steady old lady, without the jealousy.

"Should I be waiting for any calls?" Doug asked.

"There should be one around six, six thirty," Cameron replied, indicating the window for his check in. "But I'm not aware of any others that would be coming in."

By telling Doug when to expect a call, he had also provided a window in which to wait in case something had delayed him from checking in. Cameron was confident that if he had not called by six thirty, Doug would make his phone call at 6:31.

I'm just glad I've never had to put that to the test.

Doug nodded in acknowledgment but said nothing, though Cameron could tell by the look in his friend's eyes that he was dying to know the details. However, Doug was skilled enough in what Cameron was doing to never ask for any details. They also both knew that soon enough, Doug would be briefed on his own expected participation in this mission, limited though that would be. Cameron knew that would alleviate some of Doug's curiosity, but he knew it wouldn't alleviate it entirely. It had been decided that each person was to be informed of things on a need-to-know basis, and only regarding their own participation. A select few, such as Cameron and McIntyre, had a broader view, but only McIntyre and some of the higher-ups understood all of the details.

As Cameron headed to his car, he lit another cigarette. He needed every bit of reinforcement he could find to deal with DC traffic in general, but to head to one of these meetings put him even more on edge. After all, this wasn't a typical surveillance operation where he would have to be listening for details about money laundering or drug deals or something of that sort. This was back to what they had been in before, and what they had narrowly escaped from alive.

He turned up the radio as he merged into the stop-and-go metropolitan traffic: bumper-to-bumper speed for long stretches and then the blessed relief of traveling through some of the lights and making some real progress before riding the brakes once more. It was enough to make him nostalgic for the restrictions on nonessential travel, which had put much of Washington on public transportation. However, in the last year or two, the government had adopted a new approach aimed at boosting American morale and confidence, and that was a return to the way things used to be. Unless it was absolutely imperative to the war effort, restrictions would be relaxed. Embargoes on shipments of grain to the Soviet Union meant a surplus of grain in the US and, therefore, a relaxation in rationing on breads and cereals. It was the same situation with beef and dairy. The gamble came with relaxing oil and steel.

New cars were rolling out of Detroit, and people were buying them. The defense industry had employed a large segment of the population—not just in the construction of munitions but electronics and technology as well—and they needed something to spend their money on. In addition to new cars, new appliances and gadgets were coming out, which Cameron knew were in actuality obsolete military technologies.

They've surpassed the old stuff so much they can let us play with the hand-me-downs.

Cameron supposed it was a good thing. Everyone knew the Soviets were not doing that. Their traditional paranoia kept any of their technology under wraps. If the average Soviet citizen ever saw it, it was in a magazine or on the black market. This must have sat well with the KGB and the military, but no economist would endorse such an attitude. With nothing to buy, there was no way for money to be put back into the Soviet economy.

In effect, we're going to outspend the Soviets.

The armed forces drove the Russians back from their advances in the field, and now the average consumer would drive them further back in the department store. If it worked, it would be the ultimate triumph of capitalism over Communism.

If it works, that is.

That brought Cameron back to what he was about to deal with. Yes, he only had a small role to play in something bigger, but his small role could change everything. He thought back to the previous weekend when Doug had borrowed Cameron's car to take Eli to the Antietam battlefield.

That battle happened because some guy stopped for a cup of coffee and found some cigars wrapped in Lee's orders for an invasion. The Confederates could have beaten the Union if it weren't for that one guy. A small event can change the course of history. And it can change it for either good or bad.

Instead of focusing on that, Cameron made himself focus on the aspect of his assignment that did not intimidate him: the music. It was good having the band together again. Even though they had not played together in almost four years, it took very little for that familiar groove to return. Cameron was impressed that Rich had managed to expand his skills beyond what they had known and was able to bring their rehearsals to a new level. Evan, too, had kept somewhat busy by playing with a few local bands on occasion. Cameron's impromptu jams, though few and far between, had helped to keep him nimble.

The only point that he was unsure about initially was John Kendall. Cameron had been informed that Kendall was a skilled guitarist, but he had never heard him before meeting him. When it was explained that they would be selecting a new guitarist, Cameron hoped they would hold auditions and he could have some input in the selection process. Instead, as usual, the choice was ordained and he had to go along with it. In his typical fashion, Cameron resolved to make the most of it.

In the days leading up to their first rehearsal, Cameron's mind went back to the time when the band had first been recruited and another choice had been forced on him against his will.

Special Agent Gordon Dwyer, their original case officer, had selected another agent, Donald D'Lorenzo, as another roadie and even ordered him to stay with Doug, their longtime road manager. Cameron sighed as he remembered how badly that decision had turned out. Doug had an unabashed loathing of D'Lorenzo that he made little effort to curb and no effort to hide. Even Dwyer's superiors realized the injudiciousness of such a decision and ended it by recalling D'Lorenzo to Washington.

However, this time things had proven to be different. In the first place, Kendall was nothing like D'Lorenzo. Where D'Lorenzo had been brash and arrogant, Kendall was confident, respectful, and engaging. Where Doug hated D'Lorenzo to the point that sometimes the roadie had to be physically restrained from attacking him, Doug got along with Kendall quite well. But the most important thing had been the music. D'Lorenzo had no musical background at all.

He thought a G-string was only a thong.

Kendall, on the other hand, was actually not bad. It was clear that he had not been playing in some time, but he clearly had developed skills that could be drawn upon. He even had a good voice, though a lack of experience performing before a live crowd was evident in his lack of confidence.

But that can be fixed. We've just got to get him in front of a mic.

For that, Cameron had some ideas that he presented to McIntyre.

"I'm telling you, you can't throw someone that inexperienced on a tour and expect it to go off without a hitch," Cameron insisted. "He needs to be before a live crowd."

"I realize that," McIntyre replied. "But right now the logistics don't oblige themselves to setting that up."

"Logistics never oblige themselves to anything," Cameron countered. "They have to be obliged. Look, I'm not asking you to reserve Constitution Hall, but there's got to be a small club that we can use to get some folks over to listen to us play."

McIntyre was about to respond when Cameron held up his hand.

"Yes, I know that this whole thing has to be carefully handled due to security," he affirmed. "But we both know that we need to get him in front of people so he has some credibility with the public as Clyde's replacement. That is not going to happen if he remains a well-kept secret. I'm thinking of that as much as his performance."

"That also raises another issue," McIntyre admitted. "We have to come up with a new look and name for him. There is no way we can let a member of army intelligence operate so publicly with his real name or look."

"The look will be easy." Cameron nodded. "His hair is starting to grow out, and he's always got a hint of five-o'clock shadow. If he stops shaving for a day or two, he'll have a nice set of whiskers. Replace the army uniform with some T-shirts and dungarees and he will look totally different. The name, you guys can worry about."

"You've got this pretty much figured out, don't you?" she asked.

"I do my best with what I have to work with."

"Okay, maestro, I will see what I can do. I've got some ideas of my own, actually."

That was a few days ago. It will be interesting to see what she's come up with since then.

Cameron pulled up in front of the latest building designated for the meeting site. No building was ever used more than once, and they only learned the location the night before. They did not follow any set pattern to the selection though Cameron did suspect a hint at musical lyrics after the last meeting. They gathered in the back room of a Chinese restaurant, Lee Ho's.

Cameron thought back to Lee Ho Fooks of Warren Zevon's "Werewolf of London." It subliminally played to such a degree that he found himself craving beef chow mien throughout the entire meeting. This time, however, they were in a used bookstore. Nothing about it stuck out from any song lyric that he could think of. He was half disappointed and half pleased.

That means no one else is going to catch on either.

The musty, pleasant smell of old paper greeted him as he stepped inside. There were no signs of any customers in the shop, and the only person Cameron noticed was a tall, thin, bespectacled man who was placing hardcover books on the shelf by the door. Cameron noticed similarities with the description he had been given of the contact, but all of them had been just vague enough to prevent them from being entirely copied.

"May I be of assistance, sir?" the thin man asked.

"Yes, I'm looking for something on the Civil War," Cameron replied with a smile.

"I can assure you, young man, that we have a great many works on that subject. Is there a specific topic or person that you are interested in?"

"Oh, anything dealing with this hallowed ground," Cameron responded, giving a tap with his right foot. Thus far, the signs and countersigns had been given correctly. Now was the moment of truth. Cameron had been told to ask for a book dealing with the Civil War. That would be the signal. However, he had been required to research the author on his own. That would be the countersign.

"Then you would be looking for something by Bruce Catton," the thin man said, giving the correct response. "We currently don't have anything by him on the shelves, but there are some new arrivals in the back, if you'd like to check there."

"Thank you," Cameron answered. "Would you please lead the way?"

Without a word, the man turned and headed toward the back of the store. A wooden door marked Authorized Personnel Only was positioned between two large bookshelves. The man gave a series of short raps, which produced another series in response. The door opened and Cameron was admitted.

Stepping into these meetings was always a letdown. The elements of intrigue and mystery that led up to them suggested darkened, smoky rooms with mysterious figures in trench coats and low voices conveying information that could topple governments. Instead, what he always found were his colleagues in their regular clothes drinking coffee or water out of Styrofoam cups with notepads and pens on a table. This time was even more anticlimactic, as McIntyre and their liaison, Richard Carmichael, were gathered around a card table with folding chairs.

"Come on, guys," Cameron moaned. "Can't we at least try to set the mood?"

"What would you suggest? Trench coats and fedoras?" McIntyre replied.

"Actually, I was thinking more of martinis, shaken, not stirred," he suggested.

"No such luck, I'm afraid. But I've got some possible venues for the band that might ease your pain a bit."

"You are definitely singing my tune, my dear. What are they?"

"They are venues frequented by a lot of our colleagues, so we are already confident these are secure sites," Carmichael added, with his usual distasteful tone.

Cameron did not have much use for Carmichael, and not just because he worked for the CIA. To Cameron, Carmichael was another D'Lorenzo.

Seriously, were you two separated at birth?

However, Cameron knew how much was riding on their cooperation and made every effort to suppress his feelings.

"Are you seriously considering that everything we do is going to be monitored?" Cameron asked. "I can understand a little extra caution, but don't you think that is taking it to an extreme?"

"Not hardly," McIntyre assured him.

Cameron felt a chill. He could tell by her tone that she was not merely attempting to deflect an argument.

"Do you mean we've already been compromised?" he asked.

"No," she assured him. "But, if we start out with a little extra caution now, we won't need to make adjustments later when we probably *will* need it."

"You think that time will come?"

"If it doesn't, then we've done something terribly wrong." Carmichael chuckled.

I wish the hell you hadn't said that.

Cameron then gave her updates on the band's rehearsals.

"Kendall's really improving," Cameron reported. "He sounds much more confident singing in front of us now. I started bringing in Doug once or twice to listen in on things, just to get Kendall used to being out of the comfort zone of being in the band."

"He's army intelligence; he should be able to function in any situation," Carmichael protested. "He should already be ready for this!"

"You and I both know that even in their missions the army rehearses, reviews, and repeats everything until they are one hundred percent ready," Cameron countered. "Hell, even we do that! Why else are we having these meetings but to do the exact same thing?"

"That's true," Carmichael sighed. "But I just thought that he should already be able to function in something this easy."

"Oh, really." Cameron smiled at his counterpart. "Then why not make a guest appearance at our first performance? Maybe a song, perhaps? Do you play an instrument? If memory serves me correctly, McIntyre used to sing along with our songs occasionally when they were trying to recruit us. Perhaps you would be willing to be a backup singer for her?"

"There's no need to be sarcastic," he snapped.

"I'm not." He smiled. "I'm reminding you that none of this is as simple as you think. Once you are behind that mic and in those lights, it is a different world. You have to connect with people that you can barely see, that are in constant motion but still hanging on your every word, and that are waiting for you to direct their every emotion and movement on the dance floor. That's just if you are in a club, by the way. If you're in a lounge, it's worse. You watch them sit there, sometimes watching you, sometimes chatting with the people they're with, but not doing anything while you are playing, and you hope, pray even, that when you're done they at least clap."

"And your point would be?" McIntyre smiled.

"My point being that asking someone who has not played in a band in years to suddenly take a spot in a band about to go on an international tour is as difficult as asking someone who studied

Russian in their freshman year of high school to speak it at their fifteenth reunion. Yes, some things will come back to you, but you will still be rusty as hell and not at all proficient."

"Continue," she said and laughed.

"And Kendall is conducting himself with professionalism and dedication," Cameron reported. "He's rehearsing alone when we're not playing and it clearly shows. He's able to do his guitar parts better every time we play, and his vocals are a lot stronger than when he started."

"What about keyboards?" McIntyre asked, suddenly serious. "Clyde played those as well. That isn't something you can pick up overnight."

"True," replied Cameron. "However, Clyde didn't play keyboards on the songs we recorded. He would only do that as an occasional backup at the live shows. So there isn't any need for Kendall to use the keyboards because no one would be expecting him to."

"Are you entirely certain that we can get away with that?" Carmichael demanded "We can't afford for anything to go wrong on this. Any loose end that we ignore could become a noose to hang ourselves with later on."

"You say that they are listening to bootleg copies of our albums," Cameron pointed out. "Well, I obviously have *every* album we have *ever* recorded, and not *one* song on *any* album features keyboards. We didn't even use them as backup instruments because Clyde wanted to feature his guitar playing. He always felt that was better than his keyboards."

"Excellent," McIntyre conceded. "And besides, we're not about to commit the mistake of trying to actually pass him off as Clyde. That would be asking for trouble and putting our operations at a suicidal risk before we even begin. We're playing on his resemblance to him to help exploit the growing popularity of the band. I'm working on press releases now explaining the substitution so it doesn't raise awkward questions."

Carmichael was silent, but Cameron could tell he was looking for something else to complain about.

"So, getting back to these venues, when did you want us to be ready to play them?" Cameron asked. "When do we check them out?"

"Now," McIntyre told him.

"Are we taking separate vehicles and separate routes?" Cameron asked, smiling at Carmichael.

"Don't be a wiseass," Carmichael snapped.

Cameron was about to reply when a sharp look from McIntyre cut him off.

"Well, it will be separate vehicles anyway," Cameron said. "I've got some clients to do follow-up on afterward and missing those appointments will just complicate some surveillance projects you need me to set up later."

"We had better see about getting those assignments switched to someone else for the time being," McIntyre advised. "You will need to be available at a moment's notice for consultations and briefings from here on out. Things are going to pick up very soon, I imagine. We can't have any delays in anything."

"I have already anticipated that, my dear, and that is precisely what I am doing," Cameron replied with his usual smile. "It's just that I have been working with these particular situations very closely and to just up and leave would raise serious questions."

"What is it you're working on?" Carmichael asked.

"Now, now," Cameron said, wagging his finger and flashing a toothy grin, "your stuff is proprietary and so is ours. No can do, amigo."

"Now see here," Carmichael snapped, clearly offended, "we need to be working closely together and make certain that we are completely transparent about everything."

"And regarding any activity or information pertaining to this mission, we will be," interjected McIntyre. "However, about anything else, you will obviously be keeping things confidential and so will we. He's following directives and protocol, so getting upset with him is pointless."

Cameron was relieved to see Carmichael concede his question

and instead discuss what was ahead of them. It was decided that Cameron should deal with his meetings first, and have them out of the way, to enable them to deal with other issues that might require an indefinite amount of attention. Cameron was silently grateful for that opportunity. It did not matter how much he tried not to think about what was ahead; it constantly fought its way to the forefront of his mind. Therefore, to be able to lose himself, as it were, in the familiarity of his cover enterprise was a blessing.

Meeting with clients about redesigning sound systems and intercoms was a "nuts-and- bolts" environment that provided him with a sense of security. Electrical work was very cut and dried. There were few variables and few surprises. He liked that. However, even here his relief was short lived, for he knew that one of the other aspects of this was to secure listening devices for undercover work. Talking with someone that he knew was a suspect in criminal activity kept him on his guard, the ever-present reminder of what he was.

Funny, until a few weeks ago I never minded the intrusion. Now, I guess, things are different. I wonder if they will ever go back?

Cameron informed his "clients" that now that things had reached this point of development, he would be handing things over to one of the engineers who would oversee the project going forward. None of them seemed to be worried about dealing with a new person, and Cameron was satisfied that his cover story had not raised any questions. After all, it was a tried and plausible explanation that they had used before, and had even referenced at the beginning of the project.

This hand-off should go smoothly.

Of course, each solution creates its own set of new problems, and this was not any different. Now he realized he did not have the distraction that he had enjoyed when he felt himself begin to stress about the new assignment.

Oh, bullshit. I'm acting like all of this is on us, or on me. We are just supposed to play, to give the ones who know what the hell they're doing the opportunity to do it. Focus on your first international tour, man, because it's likely to be your last.

That thought made Cameron catch his breath, regretting that he didn't tell himself "only."

Just play your music, damn it, and let the ones who are supposed to worry about that other shit worry about it!

He arrived at the first location and instantly disliked it. It was relatively close to the Foggy Bottom area of Washington, and while that might enable it to draw from the nearby Georgetown University student population, Cameron knew that it was also close to the State Department offices and other such white-collar enterprises and did not think that it would be suited for their genre of music. Even the name, Chez l'Enfant, suggested something more upscale than the Roadhouse Sons were used to playing. Stepping inside the door, he knew he was right.

The club's main room was a small affair, suggestive of an English pub. The stage was located at the far end of the room, and one glance told Cameron it was clearly designed for acoustic performances. McIntyre and Carmichael were at the bar, conferring with one another, and looked up as Cameron walked in.

"No!" Cameron declared emphatically.

"Just like that?" asked McIntyre. "You're not even going to look around, check the sound system, try the acoustics?"

"I don't need to," Cameron insisted. "I doubt if it has much of a sound system because it wouldn't need one. You can hear a whisper from one end of the joint to the other! I can stand here and see that there isn't room for the four of us, plus our equipment, on that podium."

"You haven't even checked it out," Carmichael snapped. "What? You think you can just come in here and pass a judgment like that?"

"How long have you been in the music business, Hoagy?" Cameron asked him.

"What did you just call me?"

"Hoagy, as in Hoagy Carmichael," Cameron explained. "Or is

your sole musical connection simply the surname of a great American songwriter?"

"I have no idea what you're talking about," Carmichael insisted.

"I didn't think so," Cameron groused. "Look, I will spell it out for you. This place is too small. There is simply no room for four of us and all of the equipment."

"Well, you've reduced sound equipment before," suggested McIntyre. "Couldn't you do that again? You've played in small venues like this before."

"No, they weren't like this," Cameron protested. "Evan's drum set would take up two-thirds of that stage, and that is not counting his stool or monitor! No, I'm sorry but this place won't work at all."

Carmichael and McIntyre pressed the virtues they perceived in the venue, but Cameron was adamant about its unsuitability, and eventually McIntyre relented. Carmichael tried to insist on this selection, but McIntyre convinced him that would be pointless.

Cameron tried to keep an open mind as they drove to the next location, though it was difficult. As he followed their taillights, he realized they were leading him into Georgetown. At first, he had hoped it would be a shortcut to another location, but he soon realized that it was not.

These places were picked by upper management, no doubt.

Cameron had to admit, however, that this place showed some potential that the previous one had not.

The sign on the front read Barker's. The atmosphere was more relaxed, legitimately so, not the forced casualness of Chez l'Enfant. However, it still did not feel like it would lend itself to their type of music. Granted, they just wanted Kendall to have experience in front of a crowd, but Cameron would like it to be a crowd who would appreciate what they were doing.

"Okay, how's this?" Carmichael asked.

Cameron noticed the irritation in the agent's voice but chose to ignore it.

"Sizewise, it is great," Cameron said. Indeed, the seating area was well over twice what had been available in the other location. As he was studying the room, McIntyre pointed out its various virtues.

"The owner and the manager said that this particular area did not have a lot of traffic, so they could clear out the tables and let you set up your instruments here. There is plenty of power for everything and …"

Cameron cut her off with a smile. "You'll make a great Realtor if none of this works out. However, I'm noticing something this place doesn't have that would be rather important to us."

"What's that?" Carmichael sighed.

"That would be a dance floor," Cameron explained.

"What do you need one of those for?" Carmichael snapped. "Are you going to dance or sing?"

"I am going to *perform*," said Cameron. "And if my performance is adequate, the patrons will dance. Dancing patrons are something that bands love to see. So do club owners, for that matter. It means they are having fun and won't be leaving soon and will be working up a thirst. Bands like to see dancing patrons because it means they will hopefully get a return booking from the happy club owner."

"I can't see what this has to do with giving Kendall a place to *perform*," said Carmichael.

"It has a lot to do with it," Cameron explained. "Look, the thing we are trying to do is get him confident of his abilities to do this. Part of that will be watching people respond to his playing. If they respond favorably, he will be much more confident and perform his duties much better. If they just politely sit there and smile, that's another story."

"Why does this even matter?" Carmichael was clearly losing his patience.

Cameron found himself being much more sympathetic than he expected to be.

"Man, I know this is a huge irritation to you," he said. "That is why I kind of wished you folks had allowed me a bit more input into things. I would come at things from a musical perspective. You, well, let's face it. You have *other* priorities, shall we say? I'll make it clear and brief. At our concerts, people have always gotten up and danced. It doesn't matter if we are playing in a club or an auditorium. If there isn't a dance floor, then they dance in the aisles. Are you with me?"

"I'm with you," confirmed Carmichael.

Cameron noticed the man was not being sarcastic.

"Okay then," Cameron continued. "If they are getting up and dancing, that means they're digging the music and the show. You follow? If he sees that we're able to pull that off, then he'll feel more confident about his part in what we're doing. If they don't do that, he will wonder if it is him or us. Either way, self-doubt is not a good thing. Besides, I can guarantee that in Germany they are going to be expecting a performance that will make them dance."

"How can you be so sure of that?" Carmichael demanded.

"Quit spending all your time looking at surveillance photos and take a look at news coverage," Cameron suggested. "I've been following the music scene on the news since this idea was put forward, and I've noticed that they are all out there on the floor. In fact, I doubt if there is any place to sit down at any of those places. Here, we can't do that without having to take out even more chairs. That means less patrons and less trade for the place. They're not going to be any happier about it than the band will be. I am actually just trying to make your life easier, that's all."

"And do you have any suggestions of your own?" Carmichael pressed.

"Yeah, actually, I do," Cameron replied. "It's a club where I sometimes jam. It's not too big, it's a little less refined than the places you've shown me so far, but it will work. And it is in a secure location, so you won't have to worry about that."

"Define secure location," insisted Carmichael.

"Down by the Navy Yard and not far from the Marine barracks," said Cameron. "US sailors, US Marines, and within sight of the Capitol—you can't get more secure than that."

"Would it be the Muddy River Smokehouse?" asked McIntyre.

"You've heard of it?" asked Cameron, clearly surprised.

"It was the next one on the list." She smiled, holding it up for him to see.

"It was the last one on the list, too," Cameron noted.

"I haven't been with you guys this long and not noticed a thing or two," she said. "However, these were also suggested and I couldn't ignore them. But Muddy River is on the other side of the city, and it is getting close to rush hour. If we ever expect to get there in this lifetime, we'd better go now."

As Cameron made his way through the streets of Washington, he realized the truth of what McIntyre had said. Of course, after all this time of dealing with traffic in the Beltway, he had realized it long before. However, today the increasing heat and humidity of Washington made it worse. The cherry blossoms had long ago bloomed and the tourist rush had lessened, but he noticed that never seemed to make much of an impact on the traffic. For every one tourist they got rid of, two more were ready to take his or her place. After what seemed like an eternity of stopping and going, Cameron pulled onto the side street and in front of a low brick building.

Muddy River Smokehouse was a small establishment that seemed to have been started more by accident than design. The owner was originally a part-time student who was making some extra money on the side by selling pulled pork out of his apartment. As the demand grew, so did the complaints from the landlord. Eventually, the enterprise ended up in a small place near N and Capitol Streets in the southeastern part of the city. Here, there was ample space to have a place for customers to come and enjoy their meal, not just get it to take home. Someone found some mismatched tables and chairs and an old stereo to play the blues, and it soon became a popular hangout. In the beginning, it was strictly BYOB, which saved the owner the hassle of dealing with a liquor license. In time, however, some of the officials in various offices came to appreciate the food and music and, in true Washington fashion, "made things happen," and Muddy River was soon the proud owner of a liquor license.

Personnel from the Navy Yard, as well as Marines, took a liking to the place and that helped keep trouble out. As the clientele grew, the business expanded into other parts of the building and even added some outdoor seating. The stereo was replaced with live music on a nightly basis, but the original ambience was not abandoned. Mismatched tables and chairs abounded, and the raw brick walls were covered with posters of blues artists and performances from around the country. In addition, colored chalk was put out in paper cups on all the tables so patrons could decorate the walls and floors. During the war, with rationing and curfew, many feared that the place would close. However, the owner was able to place an emphasis on the live performances, and not many people resented the reduced menu. Now that rationing had relaxed, it was back to business as usual.

Cameron loved this place because it reminded him of so many places he had played in before when things were so much simpler. They even kept the old, original stereo on the shelf above the bar, a dust-covered memento of the good ol' days, before the whole world went to hell.

Noting that McIntyre and Carmichael hadn't arrived yet, Cameron decided to relax at the bar with a drink. The cool glass fit as comfortably into his hand as he did on the wobbly barstool and his foot did on the dented faux brass rail at the bottom.

"You're still on duty" came a reprimanding voice from behind him.

"Cranberry juice and club soda, my dear," he said to McIntyre's reflection in the mirror as he held up his glass and shook it. "As always, I am as professional as ever. Now, take a good look around. Don't you think this will be more suited to what we're looking for?"

"I certainly do," she said. "And, for the record, I always did. However, we do have to humor our city cousins and at least consider their suggestions, which is why we took a look at the other places."

"I thought you had something to do with those." Cameron smiled at Carmichael. The other agent did not respond. He was carefully studying the surroundings, and Cameron noted that Carmichael's expression was not one of displeasure.

"Smells great," Carmichael admitted.

"That's their St. Louis-style ribs," Cameron said. "But it could also be their pulled pork, their baked beans, or their chili. Of course, I'm biased."

"You come here a lot?" Carmichael asked.

Cameron nodded and said, "If they had a shower, I'd never leave." He smiled.

Cameron led them to the other side of the room where there was an ample stage, slightly elevated from a cleared area that, owing to the many scuff marks on it, was utilized as a dance floor.

"There are plenty of outlets for our stuff," Cameron pointed out. "There is a lot of room, and there are usually a lot of people. It would be perfect for us."

"I have to admit, it would work," Carmichael agreed. "Security-wise, we're close to the Capitol, the Navy Yard, and a lot of our own people would be here as well. There's just one thing I'm concerned about."

"What's that?" Cameron asked.

"Do they serve food during performances?" Carmichael smiled.

"Hell yes, they do." Cameron smiled back. "And, if it makes you happy, I'll be up there watching you down here, enjoying every bit of it!"

"Well, then, I think we can go with this," Carmichael conceded.

They began conferring with the manager about possible dates when someone stuck her head out of the office.

"Is there a Laura Kendrick here?" she asked.

"That would be me," said McIntyre.

"You have a phone call."

"I left word at the office where I'd be," she explained. "I'll be right back."

Cameron and Carmichael continued discussing possible dates and finally arrived at one they felt was more suitable when McIntyre returned.

"Everything okay?" Cameron asked.

"Yes, it just seems that someone phoned in about you," she explained.

"Me? Who the hell would …?" asked Cameron. Suddenly, he

looked at his watch. It read six thirty-five. "Oh shit. Look, I can explain. When I'm going to be out and taking care of stuff, I try to check in at the, um, office. If they don't hear from me by a certain time, they're supposed to call your office to, uh, arrange someone to cover for me."

"When are they supposed to call in?" McIntyre asked.

"Well, I try to call in by six or six thirty at the latest," Cameron explained. "If they haven't heard from me by then, Doug is supposed to call you."

"Then he did his job very well," she admitted. "They took his call at six thirty-one."

You're on the ball, Dougie boy.

Chapter 14

"On the Dark Side"

Petrovsky read the memo once more to be certain that he had not missed anything.

"Have you anything other than this?" he asked the officer.

"No, Comrade Petrovsky, I have not," the man replied. He stood at attention, with nervous devotion in the presence of one of the more omnipotent members of the First Chief Directorate.

"Was there any verbal message to accompany this?"

"Yes, Comrade Petrovsky, there was," the man replied, more nervous than before.

"Then give it to me," the older man demanded. "Deliver it exactly as you were taught."

"Pereplyotchik," the man responded.

"Is that all?"

"Yes, Comrade Petrovsky, that is all I was told to say."

"Thank you then; you may go."

The other man saluted his superior and waited for his response. Realizing that there would be none coming, he quietly backed out of the office.

Yakov Petrovsky sat studying the memo before him. He was stunned by what he read, at the audacity it reported. What were the Americans thinking? Would they really attempt such a thing? Under any other circumstances, Petrovsky would have dismissed this as a complete fantasy on the part of someone's overactive imagination.

However, the information came with a signal that could not be ignored. "Pereplyotchik" was the pseudonym of Felix Dzerzhinsky, the first head of the Soviet Secret Police. It was one of the names he used while undercover during the czarist era. It was the signal that such counterintelligence was genuine, and imperative.

An audacious plan required an audacious response. However, if either move were too audacious, things could quickly spiral out of control. That was how the war began—something happened somewhere and someone responded somewhere else. Petrovsky knew that if things repeated themselves, it would be all or nothing.

He noticed, with alarm and annoyance, that his hand shook as he held the paper. Was it from fear or old age? It didn't matter the cause; to him it was a sign of weakness, and it disgusted him, adding to his anxiety. He laid the paper on his desk, if only to give himself the illusion of being in control of the situation. Once more he read the communication, but this time he was not seeing the same words. He remembered intelligence communications of times past—the reports of American provocations with Operation RYaN three years ago and, the most recent, last year's Able Archer alarm. Both of those reports had detailed military exercises that Soviet intelligence insisted were plausible camouflages for an American first strike. Fortunately, in both cases their intelligence had been wrong as to American objectives. But would this third time be the ill-fated charm? Despite public assurances to the contrary, Petrovsky knew what the proletariat did not: relations between the United States and the USSR were deteriorating, and the slightest misstep could be a catastrophe.

Petrovsky took up his lighter to burn the memorandum. He paused and studied the lighter; it had been given to him during the Great Patriotic War by an American soldier he had greeted at the River Elbe. Things had been different then, he realized. Also realizing that they could never return to that, he burned the memo. Watching the flames grow to consume the entire paper, he contemplated possible courses of action on how to proceed. There was no margin for error this time. He would need confirmation on this report. He needed to move quickly but cautiously. The wrong move could cause events to flare up, and what that would cost his country, and the world if things got out of hand.

"Everything could go up in flames," he said to no one in particular. The breath from his voice caused some of the ashes to scatter.

Chapter 15

"I Can't Drive 55"

Rudolph Hertz reported to his new assignment at Schwerin and settled into his new position as part of the dormitory staff. He chafed at the thought of how much this assignment was beneath him. He was a decorated member of the NVA and, by all accounts, was destined for a successful career in the Stasi. How then did he find himself assigned as a babysitter for the overly privileged son of a Soviet official? What other reason than the ossified leadership resented the enthusiasm and drive of a younger member of the organization and sought to minimize his influence and visibility, by assigning him to this backwater.

To hell with them, he decided. He would demonstrate his abilities by exceeding all expectations. His first step toward that end was a careful observation of young Mikhail Sechenov, who had thus far defied expectations. With Mikhail's connections and privileges, he should be the center of attention and admiration of his classmates. This was not the case. With few exceptions, the other boys did not bother with him. It was easy to see why. Petulant and bombastic, Mikhail was more often the center of their jokes than their admiration. He had two or three other friends, but they would often get tired of him and hang with others for a period of time, leaving Mikhail to the confines of his room and melancholy thoughts.

Hertz decided this could be an excellent opportunity for him to make inroads with him. To assist with his objective of ingratiating himself with the boys, Fuchs had released some records pertaining to his military service. A limp from an old skiing injury became a war wound severe enough to get him a medical discharge, a complete fabrication designed to give him more status with the boys in his charge. It had some effect, garnering repeated questions from some of the boys, but none from the one he was supposed to be shadowing.

Today, however, Hertz thought he saw his opportunity to change that. The other boys were outside enjoying the free period, some playing soccer but most congregating about in their usual cliques. The protocol of the school kept things regimented enough to ensure the requisite compliance to all things Soviet, even among the East Germans, but it was unfettered enough to acknowledge the students' status among the supposedly classless Socialist state. Mikhail was in his room. Hertz had heard the sounds of an argument between Mikhail and some of the other boys, including some of his own friends, but had not been able to catch what it was about. Before he could intervene and break it up, they had dispersed on their own. As he watched Mikhail retreat to his room, he began to formulate a plan.

Waiting in his office until the strains of Mikhail's stereo made their way down the hallway, Hertz continued to flip through his magazine as his office companion shifted uncomfortably in his seat.

"How can you stand to listen to that racket?"

"I'm sorry, what did you say?" asked Hertz.

"I said, how can you sit there so relaxed with that noise?" the other man repeated.

"I guess I just got used to that type of noise on the Austrian front." Hertz laughed. "It probably reminds me of battle."

"I would take the sound of bombs over that any day," the other man grumbled. "The fact that it is decadent American music doesn't improve my impression either!"

"No, I would not imagine it would," Hertz sighed. "That part is a bit hard to take, I'll admit. Would you like me to go speak to him?"

"Yes, please do," the other man nodded. "Because if I go up

there, I will try to take his stereo again, and I don't feel like going through that anymore."

"Oh, was there a problem with it the last time?"

"Not then." The other man shook his head. "Afterward, however, there was quite a row, and I was written up for upsetting our darling boy. He's not worth my job, I'll tell you that right now, but neither is listening to that noise!"

"I'll see what I can do." Hertz smiled, arising from his chair rather stiffly and limping off down the hallway. He had already established the routine of his leg being stiff when he had been sitting and becoming less so the more he moved, which helped deflect questions about his using the stairs without much difficulty. Arriving at Mikhail's door, Hertz gritted his teeth. Like his coworker in the office, he detested the young man's choice in music. However, he was supposed to ingratiate himself with the boy so there was nothing left to do but accept it. He rapped on the door but received no answer. Waiting a few moments, he rapped again, this time louder. Still, no answer. Finally he opened the door and stepped inside.

"What the hell are you doing here?" the startled young man exclaimed. "Get the hell out or I'll have your job for this!"

"For what?" Hertz smiled. "For not receiving an answer to my first two attempts to get in?"

"You're lying; you didn't knock!"

"I knocked twice, actually."

"You're lying! I didn't hear anything."

"I don't doubt that with your music turned up so loud." Hertz smiled.

"Oh, so you're just like the others," Mikhail shouted. "You just want to give me shit about my music! Well, it won't do you any good."

"Actually, I was coming to see if you were all right," Hertz explained.

"What are you talking about?" Mikhail asked, suspicion evident in his voice.

"Well, it's such a nice day out, I couldn't imagine anyone being inside unless they weren't feeling well."

"I'm feeling fine," the boy protested. "I just don't want to hang around with any of them, and I certainly don't want to hang around with you!"

With that, the boy turned up the volume on his stereo, leaving a clear indication of his dislike of his life in general and Hertz in particular. With a smile, Hertz turned the volume down.

"Keep your hands off my stereo," Mikhail protested. "Do you know who I am? I will have your job for this."

"I don't think you'd like it very much, so why don't we just let me keep it, shall we?"

"What do you want? Get out of here!"

"Just relax." Hertz smiled. "Look, I'm going outside for a smoke. Do you want to come?"

Mikhail stared at the man, dumbfounded. "I'm a student," he replied, cautiously.

"What? Do you mean you've never smoked a cigarette before?"

"Smoking by students is expressly forbidden!"

"Ah, so you do smoke then." Hertz smiled. "So would you like to join me?"

Mikhail made no reply.

"I'm serious," Hertz insisted. "No tricks. You won't get into any trouble if you're with me."

Mikhail still did not respond, but Hertz could see the boy was considering his offer.

"I don't like those nasty Russian cigarettes," Mikhail declared.

"I don't have those," Hertz assured him.

"Then you've got those nasty East German ones," Mikhail accused. "I hate those, too! I only smoke HB cigarettes!"

"Oh, you like the British stuff, do you?" Hertz smiled, reaching into his shirt pocket and partially revealing its contents. "Well, I'm afraid I only have the American kind."

"Marlboros?" asked Mikhail, suddenly breathless.

Hertz felt satisfaction as the boy revealed a source of influence so easily, and he nodded.

"An army buddy of mine in Berlin sometimes has to travel to the American sector and picks me up a carton once in a while."

"Why?" Mikhail asked, suddenly suspicious again. "That's a lot of trouble, even for good cigarettes. So why does he do it?"

"Have you ever noticed my limp?" Hertz asked. The boy nodded in acknowledgment. "Well, I got that making certain he didn't end up with a bullet in a worse place. So, when he can, he gets me something nice."

"Not very patriotic, smoking American cigarettes," the boy accused.

Hertz shrugged. "Smoking American cigarettes, listening to American music, dressing in American clothes—what difference does it make anyway?" He wanted to laugh at the sudden flush of the boy's cheeks.

"I have special permission to listen to this," the boy protested. "There is nothing unpatriotic in what I am doing!"

"Nor in what I am doing," Hertz assured him. "Besides, I wasn't accusing you of anything; I was pointing out that we both have some innocent pleasures that just happen to come from our adversaries, that's all. There is nothing about them that make us bad people. Now, would you like to come with me or stay inside?"

The boy hesitated before answering. "Do I have to share one?"

"No, I've got a fresh pack I haven't opened yet," Hertz assured him, with a laugh. "You can have your own."

The boy leaped from his bed, a big smile on his face, and headed to the door. Hertz shook his head and pointed to the stereo.

"Turn that off first," he said.

Mikhail was about to protest but didn't. Instead he turned it off and headed out the door with his newfound conspirator. Hertz led them out the back door.

"I don't think everyone needs to know our business," Hertz muttered.

Mikhail's expression had changed from the openly suspicious one of a few moments ago to a more expectant one. Hertz was amazed that the boy could be bribed by something as little as a cigarette but was pleased nonetheless. It meant that he could be lured in with something bigger later on.

Behind the school building was a row of bushes that ran along the back wall. Hertz suspected they were remnants of a hedge or maze from earlier years. He had discovered it while exploring the school grounds on his first day. Being involved in security for so long, he instinctively searched areas that could conceal someone attempting to stake out or burglarize a location. Bushes so close to a building could conceal something nefarious. However, this did not appear to be the case here. While the bushes did create a concealed alley for someone to walk along, they did not appear to offer much else, until he came to a small ell in the building. Here, the building and the hedges converged to make a small enclosure, safe from prying eyes. There were two old crates, and Hertz at first thought that some students had been using this space. Closer examination showed a layer of dirt and moss, which indicated it had not been used in some time.

"This is a nice place," Hertz pointed out. "You can sit here and no one can see you from the building. I suppose, if you kept your voice down, no one could hear you too well either."

"Do you come here often?" Mikhail asked, impatiently eyeing Hertz's shirt pocket.

"Not too often," Hertz responded, taking his time removing the cigarettes and packing them against his hand. "If you do something too much, it makes people suspicious of you."

"You East Germans are suspicious anyway," Mikhail sneered. "Why should you care?"

"We East Germans usually have reason to be suspicious." Hertz smiled, though inwardly he wanted to slap that insolent expression off the boy's face. "We're on the front lines in this war. The Americans have their West German lackeys everywhere. It is hard knowing who to trust."

"West German lackeys for the Americans and East German

lackeys for us Soviets—that is all this country is made up of," declared Mikhail.

His voice was full of the certainty that came from adolescent reasoning, which Hertz knew was partially correct and largely full of shit. But he was supposed to gain the boy's trust, which would mean indulging his teenage arrogance; therefore, he did not argue. He only shrugged.

"I suppose," Hertz replied. "But who wants to argue politics? It ruins a good smoke."

"Indeed it does," Mikhail agreed, trying to sound worldly.

"How long have you been here?" Hertz asked, lighting the boy's cigarette.

"Two years," Mikhail replied, exhaling. "Two long, miserable years."

"If you hate it so much, why not tell your folks?"

"I don't talk to them," Mikhail said defensively.

From the speed in which the boy went from camaraderie to sullenness, Hertz knew this was a sore spot that could be exploited.

"My mother died and my father works all the time," the boy continued. "I didn't have any other relatives so they sent me to private schools. Finally, they sent me here."

"Well, do you like this place?"

"Not really, though they do let me do more of what I want than the other ones did."

"I notice that you don't hang around with the others too much. Don't you have any friends here?"

"I have some, but mostly I don't associate with them."

"Why not, if you don't mind my asking?"

Mikhail shrugged but made no other reply. Hertz let him remain silent for a while. He did not wish to make the boy uncomfortable with too many questions so soon.

"I wasn't close to my father either," Hertz said finally. "He was killed in the Great War."

"So was my grandfather," Mikhail said. "He died fighting at Stalingrad."

"What a coincidence!" Hertz laughed. "So did my father! I wonder if they shot at one another."

Mikhail laughed at first and then became somber.

"I don't suppose that was very funny, was it?" Hertz asked.

Mikhail said nothing.

"But do you want to know what is funny?" the older man continued. "Not that many years ago, we would have been bitter enemies, but now here we are, sharing a smoke. I think that's pretty funny!"

Mikhail laughed nervously.

"When you left the army, did they let you keep your gun?" the boy finally asked.

"Yes, they did," Hertz nodded. "I had permission because it was assumed I would go into security work or the police force and I would need it."

"Why didn't you do that instead of working here?"

Hertz patted his hip in reply.

"A little problem of passing a physical," he explained. "They want you to be able to chase perpetrators and miscreants, not hobble after them."

"Well, then, why didn't you join the Stasi? I hear they will take anyone."

"Maybe they'll take anyone as an informant," he said and laughed. "But, I can assure you, they are more selective about who they take as an agent. I know; I tried!"

Mikhail laughed along with him, but Hertz could see the uncertainty in the boy's eyes, and he knew the laughter was only to try to emulate him.

"Did you become an informant then?" Mikhail asked.

"Whom would I inform on?" Hertz smiled.

"I don't know." Mikhail shrugged. "Perhaps people at the school, perhaps students. Perhaps even me?"

"Why should I inform on you?" Hertz laughed. "What have you done?"

"I don't know." The boy shrugged again. "Maybe for listening to American music or wearing American clothes?"

"Now, if I reported you for using all of that American stuff, who would help me smoke my American cigarettes? Do you understand what I am saying?"

"No," Mikhail replied, shaking his head.

"It means that if I would be accusing you of something, you could accuse me of something, too. So it makes more sense for me to be nice to you than to accuse you of something."

Hertz saw the boy's eyes twinkle and realized he had taken the bait. By offering the teenager a suggestion that he would now have something to hold over the older man's head, he watched the boy's confidence increase.

"Ah, so is that what they mean by *detente*?" Mikhail asked.

"No." Hertz smiled. "It's more like *entente*, an alliance based on an understanding."

"What understanding is that?"

"That we don't always have to follow all of the rules," Hertz replied with a wink. "But we do have to follow some of them, and one is that your afternoon classes are about to start and we need to get back inside."

With that, Mikhail accompanied the man he now considered his coconspirator back inside.

Chapter 16

"I Can't Hold Back"

Alexi duly signed the reports that his secretary had placed on his desk after giving them a careful review. Each one was a standard report dealing with the imports and exports of various machine products from the Soviet Union to Poland. There were also questions pertaining to orders, quotas, and myriad other issues that needed to be addressed by the companies responsible for developing the various manufacturing enterprises the Soviets had committed to help.

Each report was as arid as a desert and, to the casual observer, devoid of anything of any particular interest. Yet Alexi was not a casual observer. He carefully reviewed each page, making notes in the margins concerning issues to be discussed with his superiors and the other embassy personnel assigned to such departments.

"Why do you read them so carefully?"

"Do you seriously want to have to deal with another uproar from Solidarity?" he replied.

That was the end of any questions as to his dedication, and so he was left to dutifully pour over each and every report, mostly because he was the one who did not seem to mind working on that unpleasant detail. They were only too happy to leave him at the mercy of each row of figures, each listing of production details, each category of quotas, and each typo that inevitably showed up when the Polish clients and agencies translated their communications into Russian.

Alexi possessed a near photographic memory, and he could recite the necessary figures and data in meetings and briefings without needing to resort to notes. His superiors appreciated that because it helped ensure that the meetings went smoothly and quickly, permitting them to attend to anything but these metallic subjects and leave any details for Alexi to handle. And handle them he did.

Alexi's attention was particularly drawn to the typos, though they ascribed it to his fastidious nature and dislike of carelessness and poor performance. They would be quite surprised by his actual motivation for noting them. Each typo was part of a message from his handler to him. They were placed randomly throughout, conceivably the result of carelessness on the part of the writer and certainly not in any way suggesting covert communication. In fact, they were so well done that Alexi sometimes had to go back and reread the reports two or three times to be certain he had detected all of them. The messages were brief, usually two or three words and never more than four. They would suggest a dish, street, or shop where he would find a more complete communication in the form of a symbol or word. Knowing how closely he was being watched, his handler never expected a reply. His presence at the indicated location would be the signal that he had received the message.

Today's message read "new tea," and Alexi knew that a message awaited him at the cafe he sometimes frequented on his way home. The rest of the day was spent in meetings and on phone calls, each one more dull and monotonous than the previous one. He was asked to stay late to handle some minor details and agreed. By pre-agreement, there was a forty-eight-hour window in which he could respond before raising suspicions. He did not think he would need that much time to respond this day. Even his bosses remarked how fatiguing things had seemed today—so much effort going into small, tedious issues and the dismal weather outside, with fog and mist rolling in from the waterfront. It would not raise any suspicions if he stopped somewhere for a cup of tea and something to eat before heading home. And it was very important for him not to raise any suspicions because he knew that he was being watched. His carefully executed behavior designed not to raise any suspicions was, in fact, raising plenty.

However, it would also be his defense. He knew they wanted him badly, so badly that they would not be willing to make any mistakes, and as long as he didn't make any, any effort on their part to arrest him would risk a serious mistake. Finally, the last phone call had been made, the last report filed, and the last form signed. He was free to leave.

"I appreciate you staying this late," he said to his secretary. She smiled at him absently and then turned back to her typing.

"I am just doing my job." She smiled. With a trace of gallows humor, Alexi wondered which job she might be referring to. With a wave and smile, he bid her a pleasant evening and left.

At the cafe, the waiter asked if he would like some coffee.

"Not tonight," Alexi sighed. "The cold and damp has settled right in me. I'm in the mood for some hot tea. Do you have any?"

"Why, yes sir, as a matter of fact we do," replied the waiter. "We have a new blend. It is an herbal variety, made with orange. Would you like to try some?"

"Yes, that sounds excellent on a night like this."

"Will you be taking it black, or would you like cream with that?"

"I will have it black but with two sugars."

The waiter left and Alexi opened his newspaper. As he did so, he quickly looked about the room, studying the pictures on the wall to disguise his assessment of the other patrons. He tried to recognize any he had seen before. There were some who were regulars, but others he had seen periodically, though not regularly. It was the second group that interested him more than the regulars. Unlike East Germany, Poland was not as likely to be saturated with informants. The people were not as inclined to support the Communist government as other countries might be. Therefore, the ones who were only occasional customers might be ones who were following him. It was safe to assume that he was always being monitored. Such an attitude prevented carelessness.

Alexi appeared to be engrossed in his paper and paid no attention to the waiter as he brought the tea.

"This is a new shipment," the waiter said. "It came in three days ago." The young man then hurried off without waiting for a response.

After a few moments, Alexi turned his attention to the steaming cup beside him. On the saucer were three packets of sugar, despite having clearly asked for two. Alexi emptied the first two packets into his tea, dropping each empty packet back onto the saucer. When he was finished, he crumpled up the empty packets, using that opportunity to palm the third packet under the band of his watch, unnoticed.

Predictably, the news was filled with vague, excellently worded reports of increased production quotas and general improvements in various sectors of Soviet life, balanced by reports of weaknesses and troubles in the West. Reports of coal strikes in Britain, previously the dominant international story, were now rivaled by reports of the kidnapping of William Buckley, the CIA station chief in Beirut. It was this report that attracted his attention. It was reported that a militant jihadist group had abducted him, but Alexi could not help but wonder if that was not simply a front for an organization established by one of his own Soviet counterparts. It was a bold move, done at a time when bold moves could be the wrong moves. Frustratingly, the article spent more time capitalizing on the propaganda value of the weakness of American intelligence security than in providing any useful information for him to evaluate.

Finally, weary of trying to figure it out, Alexi finished his tea, paid his bill, and left. The evening street was not empty. Cars and pedestrians still made their way to various destinations, and many people were heading in the same direction that he was, including the man in the dark coat who remained just far enough back to avoid being too obvious. Alexi suspected that the man was relatively new at this. He was good, but not good enough to avoid being detected. It amused him to make the man follow him without giving him anything to report on, a passive-aggressive punishment for his carelessness.

Without incident, Alexi returned to his apartment and, as was his custom, turned on the light by the window and awaited the phone call. This time the call was from his secretary with a routine question about an order from a Polish company for machine parts. He answered it patiently and told her if there were any more questions, he could address them in the morning when he returned to the office at his regular time. Being certain to be observed from the street, Alexi made something to eat in the kitchen. After clearing away the dishes from his meal, he went into the bathroom and removed the sugar packet from under his watchband.

It felt as loose as an empty packet of sugar would, and only a careful search would reveal the thin incision along one edge. Inside was a small slip of onionskin paper that, at first glance, appeared to be blank. However, by turning it slightly, he noticed the shine of the invisible ink. The only way the carefully treated message would be visible was by holding it so the light shone on it. Alexi did not waste time studying it, as he realized any excess time in the bathroom could be noted by his observers. Frustratingly, it was difficult to read at first—some of the letters were difficult to detect—but he was able to decipher the message at last.

"Going as planned."

Chapter 17

"Naughty, Naughty"

"He's just an autumn dog turd," Doug sighed. "It's no big deal."

"He's a *what?*" asked Cameron.

"An autumn dog turd," Doug repeated slowly. "You know, when you see a park or a lawn covered in autumn leaves and you just *know* there's a dog turd out there somewhere, but you can't see it. You also know that no matter how hard you try to avoid it, you're probably going to step in it anyway. I knew when I got involved with you guys again and came back here, there was the possibility that I might meet up with him at some point."

"Well, I'm just saying you *might*," Cameron repeated, wending his way through the DC traffic. "I mean, there's no guarantee he's going to show up, but it is a possibility."

"I've stepped in turds before," Doug assured him. "You make a face at the smell, wipe your feet, and go on with your life. I can handle it without having to wring his neck, don't worry."

"Look, there's no guarantee he'll show up, but I just want to be certain there isn't going to be any trouble between you two if he does."

"Are you trying to assure yourself or me? Look, I can promise you there will not be any trouble on my part," Doug said. "Even if he does show up, I doubt if he will even see me or remember who I am. Relax, the gig will go off fine."

Cameron appreciated his friend's assurance, even though he did not share it. The person they were referring to was an individual with whom Doug had a long history of bad relations but who was now a colleague of Cameron's. That person was Special Agent Donald D'Lorenzo. Even after D'Lorenzo had been pulled from the cases the Roadhouse Sons had been associated with, he and Doug still had limited exposure to one another, and that contact had sometimes involved Doug having to be physically restrained from attacking him. However, Cameron dared to hope that this time might be different. It was true that Doug had changed a lot, in ways Cameron didn't really understand, but in ways that had had a maturing effect on his former roadie. Gone were the defensive outbursts and deep suspicions of other people's motives. In their place was a self-confidence that even McIntyre felt suited Doug much better.

I'm just making something out of nothing; D'Lorenzo probably won't even show up.

But, of that fact, Cameron was not nearly so confident. Over the years since joining the bureau, Cameron and D'Lorenzo did have occasional contact, and from those brief encounters, Cameron noted that D'Lorenzo had not changed a great deal. He now colored his hair to maintain his youthful appearance but was still plagued with the insecurities that masqueraded as arrogance. He was not involved in the cases that McIntyre was usually associated with and only peripherally involved with anything Cameron had been called in to work on. However, the news that the Roadhouse Sons were going to do a reunion show seemed to have traveled, and D'Lorenzo contacted Cameron about when and where the performance would be taking place.

Oh shit.

Cameron attempted to play it down, but he didn't think that would have any effect on discouraging D'Lorenzo. The other agent waxed nostalgic with memories clearly selective as to his previous relationship with the band. The band members' feelings toward D'Lorenzo were not much fonder than Doug's, but they had possessed the benefit of having limited exposure to him. Doug, on the other hand, had to not only work with D'Lorenzo, but they also had been required to share a room together. In addition, to the band's surprise, the musicians discovered that the two men had known each other previously, and it was from that encounter that the animosity originated; it was not just a personality conflict.

D'Lorenzo had been responsible for convincing a close friend of Doug's to enlist in a top-secret project that had been sabotaged and resulted in his friend's death. To Doug, that made D'Lorenzo a murderer, and Doug never missed an opportunity to inform the world of that.

The knowledge that such a bad penny might once again turn up in their routine had a worrisome effect on Cameron. It would certainly not look good if Doug publicly attempted to bludgeon D'Lorenzo, something that was not beyond the realm of possibility. Once, during a debriefing, Doug had attacked the agent and it resulted in his being shackled. Such an event at this juncture could have a devastating effect on this assignment, and thus Cameron decided to forewarn his friend of the possibility of his nemesis's appearance.

"I'm telling you, don't worry," Doug assured him. "Yeah, I hated his guts and still do, as a matter of fact. That is probably never going to change. But I don't need to waste my time with him anymore, and I am not going to. You do not have anything to worry about."

Cameron had known Doug for years and knew when his friend was telling the truth, and this time he clearly was. That was a tremendous load off of Cameron's mind.

"Now that we've got that settled, I actually do have some questions for you," said Doug. "What are we doing about equipment? Are you going to be using the house PA or are you guys getting your own?"

Ah, finally, familiar territory!

"For this gig, it will be the house system," Cameron explained. "But we're working on the equipment we're going to need over in Germany. That is proving to be a pain in the ass."

"How so?"

"Well, for starters, everyone seems to have an opinion on what we should be using. The problem is none of them have any idea about what we are trying to do, so all of their ideas pretty much suck. Thankfully, McIntyre and even Carmichael have been telling the big shots to back off and let us determine what we need."

"Why is anyone else even concerned with it?"

"Because if it goes right, everyone wants to take credit for all of it, and if it goes wrong, everyone wants to make certain they covered their asses."

"Ah, got it." Doug nodded. "So I take it we're going to be using the same stuff as before?"

"Absolutely," said Cameron. "I hope you've been eating your Wheaties because you're going to be getting a workout!"

Cameron could tell by the look on Doug's face that the roadie was wondering how much the years of being away from the heavy lifting had made him soft, and he had good reason to worry. Handling the monitors was not easy. The stage monitors were large, cumbersome affairs; huge cabinets held the fifteen-inch speakers, with additional cabinets on top of that for the horn tweeters. The bass monitors weren't any easier. They were 750-watt, EAW BH800 monitors. Like the other monitors, these were heavy cases that held eighteen-inch speakers. On top of these were other cabinets for the fifteen-inch, mid-bass speakers; the cabinets that held the two-inch, midrange horn tweeter; and one that held the one-inch, high-frequency horn tweeter. Taking into account the number of these used as front-of-house speakers for the audience, and stage monitors and side fills for the band, it was going to be a *lot* of heavy lifting, an awful lot of it.

"They are on wheels, remember," Cameron offered weakly.

Doug rolled his eyes. Despite being on wheels, these were no easier to handle.

"There is that," the roadie muttered. "But answer me this: can any of this equipment be easily replaced if something breaks?"

"Um, what would you like to hear? I think so or I hope so?"

"That's what I thought," sighed Doug. "So that means we're going to be needing at least one or two spares, doesn't it?"

"Correct as usual, King Friday," Cameron said. "We'll be taking extras of all of them to at least use for parts in case any break down. We already thought about that problem."

"Oh, this is just getting better and better," Doug moaned. "I wonder if I ask really nice, if Value Mart will take me back."

"I doubt it." Cameron smiled. "Besides, it isn't like you'll be doing this alone. You'll have us, and I'm certain the venues will have crew on hand to help you out."

"I speak English and enough Canadian French to start a bar fight," Doug explained. "What German I know I picked up from watching 'Hogan's Heroes.' That isn't going to be much good over there."

"You don't have anything to worry about," Cameron assured him. "In West Germany they speak English and French as well as German."

"Why?"

"Uh, they lost the war, remember?"

"Oh yeah, I forgot."

Arriving at the club, Doug helped Cameron carry in his guitars. The venue had its own security detail, and there was very little equipment to unload, so Cameron assumed that Doug's upbeat attitude was the result of basically having a night off, which didn't happen often. Despite McIntyre's suggestion, Doug did seek out a second job.

"If you get one now and we have to leave, it might just raise questions," she had warned him.

"I'm a service station attendant," Doug said. "Do you have any idea the turnover rate in that? I've been there two weeks and I am considered the veteran. If I don't show up tomorrow, they'll just replace me with the first person who applies for the job."

Fortunately, Doug had earned his boss's confidence and as a result was able to have some flexibility with his work schedule in case Cameron or McIntyre needed him to attend to a detail that was not easy for them to take care of. Tonight Cameron thought it would be a nice reward for his friend to be able to just relax and listen to the band.

Muddy River had not only its own PA system but its own drum kit as well. Evan had checked it out on previous occasions and confessed to having sat in on some sets in the past. He enjoyed the setup that the club had; therefore, he did not bring his own. After making a few minor placement adjustments, he was ready for his sound check, as was Rich, who arrived with him. Kendall was the last to arrive, eliciting a disapproving look from Cameron. Doug ordered a beer and relaxed at a table in the corner as the band went through the procedure for getting their sound just right.

The crowd began arriving in various-sized groups as well as singles. Cameron had thought McIntyre would have suggested that the bar be closed for a private party, but she had vetoed the idea as one that might draw too much attention to what they were doing.

"They are always featuring various performances," she explained. "There's no reason to treat this any differently." And so they didn't.

As showtime approached, Cameron and the rest of the band gathered for their traditional pre-show shot of tequila. The four were gathered in their traditional huddle—a toast, a cheer, and knock it back. Accompanied by shouts and applause from some of the patrons, the Roadhouse Sons took their places on stage. The lights in the lounge dimmed, the lights on the stage increased, and Cameron plucked the string of his guitar. As the vibration continued, the noise in the house died down in anticipation of what was to come. The boys knew that none of the people in the house knew what they had once been capable of musically. Now they were together once more. The familiar feel of the shoulder straps, the familiar feel of the instruments, the familiar feel of the lights on their faces. However, there were also differences. There was a new man standing in Clyde's spot. He had never played with them before. This was, essentially, the band's final evaluation, and none of them knew how it would play out.

For Cameron, however, there was even more hanging in the balance. Until he had actually picked up his electric guitar, something he had not done in four years, he had never admitted how much this meant to him. Now, standing on a stage and in the spotlight, he felt it awaken. As the chord reverberated through the room, it matched the beating of his heart, and he felt both quicken the longer the note hung in the air, as though there were something coming alive in his chest and fighting its way out. He knew what it was; it was his music. It was a part of him that he had suppressed for years. Yet it had waited a long time for this moment.

And it will wait no more.

With a sweep of his hand, Cameron struck the opening chords to what they had agreed would be their ballad, Thin Lizzy's "Boys Are Back in Town." When they chose it as the opening song, they suspected that only two of the people listening would know the significance of that selection, and from Doug's hearty shout, they were right. After that song, the band went on to play selections by The Doors, Lynyrd Skynyrd, and AC/DC.

Cameron studied the reactions of the crowd, and it was what he had hoped. As usual, no one got up to dance during the first song or two, but by the third a few couples made their way onto the floor and were soon joined by others. As the set progressed, the floor filled up. Shadows moved liked specters in the background as waitresses bearing drink-laden trays made their way among the crowd. He could see the lights of cars passing by outside, like brief flares on the glass that obscured the band's reflection. Cameron's hands moved of their own accord, seeking out the familiar territory of the frets and chords of his old guitar. He hoped that he was not playing too hard and that the new strings would hold out, but he didn't worry too much. Cameron knew his guitar as well as he knew himself, and he knew that everything would be fine. He was home again. Nothing could go wrong.

Cameron glanced back at Rich and Evan and saw the same feeling reflected in their faces. It did not matter how long they had been away from this; it did not matter if they wore shields now or carried a gun. They were musicians; they were rock stars. Even Kendall had a light in his eyes that Cameron had not noticed in rehearsals, and he knew that putting him in front of a live crowd before going overseas was the right decision.

Glancing at his notes, Cameron saw that they were at the last song of the first set. He had picked this one himself: ZZ Top's "Beer Drinkers and Hell Raisers."

"This one is for all of you truants and misfits out there," he shouted. He remembered the first time he had heard that expression, many years ago in a backstage office in Burlington, Vermont, the day after his first case officer had been killed. They had been handed over to another man, Chuck Lamont, who understood their apprehension, guided them through it, and watched over them until they were ready to be on their own. Chuck had an unorthodox way of working and appreciated the Roadhouse Sons' unorthodox existence in his world and used that term to describe them. He had once told Cameron that it was a term used to describe some of the others in the bureau who did not always do things by the book. From the cheers and applause at his use of the name, Cameron knew some of his colleagues who had also heard this applied were present.

As the band played through the first stanza, Cameron wondered where Chuck was right now. As Kendall began his solo, Cameron noticed a shadow moving through the crowd. That wasn't unusual; people were getting up and dancing, and waitresses were bringing drinks. Yet this one seemed to have more of a purpose, as if it were searching the crowd for someone. Cameron instinctively focused his attention on the shadowy figure. There was something different about this one, but he couldn't place it. It weaved through the crowd, stopping and greeting people, as though it knew the people who were there. No one seemed to be upset or shocked to see this person, so Cameron allowed himself to relax, slightly.

Kendall's solo ended, and Cameron began his verses.

"The crowd gets loud when the band gets right, steel guitar crying through the night," he sang into the mic, watching the actions of the crowd on the dance floor mimic the words. They were clapping and moving along with the beat, doing everything a musician wants to see a crowd do. He had paused in the lyrics for an impromptu solo, and that was when he noticed the shadowy figure step into the edge of the light by the dance floor. It was D'Lorenzo.

The agent smiled and waved at the band. Cameron, realizing that D'Lorenzo was looking straight at him, had no choice but to give a brief nod in return. D'Lorenzo stepped back outside the ring of light and once more became a shadow. As Cameron began the next line, he was gripped with apprehension as he noticed D'Lorenzo heading to where Doug was sitting. The roadie, enjoying a beer and the music, did not seem to notice the man approach him.

"Yeah, tryin' to cover up the corner fight ..."

Life, please don't imitate art!

"But everything's cool 'cause they's just tight."

Hopefully, neither of them is too tight!

The band belted out the chorus as D'Lorenzo tapped Doug on the shoulder. Cameron could see the roadie turn and face him and pause for a moment before getting up. Doug rose slowly, which Cameron took as a good sign. He wasn't lunging or swinging. D'Lorenzo extended his hand, and Doug took it. Cameron waited to see if Doug would do anything past that, but there was no sign of a confrontation. Relieved, Cameron threw himself into the final verse, and like the words he sang, the place became even livelier as the dancers cheered on the band, clapping and laughing at the reference to Congress and whistling and whooping at the declaration of being both professional and experimental. They gave the Roadhouse Sons a standing ovation as the song ended, and Cameron announced they were taking a brief break.

As he unplugged his guitar, Cameron noticed out of the corner of his eye that D'Lorenzo was still standing with Doug, and since Cameron was not certain how long the roadie's long-suffering would extend, he decided he had better get over there.

"Hey there," D'Lorenzo greeted him. His tone was that of someone greeting a lost classmate at a reunion. Cameron felt annoyed by the falsity of the warmth, because he had been in a conference with D'Lorenzo only a month ago and had talked to him on the phone less than a week ago about this performance. He didn't say anything, however, because he knew that was just how D'Lorenzo was. Cameron cast a glance over D'Lorenzo's shoulder as the two made small talk and saw Doug make a face and, with exaggerated motions, wipe his foot on the floor. Despite his efforts, Cameron could not hide a smile. D'Lorenzo followed Cameron's gaze and noticed Doug's movements.

"What are you doing?" D'Lorenzo asked.

"Oh, nothing," Doug replied, with complete innocence and sincerity. "I just thought I had something on my boot, that's all. If you'll excuse me, I'm going to go get another beer."

"Just like the old days, eh?" D'Lorenzo laughed, giving Cameron a playful punch on the shoulder.

Cameron halfheartedly agreed, and the two spent the next few minutes reminiscing over the brief time that D'Lorenzo was involved with them.

"Well, I've got to get going," he finally said. "I just stopped in to hear you guys and give McIntyre a message."

"About what?" Cameron asked.

"Oh, nothing really." D'Lorenzo shrugged. "They just scheduled a meeting for tomorrow and wanted to make certain she got the message. Well, I've got to be off."

Cameron watched him leave and wondered what the meeting might be about.

Probably nothing, like he said. He's always trying to make things sound bigger than they are.

The band played their second set as skillfully as their first, and the crowd seemed to be even more enthusiastic. As the crowd left after the final song, people made their way up to the stage to compliment them on their performance and inquire as to any future dates. Cameron and the others deftly avoided any definitive answers, and despite that, the band's newly discovered fans left in a warm afterglow of a great evening.

Finally, it was just the band, Doug, Carmichael, and McIntyre.

"I've got to admit, I'm pretty damned impressed." Carmichael laughed, ordering Cameron a drink. "Maybe when all this is over, you can play here again?"

"Man, I'd love that," Cameron agreed, still buoyed by the evening's high energy.

He allowed himself the fantasy of being back on stage as the company enjoyed a few quiet moments before last call. Everyone felt confident of the band's ability to perform, and both Doug and McIntyre, so familiar with the Roadhouse Sons, agreed that this combination was easily the equal of anything they had done in the past.

"You guys shouldn't have any problems, man," Doug said, tipping back another beer.   Cameron noticed that his friend was relaxed and in a good mood, and if there had been any residual resentment about seeing D'Lorenzo, it was forgotten in the good feeling of the moment.

He's right; I don't think we've got anything to worry about.

Cameron, swept up in the exhilaration of the moment, ordered another round of drinks for everyone. They all asked for beer, except for McIntyre.

"I'd love another dry martini," she said.

While they waited, the band joked about the evening's experiences, about missed lyrics and dropped chords and solos that either went too long or too short. Everyone agreed that Kendall's performances of Clyde's usual songs were so nearly identical that they would not be noticed. When their drinks arrived, Rich proposed a toast to the reuniting of the band and the success of their future performances, to which everyone gave hearty approval. As McIntyre raised her glass to her lips, Doug grabbed her wrist.

"You didn't order a dirty martini," he said, giving her a warning look.

Cameron, shocked at his friend's behavior, looked at the glass in McIntyre's hand and realized Doug was correct. Instead of the usual, clear beverage she had been drinking all night, her glass had the slightly clouded appearance that was caused by the addition of the olive brine.

Or something else?

Chapter 18

"Do It Again"

Yakov Petrovsky wanted to lose his patience with the man seated across from him, but he could not. The man did not outrank him, nor did the man possess more influence than he did. He couldn't lose patience with him for the simple reason that he was voicing the same concerns that Petrovsky shared.

"Are you entirely certain that this source is reliable?" the man insisted.

The man in question was Georgi Malinovsky, another high-ranking officer in the First Chief Directorate and a peer of Petrovsky's. He had shared with Malinovsky the communication he had received from a former asset in the United States.

"I am entirely certain," Petrovsky assured him. "All of the information we received from him prior to this has been impeccable."

"Yes, prior to this," Malinovsky insisted. "How long has it been since he's had access to the information we've wanted? The intelligence we received from him did not help us locate American submarines, did it? How can we be certain that he hasn't been discovered and isn't being used to feed us false information?"

"I will admit, all of those issues are a concern of mine, as well," Petrovsky conceded.

"Then what are you going to do about it? What you've described to me is fantastic, if not utterly preposterous. Not even the American President Reagan would countenance such an action!"

"Wouldn't he?" asked Petrovsky with a smile. "And why not? Isn't he the embodiment of the American cowboy and the architect of their cowboy diplomacy? Isn't that why they voted him into office? An enterprise such as this is entirely credible in that light. Even you have to agree to that."

"Yet, in the light of certain other incidents, no, I certainly would not agree! To do so is too risky."

"What incidents?"

"How quickly we forget what we don't want to face," sneered Malinovsky. "Five months ago you were as certain as everyone else that NATO forces were preparing an attack on us during training exercises in the North Atlantic. As I recall, you have always believed they would make the first strike. You personally made significant contributions to Operation RYaN for Chairman Andropov, did you not?"

Petrovsky fumed at the reminder of those events. In 1981, Yuri Andropov, then chairman of the KGB, announced that the United States was preparing a first-strike initiative against the Soviet Union. This gave credence to the whispered paranoia of the Kremlin following their reversals of fortune in the war, and they authorized Operation RYaN—from the Russian acronym for "nuclear missile attack"—to collect evidence of such an action, and Petrovsky was a major contributor.

In November 1983, Soviet military and intelligence analysts seemed to confirm these suspicions when they declared that the United States was imitating Nazi Germany and preparing an offensive against the Soviet Union under the guise of an operation they called Able Archer 83. The Kremlin, equally exulted and terrified that their paranoia was justified, accepted this conclusion unilaterally. Each day, new NATO developments reinforced their beliefs. The radio silences between various bodies involved in the exercises and the new forms of coded transmissions were startling enough in and of themselves. With the addition of the involvement of various heads of state, and a marked increase in diplomatic communications between the United States and their British counterparts, suspicions were fueled and confirmed when the United States put all of their forces on DEFCON 1 status. In response, the Soviets declared State Orange, signaling a nuclear strike within thirty-six hours. Air forces in Poland and East Germany were placed on alert. Soviet nuclear forces in the Balkans and Czechoslovakia were also readied for attack.

In the end, it had all been a NATO exercise, after all. The diplomatic chatter had been between President Reagan, Queen Elizabeth II, and Margaret Thatcher regarding the Falkland Island crisis, not global nuclear annihilation. The supposed military buildup around Supreme Allied Headquarters in Casteau had been to see how they would respond in the event of a Soviet nuclear strike, not preparation for a strike against the Soviet Union or the Warsaw Pact. The KGB had told the Kremlin that there was a monster in the closet, and it had turned out to be a coat. Petrovsky loathed Malinovsky even more for the reminder of his involvement in that embarrassment.

"Then what would you suggest that I do?" Petrovsky demanded.

"Nothing."

"Nothing," cried Petrovsky. "Didn't you hear a word that I said?"

"I heard every word," assured Malinovsky. "But I can't believe that it is anything but another American trap."

"I have not overlooked that possibility either," Petrovsky replied coolly. "Yet, neither can I overlook that this has come from a highly reliable source."

"You mean a *previously* reliable source," Malinovsky corrected. "However, that is irrelevant. RYaN's information came from reliable sources as well, as you recall."

"They came from our own reliable sources," Petrovsky shouted. "There were no outside corroborations."

"Are there any here?"

"I believe so, yes," Petrovsky said. "Alexi's controller has been increasingly suspicious of him and has increased surveillance on him."

"Really? That is incredible! What has Alexi done?"

"Nothing," Petrovsky said. "His performance is exemplary, his conduct impeccable, and his work efficient. He has done nothing out of the ordinary, nor has he done anything to draw attention to himself."

"And for this reason you are willing to give credence to an isolated report from a former asset?"

"Do you see anything wrong with that?" demanded Petrovsky.

"Do I see anything right with it, you mean? Frankly, no I don't. What I see is someone so terrified of making another mistake that he is rushing headlong into doing exactly that. You're believing this report because it reinforces something you want to believe, that the Americans are up to something."

"And you are refusing to believe that because you don't want to admit that they might be."

"All right, yes," Malinovsky confessed. "Do you realize how close we came to annihilating ourselves over a mistake? No, I do not want to run that risk again, ever!"

Petrovsky could not deny having the same concerns as the other man. However, it was because of these very concerns that he insisted on action.

"Then what about Alexi?"

"What about him?" Malinovsky demanded. "Surely you can't have been so close to the purges that you don't believe he isn't trying to be an exemplary employee just to be an exemplary employee?"

"I remember the purges quite well, comrade," Petrovsky protested. "And it is because of that fact that I cannot believe that a man who once was the toast of the directorate will so quietly accept being a lowly subordinate of a mere trade delegation, with no intelligence-gathering activities whatsoever. Or of any hope of future prospects for redemption."

"Khrushchev fell out of favor and was content to grow turnips," Malinovsky countered. "Perhaps Alexi is just waiting for a new assignment. He's experienced enough to understand that sometimes there are long periods of inaction until the opportunity to utilize his talents arise."

"Khrushchev's grandson said the old man spent his retirement crying," Petrovsky corrected. "However, like Khrushchev, Alexi understands that there will never be any such further opportunities again. No, Alexi is what the Americans would call 'damaged goods.' Furthermore, he is well aware of that fact."

"Then he knows that only by doing nothing counter to what he is asked is the only way to rehabilitate himself and restore his reputation."

"That is a consideration," conceded Petrovsky, "albeit a remote one, which even you must admit."

"I must admit nothing, nor will I admit it. I assure you that I am correct in my assessment, and you are not," Malinovsky insisted. "I assure you it is more than a consideration; it is how it is. Now you asked for my recommendation, and I have given it to you. Do nothing on this. Certainly not until we have received any outside corroboration of this intelligence."

"Perhaps you are right," sighed Petrovsky.

"I am certain that I am," said Malinovsky.

After his colleague left, Petrovsky considered their conversation. He seethed at Malinovsky's arrogance, which had only grown worse since the events of Able Archer. Malinovsky had been part of a group that questioned the conclusions of the studies and urged restraint. Because of this—coupled with the patriotic memories conjured up by the association of his patronymic with that of General Rodion Malinovsky, the famous hero of the Battle of Stalingrad—Malinovsky had enjoyed a rapport with members of the Soviet military that other members of the KGB did not possess.

Petrovsky and others in the directorate knew that there was no relation between the two men, and while Malinovsky never claimed a relationship, neither did he discourage the association. Instead he basked in the military favor that he seemed to possess and used it to be the presumptive director. However, even Malinovsky was not so bold as to be too obvious with his delusion of grandeur and saved it for such personal moments as these.

"You talk like those who said Hitler would never invade," he muttered to the empty room. No, the Americans would be bold enough to attempt something, and it would be up to him to do something. Yes, Malinovsky was correct that nothing should be done, at least as far as causing a major alarm, but to do absolutely nothing would be madness. Indeed, that was what Petrovsky had already concluded. That did not mean he was entirely without options, however, and he realized that this could be taken care of discreetly with a few phone calls. He smiled with satisfaction as he dialed the first one.

Chapter 19

"Back Where You Belong"

Cameron knew this assignment was going to be unlike anything he had previously experienced, but he didn't know it was going to involve quite the attention to detail that it was turning out to be. Understandably, the issue of cover names or the lack thereof was raised and discussed at length. It was decided that cover names would necessarily have to be devised for McIntyre and Kendall. Both of them worked, to a greater or lesser degree, in counterintelligence and therefore would need to keep their true identities concealed, and their respective agencies developed their covers. The bureau transformed McIntyre into publicist Laura Kendrick and naval intelligence transformed Kendall into itinerant guitar player Ed Collier. The three original members of the band would keep their own names, as the band's popularity was based upon their identities as the Roadhouse Sons.

Cameron had raised concerns about he and Evan being special agents and the potential risk of exposure. However, in the final meeting with Vernon Gray, he was assured by both McIntyre and Carmichael that he had nothing to be concerned about.

"You have never worked closely in the area of counterintelligence before, so it is unlikely that your identity with the bureau will be known to any Soviet or Stasi operatives," Gray explained. "Evan Dixon is an analyst, so he would not be known to them either."

Gray went on to explain that Doug, likewise, would not be

required to have a cover, as there would likely be no previous knowledge of his identity. Cameron and McIntyre took exception to that conclusion and raised the issue of Doug's identity having been known to a former Soviet recruiter.

"We're aware of that," Gray had assured them. "However, we don't feel that, in itself, will be a deterrent."

"Why not?" McIntyre demanded. "I should think that would be a major concern!"

"Because we have a greater concern that we feel your friend will help us with," the CIA agent explained.

"Doug? What on earth could he help you with?" she asked.

"Although it is true that Courtland was the subject of an attempted recruitment, the fact is it was due to his proximity to their real target," Gray explained.

"You mean Gus Kalbe?" asked Cameron.

"That's precisely who I mean." Gray smiled.

"But nothing came of that recruitment," McIntyre protested. "Our investigations showed that everything was cleared up."

"Nothing came of them trying to recruit Courtland," Gray explained. "However, we've taken a closer look at that case and have come to a different conclusion about Kalbe."

"What kind of a conclusion?" Cameron asked, though he was almost certain he knew the answer.

"We believe that the Soviets were, in fact, successful in recruiting Kalbe."

Shit, I knew it.

Cameron thought back to the last time they had all worked together in Seattle four years ago. Someone had approached him, claiming to be Gus Kalbe. Kalbe wanted to reconnect with Doug, in order to recover some things he had left behind when being deployed on the *Mustang*. When Cameron confronted the man with his supposed death and disappearance, the faux Kalbe concocted a less than plausible explanation for it before luring Cameron into a trap with a ruse about kidnapping his then girlfriend and turning him over to a sadistic Soviet agent once they had caught him. Before that evening was over, the fake Kalbe was dead, Doug was nearly killed, and Cameron's hand was smashed.

That was probably why they posed a phony Kalbe in the first place; he had been their guy all along.

"How can you be so certain?" McIntyre demanded. "We analyzed all of that information thoroughly and found there was nothing to indicate that Kalbe had betrayed the *Mustang* in any way!"

"I am certain that insofar as your analysis went, that was correct." Gray smiled, his tone dripping with his patronizing attitude. "However, we came to a different conclusion, one that suggested that Kalbe not only was a Soviet spy but also destroyed the *Mustang* rather than allow the captain to get it out of reach of NORAD defenses."

"I'll ask again, how can you be so certain?" McIntyre repeated. "We reviewed every aspect of that incident and found nothing that would corroborate that conclusion. Are you trying to tell me you had information that you withheld from us?"

"Come now, Barbara, don't be so naive," Gray said condescendingly. "Surely you don't believe that a mission of that magnitude would have everything made public, do you? Both our agency and the NSA worked with military intelligence to keep that entire situation monitored. That was how we were able to detect the final transmissions of Captain Pickering. In them, he indicated that a spy had been uncovered and the vessel was in danger."

"And?" demanded McIntyre, barely able to contain her anger.

"And nothing." Gray shrugged. "That was the last transmission before the destruction of the *Mustang*."

"How do you know that he wasn't the spy and sending that to his contact?" Cameron asked.

"Because he sent an encrypted message on a secure channel to naval intelligence," Gray replied. The man waited, calmly smiling. "Surely you don't think that naval intelligence would be an answering service for the KGB, now do you?"

McIntyre seethed but said nothing; however, Cameron could tell by the flash in her gray eyes that once more the sidewalks of DC would bear the focus of her wrath as she took her daily jog.

If this assignment doesn't get over quickly, you'll either develop plantar fasciitis or high blood pressure.

"Courtland is going to be bait, to see if anyone tries to contact him," Gray said and sniffed.

"I thought you agreed that they hadn't recruited him," snapped Cameron.

Throughout this assignment he had been well aware of his lack of experience and seniority in this field and had tried to remain respectful when dealing with their counterparts in the CIA. However, like McIntyre, his patience with the games and insinuations was taking its toll on him as well.

"We don't believe they had," Gray admitted. "However, we can't be certain they might not try again."

Surprisingly, it was Carmichael who interposed himself in the conversation and changed the subject.

"I think this is a topic that should be discussed by people with more seniority than us," Carmichael said. "We should really be focused on the topic of this meeting, which is the upcoming assignment to Germany. So, when you get to Bonn, you will be working with our BND counterpart, Hagan Krug," Carmichael said.

He read from his notes and didn't look at anyone. Cameron, however, saw the steely glare that McIntyre and Gray passed between them.

"Krug is a former officer in the Bundeswehr and has been in West German intelligence since 1973. We've worked with him in the past, and he is one of the best," Carmichael continued.

"What will he be doing?" Cameron asked.

"He will be working mostly behind the scenes," explained Gray. "The East Germans are well aware of most, if not all, West German intelligence officers, and therefore he's too well known to them to be working with you directly. However, the West Germans aren't about to have anything like this operation even mentioned on their soil without someone from their office watching it closely. He has a team that will be his public face, so to speak, acting as agents for various West German news outlets."

"Barbara, has your team taken care of their details?" Carmichael asked.

"You should probably refer to her by her cover, at least in private while you are here," interrupted Gray. "You should all be getting used to it from now on. We can't afford to have any mistakes, anywhere, during this mission."

"Will you be accompanying us?" asked Kendrick.

"No," explained Gray. "However, as you are well aware, when using a cover it is a wise idea to start familiarizing yourself with it from the outset so it becomes second nature. You all need to be used to calling her that, and she needs to be used to being called that."

She's been doing this how long, and she needs you to remind her of that?

"Let's start over then," Carmichael muttered. "Laura, has your team taken care of the final details you were discussing?"

"Yes," Kendrick began, before being interrupted by Gray.

"What were they?" Gray asked, directing his question at Carmichael and totally ignoring Kendrick.

"That was in regard to the necessary vaccinations they required before traveling," Carmichael explained.

"Not all of us," clarified Kendrick. "Obviously, Special Agent Walsh, Special Agent Dixon, and I are all up to date on required vaccinations, as is Major Kendall …"

"As is Mr. Collier," Gray corrected, with a condescending smile. Kendrick, who had been reading from her notes, continued to do so without looking up.

"As is Mr. Collier," she repeated, the flow of her conversation betraying no evidence of the interruption. "Mr. Webster has had the standard childhood vaccinations with boosters at regular intervals. Mr. Courtland, however, required the full slate of vaccinations and medications."

"The full slate," gasped Gray. "You mean he hasn't had any at all?"

"He wasn't certain he had ever had any of them in the first place but was certain he'd never had any boosters," Cameron explained. "His home life was a bit touch-and-go growing up."

"Even so, weren't these required for attending public school?" Gray insisted.

"That is presumed," explained Kendrick. "However, no records could be located, and even if they had been, that would have been almost thirty years ago. They would need to be repeated. As Special Agent Walsh has indicated, Mr. Courtland admitted that he had never had any immunizations since leaving school."

"I would like to put in Special Agent Walsh for a citation for accomplishing that," said Carmichael. He chuckled and cast a glance at Cameron.

"Indeed?" asked Gray, failing to see anything humorous in the discussion. "And why would that be?"

"Doug is a former professional wrestler with a deep dislike of needles," explained Cameron. "Getting him to go was somewhat, eh, problematic, shall we say. He kept insisting that he didn't need them, and he was probably right."

"Why do you say that?" Gray demanded.

"Well," said Cameron, "I heard a story once that Doug got bit by a rattlesnake and the snake died. If you knew him, you would give credence to that story."

"Has he started speaking to any of you again, yet?" Carmichael smiled.

"Mr. Courtland has begun making three-word replies," replied Cameron, with a wink. "In a few days he'll be back up to full sentences."

"What was the matter? Did he experience some kind of a reaction to the vaccines?" Gray demanded.

"No, he had a reaction to the needle," Cameron explained. "He does not like needles at all. In fact, threats and orders to have it done were totally ineffectual, even when they came from Mr. Stoughton."

"How were you finally able to get it done then?" Gray asked in amazement.

Cameron could tell by the man's widened eyes that learning someone did not immediately subordinate themselves to Evander Stoughton was exceptional.

"It cost Mr. Stoughton a steak dinner at the Mayflower." Cameron smiled. "Even then, to hear Doug tell it, the nurse attacked him with a harpoon."

"But the required result has been achieved?" Gray demanded, clearly losing patience with the conversation.

Kendrick, not wishing to be in communication with him any longer than was required, confirmed everything.

"The next thing to discuss is your itinerary then," continued Carmichael, handing Kendrick and Cameron a sheet with a list of cities and dates. "You will be arriving in Bonn where we have already scheduled a press conference and publicity appearances. From there, you will be traveling to Stuttgart for your first performance."

"Why not do a performance in Bonn when we arrive?" asked Cameron.

"Because we are going to need time to review your equipment and coordinate with your BND assistants. A publicity appearance can provide us with ample time to make certain that your equipment has not been tampered with and detect any possible Stasi informants posing as reporters or fans."

"Do you think the East Germans will suspect anything that soon?" wondered Cameron.

"We're certain of it," confirmed Gray. "The East Germans are suspicious of anything that hints at Imperialist America, and if it is something that their youth are enjoying without state sanction, it is going to be even more of a concern to them. That is why, in addition to one of our agents, you are going to have a BND detail posing as reporters and a photographer to follow you every step of the way. While the average person will think they are taking publicity photos, they will actually be surveilling the crowds at your appearances and performances to detect any known Stasi agents or informers."

Holy shit, this is heavier than I thought.

"From Stuttgart, you will be heading to Munich for another performance," continued Carmichael. "Hannover is your next stop, and from there you will be traveling to East Berlin for a one-night performance and immediately crossing back into West Berlin following the show."

"In West Berlin, you will be staying for a few days while the objective is being undertaken," Gray explained. "There, you will be making the rounds of the media outlets and performing at one of the venues there. This will give us the time to distract East German attention, by having them focus on what else you might possibly be doing there."

Okay, so far, so good.

"After East Berlin, you are scheduled for a performance in Hamburg, then Frankfurt, and finally, Amsterdam," Carmichael informed him.

They seem fairly confident that we will make it out of East Berlin. Cameron felt some of his tension lessen as they mentioned other locales following the focus of their efforts.

"Well now, Amsterdam will be a perfect place to finish this tour." Cameron smiled. "I know the guys will love the chance to unwind there after all of this is over." Images of Amsterdam's famous Red Light District played through his mind, and he began to consider ways to slip away from Kendrick and enjoy some much-deserved R&R, as well.

"All venues subsequent to the East Berlin performance are merely for diversionary purposes," declared Carmichael. "Following the success of our objective in East Berlin, you will be conveyed to a secure location for debriefing and repatriation. News services will carry a prearranged story detailing an unanticipated conflict with dates back here in the US, explaining why the last three shows were canceled."

In one stroke, Carmichael had succeeded in destroying not only Cameron's dreams but his relief as well.

You are, essentially, an asshole. You realize that, don't you? No? Well, you are.

"I know it might seem superfluous," said Cameron. "But what happens if we don't achieve our objective?"

"In the event of that outcome, none of you will be around to worry about it," explained Gray.

Chapter 20

"The Heart of Rock and Roll"

Hertz knew that this was a risky move, even with trying to justify it under his mandate of winning the boy's trust. His superiors would not appreciate being the scapegoats for this action, and retribution would be swift if any problems arose over it. However, the risk was certainly worth the reward. The boy would be far easier to manage and control if he felt he had a partner in crime. Still, Hertz debated the wisdom of going through with his decision. He did, technically, have his superiors' blessing for this, but in actuality, he had not been entirely forthcoming with his plan.

"It is a cassette tape of a rock band," he had explained to Fuchs. "I got it from a friend of mine. It is a little old and hard to come by, but he would like it and that would help him see me more as an ally than an adversary."

"Why is it hard to come by?" Fuchs demanded.

The younger agent had a response already rehearsed for such an occasion, but he did not expect to have to deliver it so soon and was momentarily caught off guard.

"Oh, you see, it is a band that does not exist anymore," he explained. "So their albums are no longer produced. This is a copy of one that I got from a friend. The quality isn't so good, but it is loud and sounds Western, so the boy will most likely lap it up."

Hertz convinced himself that he did not, in fact, lie to his superior *per se*, but neither had he told the complete truth. Yes, it was true that the band, the Klaus Renft Combo, did not exist anymore. However, what he had neglected to mention was the band's name or that the reason they no longer existed was because the East German Culture Ministry said so. The Klaus Renft Combo was too radical for the GDR.

At first, the combo did not attract too much attention from the authorities. They played the music that they heard on Radio in the American Sector and recorded the songs in order to imitate them later, which they did, successfully. Crowds of young people thronged the clubs and areas where they performed, listening to the Rolling Stones and various other bands. However, as the combo's popularity grew, so did the attention they received from the authorities.

Not being permitted to play in the larger halls, the combo performed in the villages to ever-increasing crowds. In time, they did not content themselves with cover songs but began performing more and more of their own works. Their popularity bred courage, which they displayed at their concerts and performances, seeming to bait the Stasi and police by joking about secret listeners or the band's possible disappearance. Like their counterparts in the West, social commentary did not escape the band's purview to the ever-increasing discomfort of the GDR. This discomfort bred popularity among East German youth and their albums became highly sought after. Finally, in 1975, things came to a head.

Klaus Renft and the other members of the combo were ordered to appear before a representative of the Ministry of Culture to renew the necessary documentation that would permit them to keep performing. When they arrived for the meeting, however, things took an unexpected turn when the woman in charge informed them they would not be performing—not there, not then, and not ever.

"Your music is insulting and libelous," she informed them. "Therefore, you will not be performing it again."

"You mean we've been banned?" demanded the band's founder and namesake.

"No," she replied. "I'm informing you that you no longer exist."

And with that, an increasingly popular expression of East German angst was silenced. Overnight the labels that had recorded their albums stopped carrying them and they became quite valuable on the black market, forcing many fans to record them onto tape.

Eventually, some of the members of the Klaus Renft Combo did make their way to the West, but only after having served time in Stasi custody. The more socially cooperative members of the band regrouped under a new manager, who happened to be a Stasi agent, and called themselves Karussell. They performed former combo songs, but without the social commentary or charged political atmosphere. Hertz knew that he could have gotten those tapes, or albums, but he remembered the original band and knew that, somehow, the music just wasn't the same. He doubted, however, that he could have had such a conversation with his superiors.

"Do they do American songs?" the boy demanded when Hertz gave him the tape. "I only listen to American bands."

"You listen to some other ones, too," Hertz pointed out. "You like the Rolling Stones; they're a British band. You also like AC/DC and they are Australian. Maybe these are German, but they do a lot of cover songs of your bands. Give them a listen; you might like them."

Mikhail sniffed and reluctantly took it from him. Hertz bristled at the boy's arrogance and resented giving him the tape. Even though he never dared mention it, Hertz had been a fan of the combo as well and that particular tape was his. Being raised in a very loyal Communist household and groomed for a life in state service, Hertz never dared draw too much attention to any activity that might raise an eyebrow. Record albums of unapproved bands were too difficult to make inconspicuous, but a supposedly blank tape wasn't. To be safe, he only had one. And he had just cast that pearl before this swine of a boy.

"Do you have a cigarette?" the boy asked, flicking the tape onto his nightstand. He had never even bothered to sit up to acknowledge Hertz's presence or his gift. Now he didn't even look at the man when he asked him a question.

"I only have a couple," Hertz replied, keeping his anger in check.

"I want one," the boy said, finally looking at him.

"I said I only have a couple," Hertz explained. "I don't know when I'll be getting more, so I'm hanging on to these."

"If you have a couple, you can give me one," Mikhail pouted.

"Aren't you a good little Marxist." Hertz smiled. "Even distribution of goods among the people, is that it? Well, even that policy gets curtailed when there isn't enough to go around."

"You mock the Communist ideal," Mikhail warned. "I could report you for that! I could make serious trouble for you if I wanted to. You should be careful if you know what's good for you."

Hertz leaned down to the boy's face and smiled a feral grin. "I'm not some lackey that you can intimidate with your position," he whispered. "I don't have anything to fear, but you are on everyone's list for being a pain in the ass. Who do you think they're going to give credence to? Now, if you want threats, let me give you one. I can get you plenty of contraband, or I can make certain you never get any again. Which is it going to be?"

Mikhail sank back onto the bed, his eyes wide with fear. "You can't talk to me like that," the boy whined. "Do you know who I am?"

"Yes," Hertz said. "You're a spoiled troublemaker that none of the other students want to be bothered with and the staff would like to ignore, in case you hadn't noticed that reality."

Mikhail pushed himself back toward his wall and was about to protest when Hertz cut him off.

"Shut up," the man snarled, leaning closer into the boy's face. "I'll point out something else you might not have noticed. I'm the one who does make the effort to be nice to you. I don't mind doing it either. I think the others are being unfair to you and that bothers me, at least a little. But I don't intend to be made a dispensary for you. Do you understand? If you don't give me any grief, I will see to it that things continue to find their way to you and no one complains about it. If you do give me grief, I will see to it that nothing ever finds its way to you again and complaints get listened to. Are we clear?"

"Yes," Mikhail whispered, after a moment's hesitation.

"Good." Hertz smiled and stood up. "Get your coat."

"Why?" the boy whined, suspicious of the sudden change in Hertz's demeanor.

"You want a cigarette, don't you?" Hertz said. "Well, come with me. I bet I can get some more from one of the other staff later, so we can have one of these."

Mikhail remained on the bed, still trembling.

"I'm not tricking you," Hertz assured him. "I meant what I said. I don't like the way you've been treated, but I'm not going to be taken advantage of. You're a good kid, and I don't mind being nice to you. But if you treat me like you treat the rest of them, then I will respond in kind. Am I making myself clear?"

Mikhail studied the man suspiciously and then nodded.

"I can't hear you," Hertz warned.

"Yes," the boy replied bitterly.

"That doesn't feel so good, does it?" Hertz asked.

The boy shook his head. "No, it doesn't," he replied.

"Then don't make me do that again," the man said. "I don't like doing it at all. Now get moving if you want a smoke. My break is almost over and I'm dying for one."

Outside, in their isolated niche, Hertz passed the boy a lit cigarette.

"We'll just share it," he muttered.

"Did you mean what you said up there?" Mikhail asked. "About not liking to be that way?"

"Yes, I meant it," Hertz assured him. "No one likes to be an asshole if you stop and think about it."

"People around here certainly seem to enjoy it," Mikhail exclaimed with bitterness.

"The people we deal with are always a reflection of ourselves," Hertz sighed. "They are going to treat you how you treat them. Let's face it, you are not always easy to get along with!"

"That's not true," Mikhail protested, but Hertz cut him off.

"Every conflict you have had here could have been avoided," Hertz insisted. "You just choose to be difficult when you don't have to be."

The boy glowered but said nothing.

"Look," Hertz said. "I can understand your frustration. It is not easy living in an environment where everything you do or say has to be approved first. It is a little easier for us Germans because we are used to it. You have a little bit of privilege and don't like having that interfered with. I understand. But you don't need to be as disagreeable about it with people as you have been in the past. Certainly not with me!"

"This is the way I am ..." the boy began to protest, but Hertz cut him off.

"Bullshit," the man said. "It's the way you choose to be because it's easier than taking responsibility for yourself. And frankly, it is getting a little tiresome. Stop it, and I mean now! You're not going to make things any easier for yourself and, in fact, might make them worse, and that will make it harder for me to do anything nice for you."

"You don't know what you're talking about," Mikhail pouted, holding out his hand for the cigarette. "You just hate me because you're jealous of me!"

"Hardly." Hertz yawned, ignoring the boy's gesture.

"It's my turn!"

"For what?" asked Hertz, taking another drag from the cigarette.

"You can't do this; it's not fair," Mikhail protested.

"But aren't I supposed to be jealous of you?" Hertz sneered. "What is it about you that is supposed to make me jealous, exactly? All of your privileges? Or how you manage to get them all revoked? Please, tell me, because I'm dying to know. I'll listen to your whole story while I finish this cigarette you so desperately want but can only have if I grant it to you."

The boy's face flushed with anger and embarrassment as the older man's grin widened. Mikhail knew that he had no counter for any of the things Hertz had just said, and that impotence was maddening. In his frustration, Mikhail began to cry.

"Don't waste the tears." Hertz laughed. "They don't help and only make you look more foolish. If you want to be smart, you'll start to listen to me."

"Why should I?"

"Because I can make sure things get easier for you," Hertz said, offering the cigarette. "Trust me."

Chapter 21

"It Can Happen"

The flashing of bulbs and the flurry of reporters' questions made Cameron's head spin. The Roadhouse Sons had not been in the midst of such a media frenzy since their days in Seattle and their tour with the band Boney Jack. Then it was in the fabricated world of "battle of the bands" with the All-American Roadhouse Sons pitted against the antiestablishment punk rockers. This time, however, the attention was all theirs.

Despite assurances from Kendrick and the others that the Roadhouse Sons were quite popular in Germany, the band had taken it with a grain of salt. Those doubts were dispelled when they arrived in Bonn. Stepping from the plane, Cameron and the others found themselves in a sea of photographers and reporters. He noted with some amusement that the guys were taking their time descending the stairs to the tarmac.

Why the hell not? I'm taking my sweet time, too!

At the bottom waited the band's security detail and among them Cameron spotted the face of Hagan Krug, easily recognized from the file photos Kendrick and the others had provided at the briefing. Square jawed, with closely cropped hair and broad shoulders, Krug reminded Cameron of his first mentor, Gordon Dwyer. However, the slightly silvered hair and dimpled chin gave the impression of a matinee idol, an impression that lent credence to his role as a talent agent.

At the bottom of the stairs, Krug greeted them and carefully directed them through the sea of photographers, pausing briefly for a few quick photos and allowing the band to take a few questions from the reporters before ushering them into a waiting limousine.

Inside the limousine, Cameron sat in stunned amazement. The interior was well appointed, with wooden paneling and leather seats. In the middle of the group sat a large bucket, filled with three bottles of champagne.

"This is like something out of the magazine stories," Evan said and chuckled. He grabbed one of the bottles. "I feel like Led Zeppelin!"

"They're treating us like rock stars." Rich laughed, holding out a glass to be filled.

"Uh, man, we *are* rock stars." Cameron winked, taking a glass from Krug.

"Yeah, but we've never been treated like it before," Rich replied, downing his champagne in one gulp. "Except by club owners who were always convinced we'd drink too much or make too much noise. If I had ever been treated like this, I'd never have worked in a music store!"

"Gentlemen, I am happy you appreciate your reception." Krug smiled. "I assure you, it is genuine and not contrived merely for appearance's sake. Though, obviously, we must keep up appearances. However, we need not discuss that at this time."

Cameron noticed the glance Krug gave in the direction of the driver and wondered if this man was an enemy operative or a civilian. In either event, Krug kept the conversation going, discussing promotional details with Kendrick and the others and offering suggestions as to clubs to go to for recreation.

"You will find Bonn to be a bit more untouched by the war than some of the other European capitals," he explained. "We Germans mostly stood at the border and glared at one another. We fought like hell everywhere else though."

"Then here's to a relatively untouched capital," said Cameron, raising his glass. Krug had touched upon a subject that Cameron was determined to avoid, at all cost, the so-called secret agreement of the East and West Germans.

At the outbreak of the war, both Moscow and Washington were stunned when they discovered that neither German army would cross the border into the other's territory. They poured into other countries and fought like demons, but on their own soil they showed but token conflict. The closest things came was when overzealous East German generals captured West Berlin. However, secret negotiations helped defuse that crisis and resulted in the Western diplomats and personnel being "paroled" back to the West, and West Berlin being declared an open city. From the beginning of the cold war, Germany, and Berlin in particular, had been both the pressure point and the release valve in tensions between NATO and the Communist bloc, and they were determined its status would not change.

In the heady early days of the war, it became an almost quixotic hope that if Germany was stable, then possibly no one would be incited to make the final roll of the dice and launch the missiles. The world held its breath when West Berlin fell, but tensions relaxed when it was opened once again.

There were many who felt that the German negotiations helped the East Germans save face in backing away from a total onslaught, and helped provide the Soviet leadership with the opportunity to do the same when the war began to turn against them. However, Krug's reminder to maintain secrecy only brought home how precarious situations still were. Cameron drained his glass and held it out once more for a refill, pointedly ignoring Kendrick's disapproving glare.

Krug, perhaps sensing the tension that subject produced or simply wanting to show off German engineering, demonstrated the sound system of the limousine. With a push of the button, Evan's rendition of "Statesboro Blues" filled the car, accompanied by faint cheers and clapping.

"That's from 'Live at the Battenkill'." Evan laughed. "Holy crap, that made it over here?"

"I assure you, gentlemen, all of your records made it over here." Krug smiled. "I would like to point out to you that this is my favorite one. All of the albums have been made into cassette tapes, as well. You are genuinely quite popular."

"Popular enough to discuss royalties?" Rich asked with a smile.

"Now, gentlemen, we don't want to be discussing business so soon," Krug replied, returning a smile. "There will be time enough for that later. Right now, let us enjoy a brief period of relaxation. I assure you, you will find yourselves quite busy, beginning tomorrow morning."

So, there's a subject you guys don't like to discuss either.

Taking the not-so-subtle hint, Cameron led the band in reminiscing about the live performance they were listening to. They talked about the owner of the Battenkill Roadhouse, where the event took place, and remembered how he had once been such a supporter of the band, but eventually they had a falling-out, which set them on the road that led them to this moment. They talked about some of the people who used to be devoted fans and wondered which of the whistles and cheers they heard might have belonged to them. Krug was fascinated by some of the stories the band told about their adventures on the road and laughed heartily, and genuinely, at some of their escapades.

The limousine pulled to a stop in front of a modern-looking building, which Cameron correctly assumed was the hotel.

"While Bonn was relatively untouched, we were not entirely untouched," Krug explained. "This building was destroyed in a bombing at the outbreak of the war, but since it had enjoyed such popularity among the diplomatic corps, it was quickly rebuilt. If you will follow me, I have taken the liberty of already checking you in and have your hotel room keys. The bellman will take your things."

Cameron noticed that the lobby and hallways were quite elegant, as were the elevators. Everything was equal to any of the finer hotels in Washington, and he understood that this was not the hotel used by ordinary businessmen. He remembered what Krug had assured them on the way over: the Roadhouse Sons were not trying to create an image; they were taking advantage of one that already existed. Clearly, here in Germany, the Roadhouse Sons were on top.

I suppose, if I had to, I could get used to this.

When they got to their suite, a man, who Cameron suspected was one of Krug's assistants, opened the door. Stepping inside, Cameron was taken aback. The room was eerily reminiscent of the safe house where the band had first been sequestered when they were reluctantly recruited six years before. From the door, there was a platform that went around the perimeter of the room on three sides, with steps going down to the sitting area. Doors on either side opened onto bedrooms, and to the left of the entrance there was a kitchen and dining area. A large console was against the one wall that the walkway did not touch, and that was open to reveal a large television, stereo, and liquor cabinet recessed into it.

The furniture and carpets are even in white.

"I trust this will be to your satisfaction," Krug said, breaking Cameron's train of thought. "For convenience's sake, we felt it would be best to have you all in one suite, with the exception of Miss Kendrick, of course. She will be in a suite across the hall. Your road managers will be in a room elsewhere in the hotel. You will only be here for a day or so, and then we will be commencing with your tour. All subsequent accommodations will be adequate but not as opulent as these, I'm afraid."

Krug's assistant closed the door and things got down to business.

"The entire suite has been swept for listening devices," Krug explained to Kendrick. "Likewise, your accommodations and those of your crew. We took the liberty of posting people in the rooms until your arrival to ensure that nothing was done while we were away."

"Thank you," Kendrick said. "Your reputation for thoroughness precedes you, and I would not have doubted your measures."

"*Vielen Dank,*" Krug replied, with a smile and a small bow. "Then I trust you will not be surprised that, despite your long trip, I suggest we have a briefing?"

"I am neither surprised nor opposed," Kendrick assured him. "The sooner we start to grasp this, the better."

Speak for yourself!

"Very good then," Krug said, his voice adopting a more martial tone. "If everyone could have a seat, I will begin explaining how things will be proceeding from here."

Krug's associate produced a briefcase from which Krug produced three glossy eight-by-ten photos of two men and a woman.

"These are the operatives who will be accompanying you on this tour," Krug explained, handing the photos to Kendrick. "They will be the means by which we will be able to communicate in case of an emergency or any change of plans. Two of them, Reinhardt Wessel and Elsa Scholl, will be representatives of a West German newspaper. She will be posing as a reporter doing a story on the famous Roadhouse Sons, and he will be a freelance photographer doing the accompanying photo shoot for it."

Cameron studied the two photos closely. The first one was of the woman. Tall, blond, with Nordic features of an oval face with high cheekbones, a narrow nose, and what he suspected were intense blue eyes. Her hair was pulled back, and her posture suggested someone who was constantly alert and not easily intimidated. Her arms were folded across her chest, fingers resting on the outside of her arms to enable her to respond to a situation quickly, and her head was tilted slightly forward, causing her to cast a warning glance at the photographer.

The photo of the first man showed someone with a round face and unruly hair. He was slightly heavyset, with broad shoulders, a wide smile, and sparkling eyes, which suggested an exuberant personality that Cameron had found typical among photographers who covered rock bands. Reserved and formal types were not able to adapt to the unpredictability of musicians, but photographers who always seemed up for whatever might happen did.

Hopefully, this won't be too much of a drag.

The third photo was of a man in a suit, more formal but not noticeably reserved. Cameron wondered what his function in this operation would be.

"This man is Ernst Eberhard," Krug explained. "He will be posing as a representative of the talent agency that has put together this tour. He also will be making periodic visits to the venues where you will be performing, as well has having regular briefings with Miss Kendrick. Unofficially, he will be representing me and enabling us to monitor these proceedings closely."

"You're not going to be traveling with us, you mean?" Evan asked.

"I'm afraid that I am too well known to our friends in the East." Krug smiled. "My being with you folks here, at your arrival, will not raise any suspicions. I'm with the foreign minister and my job is to meet with high-profile visitors to our country. You, as a major attraction, therefore fall under my auspices. However, for me to be accompanying you throughout your tour would raise far too many questions and defeat the entire enterprise."

"What is it that we are expected to do, exactly?" Rich asked.

This irritated Cameron. How many briefings had they already had regarding this? How many times had it been explained, in great detail, what was going to happen? Did Rich see anyone else asking this question? Hadn't he been part of operations like this long enough to know what was expected of him? Then Cameron realized that no, Rich hadn't. Not anything similar to this, at least. In fact, he doubted that any of them had.

"You are expected to do what you do best, my friend," Krug said. "You are expected to play music and entertain the masses."

"That's it?" the bass player asked.

"I assure you, my friend, there is no room for improvisation in this affair," Krug warned.

Chapter 22

"Go Insane"

The next morning came far sooner than Cameron would have wished. Still adjusting to the time difference, as well as the previous night, it took several cups of coffee for him to wake up. Listening to the mumbled conversations of the other men around the table, it was obvious that he was not the only one suffering. However, it was also obvious that any pleas for mercy or leniency would be ignored, as Kendrick had made it perfectly clear that they would be hitting the ground running. In fact, Cameron had to finish his toast on the way to the car.

The morning was a whirlwind of radio and magazine interviews, photo shoots, and publicity appearances. Somewhere he managed to grab a sandwich and a bottle of water, but he was shocked to realize when he sat down that it was almost three o'clock in the afternoon.

Shit, time really does fly when you're having fun.

"What's next on the agenda, Commodore?" Cameron asked.

"In a little while, you'll be meeting with your road crew to review the equipment," Kendrick said. "Then it is back to the hotel for a quick change and off to Das Tor for some limited R&R and a publicity appearance, after which we head back to the hotel where you will settle down for a good night's sleep before I get you up at the crack of nine to head to Stuttgart for your first show."

I'm exhausted already.

"Okay, maybe this whole rock star thing is going to take a bit more getting used to than I thought," he sighed. "Just for curiosity's sake, what is Das Tor?"

"Oh, it's one of Bonn's best nightclubs," interjected Reinhardt Wessel. "If you get there, you should try to get one of the bands to let you sit in with them. That would be a great opportunity! Think of the publicity you could get from that!"

Cameron noticed Kendrick give Wessel a disapproving glance, but she said nothing. Cameron had to agree with her. At first, Wessel's enthusiasm and excitement was nice. However, his energy level never seemed to deplete, even when theirs did. Now, as Cameron and the others were hoping to adjust to a hectic schedule, Wessel was becoming annoying, and, with increasingly menacing glares from Doug, potentially dangerous.

"You don't just ask a band to let you play in or even sit in." Cameron smiled weakly. He knew he needed to be polite so was pleasant but firm. "But it will be nice to hear some of the local bands and maybe have a drink or two with them."

Wessel's expression seemed to deflate, and for the first time, Cameron was convinced that he had finally gotten the photographer to run out of energy. His belief was soon dashed when Wessel seemed to recollect himself, and his smile burst out again in full force.

"I know some of the acts that play there," Wessel assured him. "If any of them are on tonight, I can talk to them if you like!"

"I would prefer to keep everything through the publicity Mr. Krug has established," Kendrick cut in. "I would hate to complicate things unnecessarily."

Cameron noticed the finality in her tone and suspected that it was not lost on Wessel either, as the photographer did not press the subject further.

Thank you, my dear. I owe you a martini for that.

"So when are we going to meet the reporter?" Cameron asked.

Wessel was about to respond when Kendrick spoke.

"She's already been covering you," Kendrick said. "She wanted to observe you, undetected, for a day or so, and then get your impressions. Don't worry, I've been in regular contact with her."

"I wasn't worried." Cameron yawned. "I was merely curious. Wessel has rolls of photos of us; I was wondering if they were going to get into print."

"You have to do the rolls of photos so you can get a few good ones," Wessel explained and laughed. "I'm trying to make certain that I have what I need. I don't want my bosses mad at me for not taking advantage of a popular American rock band. The Roadhouse Sons are not unknown here!"

"That has been evident," Cameron agreed. "I saw us on the news last night and saw a rather unflattering photo of us this morning."

"What do you mean by unflattering?" Kendrick asked, concerned.

"I mean it made Rich look like a zombie," Cameron assured her. *Don't worry; nothing you need to be that concerned with, my dear.*

"But that is understandable," Cameron continued. "We'd been on that flight for how long? I'm surprised the rest of us didn't look like death warmed over either. Don't worry, I promise you that there will not be any inappropriate photos of us whooping it up."

"I doubted there would be." Kendrick smiled.

"Why's that?" Cameron asked, suddenly suspicious of the change in her tone.

"I'm counting on you fellows being off the circuit so long that you're too pooped to whoop, if you know what I mean."

"Never." Cameron laughed.

A knock at the door informed them that their limousine had arrived to take them to the hotel. From there, they left to meet up with Doug and his new assistant; they had been familiarizing themselves with the equipment for most of the day. Cameron found Doug to be animated and jovial at the prospect of a tour and felt relieved. Knowing how touchy and sensitive his roadie could be in unfamiliar circumstances had Cameron quite anxious that this assignment would have him in a foul mood.

Instead Cameron discovered Doug in the hotel bar enjoying a beer with a man who Cameron at first mistook for Ed Collier, until he saw the guitarist move past him. Doug waved when he saw his boss and motioned for Cameron to come join him.

"Hey, man, I'm glad you showed up," said Doug. "This is Ryan Casey; he's the fellow they hired to help with the equipment. He got stuck over here in Germany when the war broke out and has stayed. He and I were sharing some stories about having to live on the road."

"Oh shit, I can imagine what that must have been like," said Cameron, offering his hand to the other man. "Nice to meet you. So, judging by the way Doug is reacting to you, I assume you are familiar with light and sound setups? Dougie hates on-the-job training."

"Yes sir, I am," Casey assured him. Then he listed some of the systems he had worked with in the past. Satisfied that Casey did, indeed, know what he was doing and was not merely someone recruited for the assignment, Cameron joined them in a drink.

"What the heck is that?" Cameron asked Doug, pointing to a small glass in front of the roadie.

"Oh this?" asked Doug. "It's something Casey ordered. I've never heard of it before, but it tastes good."

"It's called Jägermeister," Casey explained. "It's pretty good. I don't drink it a lot, but since Doug had never heard of it, I thought he might like a change from German beer."

"Bite your tongue." Doug laughed. "You never change from good beer!"

"Except for tequila," Cameron reminded him.

"Unfortunately, I'm afraid you won't find a lot of that here in Germany right now," Casey informed him. "Some of the fancier bars might have it, but not the ones that cater to our clientele."

"Damn," muttered Cameron. "Well, then I guess there's nothing else but to try your Jäger ... whatever it is."

Casey ordered them another round, and while they were waiting for it, he began to tell Cameron his story.

"I originally came here in 1977, planning on taking a year off of college and doing the typical backpacking across Europe. I started in Spain, deciding to do the Camino in reverse. I took my time moving through France, stayed in Paris a few months, and then kept on heading east. I made it to Munich when the shit hit the fan and

I never left Germany. For a while, anyway, I couldn't have even if I wanted to."

"What did you do?" Cameron asked. He wondered if Casey had really been a student or if he had been stationed here. He suspected the latter and accepted Casey's legend as fact.

"I had to report to the American embassy here in Bonn, hoping to apply for evacuation back to the States. But, being a single guy with no dependents, they had no idea when the Red Cross could get me home, or even if they could. So I got an extended visa from the German government and stayed here. They required me to do some home guard duty for the German army, but in noncombat situations, because I was a foreign national. I did some work in the hospitals and stuff like that, freeing guys up to go to the front. Then, when things started to settle down, I found work in the music scene. Luckily, that area has grown the longer the war has dragged on."

"Why do you think that is?" Cameron asked as the waitress brought their drinks.

"I think they're just sick of it all," Casey explained. "They already went through two huge-ass wars already. No one wants to go through another one. They want escape. Music gives that to them. Add to that the possibility of being blown to smithereens, and well, you get the idea."

I sure as hell do.

"Oh, well then, here's to helping with the war effort," said Cameron, raising his glass. The other two men joined in with a hearty "hear, hear" and began discussing music, bands, and previous adventures. Cameron was amazed at how easily Casey seemed to fit into a sense of camaraderie with Doug. It seemed like he had been with them for a long time.

"So you're the one rooming with Doug, eh?" Cameron asked. "You seem to be doing well. Dougie doesn't usually take to strangers."

"We seem to have hit it off pretty good." Casey laughed.

"He promised to let me out when I scratch at the door," Doug joked. "I think it will work out fine. Besides, he has some cool ideas about how to modify some of the speakers for improved performance. I'm going to like working with him!"

"It's nothing big." Casey shrugged. "But I have found out how to get some better use out of those BH800s. Sometimes the acoustics in the venues don't lend themselves to the best sound. When the time comes, I know how to make some modifications so they will do some things you never thought they could."

"I'm looking forward to it," Cameron assured him.

If your other credentials are as impressive as your musical ones are, this whole thing might actually work.

One by one, the others arrived, and Cameron made the introductions. To his relief, Wessel was not with them. *Thank God—I need a break from the shutterbug for a bit.*

"So, do you guys want to go take a look at our stuff now, or what?" asked Doug.

"Where's Kendrick?" Cameron asked.

"She just came through the door," Doug said and winked. "I didn't want her to think we were slacking; that's why I suggested we take it outside."

Cameron appreciated the wisdom of Doug's suggestion; unfortunately they were not able to implement it before their manager arrived at the table.

"Gentlemen, I see you've met your new engineer," said Kendrick, laying a hand on Casey's shoulder. "I see he has been properly toasted into the group."

With a nod, she indicated the beer bottles and glasses that covered the table.

"We made an appropriate beginning," Evan assured her. "The procedure will most likely continue later this evening."

"Don't get too carried away," Kendrick admonished. "You've got an early start and two shows tomorrow. Big heads will not enhance your performances."

"Two shows," gasped Cameron. "I thought it was only one!"

"The first one is basically a matinee performance for some of the members of the press and some German television stations," she explained. "They wanted to get a behind-the-scenes look at you guys and doing so at the show itself would not work out."

"But, for God's sake, we haven't even rehearsed," Cameron protested. "Will we have time enough to do that before you plaster us all over television?"

"Calm down. This isn't the first time I've done this." Kendrick laughed. "Your matinee performance will actually be your rehearsal. They want to see all of the nuts and bolts of how the Roadhouse Sons get ready for a performance. They want the sound check, the tuning, everything. So just be yourselves. But with cleaner shirts, if you don't mind."

"Ha-ha," muttered Cameron. He hated having people wander around and watch him as he was getting ready for a show. He wanted to be able to make certain that his first performance in Germany would be flawless. He didn't feel he could do that with reporters asking him questions and cameras making him self-conscious. The idea that Kendrick would have made that decision without discussing it with him infuriated him. However, now was not the time or the place to discuss this.

But we will *discuss it, my dear.*

Outside, Casey unlocked the back of the truck and smiled at the whistles and comments of the band.

"I helped pick out this stuff," he explained. "I got the shopping list you provided and found it all. I did have to call in some favors on some of the monitors, but for the most part it wasn't that difficult."

He pulled out the various speakers, and Cameron noticed that nearly all of them were brand-new, except two that were in the far corner. Those systems had clearly seen better days. The fronts were held on by gaffer tape, and there were scuff marks and the remains of old tour stickers on the cases. Personally, unless he had a deep, sentimental attachment to them, Cameron thought he would have tossed them long ago.

"I hope *those* aren't the ones you had to call in favors for," he told Casey, pointing to the old speaker. "What the hell is holding them together—spit?"

"Oh, them?" Casey said. "They're the ones I picked up for parts, just in case we needed any. You never know when that might come in handy. Yeah, the outsides sure as hell have some miles on them, but the insides are pretty good."

Damn things are marked by road years. I can certainly sympathize.

"Do you guys have any questions?" Casey asked.

"You're certain all of this will be compatible with our instruments?" Rich asked. "No feedback, no shorting something out or blowing something up?"

"These are all the exact same things you guys use back in the States," Casey assured him. "The outlets all work on the same wattage, so you won't have any misfires at all. It will be just like your Battenkill days!"

"Not hardly," Rich snorted.

"Why not?" Casey asked.

Cameron could see that the engineer was visibly concerned, and for that matter, so was he. Why was Rich suddenly copping an attitude?

"Because in those days we got fed from the bar and had to sublet the band house from the cockroaches, who did not like to share," the bassist explained. "Plus, the groupies usually had more road wear on them than the bald tires on the band truck. So far, Germany has been a bit of an improvement over that!"

"One can only hope," said Casey, visibly relieved.

"Listen—we're due at the club in a few hours," Kendrick reminded them. "Unless you want to get by with bar food, you might want to change so we can grab dinner and get going."

"What about us?" Doug asked.

Typically, the road crew did hang out with the band after performances and so forth. They worked the same schedule as the band, often more, and were usually just as hungry or in need of relaxation after a show as the band was. This time, however, it was not a performance but an appearance, and therefore, the press might just want only the band. Cameron was about to suggest they come along when someone beat him to it.

"I think it would be great to have them all together," said Wessel.

"Where the hell did you come from?" asked Cameron. He hadn't heard the photographer approach, and as much for that as for Wessel interjecting himself into a band conversation, Cameron was quite annoyed. He realized that annoyance probably showed in his tone.

I don't give a damn.

"I was up in the room waiting for you guys to come back," Wessel explained, with his typical smile. "I thought I might do a shoot of you guys relaxing on your afternoon off."

"You mean our suite was unlocked this entire time?" Cameron cried.

"No, no, no, no, no," Wessel quickly assured him. "Krug got me a key as well so I could have access to you guys for the photo spread. That way, I wouldn't be bothering you all the time or having to explain to the hotel why I needed to be in there."

"And so you could be in there when we weren't," Cameron snapped. "Krug or no Krug, that ends *now*! Give me the key."

Wessel took a step back; the expression on his face was one of hurt. Cameron was reminded of a small child but was unmoved.

"I don't think I should," Wessel protested. "I mean, I have my orders ..."

"The Nuremberg defense didn't work the last time you guys tried using it!" warned Cameron.

The shocked look on Wessel's face, as well as the gasp from Kendrick, told him he had gone too far in his response. Quickly, he searched for a way out of it but could find none. Mercifully, Kendrick took charge of the situation.

"I'm afraid that Cameron is right, Reinhardt," she said. "That is a security issue that we really can't allow. I wasn't aware that Mr. Krug had given you a key. I'm afraid I'm going to have to ask for you to return it, please."

Kendrick held out her hand for the photographer to give her his key. Cameron knew that she was not about to take no for an answer and that if the photographer did not comply with her demand, she would be on the phone with Krug, raising hell. Apparently, that same realization occurred to Wessel, who reluctantly handed it over.

"From now on, if you want access to the band when they are in their room, you inform me," Kendrick said. "Otherwise, all access to them will be limited to their performances and public appearances, such as the one tonight. That should be more than adequate for any of your promotional needs."

Wessel nodded but said nothing.

Cameron was relieved but still felt bad about his previous remark. He wanted to say something but feared that now was not the appropriate time. Fortunately, Kendrick came to his rescue once more.

"Now, we really should be getting ready for tonight," she reminded them. "This isn't just a night out; this is the first time the public will be seeing you guys up close and personal. Be on your best behavior, look your best, and do your best. And, Doug, to answer your question, yes, I think it would be a good idea to have you guys out with us too. You're going to be doing a lot of driving and hard work, and you should have a chance to enjoy yourselves at least a little bit."

"Oh, music to my ears." Doug smiled. "Well, the 'enjoy yourselves' part anyway."

As they moved off to return to the room, Wessel held back a little. The photographer said nothing, but Cameron felt the man's eyes boring into his back.

Chapter 23

"Nobody Told Me"

Adalrich Fuchs listened as his Russian counterpart explained the reason for his call. He heard the insistence in the KGB officer's voice but privately conceded the same doubts that the directorate shared.

"Are you entirely certain that they will attempt such a thing?" Fuchs pressed.

"Entirely? No, I must admit, not entirely," Petrovsky sighed. "However, I have enough of a suspicion that I think at least some steps should be taken, and that is where I need your assistance."

"What is it that you wish me to do?" Fuchs asked guardedly. His being a member of East German intelligence would not preserve him from any repercussions if his counterpart's concerns proved to be unfounded.

"If any move is going to be taken against the one they are targeting, we still have leverage over him," Petrovsky explained.

"You mean his son?"

"Precisely."

"He is currently being monitored by one of my own men," Fuchs reminded him. "I believe that was a wise move, as we have not had any reports of his causing trouble for the school, or anyone else, for that matter."

"That is a relief," sighed Petrovsky. "The little shit was becoming my worst headache. We all deserved a reprieve from his antics. But I'm afraid we need to keep a closer eye on him."

"Do you think they might make an attempt on him, as well?"

"I highly doubt it. We've kept his parentage matter of highest priority for just such an event. His mother was the darling of the Soviet people. However, his father remains a mystery, not only to the Soviet people but most especially to the West. Only we know who he is, and I intend to keep it that way. That was the guarantee for Alexi's good behavior, and I see no reason to discount it now. I will need you to take steps to ensure that he is monitored at all times."

"He is in an elite school with children of East German officials and Eastern Bloc diplomats," Fuchs insisted. "Security at such a facility is quite rigid, I assure you!"

"I'm certain it is under normal circumstances," Petrovsky assured him. "However, these circumstances are not normal."

"What is it that you wish me to do then?"

"I want the boy removed from his school, at least for the time being," Petrovsky explained. "You say you have one of your men monitoring him? Excellent. Have him be the boy's tutor or something. Have him arrange a field trip or excursion for him for a few days. Keep him moving; keep him close."

Fuchs had worked with Soviet intelligence for many years and was quite used to their sentiments that the East Germans were merely subordinates to their own directorate. However, he never ceased to resent it, and this was no exception. He had developed a workable plan that accomplished everything they needed to accomplish; now he had to risk having it all upended because of someone's paranoia, and he was without suitable grounds to protest. What Moscow wanted, Moscow got.

"Do you know how long we will need to do this for?" Fuchs asked resignedly.

"Our intelligence says that this plan was only recently decided upon. If that is the case, the Americans will not want to wait too long before they make their attempt, if they are going to make it at all. I should say we should know, for certain, within a week at least, if anything is going to come of my suspicions."

"A week does not seem like very much time," Fuchs cautioned. "Are you certain they are going to make a move that quickly? Even the Americans can't have things that planned out so soon."

"I have not been able to determine how long this has been in the planning, but what I have heard suggests that something is already planned. I am putting in paperwork for Alexi to be recalled to Moscow immediately," Petrovsky explained. "I'm not going to take any chances. He will be here within a week. If they are going to attempt anything, they will have to attempt it by then."

"You have to wait for paperwork?" gasped Fuchs. "Why don't you just make a phone call? Isn't that how it is usually done?"

"I'm afraid my hands are tied," lamented Petrovsky. "I have been told I am overreacting and ordered not to raise alarms or take any action whatsoever in regard to this. Even my request to have him recalled was made subject to review by the directorate."

"How did you convince them then?"

"By explaining he would be required to fill a bureaucratic position here in the directorate regarding previous cases and agents that he had worked with. Since he does not fill a vital function in our delegation in Poland, there were no practical grounds to oppose my request. However …"

"However, they are suspicious of you?"

"Yes," Petrovsky grumbled. "They are suspicious of me but not suspicious of anyone else. Can you believe that? We are not that far removed from the days of Stalin and Beria, it seems."

"Now, comrade, let us be sensible," Fuchs assured him. "Stalin and Beria have been dead for over thirty years; surely their influence can't still be felt!"

"Ghosts are immortal," muttered Petrovsky.

It was obvious to Fuchs that such threats of retribution were quite real to his Russian colleague and that, even now, he fully realized the danger that his actions had placed him in.

"And yet you pursued this? Why?"

"Because, if I am wrong, the only thing I have done is have someone push papers in Moscow instead of Gdansk."

"And damaged your reputation significantly, if not irreparably."

"That is a risk I am willing to take."

"Again, *why?*" Fuchs pressed. "Such damage is costly, extremely costly."

"Because I am convinced I am right!"

"So, what if you are right? What then?"

"If I am right, I have prevented the West from winning this war," Petrovsky said. "I have exposed their warmongering and shown the world that their overtures for peace are only so much propaganda. We will recapture ground in the court of public opinion that we have been unable to recapture on the battlefield."

"Then, comrade, can you assure me that my removing the boy will not be subject to the same examination?"

"What do you mean?"

"He is not an East German national," Fuchs reminded him. "He is a Soviet citizen and one that we do not have direct jurisdiction over. I can't just move him from place to place without a reason."

"Like I said, say that he is going on a field trip associated with a class. Perhaps a holiday?"

"Alone? Without the other students? I may as well have him accompanied by a brass band and military parade. That is certain to raise suspicions!"

"Then perhaps a health issue can be arranged," suggested Petrovsky. "Let's be honest, my friend, it would not be the first time that either of us have resorted to such measures."

"Yes, that would be more easily explained," agreed Fuchs. "Something requiring him to be brought back to East Berlin for monitoring."

"I will leave those details to you," Petrovsky said. "But nothing too serious, please. For the moment, the brat is still useful to us."

"For the moment?"

"Yes," said Petrovsky, smiling. "You see, if I am correct, there is the possibility that Alexi has been in contact with the West. In so doing, he has made himself a traitor and one too dangerous to have on trial or in prison. A brief visit to the Lubyanka prison will solve that problem. With him gone, his offspring has no value and can be sent off with the rest of the proletariat and we don't have to waste any more time or resources on him again."

"And if you are wrong?"

"Then we were incorrect in assuming the value that the West placed on Alexi and can still dispose of him and be rid of his troublesome son, as well."

"There is still another possibility," Fuchs reminded him.

"What is that?"

"That you are, in fact, correct, but the Americans are successful."

There was a moment of silence on the other end of the phone.

"That is best not to be considered," whispered Petrovsky.

"But why not?"

"Because Stalin and Beria haven't been dead that long."

Chapter 24

"Against All Odds"

The lights of the club throbbed in time to the music that blasted through the speakers, making it almost impossible to hear anyone speaking. However, here and there throughout the club were booths set into small alcoves that provided enough respite that one was able to have a conversation as well as order drinks.

The band had been shown to a special alcove near the stage, where they had an unobstructed view of the dance floor, and the patrons had an almost unobstructed view of them. The band members had been accompanied by reporters and photographers, in addition to Wessel, and found themselves the focus of attention they had not received in a long time.

"This reminds me a little of Seattle." Evan laughed as the flashbulbs went off around him. "Say, the Germans aren't into that punk stuff, are they?"

"I have no idea." Rich shrugged, smiling at one of the female patrons. "But at least we don't have to go through any more of that battle of the bands shit like we did with Boney Jack. This time, the attention is all ours!"

A round of drinks was ordered, and when it arrived, it was accompanied by a bottle of champagne on ice.

"Compliments of the house," the manager said.

The band dutifully toasted the generosity of the establishment and sat back to listen to the music. To their disappointment, on this particular night there was no live music, only a DJ playing a mixture of American and British records, as well as recordings of German bands. The patrons did not seem to mind, however, as the dance floor was never empty.

"I thought Wessel said he knew the bands playing here?" Rich grumbled. "I was hoping to get some playing in before our big shows."

Cameron nodded and shrugged at this exposure of the photographer's bluster, but he didn't say anything. He had long ago lost count of how many times someone would talk big, only to be shown a fool. It was never worth pursuing, as he never put stock in any of those statements. To his chagrin, however, Rich was not so willing to let it go.

"Hey, Wessel," the bass player shouted over the music, "didn't you say you knew the guys who played here?"

The photographer paused in his shooting. If he had missed the angry, accusatory tone of the bassist's voice, there was no mistaking the displeased expression on his face. In the pulsating light, Cameron could tell by Wessel's expression that he had not seriously expected to have been taken seriously in his offer and was now searching for a plausible excuse.

"Oh, I guess they aren't playing tonight," he explained. "I'll check the schedule to see the next time they're here."

Big deal, we're only here tonight.

"Let it go, man," Cameron whispered into Rich's ear. "It's not worth it."

"I know, but it pisses me off when people make these claims and nothing comes of it," Rich grumbled.

"Look, we're being treated like kings here," Cameron explained. "Don't let that asshole turn you into the ugly American."

"I'll do my best," Rich assured him, pouring the last of the champagne into his glass. "But no promises!"

The Talking Heads, The Doors, and the Allman Brothers all kept the club hopping, and some of the ladies even talked Cameron and the others onto the dance floor. The spinning of the mirrored disco balls and the pulsating colored lights gave the room a psychedelic feel that both pleased Cameron and made him edgy. It was too hard to distinguish faces and features in this changing light, which meant it would be too difficult to monitor what was going on in the room.

Why, then, did they pick this place as our first appearance?

As he pondered this, the song stopped and the lights ceased to pulsate. Murmurs from the crowd made it clear that this was not a usual occurrence, and Cameron became truly alert. Despite the effects of the strange lighting on his eyes, he had been able to keep close to the booth they were in and keep the exit in sight, in case of an emergency. Was such a circumstance happening now?

"Meine Damen und Herren" came the DJ's voice, causing all eyes but Cameron's to focus on him. Cameron monitored the crowd while slowly backing toward the booth. "Unsere besonderen gäste, die Roadhouse Söhne!"

Suddenly, the lights dimmed and a spotlight shone on Cameron and the band as the room erupted into wild applause and whistles. To his relief, the lights did not shine directly into his eyes and he was able to still see without being dazzled.

"They just introduced you guys as their special guests," Wessel whispered into his ear.

"Am I supposed to go up there and say something?" Cameron muttered.

"No, just wave back and smile a lot," the photographer assured him.

Cameron obliged to the satisfaction of the crowd and turned to make certain the other band members did so as well. Then he suddenly heard his own voice coming over the speakers, singing "Won't Get Fooled Again."

"That Battenkill album must be a huge hit over here," Cameron muttered to Collier, only to discover that he was actually talking to Casey.

"Oh shit, man, I'm sorry." Cameron laughed. "I thought you were Ed!"

"Don't worry about it, man," Casey said and laughed back.

"You're not the first one to make that mistake tonight. If it helps me get a date, I might go along with it!"

"Seriously, you two do look a lot alike," Cameron admitted. "Are you two secretly brothers or maybe cousins or something?"

The roadie shook his head. "No, I'm reasonably certain my dad never jumped the fence on my mom." Casey laughed. "The only way Ed and I are related is through Adam!"

Their conversation was interrupted as they were approached by the other patrons, who wanted an autograph or a picture. Young women wanted to dance with them, and young musicians wanted to talk about how to be a success in the business. There were the customary offers of drinks, many of which the band deftly deflected so as not to cloud their judgments.

"I see you are adjusting to your celebrity status well" came a woman's voice from behind him. Cameron turned to see a woman, roughly his age, standing behind him. She was dressed smartly but did not entirely blend in with the demographic of the establishment.

"I'm Elsa Scholl," the woman said, extending her hand. "I believe you must be Cameron Walsh?"

"Oh yes." Cameron smiled warmly, drinking in her throaty voice. "I remember them telling me about you. Yes, I'm Cameron. Let me introduce you to the others."

Cameron duly introduced her to the band members and crew, and Kendrick, having talked to her on the phone earlier, introduced herself. Cameron ordered her a drink and got acquainted as the DJ concluded the band's Battenkill album and went on to one of their subsequent ones. Cameron recognized the tune as one of Rich's original songs.

"Holy shit," Cameron remarked. "Do they have all of our stuff over here?"

"How many did you make?" Elsa asked.

"I'm not sure," Cameron replied, trying to recall.

"Didn't we do seven in all?" Evan remarked.

Rich replied in the affirmative.

"Well, I know that there are four of your albums that are quite popular right now," Elsa explained. "However, I'm afraid I couldn't tell you their names."

That's all right. Right now I can't remember their names either.

"Did you just get here?" Collier asked.

"Oh, I've been watching you folks since you arrived." She smiled. "That was one of the reasons I suggested this location because it is easy to blend in if you want to."

That is not necessarily a good thing. Cameron was annoyed that someone who was supposed to be a fellow operative would do something that would put the rest of them at such risk. However, this entire operation had been planned and approved by people more experienced that he, so there wasn't much that he could do about it.

Elsa displayed a remarkable talent for being able to direct questions to each of the members that highlighted their areas of expertise and personal experiences. She had clearly done her research, though Cameron noticed that occasionally Elsa would lean in to Kendrick and share some private aside and laugh, so he suspected that their manager had provided her with certain talking points. She had even made a point of including Doug and Casey in the conversations.

"I hope you don't mind that I decided to observe you all from a distance," she explained. "But I wanted to get a sense of how you would be received here and how you were going to react."

"And did we pass inspection?" Cameron laughed, though privately he was still annoyed by it.

"It wasn't a test, really," she assured him with a smile. "I just wanted to see if you were going to be any different from other bands that have toured here."

"Were we?" he asked again.

"Yes, actually," she replied. "And I must admit I was both pleased and surprised at that."

"How so?" Evan inquired.

"Well, other bands that have come here already have enjoyed a great deal of popularity in the United States and elsewhere," she explained. "For them, it was simply a continuation of everything they'd already done, and such acclaim and attention seemed to be expected. But you were different. You had been out of the public eye for a long time and are coming into a resurgence of popularity. You seemed to appreciate it more, and it showed. I liked that."

"I'm glad to hear it," Cameron said, smiling warmly.

She returned the smile, and for a moment, their eyes met; he was convinced she smiled a bit more, before turning to the others to continue their conversation. To everyone's relief, she did not have a notepad with prepared questions but allowed the conversation to continue naturally. She did not write anything down, but judging from her follow-up questions to things that had been discussed some time previously, Cameron saw that she had a detailed memory.

As the evening wore on, Kendrick finally suggested that it was time they returned to the hotel to be ready for their performances the next day.

"Will you be joining us?" Cameron asked. Elsa smiled and leaned against him.

"That is sweet of you to think of me," she said, "however, I need to get home to begin working on my story. But, no worries, I will see you again tomorrow at your rehearsal."

"More observing from afar?" Cameron winked.

"Hmmm, possibly," she said, "but only because I don't want to be in the way."

"We can be very accommodating," Cameron assured her.

"I have no doubt," she replied with a smile.

Cameron enjoyed the relative stillness of the ride back. Relative, because the others were intent on chatting and playing music, which did intrude on his thoughts though, mercifully, not as badly as the din of the nightclub. Before they had taken their leave, there was another introduction from the DJ and a bottle of champagne from the management. It seemed to take forever for the band to make its way through the crowd of well-wishers and fans.

But it was worth every inconvenience.

Back at the hotel, the band headed for the elevators. Looking over his shoulder, Cameron noticed Wessel following them.

"We're calling it a day, man," Cameron said. "Why don't you give those shutters a rest and catch up with us in the morning?"

The pained expression on Wessel's face did not soften Cameron's feelings; if anything, it seemed to make him angrier.

Quit pouting, for Christ's sake. You're a grown man!

"What about them then?" Wessel asked, pointing at Doug and Casey.

"Our room is up near theirs," grumbled Doug.

Cameron knew that when the roadie got tired, he tended to develop a short temper, and it was beginning to show.

Don't press it, Wessel. I can't deal with the carnage now.

"Okay then, I guess I will see you at breakfast," said Wessel. "Around nine?"

"That works for me," mumbled Cameron as the elevator doors closed.

"He's an annoying bastard," Rich snapped as the elevator rose.

"No arguments here." Evan yawned.

"Nor here," agreed Kendrick. "However, remember that he is part of our team and we have to work with him on this assignment."

"Yes, let's just remember that we don't have the monopoly on guys like D'Lorenzo," said Doug, earning himself a disapproving glare from Kendrick.

"I'm hoping you all have at least a few minutes to go over things before we call it a night?" asked Kendrick.

"Do we have a choice?" asked Rich, with a stretch and a yawn.

"As a matter of fact, no." Kendrick smiled.

"Then, my dear, would you care to join us for a nightcap?" moaned Evan.

Before entering the suite, Cameron stopped them at the door.

"Listen, Wessel said he had been up here earlier," Cameron said. "I don't know if he was with anyone or not, but I don't like it. Yeah, I know we're supposed to be working with him, but there's something about him that isn't sitting right, and it isn't just because he's an annoying bastard."

"What are you getting at?" Rich grumbled, clearly exhausted.

Cameron put his finger to his lips and ran his other hand over the doorframe, indicating they should check for listening devices. The others reluctantly nodded in agreement.

Inside Cameron turned on the radio to provide noise to cover their movements, and each one took a section of the room before going into their own rooms. A few minutes later, they gathered again in the living room.

"Anything?" Cameron asked. He was as much relieved as he was disappointed when they shook their heads.

"In light of what I discussed with Elsa tonight, that was probably a wise move on your part," Kendrick admitted.

"Why?" Cameron asked.

Why couldn't it just be my paranoia, and why couldn't you just say I was overreacting?

"Because, according to her, your visit has produced a lot of chatter," Kendrick explained.

"Well, no kidding," snapped Rich, collapsing in a chair. "We're on all the news shows and in all of the papers. Isn't that what you wanted?"

"I'm not talking about the chatter in the entertainment world," Kendrick replied. "According to her, a lot of intelligence chatter has been swirling around your arrival."

"Do you think someone has been tipped off?" Cameron asked. He did not know if he was more relieved that he might not have to be part of such a risky mission, or more disappointed that their tour might be cut short.

To his relief, Kendrick shook her head. "A certain amount of this is to be expected. You are, after all, American performers suddenly showing up here, and the East Germans do have an eye out for any Western presence that might show up on their radar at any point. Since you are as popular there as you are here, they are trying to determine your itinerary to see if you will be going into their territory at all. Since that was handled through the talent agency Eberhard represents, your complete itinerary has been laid out already, so all necessary permits could be acquired and so there will not be any surprises that might complicate things."

"Was that such a good idea to tell them everything?" Cameron asked.

"They don't know everything," Kendrick assured him. "They only know dates and locations. They had to know that to issue permission for you to perform in East Berlin because that all had to be submitted in advance. However, since we're not staying in East Berlin, we didn't have to list any accommodations and so those have been kept confidential. In fact, they will only be revealed to us when it is time to leave one for the other."

"So, in other words, there isn't anything to worry about?" Evan yawned.

"I never said that," replied Kendrick.

"If they've been chatting about us, do you have any idea what they've been saying?" Cameron asked.

"As I said, they are just talking about you being here and the need to see what you are doing," Kendrick reiterated.

"Nothing specifically tied to what we're doing?" Cameron pressed.

"Not at this point," she assured him.

Though that is hardly reassuring.

Chapter 25

"Eyes without a Face"

The boy's moaning and crying had taken their toll on Hertz. He had given the prescribed dosage to the boy and was quite aware of the effect it should have. Mild cramps, severe diarrhea, and nausea—nothing like the symptoms the boy was demonstrating right now. Mikhail rolled about on the bed as if in convulsions, screaming in pain, clutching his midsection. He was ashen white and sweating. Despite his irritation at the boy's behavior, Hertz was still concerned. What if something happened to him? What would be the repercussions? Just then Mikhail noticed Hertz watching him and began to whimper, a pleading expression on his face.

"Good God," Hertz muttered contemptuously under his breath. "Are you that effeminate?"

Under orders from East Berlin, Hertz had slipped a powder into Mikhail's drink at dinner. He had done this many times in the past. It was not a serious poison, merely something to incapacitate an individual for a brief period of time. It would manifest a few hours after being administered and be disguised as either a severe cold or mild case of the flu. The victim would be back to normal within a day or so. This time, however, things seemed to be more severe than usual, though Hertz did not know how much was genuine affliction or genuine theatrics.

"We want to have a reason to bring him back here where we

can monitor him closely," Fuchs explained. "A case of mild food poisoning would justify moving him to one of our hospitals here in Berlin, without raising suspicions. I doubt if the infirmary at that school would be equipped for anything too serious, and even if they were, the possible embarrassment of the situation would make them compliant with our wishes."

"Wouldn't food poisoning need to affect more than him?" Hertz asked. He did not want the responsibility of having to administer a mild poison to the children of influential Stasi families.

"Of course not," Fuchs snapped, no doubt having considered the same thing. "We can attribute it to some of that Western excess he is noted for. He is always getting special privileges, isn't he? Special foods included? No, no one will suspect a thing, or be sympathetic for that matter."

And so Hertz had followed orders. To his amazement, the drug took effect faster than usual, almost instantly, with the boy collapsing in the dining hall instead of his room as Hertz had intended. With the help of one of the other staff, they carried him to the infirmary, where, as predicted, the doctor felt this was more than what he could attend to.

"It could be something he ate," the doctor told Hertz, "or it could be appendicitis. He's complaining about severe pain in his abdomen, but I can't tell if it is localized or general. He won't remain still long enough for me to make a thorough examination. I feel the boy should be X-rayed and I do not have that equipment here."

"How far is the nearest hospital?" Hertz asked. For a moment, he hoped that it would be serious enough to need to hospitalize the boy here, thus sparing him the torture of listening to his wails on the two-hour drive to Berlin. Alas, it was not to be.

"I do not suggest taking him there," the doctor advised. "They are rather provincial. A case of this seriousness requires the attention he would receive in a better-equipped facility in Berlin."

Despite the doctor's medical explanation, Hertz realized it was because no one would want to be responsible if the child of an influential dignitary were to take a turn for the worse under his or her care.

"Do you have an ambulance, at least?" Hertz sighed.

The doctor shook his head. "No, I'm afraid that you will have to drive him yourself."

"What? Are you serious? You just said that it was his appendix!" cried Hertz. "If that is the case, he might die before we reach Berlin!"

"I said it might be," the doctor insisted. "He does not seem to be running a fever, so I doubt that it is ruptured. It might just be inflamed."

"And how will I know that it has gotten worse?" Hertz demanded.

"He'll stop crying," the doctor muttered.

"If anything goes wrong with him, it will rest solely on your head, and I'll ensure that everyone from Berlin to Moscow knows it," Hertz said, stepping into the doctor's face. "Do you understand me?"

"Perfectly," the doctor replied.

From his close proximity to the doctor's face, Hertz smelled the liquor on the man's breath and made a disdainful face.

Wrapping the boy in a blanket, they loaded him in the back of Hertz's car. Hertz gave the doctor the name of the hospital that he would be going to, with instructions to have all preparations made ready for their arrival. From the widening of the doctor's eyes, Hertz realized that the man recognized the name of the hospital as one frequented by members of the Stasi and officials of the East German government. Hertz decided that he would stop along the way to phone Fuchs and update him on the situation.

They drove through the night, Hertz wending his way among the few cars that shared the road with them. Mercifully, they were not stopped. In Neustadt-Glewe, Hertz found a phone and made the call to Fuchs.

"Are you certain you gave the correct amount?" Fuchs demanded, when informed of the boy's condition. "This onset is far more rapid that usual. Something is terribly wrong!"

"I'm certain of the amount," Hertz insisted. "You only sent a single dosage and that was what was administered."

"We can't afford to have anything happen to him," Fuchs reminded his subordinate. "There will be no way to avoid the consequences if it does."

"I would not be overly alarmed," Hertz grumbled. "The boy seems to be calm enough if he thinks he has my attention. He only relapses if he thinks he's being ignored."

"We cannot be too careful at this point," the other man insisted. "What is it you expect me to do?"

"Make the necessary arrangements at the hospital," Hertz told him. "I can't trust that fool of a doctor to get it right. From the way his hands trembled, it was obvious that he has not had enough to drink today, and he was in a total panic about everything. I need someone with their wits about them to ensure nothing goes wrong."

"I see," mumbled Fuchs. "Don't worry then. I will have everything prepared for your arrival. Where you are calling from, you still have well over an hour to get there."

"Yes, but the traffic is light this time of night. I wouldn't worry about it."

"All the same, you should make all haste, just in case it is something serious. What is the number of your car? I can ensure that no one stops you."

Hertz gave his superior the number of his license plate and hung up the phone. Approaching the car, he heard the cries of his passenger ringing through the night air and a hot rage came over him.

"Stop that noise this instant!" Hertz shouted as he opened the door. "You're screaming like you're being eviscerated, and I won't listen to it anymore! I've heard soldiers on the battlefield with their legs blown off cry less than you with your damn bellyache."

"Where were you?" Mikhail gasped and writhed. "I'm dying here and you left me! You left me to die, all alone. You don't care what happens to me, you bastard!"

"If I were going to leave you somewhere to die, it would be on an abandoned stretch of road and not in the middle of a town," Hertz snapped. "Now shut up before I do just that!"

The boy began to wail once more but noted the expression

on Hertz's face and realized the man was sincere in his threat. Reluctantly, Mikhail settled into a steady whimper as they continued on through the night. A few miles outside of town, a light rain began to fall. Hertz pushed the car to go as fast as conditions would permit and was relieved that they did not encounter any police. It would be difficult enough explaining why he was out at this hour, but to have to do so with a screaming youth who was not his in the backseat would draw far too much attention to them, and even though his Stasi credentials would be enough to avoid any complications, he would prefer to be unnoticed.

Hertz was relieved to finally see the lights of Berlin in the distance. Mikhail had stopped crying some time before. Hertz had become anxious as the boy's moans became weaker but was relieved when he began to snore. Hertz decided to maintain his speed instead of slowing down, so it was not that long before they reached the hospital. Rousing a nurse and orderlies from the building, they loaded the boy onto a gurney. Awakening to find himself surrounded by people in white frightened Mikhail enough to begin an encore performance of his earlier screaming, though Hertz noticed a difference this time. Now it was genuine fear, but once he realized he was at a hospital and was the center of a rush of activity and attention, he settled down.

Mikhail was wheeled inside for tests, and Hertz made himself as comfortable as possible in the waiting room. Some time later, the doctor approached him with the results of the examination.

"Well, sir, I am happy to say that it was not his appendix after all."

"That is a relief." Hertz smiled, trying his best to sound genuine. "Do you have any idea what might have caused this?"

"He seems to have been suffering from a severe intestinal blockage," the doctor explained, "which was, in fact, applying pressure to his appendix and causing irritation. Once we administered a suppository, the bowels were evacuated and the pressure was relieved."

"You mean, this was brought on by his being full of shit?"

"Well, yes, I suppose that is a way to phrase it." The doctor smiled. "We've got him sedated and have administered some mild laxatives, but we would like to keep him under observation for a day or so to ensure that the appendix does not become inflamed again. He is still complaining of nausea and seems dehydrated."

"I think that would be best," Hertz agreed.

Hertz went to his parents' house in Berlin and from there phoned Fuchs to give him an update.

"We can see an analogy for the quality of Western life in that diagnosis," Fuchs muttered.

Hertz rolled his eyes. Like many of his generation, Fuchs was a devout Communist who decried anything that smacked of the West. Recent thawing of relations between the Soviet Union and her traditional adversary left many of them feeling abandoned and resentful. Anything that would serve to justify their previous contempt was seized upon with great relish. To Hertz, and others of his generation who had resented the stranglehold the Old Guard seemed to have on East German society, this attitude was tiresome.

"I will go back to check on him in the morning," Hertz informed Fuchs, without commenting on his superior's remark. "They said they wanted to keep him for observation to ensure that there was nothing actually wrong with his appendix."

"That is quite helpful," Fuchs mumbled. "I would like you to come to my office to obtain more dosages, in case we need to keep him there for longer."

"Wouldn't it be less likely to raise suspicions if you simply ask the doctor to keep him under observation until further notice?" Hertz asked. He had long ago become impatient with Fuchs's attempts at micromanaging situations and did not wish to be a part of it anymore. "If we take too much into our hands, it is likely to complicate matters and draw far more attention than we want."

"Yes, I suppose you are right," Fuchs sighed. Hertz smiled at the disappointment in his superior's voice. "Very well, I will have a talk with the administrator in the morning. Nevertheless, I expect a full briefing after you have visited the boy. You are not removed from this assignment yet!"

"I did not expect so, sir," Hertz commented, making a face into the phone. "I assure you that I will be by your office personally to update you on the situation as soon as I have discussed it with his physician."

The two men gave their perfunctory farewells and hung up.

Hertz poured himself a drink from his father's bottle of schnapps and drained it in one gulp. Pouring another, he tried to think of what to do next.

Chapter 26

"Flesh for Fantasy"

To Cameron's disappointment, the tour schedule was almost too fast for him to really absorb what was happening to them. On a personal level, he regretted the underlying reason for their presence in Germany. It prevented him from throwing himself, feet first, into what would prove to be his opportunity to immerse himself in his lifelong dream of being a rock-and-roll superstar.

Trying to catch a few minute's rest as they drove from one venue to the next, he fantasized about how they could have capitalized on this popularity if things had been different. Yet, after each scenario, he always arrived at the same conclusion.

None of this would have ever happened if it weren't for the real reason we're here.

So, with a sigh, he always resigned himself to how things were going. If nothing else, he comforted himself with the ever-increasing stack of articles that were appearing about them, which he could add to a scrapbook and look at when he was old.

I hope that doesn't jinx the possibility that I will get old.

They had had their rehearsal and show in Stuttgart, which was well received by the critics. A German TV station had filmed the rehearsal, but they had not been able to watch it when it came on.

"I assure you, it was very well done," Elsa had told him. "You would have been very pleased with it."

"Well, if you say so, then I'm sure I would have been," Cameron said. He was under no illusions that a woman of Elsa's influence and prominence had not been charmed by the best and brightest of the entertainment industry and that his efforts would not exceed any that had come before.

Still, why not have some fun trying?

However, it was Elsa who brought that to a close during one of the private "interviews" she had requested with him.

"I would recommend saving your charms for the women who attend your shows, Mr. Walsh," she declared. "Despite the smiles and conviviality of my interactions with you and your band, my function here is entirely professional on several levels. I don't think I need to remind you that we have no margin for error in this operation, do I?"

"No, you most certainly don't," Cameron assured her. "I'm sorry if I gave offense; I was just trying to play my part."

"I am sure you were," Elsa replied dismissively. "I am aware that you did not enjoy the level of notoriety in the United States that you are enjoying here; however, I would advise you to not let it go to your head if I were you. Conceit breeds carelessness; remember that."

"Thank you for that advice. I will keep it in mind," Cameron said.

"Good." She smiled. "Now I will keep my briefings simple and conduct them with your manager, Ms. Kendrick. My interactions with the band will be exclusively as a reporter covering your tour. I will ask questions, mostly about your impressions of things, your plans, and so forth. I can neither afford to have briefings be too widely involved, or to have my time monopolized by Ms. Kendrick. She and I have already discussed this; I am just informing you of this. In addition, I want you to know that it is unlikely I will talk with any of you privately after this. However, I reserve the right to change my mind if circumstances dictate it needs to be done. Are we clear on this?"

"Perfectly." Cameron smiled.

To his relief, Cameron discovered that the band would be allowed to host after-parties, where they would be permitted to mingle with the crowds. This permitted him enough of an opportunity to indulge his fantasy so the reality of the situation did not become burdensome. Kendrick and Elsa had devised a plan for the roadies to offer special passes to attendees, enabling them to meet the band at these special events. Wessel would capture photos of the fans with various band members and collect a mailing address so the developed photos could be sent to the participants.

"This will assist us in keeping an eye on the crowds and comparing them to any known Stasi agents working in the West," Wessel explained.

"Do you think they will be that obvious?" Cameron asked. "That sounds incredibly naive, if you ask me."

"We have a database of East Germans on file in Bonn," Wessel explained, his enthusiasm undeterred. "The images will be compared to the ones that we have as will the addresses. At the very least, it will provide us with additional information on possible operatives here."

"Do you really think we are being watched?" Rich demanded. "We're just supposed to be performing here. Why would they watch us?"

"We are watching everyone, in the event they are acting against us," said Wessel, his characteristic smile finally fading. "We aren't half as paranoid as they are. You guys are going to be playing in East Berlin. They aren't going to permit you within a meter of the border without having a good idea about you first. Nor will they take your clearance at face value. As far as they are concerned, there is always the possibility that you could be a threat to them on some level. If only for the fact that you are an American band and playing rock-and-roll music."

"They really hate all that, that much?" Rich asked.

"In East Berlin, ask them about the Lipzi." Wessel winked.

"What the hell is that?"

"It was a dance they developed to be a counter to decadent Western dance moves," the photographer explained. "You only moved your feet, you never made any contact with your dance partner and the top of your body stayed still."

"Sounds boring as hell," Rich mumbled.

"It was." Wessel laughed. "However, it was designed to be done in quarter time, so the authorities figured that it would be fast enough to appeal to the East German youth and be a counter to the dances of the sixties and seventies."

"Did it ever catch on?" Cameron wondered.

"Only with the kids trying to kiss the state's ass," Wessel said. "It had two things going against it. The first was that it was just plain boring. The second was that it was approved."

"Why would that make a difference?" Rich wondered.

"How many of your fans do you think like doing what they are told?" Wessel replied.

The bassist conceded that the photographer had a valid point.

The party at Stuttgart proved to be an excellent means for starting the tour. Roughly forty people, including venue personnel, congratulated the Roadhouse Sons on their German debut. Cameron was grateful that the only instructions Kendrick had given him were to smile, be pleasant, and not drink too much. It took little effort to observe two of those conditions and more effort than he previously thought to observe the last one.

Whenever he had empty hands, someone was pressing another drink on him. Remembering incidents in the band's past, where substances had been slipped to members, Cameron learned long ago how to discreetly set these offered beverages down and forget about them. He quickly fell back into an old habit he used to have of always carrying a beer bottle around with him. No one could tell if the dark bottle was full or empty, but its presence suggested that he already had a drink, so people did not feel the need to get him one. Looking about the room, he saw that the other guys were doing the same thing.

Training shows, I guess, doesn't it?

The first party broke up past midnight. To the band's amazement, curfew restrictions were far more relaxed here than they were in the United States.

"Well, here in the West anyhow," Wessel confirmed. "In the other half, it is business as usual."

"What do you mean?" Doug asked.

"They've always had a curfew, official or not," the photographer explained. "Even if there isn't an official one, if you are out too late, you are suspicious and are questioned."

"Wow! Do they check to see how many times you wipe, too?" the roadie wondered.

"Only if you use more than two squares of paper." Wessel laughed.

Doug was not certain he found that answer entirely facetious.

Munich was a town that Cameron and the others wished they had been able to see more of. Rich had hoped to have a beer in the hall where Hitler attempted to launch his famous grab for power in the 1920s but was dismayed to find out that would not be possible.

"They tore it down about four or five years ago," Wessel said.

The photographer told them of many other notable sights, including the site of the Olympic village, but Kendrick ruled out sightseeing.

"You're really not going to have a lot of extra time on your hands," she informed them. "Publicity appearances, performance, and after-party will be taking up a lot of it. You might want to use the free time to get some rest."

Later, at the show, Cameron was grateful for her suggestion. Almost as soon as he was at the hotel, he was asleep. Following a light dinner, he and the others went for their sound check. Following that was an interview that Elsa had set up, though Cameron was surprised not to see her there. Wessel was surprised by that, too, and Kendrick asked him to check on her.

"I haven't been able to reach her at any of the contacts I have," she explained.

As the time for the show approached, Cameron noticed that Wessel had not returned. The time came for the band to take the stage, and they did so without their official photographer. When Kendrick was not there during intermission, Cameron knew something was terribly wrong.

Despite their concerns, the band went through their established procedure, including the special after-party. Other than the band

and the roadies, no one seemed to suspect that anything was out of the ordinary. The band members made their usual rounds of the guests, greeting all of their well-wishers and posing for photos. To Cameron's embarrassment, any photos that were taken had to be taken on cameras the guests had brought.

Pretty damn hard to carry out your objective with those, isn't it? Maybe I should ask if they'll send us the pictures?

To his relief, Cameron finally saw Kendrick come through the door and make her way through the crowd. He could not tell by her expression if anything was wrong—she had long ago perfected the art of the poker face—nor did there appear to be any urgency in her movements. She smiled and greeted various guests while continuing her purposeful movement toward him. As she approached, he gave her a big smile and held out his arms to give her a big hug. Scooping her in his embrace, he whispered in her ear.

"What the hell is going on?" he asked.

"Krug's been murdered," she whispered back.

Chapter 27

"Rock You Like a Hurricane"

Alexi studied the report in his hands carefully. The last two communications had not had any messages in them whatsoever, and he was beginning to suspect that this one would likewise be devoid of any. However, he finally noticed one error and then a second, indicating the letters *t* and *a*. Before Alexi could notice any others, his supervisor entered his office.

"Congratulations," the man said, nodding to the paper Alexi was studying. "You're about to be shed of that."

"What do you mean, comrade?" Alexi asked, rising from his chair.

"I've just received word that you are to return to Moscow," the man replied, motioning him to sit back down. "No more having to decipher Polish attempts at Russian will be a welcome change, eh?"

"Not necessarily." Alexi smiled. "Have you ever had to decipher Russian attempts at Russian?"

"Well, I doubt that this assignment will be so frustrating," the other man said. "You will be back at your old office."

"At the directorate?" Alexi asked.

The other man nodded. Alexi waited for any explanation that might be forthcoming, but there was none.

"Why do they want me back there?" Alexi asked, trying not to sound too concerned.

"There was nothing specific," the man said. "They just informed me that you would be recalled soon. Something about a review of your old cases."

Alexi's apprehension grew. He was well aware of his agency's practices, and to be recalled did not necessarily mean it was for a good reason or that he would be doing the reviewing.

"Soon? You mean, they didn't say when?"

"No," the man said and shook his head. "Just that they would be informing me that you would be returning to Moscow and that I was to find someone to replace you, so there would be no interruption of your duties."

"Well, that shouldn't be too difficult." Alexi smiled. "I mostly review the reports from Polish factories about the machinery we've supplied them and make certain everything is running smoothly, or else I put them in touch with people who can correct problems if they arise. There is nothing too taxing in that. I'm certain you won't have any difficulty in finding someone."

"I have no concerns," the other man said, studying him.

It was obvious to Alexi that this attempt at small talk was a front to observe his reactions to the announcement. But was he directed to do this observation, or was it the other man's own perverse sense of humor?

"Is there anything else?" Alexi asked.

The other man shook his head. "No, nothing," he assured him. "I was just informing you, in case you needed to get anything together before you left."

Alexi held out his hands to indicate his office.

"Everything is right here; I brought nothing with me but my clothes," he explained. "I haven't socialized outside of embassy functions. I've tried to be very quiet and low key while assigned here."

"That has not been lost on anyone," the other man confirmed.

"Is there a problem with that?" Alexi asked.

"No," the other man assured him. "Why should it be a problem?"

Alexi refused to be drawn into a defensive conversation and made no response. Instead he was thinking of how to get a message to his handler. He needed to get home, but then he remembered the report on his desk. There was a message in it. He needed to decipher that as well.

"Are you doing anything this evening?" his supervisor asked.

"I have no plans," Alexi informed him.

"Good." The man smiled. "Then why don't we go out for a drink? What do you say?"

"I'm flattered," Alexi said. "Let me conclude this report and I will be right with you."

"Oh, I'm sure we can get someone else to handle this." The other man smiled, taking the folder off his desk. He walked to the office door and handed it to the secretary. "Elena, can you give this to Victor Polacov? He'll be taking over these clients, so he might as well get acquainted with them now."

"So you already had my replacement considered," Alexi said as the man once again sat opposite him.

"You should know that we leave nothing to chance," the man said. "Everything is always thought several steps ahead. It would have been idiotic to think that a man of your background and experience would remain in such an obscure posting indefinitely. I always knew you would be recalled and had considered a replacement for you."

"Victor is very capable," Alexi began, but the man waved him off.

"I don't need capable for this; I need competent," he replied. "You were competent, Victor will be competent, and if I need to replace him, someone else will be competent as well. Now grab your coat and let's go. I know a nice little restaurant near the center of town where we can get a good meal."

Alexi knew that protesting would only raise suspicions, and that was the opposite of what he wanted to do. There was no choice but to go. He remained calm, but he knew that somehow he needed to get a message to his handler. He wondered what the message was that they were trying to get to him. Had they learned of this recall? Were they trying to inform him of how to get out of Poland? He did not waste time speculating about the meaning behind the recall.

There was no need to. He had issued enough of them to know their implications.

His superior waited for Alexi to grab his coat and follow him. As Alexi went for his briefcase, the other man shook his head.

"You won't be needing that tonight," the man said. "We might as well start getting other people used to handling your assignments. No time like the present, is there?"

"I suppose not." Alexi smiled and left the briefcase on his desk. This he did not mind doing, as there was nothing incriminating in there.

The two men stepped outside where a car was waiting for them. Alexi noted that it had been running and suspected that it had been running the entire time they had been talking. He thought to the times that he, too, had been sent to pick up someone on behalf of his superiors. Rarely had they ever taken someone home. However, now he was only mildly concerned. He knew that except for one liaison with the Soviet embassy, he was the only member of the trade delegation that actually worked for the directorate. The others were actual office staff and personnel assigned to the projects that were being developed in Poland, and this included his superior in the delegation.

Other than the driver, there was no one else in the car with them, another factor that allowed Alexi to relax, just a little. The driver was given the address of a restaurant that Alexi was familiar with, and it was located where he had been told it was. Once there, they were shown to a table for two, located near the center of the room in plain sight of everyone. Again, some of Alexi's concerns were abated. The meal itself was delicious but not exceptional, nor was the conversation. This was hardly unexpected, as Alexi did not socialize much with anyone, so he was a bit of the odd man out. However, he admired how his superior valiantly tried to make conversation.

"You were a conscientious worker," he commended him. "Your attention to duty and patience in working with some of our more troublesome clients did not go unnoticed."

"Thank you, I appreciate that," Alexi replied, toasting his

companion with his water glass. While many glasses of vodka were ordered, Alexi tempered his consumption. He might be more relaxed now than he had been, but he still intended to keep his wits about him. After a few glasses, his superior decided not to wait for Alexi to catch up to him and proceeded to indulge himself more and more. This is what Alexi hoped for because, if the man were drunk enough, he would let something slip if there was anything he was trying to hide. Alexi kept bringing the conversation back to work.

"I do still have a few clients that I am working with," he admitted. "These were big accounts that I would hate to see anything go wrong with. Their success could be quite a good reflection on the delegation. Do you think there is any way that Moscow would let me see these through?"

"Why the hell worry about machines and parts?" his companion slurred. "You're going to be back in Moscow dealing with more important things. Everything is changing in Moscow!"

"Like what?" Alexi pressed, convinced he was on the right path. "What are they going to have me working on? I'll just be doing the same thing there as here."

"Parts are parts." The other man shrugged. "You get the chance to make someone else look good instead of us. You are good at what you do; that is what I kept telling them!"

"Telling who?"

"The people in Moscow who want you back," the other man snapped. "They always ask how you are behaving, what you do, where you go, and who you talk to. I tell them you work, you go home, you come back to work. You never give anyone any trouble; none of us have any complaints. You deal with the Poles and the East Germans and never get frustrated with any of them."

"Then possibly you could persuade them to let me stay?"

"The bastards got upset when I kept telling them you were the best one we had," he muttered as if he hadn't heard Alexi's question. However, that statement was telling in and of itself. Alexi knew that he had been constantly monitored—no one could be so naive as to think he wouldn't be—though he had not suspected they were going to such lengths to find something negative about him. Failing to find out anything to be suspicious of could only mean one thing: they had finally decided to manufacture something. If he were being called back, it would be on such a charge. This turned his blood to water. That would also mean that there was no way for him to defend himself.

"My friend, it is getting late." Alexi laughed. "What do you say we have one more drink and then you take me home? I have had a long day."

"Ah, yes, one more drink then." His companion laughed loudly, motioning for the waiter.

When their drinks arrived, Alexi proposed a toast to his host and carefully sipped his vodka, while his companion tossed his back. They paid for the meal, and Alexi helped his friend to the car. Alexi was dropped off at his apartment, and as he emerged from the backseat, he noticed the familiar figure waiting by the corner. He wondered, with a grim sense of humor, what the man would do when Alexi was gone.

Once inside his apartment, Alexi turned on his light, as usual, and then waited for a few moments. Bending over, he wiggled the cord from the outlet, causing the light to flicker a few times. Then he plugged it back in and the light came on. Withdrawing it once more, the light went out. He partially inserted it once more, and it flickered three times before he unplugged it entirely and sat by the phone. He did not have long to wait before it rang.

"Good evening, comrade" came a man's voice. "Is everything all right?"

"Of course it is," Alexi replied. "Why shouldn't it be?"

"We noticed something wrong with the light in your window," the man explained. "We wanted to make certain that you were all right."

"I'm fine," he assured them. "The bulb is probably burned out, or else the plug is loose in the outlet."

"Perhaps you should check them," the voice said. "Such things can cause an electrical fire, and that would be most tragic if such a thing were to take place so close to your return to Moscow."

"Yes, indeed it would," Alexi agreed, not missing the warning hidden in the statement. They not only wanted him in Moscow; they wanted him alive. "Wait just a moment while I check it."

Alexi set the receiver on the end table and made a point of exaggerating the effort required to move the chair. He plugged the lamp back into the outlet and the room was illuminated once more.

"Yes, the plug had come loose," Alexi explained. "I've secured it once more. I'll be shutting it off now, anyhow. I'm about to prepare for bed."

"Very well, comrade," the man said. "We wish you a good night then." And with that, he hung up.

Alexi, not wishing to raise any more suspicions, did as he said he was going to and turned off the light. Only the light from his kitchen area shown into the room, giving everything a half-light. He thought about getting up to check his apartment, to see if anyone had been there while he was away. There hadn't been enough time to do so when he returned home; they expected the light to be on within a certain period of time after his arrival. However, before he could get up, there was a knock at the door.

Chapter 28

"Born in the USA"

Cameron and Kendrick made their way through the crowd to a small changing room. As they did so, Cameron grabbed Doug and told him to stand by the door while he and Kendrick discussed something. Without a word, Doug nodded and took up his position. Cameron knew that the folded arms and stern expression would be a sound deterrent against any unwanted interruptions. This practice had seen ample use for sensual liaisons in the past, and Cameron knew it would be successful for something of a more serious nature now.

"What the hell is going on?" Cameron repeated.

"I was contacted by Ernst Eberhard," Kendrick explained. "Krug was murdered in an automobile accident earlier today."

"Now, come on, don't jump to conclusions," Cameron warned. "I know we're all on pins and needles here, but just because someone died in a car accident doesn't mean they were murdered. Accidents happen all the time!"

"Accidents, yes," Kendrick agreed. "But brake lines do not get cut all the time. No, it was murder."

"The brake lines were cut?" Cameron gasped. "Isn't that a bit amateurish?"

"Not really," she explained. "It is the quick fix, and you hope that the car crashes and burns to hopefully hide things. But, if it doesn't, it does serve notice as to who was behind it."

"Who was behind it?" he asked.

"Odds are pretty good it wasn't the Campfire Girls," she snapped.

"Well, excuse me," he said. "I just didn't think they would be that obvious!"

"On the contrary, they would not mind at all to be that obvious. It serves notice to the BND that the Stasi's reach can extend anywhere. Remember Willie Brandt?"

Cameron recognized the name but couldn't recall its relevance to the conversation. "Wait, wasn't he the mayor of West Berlin, or something?" he asked.

"Yes, he was, but he also went on to become chancellor of West Germany until he was forced out by a huge scandal involving someone on his staff who was a Stasi agent and had been for years. Trust me, that wall in Berlin only keeps the people in that Honecker wants it to keep in; their agents can move through it whenever they want."

Cameron felt his stomach flip. "We're going through that wall soon, aren't we?"

"In about three days," she confirmed.

"What do we do?" Cameron wondered.

"First, we get out of this closet before people start talking," Kendrick explained. "Then we wrap this party up as soon as we can and get back to the hotel. I'm hoping that we will have received some word from someone in Bonn to give us a direction to go in. Until then, we have no choice but to carry on as planned."

"Is that wise?" Cameron asked. *Or safe?*

"We are only supposed to be a peripheral action," Kendrick reminded him. "Other parties are going to be doing the main actions. For us to change anything, for any reason, could jeopardize their missions. We need to keep on task, at least until we get to West Berlin. If anything changes, we will know by then and can easily fabricate some excuse for why we had to cancel our planned trip into East Berlin. There is always some bureaucratic snafu when dealing with the East Germans, so it won't raise any suspicions with anyone if our proposed performance doesn't happen."

Cameron only felt partially relieved by her explanation. While it did present a possibility that they would not have to risk going into East German territory, it did not assuage the concerns that someone directly responsible for bringing them to this country was now murdered, by a person or persons officially unknown but clearly suspected.

"Well, if we're going to keep calm and carry on, then let's be doing it," he murmured. "I need a drink, and I owe you a martini."

"We'll start with one," Kendrick muttered.

Outside, Doug was still at his station, and Cameron was relieved to see that there was still a clear area outside the door.

"Thanks, man," Cameron whispered to his roadie. "Did anyone try to get in?"

"A couple of people did ask where you were, but they left when I shrugged," Doug explained. "I only had to snarl at dipshit once when he didn't take the hint the first time."

"Who?" Cameron asked.

"Wessel," explained Doug.

"He's back?"

"Yeah, came in a few minutes ago." Doug yawned. "All apologetic about not being here and wanting to explain to Kendrick in person."

"You know you should have let him in," Cameron reminded him. "He's not just a photographer."

"You said no one got in," Doug snapped. "No one did. You guys want exceptions to be made to your rules, make them clear to me ahead of time! I'm not a mind reader, and my crystal ball blew a tube."

"Calm down," Cameron whispered. "I'm not riding your ass; you did what you were told to do! I'm just saying that, in the future, if he has to talk to us urgently, let him. It's okay."

The roadie shrugged and headed to where Casey was sitting. Cameron noticed that they had a small group around them, with everyone laughing and clapping. Periodically, Casey would put his hands in the air and wave them before plunging them back down into the group. Kendrick had paused to see what was going on, so Cameron joined her.

Casey had three Styrofoam cups and lifted one to reveal a coin underneath. He then began to quickly slide the cups about the table, periodically pausing to wiggle his fingers and crack his knuckles or snap his fingers before resuming his performance. Cameron watched as several people attempted to guess where the coin was, and all failed to do so. Even Cameron had to acknowledge that his other roadie was very good at this, as even he was unable to follow the coin's path.

"Come on now, what's your secret?" someone asked, only to be answered by a shrug.

"A magician never reveals his secrets." Casey smiled, holding up his hands. "Then what good is he for?"

Cameron felt a nudge in his ribs and caught the slight nod from Kendrick.

"Hey, guys, I hate to put a damper on things, but we've got to wrap this up," Cameron said to the crowd. "We've got a busy day tomorrow and have to get ready. I'd like to thank you all for coming out and making this a great show!"

Before anyone could say anything, he made his way to the door, positioning himself there so the could sign last-minute autographs and shake hands with the guests. To his relief, the moaning and complaining about the early ending of the after-party was minimal and was eased, somewhat, by members of the band giving personal attention to those complaining.

"All right, what's up?" demanded Rich.

"Not here," Cameron whispered. "Back at the room."

Rich nodded and grabbed his coat. Cameron waited until the others had gathered. Wessel was trying to get his attention.

"I kept trying to talk to you, but *he* wouldn't let me in!" the photographer sputtered, nodding at Doug.

"He follows orders," Cameron informed him. "And he follows them to the letter! I told him not to let anyone bother us, and he didn't. We'll talk about this later."

A slightly sullen group made its way back to the hotel. They knew it was for a reason, and that made them uncomfortable because it was unlikely that it would be a positive situation that brought about this change.

"That was a good trick," Cameron said to Casey. "I can usually follow them pretty good, but I couldn't keep up with you!"

"It is all in the hands." Casey laughed. "The hands I wave around, I mean, not necessarily the ones on the cups."

"What are you talking about?" Cameron demanded.

"Didn't you see me snapping my fingers, waving my hands, and popping my knuckles?" Casey asked.

Cameron nodded.

"Then your attention was divided between that and my hands on the cups. Your brain couldn't keep track of them all, so it split its attention and you lost track of the coin. It is as simple as that."

"That's pretty damn easy for you to say," said Cameron. "I'd have lost track of that stupid coin after the first few switches if I had been doing it!"

"I guess that's why you pay me the big bucks then, isn't it?" Casey laughed.

"We pay you for that?" Cameron teased. "Then I want a cut of anything you take in!"

"If I ever start doing it for money, you will." Casey winked in reply.

Cameron was actually relieved to hear that. When he saw Casey doing it, he was at first concerned that he might be trying to do it for money, and that could cause unnecessary attention to them. Then he reminded himself who, and what, Casey really was and realized that he might just have been doing this longer than Cameron had been.

"So you don't use it to make money?"

"Oh, hell no," Casey assured him. "That would just cause a lot of hard feelings and resentment and bring down the whole vibe of the parties. I just like doing it to make people laugh. Yeah, they make bets on it, but just verbal. I kind of discourage anything else. Too easy for people to get pissed off."

At the hotel, Kendrick brought them all into Doug and Casey's room, where she turned on the television and turned up the volume.

"I have not had the opportunity to check either my room or the band's since I received the news," Kendrick explained as quietly as she could. "I figured this room, being the smallest, would be easier for us to check before talking about anything."

"What news?" Rich asked, but Kendrick only shook her head in reply.

They gave the entire room a thorough going over, carefully checking the lamps, door casings, and table legs. There were some vases on the shelves, along with other items, but they proved to be untouched as well. Doug carefully took the books off the shelves and checked the spines of each, while Casey carefully unscrewed the phone receiver. Rich and Evan checked the bathroom while Kendrick and Wessel checked the radio and the television. Cameron slid his fingers along the picture frames to detect any possible signs of a listening device being installed in them. No one found anything.

"Are those your lighters?" asked Kendrick.

"Yes," replied Casey. "The packs of cigarettes belong to us, too. I checked them. They're clean."

"All right then," sighed Kendrick. "Let's get down to business. I was notified this evening that Krug had been killed. As the brake lines were cut, we believe it to be intentional. Have you received any further notice, Wessel?"

"Nothing about that, I'm afraid," the photographer sighed.

Secretly Cameron wished that the annoying buoyant spirit he customarily displayed would return. Life seemed less foreboding then.

"They did say that Eberhard would be meeting with us in Hannover tomorrow night to relay any possible developments that have occurred since then and to brief us on any possible change in plans," Wessel added.

"Collier, has anyone attempted to contact you?" Kendrick asked.

"I'm totally under your aegis on this," he said. "No one would be contacting me for any reason."

"Casey, what about you?" she asked the other roadie.

He, too, shook his head. "Not yet," he replied. "However, they would only be with me in case of extreme emergency. I am supposed to be totally underground until we get to West Berlin."

"So that means things might not be as serious as we think?" Evan said.

"No," Casey replied. "It means they haven't finished processing any information yet, or they haven't remembered I'm here yet. Things get done by the pony express sometimes."

Cameron felt the disappointment in Evan's eyes. This was serious. Though it was not like a surveillance operation that had gone bad and could be redone with a different crew at a different time and location. This time, there was far more involved and far more at stake.

"So what do we do?" asked Doug. His voice sounded small, as if he did not dare ask the question.

"We keep doing what we are doing," Kendrick replied. Her voice was equally as quiet.

Cameron was surprised. Kendrick had not, and did not, make any secret of her disapproval of including Doug in this operation. She considered him a loose canon and not without reason, based upon her past experiences with him. Doug's history with her was almost as rocky as his history with D'Lorenzo. Accordingly, they had dealt with each other as little as possible, though Cameron had noticed a definite thaw in their attitudes toward each other since their arrival in Germany—cordial, if not open.

That is progress, I'd say.

Doug did not seek any further clarification, neither did anyone else, and that reason was perfectly evident to Cameron. It was the same reason he didn't say anything. Cameron was glad they were still doing what they were supposed to. This relief did not carry as far as the mission itself. For the moment, Cameron had decided that could go to hell. Right now he needed his music, and he knew that the band, including Collier, probably needed it as well. It was how a musician would respond to a situation; they would embrace something that suggested normalcy, and that was their music. Despite all of the claims that the musicians on the Titanic played to keep the passengers calm, Cameron always suspected that the reason they did what they did was because they needed it as much as anyone.

And once again, the band plays on.

Chapter 29

"Lights Out"

Alexi counted the knocks on the door. There were four: two slow knocks, then two knocks in quick succession. This he knew to be the signal from his contact. Waiting a few moments, he returned the same number of knocks, except in reverse order. Then he slowly opened the door.

In the hallway stood a man of practiced non–descriptiveness. His overcoat was gray and worn about the collar and elbows. The pants that showed beneath it were a dark color, as were his shoes. The man was average height and weight, with no distinctive features in his face, dark hair, and black–rimmed glasses. In their meetings, he had never spoken with any inflections or changes. All conversation was conducted as if making small talk, nothing to elicit either a reaction or a response. He never smiled or betrayed any facial reaction to anything that was said. If the man were in an empty field or a crowd, there was nothing that would make him stand out in anyone's mind, and even Alexi, with all his years of practiced experience, often found it difficult to recall anything about him after their meetings. Further, Alexi had never known the man's name, nor was he given a code name for him. He was simply "your contact."

"We missed you," the man said in his soft voice. His tone was dull, disinterested. It was as if he were simply stating an obvious fact, such as "This is Poland," or "You are wearing clothes."

"I was called away," Alexi explained. "I'm being recalled to

Moscow and my boss insisted on taking me out to a dinner. They gave my files to another person in the office. I have no idea when I will be leaving."

"We have to leave now," the man said. Alexi's heart froze. Was this the plan all along? Had these people actually been members of the KGB, and was this an attempt to gather sufficient evidence to convict him of crimes against the state? He tried to think where he could have gone wrong in his plans. With his extensive knowledge of foreign intelligence operatives, he had known who to contact in British intelligence and made careful overtures to MI6. It had been nearly three years of carefully orchestrated maneuvers that brought them to the point where he could escape to the West. Then, at that moment, he received notice that he was being recalled to Moscow. A coincidence? That would be too fantastic to be believed.

Alexi quickly thought of how he could escape. There was no back door to the apartment; the only other means of egress was the fire escape. That choice was, in fact, not a choice, as it could be clearly seen from the street where the agent stationed to monitor his apartment always stood. There would be agents waiting at the bottom by the time he reached it, if they didn't shoot him first. The man in the doorway had his hands in his pockets as always, and Alexi wasn't certain which pocket held a gun, or if both did.

"We have no time," the man said calmly. "By now they are pulling up in front, and if you listen closely, you can hear someone on the fire escape. You can come with me now, or I can shoot you now."

Alexi hesitated for only a moment, then stepped into the hallway, and closed his door. He did not even bother to retrieve his coat, still draped across the kitchen chair. The man displayed no reaction to Alexi's choice but turned and hurried to another apartment just down the hall. The door had been left ajar and they entered it quickly, with the man locking the door behind him. Inside, an elderly Polish woman was preparing dinner at the kitchen stove while her husband watched television. Neither of them acknowledged the intrusion, giving the moment a surreal aspect.

The man continued through the apartment to a bedroom in the

far corner. There, he went to a bookcase and slid it back, revealing a ladder that extended both through the ceiling and through the floor.

"Go down," the man said in his same, disinterested voice. "Hurry."

Alexi did as instructed, and after he had descended a few feet, the other man stepped onto the ladder and pulled the secret panel behind him, extinguishing any light. In the darkness, Alexi was not certain of his footing and moved cautiously. The other man moved with uncharacteristic speed and stepped on Alexi's fingers, causing him to utter a quick exclamation.

"Quiet," the man said in a low voice. "Hurry."

Alexi picked up his pace, though still moving cautiously, and they continued down into the darkness. Alexi knew that since his apartment had been on the second floor, they should not have to descend too far to reach the basement, if that was their destination, and he felt the floor almost as soon as he had that thought.

"Step back three steps," the man said, and Alexi did as he was instructed. The man reached the bottom of the ladder, and in the darkness Alexi heard him feeling along the wall and then stop. He made a series of knocks similar to the ones he had made on Alexi's door and was greeted by the same countersign. Another smaller panel opened to reveal muted light, and from the small view he was afforded, Alexi discovered that they were in the other building's garage.

"He's here," the man said.

"So are the others," another voice replied, and Alexi considered making a dive for the other man. In the darkness and closed quarters, he would have a chance to overpower him and get away. His years of experience and skill in these situations would give him a distinct advantage. However, how long would that advantage last? A few moments? There was no way of knowing how many others were waiting on the other side of the panel, but no matter the number, Alexi knew for a fact that they were armed. He decided to wait until he knew for certain what he was up against.

"Is the car here?" the man asked.

"No, they kept going when the others pulled up in front" came the reply through the opening.

"That is unfortunate," the man said, still betraying no emotion.

"But not unexpected," the disembodied voice assured him. "We have an area for him to wait in. Follow me."

The panel opened to reveal the basement and two men standing outside, each with a gun trained on them. Alexi did not recognize any of the men as being from the KGB detail with either the embassy in Warsaw or the trade delegation in Gdansk, nor could he remember ever seeing them with the Polish State Security, but that meant nothing. Both agencies possessed thousands of agents, and there was no way to know who all of them were. The man Alexi had been following stepped through the door first, without saying anything. The other men waited for Alexi to move but made no threatening gestures.

"We're safe here for the moment," the man said, "but only for a moment, I'm afraid. If you will follow me, we have a place where you can hide until the situation dies down."

The gunmen watched Alexi and waited for his response. Alexi decided that it would be wise to follow his companion and noticed that the gunmen remained at their station. Alexi was led to the far side of the basement that connected to the furnace room, where he was led.

Inside, the other man pushed a filing cabinet away to reveal an opening and motioned for Alexi to enter.

"Don't be alarmed," the man said. "This is simply a room where you will wait until we can come for you. Get inside, and I will return as quickly as I can."

Alexi hesitated for a moment; he had no assurance that this was not a trick of some kind. However, he also knew that there was only one means of escape from that room, and it would lead him out to where the other two men were, no doubt, still waiting and armed. To further reiterate that point, the other man's right hand was still in his pocket. Alexi stepped into the opening and felt his foot bump into a chair when the door began to close, plunging the room into darkness.

"It will not do you any good to try to force your way out," the other man said. "This will be securely locked once this door is closed."

With that, he closed the door and Alexi heard the click of the lock. Feeling his way in the darkness, Alexi sat down on the chair and waited. There were no sounds from outside. He stretched his leg but did not connect with the wall. He extended his leg to its full extent, but still nothing. Alexi realized that he was probably sitting with his back to the door and panic began to set in. He wanted to get up to move, to shift his position, and began to do so. But in the darkness he could not be certain if this would correct the situation or make it worse. So he sat back down and waited. He had no way of determining how long he had been there. Neither the numbers nor the hands on his watch were luminescent, and there was no light by which to see them. Despite his efforts, he could not seem to find the will to control his thoughts.

As the darkness seemed to grow deeper, he recalled all the people that he had put in similar situations in the past and wondered if, somehow, this was their revenge. His thoughts traveled to Lubyanka Prison and the basement passages and holding cells there, and to all the interrogations he had witnessed and conducted there. He recalled with graphic vividness the beatings inflicted on the enemies of the state. He felt the rubber truncheon in his hand once more, the feel of his knuckles making contact with the soft flesh of his prisoners. Is that where he would be sent? If he were, would he be put in one of the cells or just be taken out back? Which would be the best outcome to wish for? Just then he heard the click of the door.

Chapter 30

"Deeper and Deeper"

Fuchs closed the report from the Hauptverwaltung Aufklärung (HVA), the branch of the Stasi responsible for foreign reconnaissance. The report included a series of photographs provided by their agents in the West. In an effort to assist his friend in this task, copies of the photos had been provided via special courier to Petrovsky and the KGB man was only too delighted to receive them. Petrovsky had revealed more evidence obtained from his source in Washington. In several points, the evidence obtained by some of Markus Wolf's agents corroborated the suspicions of his KGB counterpart, leaving some troubling gaps.

The first photograph was that of a woman, listed in HVA files as Special Agent Barbara Ellen McIntyre of the Federal Bureau of Investigation, with fourteen years of service. From the photograph, Fuchs could see that she was not like some of the other individuals whose photographs covered the top of his desk. She was professional in her bearing and appearance, as opposed to people depicted in the other photos. Randomly, he selected one and perused the accompanying biography.

"Richard Webster, musician; founding member of the group, unemployed before being rehired to perform on the current tour of Germany, single, no dependents, no permanent address.

"Evan Dixon, musician; founding member of the group,

employment history unknown, married, father of one. Resides in Calverton, Maryland.

"Cameron Walsh, musician; founding member of the group, occupation: light and sound technician, no known dependents. Resides in Washington, DC. Has been frequently sighted with subject Barbara Ellen McIntyre and is believed to be a federal agent.

"Ryan Casey, technician and engineer. American residing in the BRD since the outbreak of hostilities, unsuccessfully applied for a relief visa, granted refugee visa by BRD. Employed by the Bundeswehr in nonmilitary capacities from 1978 to 1981. Employed by various electronics entities from 1981 to the present. Subject has no known address and no known dependents."

The photos depicted young American men in much the same way he expected to see them: disheveled hair, unshaven, and generally unkempt in appearance. Torn pants, battered shoes, and stained shirts were more reminiscent of the refugees following the fall of Nazi Germany than they were of a country that had only recently gained military and diplomatic advantages against the Soviets. He stared at the photos, his bilious contempt making his hands shake as he reached for the photo of Barbara McIntyre. She had clearly been identified as an American agent, but what was curious was the fact that she worked for an agency that did not possess a mandate to operate on foreign soil. The Federal Bureau of Investigation was only authorized to operate in the United States and its possessions. The only agency permitted abroad was the Central Intelligence Agency. However, no CIA agent had been identified among these other individuals, which made him certain that one of them had to be.

Fuchs referred back to the file and examined two more photographs contained within it. The first one was of a man with rough features framed by a black beard and unruly, dark hair. The description that accompanied the photograph listed him as Douglas Courtland.

"Douglas Courtland; subject has numerous arrest citations for violent behavior. Has worked with the members of this group for many years. Last known residence was Wilmington, Delaware.

Currently resides in Washington, DC. Subject has one dependent, a son from a previous relationship. Subject has appeared in relation to investigations involving the USS *Mustang* and crew member Augustus Kalbe. Subject was the focus of previous recruitment attempts, all unsuccessful. Subject was last known individual contacted by Augustus Kalbe in relation to the USS *Mustang*. Suspect has been under observation by the American government as a result of prior relationships and recruitment attempts."

The other photo that attracted his attention was one that he had mistaken for one of the other subjects until he examined it closer. The description indicated that this subject was one Edward Collier.

"Edward Collier, musician, employment history unknown, newly hired to replace former musician Clyde Poulin. Reportedly resides in Harrisburg, Pennsylvania; subsequent investigation indicates that is false. Suspect has no known dependents. Contact advises that Edward Collier was the name of a member of the Seattle network who had attempted to defect to the Americans. Before making contact, subject died under mysterious circumstances. Investigation uncovered no indication of American involvement in subject's death."

Fuchs held the photos like a hand of cards, and he realized that Petrovsky was right, though it was impossible to say about what. Something was happening; one or perhaps two American agents, who had no business in Europe, were now here. The one named Collier had no detectable past and no attachments to anyone. If that were not sufficient grounds to consider him an enemy operative, there was the use of a cover name of a known Soviet agent. But the one that concerned him the most was the third one. The one they had attempted, unsuccessfully, to recruit. He was involved with the *Mustang*, the American provocation of this war. One of the individuals that Soviet intelligence had made repeated reference to in relation to that project had been a close friend and contact. What was it the Americans were hoping to bait them with by sending this person here? It was obvious that something significant was taking shape, but at the moment it was impossible to determine what it was.

One thing was clear, however. It was no longer simply a matter of humoring his Russian counterpart; now there was something for them to worry about. But what? Fuchs reached for the phone. He might not know what he was dealing with, but he did know whom he needed to contact about it.

Chapter 31

"Union of the Snake"

Cameron was glad that they took their time going through Hannover. It was just what he needed. The weather was sunny and pleasant, and it was a relief to see the reflection of the rebuilt buildings on the river. The so-called New Town Hall shone like a wedding cake against the blue sky, and many pedestrians, all in bright colors, took advantage of the weather and were walking along the sidewalks, or in the cafes.

Cameron was looking forward to this performance. Hannover was one of the largest cities in Germany and, despite its proximity to the East German border, had been relatively untouched by the war.

Both sides want the other half in one piece, I guess, no matter which side wins.

However, his appreciation for the sightseeing they were being allowed to enjoy did not mitigate the anxiety he felt about the situation they were in. Kendrick and Wessel still had not learned anything new, and they had not been given any directives, which meant proceeding as planned with their original directive. But where would that place them? What, if anything, had changed in areas they had no control over? Cameron realized that constantly changing variables were a factor in any operation, but this particular instance drove that anxiety and frustration home more than he had anticipated. This one would place them directly in harm's way in

East Berlin and not simply by possibly having a cover exposed, but by ending up in a Stasi jail, if they were lucky, or quite possibly dead.

He thought about all of the times that the reality of being killed in the line of duty had seemed to merely lick at their toes while it washed over the ones around them. Dwyer was the first one, a skilled and capable agent, murdered at close range by someone he knew. Then there were all those people in Seattle, from Boney Jack to Doug's girlfriend and her family and, Cameron recalled with a shudder, nearly him as well. Absentmindedly, he flexed his right hand, the one smashed the night he was captured. It had taken him months to get over the injury and longer to get over being a prisoner. Still, to this day, things would trigger a memory and bother him, though, for some inexplicable reason, not on this trip.

They arrived at the venue and began unloading their gear. Kendrick had often complained about the band assisting the roadies, as it did not complement the image that the German press had been trying to create of American rock stars.

"If they see you unloading your equipment, they think you're not one of the major players and they'll feel cheated," Kendrick explained. "The guys can handle it, and besides, each place has people on board to assist them. Stay out of the back of the truck."

To ensure that they complied, Kendrick arranged for their guitars to always accompany them in the car. Most of the time Evan used the drums provided by the venues, but they did have a set for him as a backup in the event the house sets ever proved unsatisfactory. So far on the tour, things had been perfectly acceptable, but they had reservations about what they would find in East Berlin.

Oh hell, yes, what will we find in East Berlin?

Cameron withdrew his guitar case from the trunk of the limousine, the familiar grip of the handle imbuing him with confidence once more. He was going to go through with his assignment, of that there had never been any question, but as he seemed to get his second wind, it became obvious that what little time he'd had for any type of anxiety over it was long gone. They were in Hannover, the next stop was Berlin, and after that, the jaws of the beast.

This ain't no party, this ain't no disco, this ain't no fooling around. Yes, Mr. Byrne, you are right. This is life during wartime.

Inside he was greeted with the usual activity of trying to find out where the entrances were for the equipment, where they were supposed to set up, where the band was to change, etc. Cameron was always reminded of a hen yard. The crews, the roadies, and the engineers all rushing about trying to get things done and establishing their spot in the pecking order; the traveling roadies working to ensure their positions are respected and the ones who work at the venue struggling to accomplish the same thing. In the background were the managers, strutting like the proverbial rooster. Occasionally they would bark an order like a rooster crowing at noon for no apparent reason, and usually accomplishing the same end—letting everyone know they were present but contributing nothing to the situation. However, after a few minutes, everything would inevitably settle down into a routine that enabled the show to go on.

This will be just like all the other setups, except with a German accent.

"Mr. Walsh, I am so glad that I found you" came a pleasant voice. Cameron turned to find Elsa Scholl waiting for him.

"Well, hello there," he said and smiled.

Don't look too friendly; remember the other time.

"I was hoping to get a few moments with you, if you don't mind," she said.

"Well, I really need to be getting to the stage and getting started." He smiled, raising his guitar cases for her to see and hoping she took the polite hint. She didn't.

"I can assure you, I won't be long." She smiled back, pleasantly.

Cameron was suspicious, considering their earlier interaction, but realized that Kendrick expected him to ensure there would be no additional tensions.

"Okay then," he said, surrendering to the inevitable. "Lead on!"

Elsa led him down the corridor to a small office and then closed the door after they were inside.

"First, let me start by apologizing for my behavior the other day," she said. "I could just as easily have brushed off your advances with a smile as with a snarl. I'm sorry that I chose the latter."

"I understand, and I appreciate that," Cameron replied. "I'm sorry my personality seemed to have had that effect on you. I assure you, it wasn't intentional."

"Very well." Elsa smiled. "Now that we've gotten our apologies out of the way, I was wondering if we might have a talk?"

Cameron nodded.

"I'm certain you've learned about Krug."

"Yes, I have. Have they discovered any more details?" he asked. Reluctant to discuss something this sensitive in an area he was not entirely certain was secure, Cameron decided to keep his remarks broad and not specific.

"None, I'm afraid," she replied. "Have you received any further instructions?"

Ah, we seem to be on the same page.

"Only that the show must go on." He smiled. "I know that Kendrick met with Eberhard, his assistant, but no one has provided any further details about anything."

Elsa nodded as she considered what Cameron told her. Her intense expression and lack of response caused him to think he had misspoken, but her sudden smile broke the tension.

"Of course," she replied. "There has been no change in anything; therefore, there is no reason to change anything."

Cameron smiled and nodded in agreement but wondered at her odd reaction.

"Is there anything else?" he asked.

"No, nothing." She smiled again. "I was only wondering if you had been brought up to date on the situation."

"I have a good manager," he assured her as he opened the door. "If I need to know anything, she will see to it that I do. Now, if you'll excuse me, I have to go get set up."

Before she could respond, he stepped out into the hallway and headed toward the stage.

Cameron had no idea why she would make such a point to

apologize for something so trivial and then be so concerned about information she no doubt already had. Something seemed odd to him, but he put it out of his mind. She was their contact here. She had been thoroughly vetted by the West Germans and his own people. She was cleared, he told himself. Still, he remained unsettled. He tried to convince himself that he was just dealing with residual nerves about the operation, but he was hardly surprised when his concerns didn't abate.

Always trust your gut, old boy. But what the hell are you going to do about it?

At the stage he helped oversee the setup of the monitors and the sound system. The familiarity of this routine was what he needed at the moment. The unraveling of cords, the initial feedback when they turned on the microphones, and the familiar sounds and sights of every stage he had ever been on was like a balm to him—soothing, comforting and assuring. He took a deep breath and slowly released it, feeling his tensions slip away. Opening his guitar case, he selected his favorite and, after plugging it in, began the customary semaphore hand signaling to the engineer in the sound booth indicating if something needed to be turned up or down. He didn't worry if it were Casey in the booth or not, these things were a universal language.

The band was halfway through their setup when Cameron noticed someone out of the corner of his eye and heard the familiar click and whir of a camera. Wessel moved to the front of the stage, and Cameron fought the sense of annoyance that came at the sight of the photographer.

He's supposed to be on our side, too, remember?

"Well, what's new?" Cameron asked.

Wessel's eyes widened and he looked about nervously. "Not so loud," he whispered.

"What, you don't anyone to hear me asking how you are?" Cameron snorted. "Fine then, piss off! Is that better?"

"There's no need to be testy!" the photographer protested.

"Then quit being such a pain in the ass!" Cameron barked. "I simply asked you how you were and you suddenly get all mysterious. Fine, if I'm asking you something the wrong way, I just won't bother talking to you! Does that work?"

The photographer gaped at him as did some of the other band members. No one understood why Cameron reacted the way he had, and frankly, neither did Cameron.

"Look, let's get back to work and get this wrapped up," he muttered. "It was a long drive and I'd like to get some shut-eye before the show."

The band returned to their routine, though with less enthusiasm than previously. When they were finished, Cameron arranged for a ride to their hotel. He did not ask if anyone else wanted to go with him; he was tired and wanted to be alone.

I hope the hell Kendrick got us checked in.

To his relief, she had. She was also waiting for him when he arrived.

"I hope you have a minute," she said.

He nodded in agreement, knowing full well that resistance was futile.

"Let's talk up in the suite," she said, leading the way. Once they arrived, she turned on the television and began to ask about the incident at the hall.

"Why did you bite his head off?" Her folded arms and stern expression reminded Cameron of a schoolteacher, and it was this notion that made him reach his limit.

"Because it was easier than knocking him on his goddamned ass," he snapped.

"There is absolutely no reason ..." she began, but Cameron cut her off.

"There is every reason," Cameron shouted. "This bullshit comes to an end *now*! If things are so delicate that a simple question as to how someone is doing makes them freak the hell out, then things are too delicate to continue. Pull the plug on this thing, end the tour, and go home!"

"Cameron," she said in a voice that was intended to be calming and soothing. In light of the circumstances, however, it was patronizing and further infuriated him.

"Don't waste your breath," he warned. "This isn't Rutland, this isn't Burlington, this isn't Seattle, and I'm not some raw recruit and neither are the others. If we were, none of us would be doing this and you know it! We're all experienced enough to know that the way you draw attention to yourself is by panicking every time you think someone has exposed you. I asked that dipstick how he was, pure and simple, and you would have thought I had shone a spotlight on him and detailed everything! I'm telling you right now that I've had enough of this walking on eggshells around you people."

"What on earth are you talking about?" she demanded.

"That idiot photographer jumps at every sound, and that so-called reporter can't make up her mind if she wants to be a Rhine maiden or Ilsa the She-Wolf of the SS, and you are getting worked up when I'm sick and tired of everyone's mind games. Like I said, if everything is as delicate as you say, then you had all better start acting like it because you're all behaving like high school kids trying to skip class!"

"How dare you! Do I need to remind you that we're all trained professionals?"

"Apparently, yes, you do," Cameron barked. "Because for the first time since I've known you, a damned cover band has its shit together more than the rest of you! I'm serious. I've had it. If things are too much for you, then put me on the first plane back to the States right now. I'm here to do my job, and that is what I am doing, playing music. That is what the rest of them are doing, too, by the way. The only flies in the ointment are the rest of you!"

"You need to understand that Krug's death has really upset a lot of things," Kendrick explained.

"I can imagine it has," Cameron agreed. "But, if it has upset things to the point that everyone is jumping at every single mouse fart, you need to eighty-six this before the body count starts mounting!"

Kendrick was about to reply when she held up her hands in

surrender. "You're right," she conceded. "You're absolutely right on all points. I'm sorry."

"Never mind that," Cameron grumbled. "Exactly what is going on and what are we going to do?"

"Well, for starters, it should come as no surprise that we've uncovered more information surrounding Krug's death."

"A double agent," Cameron said. It was a statement, not a question.

"Correct, but do you mind explaining to me how you know that?"

"I figured that out as soon as you told me how the accident happened, due to cut brake lines. When you mentioned that Stasi had agents here in the West, and in the BND, it seemed obvious that that was how it happened."

"How far do you think the double agent's reach went?"

"They've probably been watching Krug forever," Cameron snapped. "He said as much when he said he couldn't be too public on this tour because of the attention he'd attract. It's simple: they saw a chance and took it."

"As elementary as they are, your deductions are nonetheless accurate," Kendrick allowed. "However, there is something you're overlooking."

"What is that?"

"While it is true they'd had Krug in their sights for years, it was actually this particular mission that signed his death warrant."

"How the hell do you know that?" Cameron asked, the familiar sick feeling returning.

"They aren't the only ones to have double agents, dear one," she said. "Ours have been reporting back to us details of what we're doing here."

"Exactly how much do they know?" Cameron asked, his mouth dry.

"I'm afraid just about everything."

"You're shitting me, right?"

"Oh, how I wish I was," she sighed.

"Let's just back up for a second," Cameron said. "You said 'just about everything.' What exactly have we discovered about what they know?"

"They know our itinerary for starters," she replied.

"That's really not surprising, considering we had to fully disclose it," he reminded her. "Both concert venues and cities, remember?"

"I remember," she assured him. "However, they also know all of our hotel information and some things that we only talked about in DC."

"Like what?"

"Like Doug," she explained. "His name is still on their radar, it seems."

"Do you think he's the double agent?" Cameron asked.

The question seemed foreign to him, as if someone else had spoke the words using his own vocal cords. However, he was not shocked by it. Things were too close and too dangerous now to be moved by sentiment. Yes, he had known Doug for years and had proof of his courage and loyalty, but he also knew that his roadie always seemed to be connected to these covert investigations. Was there truly fire where there was smoke?

"No, all of this information is coming from here in Germany, both west and east," she assured him. "He is just the one who has triggered their attention."

"Do they know about anything else?" Cameron pressed.

"Apparently, someone else has also attracted their attention."

"Who?" Cameron doubted strongly that either he or Evan would be blown; their work had been largely outside of anything involving espionage. However, that was no guarantee. He was concerned, however, that Kendrick would be known, given her involvement with counterintelligence work with the bureau. He was not prepared for the name she gave him.

"Ed Collier," she said.

"What? What the hell would they want to look at him for? He's a guitarist for Christ's sake!"

"Oh, how well he fits his cover." She laughed. "Even you forgot!"

Cameron felt his face burn. Ed Collier's name was part of his legend as a musician and substitute for their former band member. In his real life, Collier was known by another name and had a career in army intelligence.

"Did the blush start from my neck and gradually go up?" he muttered sheepishly.

"Nope," she said and smirked. "Bright red from the start, just like a traffic light."

"Appropriate," he moaned. "So why are they interested in him? Do you think it has anything to do with what he, uh, does on the side?"

"That, we really have no idea," she confided. "It is just that, of the entire band, he and Doug are the ones whose names come up most in the chatter that we listen in on and what our contacts are revealing."

"Do you think Ed's a mole?"

"He was carefully vetted from the beginning and practically handpicked for this job. I would need a lot of evidence to believe it," she protested.

"That doesn't necessarily mean anything," Cameron pointed out.

"What is that supposed to mean?"

"Jesus picked Judas; look how that turned out."

"I hardly think this is comparable," she said. "Besides, the type of information that we're hearing comments on and is being reported comes from pretty high up, things that were not even discussed with you."

"Then that means someone at the top is the possible leak!"

"I'm afraid so," she agreed

"Then wouldn't it make sense to shit-can everything and go home?" Cameron demanded.

"That would be the expected reaction, yes."

"But, I take it, that is not what we're going to be doing?"

Kendrick shook her head.

"Please tell me there is at least a logical explanation for why not," he pleaded.

"Several," she sighed. "First, we really don't know how much they do or do not know. If we cut our losses and run, it will only tip our hand that we know they have someone. They will likely roll up whatever network they are running for this, and we'll never know who or where the leak was. Second, we know that they are aware we're here as part of something. We don't know for certain if they know about anything else or not. If we leave now, we could be putting something else in jeopardy."

"So business as usual then?" Cameron asked.

"Not quite," she replied. "Now we need to try to find out who might be the leak."

"Any suspects yet?"

"To be honest, everyone," she admitted. "Moscow rules, remember."

"Trust no one," he sighed. "I admit that might be the most elementary approach, but I do think we need to have a more specified focus."

"I take it you already have some people in mind?" she asked, without a trace of surprise.

"Oh, hell yeah," he admitted. "Wessel, first of all, if you want to know the truth. I don't like the way he is always trying to put himself in everything and make himself indispensable. The fact that he has access to our suites is also something I do not like one bit!"

"I have taken care of that, haven't I?" she protested.

Cameron nodded.

"Yes, but we still have to deal with him," he grumbled.

"There's nothing I can do about that. He's part of this assignment, and that didn't come from me."

"Fine, but there's still the reporter to consider."

"Elsa?" Kendrick exclaimed. "She's a senior operative of theirs, highly placed and highly regarded. Just because she didn't fall for the famous Cameron Walsh charm doesn't mean she's working for the other side."

"It's the way she keeps asking questions," he insisted.

"She's a reporter! That's what she's supposed to do."

"I'm not talking about questions about the band or the tour; I'm talking about when she takes us aside and starts asking questions about what we know about what's going on."

"When has she done that?" Kendrick asked, obviously surprised.

"Well, she just did that with me today," he explained. "I haven't found out yet if she's done that with any of the others."

"Let me investigate that," Kendrick told him, "though I believe even that has a logical explanation."

"Which is?"

"Eberhard told me that they're looking for the leak as well," she said.

"That's another one, Eberhard," Cameron snapped. "He just showed up suddenly out of nowhere, taking over Krug's spot."

"It was hardly that sudden," Kendrick replied. "We've been in contact with Krug and Eberhard from the very beginning. When Krug showed the photos, he was bringing the rest of you up to speed, not me."

Cameron said nothing, but Kendrick could see he was not convinced.

"You realize that you have just put our entire West German contingent on your list of suspects?" she asked.

"Along with almost half the band," he sighed. "I can see the expediency behind those Moscow rules. It's easier to not trust anyone."

Chapter 32

"We're Not Gonna Take It"

Hertz could barely stop himself from slamming down the phone in frustration. Fuchs continued to speak, but Hertz could no longer register the words. It droned on like so much banality.

"Are you listening to me?" Fuchs demanded, sensing a lapse in his subordinate's attention.

"Yes sir, I'm listening," Hertz assured him. He could only hope that he sounded convincing.

"Then, what do you think of my plan?" his senior demanded.

"I think that what you are proposing is both extremely risky and possibly unnecessary. Surely I can't be the only member of this agency available for this?"

"No, but you are the only one who would be able to successfully take advantage of the situation under your circumstances."

"Exactly what circumstances are you referring to?"

"The boy," Fuchs spat, his dislike for the young man under his charge unmistakable.

"How is that going to help? This isn't a children's show! It's a rock concert. We've had people monitoring this demographic for years; we have agents already in place who have been following the movements of groups like this for a long time. They will already be placed in the audience, they have already established a presence, and they will not draw attention to themselves. I have not been to any of these events since being transferred to your office and will hardly be able to blend in effectively. Having to monitor Mikhail will be even more of an additional constraint to any possible surveillance you want me to do."

"Your previous experience with our agents monitoring this segment of the population is the other reason I expect you to do this. Your knowledge of who they are will be an asset in establishing a security perimeter to prevent them from attempting anything," Fuchs warned.

"What exactly is it that you think they are going to attempt to do?" Hertz insisted. "What are we supposed to be watching for if we don't know what it is they are going to attempt?"

"We have received intelligence from our KGB comrades that this concert is being held in conjunction with another operation," Fuchs explained.

"Another operation here?"

"That is not something to be revealed except on a need-to-know basis," Fuchs snapped. "You are to be *there*, and to ensure that in the event they attempt anything extraordinary, your agents will be able to respond instantly. That is all you need to know!"

"You said the event was going to be held at the Gendarmenmarkt," Hertz protested. "There will be an abundance of Vopo present, and there are numerous other agents who run these networks that will also be there."

"Comrade, I don't think I am making myself clear," Fuchs said, the icy calm of his voice coming over the phone. "You are a senior agent and the one that I want there, and I want you to participate in the function they have afterward. Monitor it closely for anything resembling suspicious activities. Keep the boy with you; say he is your brother or some such excuse. Having him there would be less suspicious than a single man on his own, even in that degenerate mob."

Hertz sneered into the receiver at Fuchs's attitude, so typical of his generation.

"As you wish, comrade," Hertz said finally. "I will make

arrangements to be there. Should I contact any of my former network?"

"Yes, absolutely," Fuchs replied. The undisguised joy in the senior agent's voice at his victory over Hertz nearly made the younger man slam the phone down once more. "Coordinate your efforts and objectives and report any findings back to me."

With that, the older man hung up, leaving not only the dial tone but also the dangling question in Hertz's ear. What objective? What did Fuchs expect to have done except to have his subordinates, once again, sort out his idiocy? Hertz realized that he was still holding the receiver in his hand, so tightly that his arm was trembling. He replaced it before letting loose with a stream of profanity, as there was no way of knowing who might have been listening on the other end.

With each word, he gave vent to his increasing frustrations, not only with his assignment but also with his life in general. He recalled driving through the towns in the countryside, seeing the buildings painted only halfway up the fronts because that was the only part visible to Honecker and his cronies from the backseats of their cars. Carefully constructed fantasies in the face of crushing realities. Fuchs was cut from that mold, and his cognitive dissonance was affecting his judgment. Like the production figures that were boasted over East German media, vague wording was used to suggest an atmosphere of competence and success, when the truth was hardly as ambiguous. Increased factory output never materialized into increased standard of living, no matter how many percentages egg production had increased over previous periods.

"You want me to coordinate efforts and objectives?" Hertz grumbled aloud. But he didn't vocalize the opinions that he shouted silently in his mind. He never said those aloud. Someone might be listening. Someone was always listening.

Hertz paced the room of his parents' home, trying to figure something out. It was obvious to anyone that the appearance of an American band in East Berlin was quite likely not simply a publicity appearance. But what was behind it then? It couldn't simply be to contact an agent in East Berlin. On both sides of the wall, the city was so filled with agents that if they all suddenly disappeared, Berlin would be nearly deserted. Information from the West was limited to him in his current assignment, but it was reasonable to conclude that this group would not simply be performing in East Berlin. There would be performances in other cities; there always were. However, East Berlin was the only city scheduled in East Germany, so on that basis alone, there were some grounds for Fuchs's suspicions, other than geriatric paranoia. A glance at the clock reminded Hertz that he needed to be at the hospital for the daily briefing with the doctors.

Mikhail was long past the point of danger, yet the hospital complied with Stasi demand that he be kept for observation. Hertz sympathized with them, to a point. It was clear from their detailed reports and briefings that they were as adept as anyone else in East German society at taking nothing and contorting it to suggest something. He could only assume that these meetings were as tedious for them as for him. At least today there would be good news that might provide everyone with relief.

However, that news would have to wait, he decided as he rushed out the door. An idea began to form, and he needed to pursue it as quickly as possible. The weather was pleasant and even managed to minimize some of the bleakness of the East Berlin neighborhood. Hertz's family did possess some influence in the East German government, however, not enough to achieve residence in the more affluent neighborhoods of the ruling elite. His parents, die-hard Communists from the days of the Nazi regime, did not complain about the situation, but Hertz resented it. Today, the resentment burned harsher than ever. It was he who was doing all of the work for an out-of-touch superior with delusions of infallibility so common to his position and generation. Small citations with intricate wording might assuage the insecurities of his parents' Socialist belief system, but it was having less and less of an effect on him.

Hertz had been spending the past several weeks playing nursemaid to a dilemma of his superiors' own creation, accomplishing nothing other than to give them the satisfaction of having a focus of criticism whenever they were being criticized. Now Fuchs, in his senile delirium, had come to the conclusion that there legitimately was a problem, as yet unnamed and unidentified, that Hertz was now required to identify and address. Hertz thrust his hands deeper into his pockets as he realized that if he were able to achieve that objective, Fuchs would claim the credit. And if he were not, he alone would bear the responsibility.

"Very well then," he muttered as he stormed down the sidewalk. He had considered taking his car, but he knew it would be unwise to use up his gasoline for traveling in the city, if it could be at all helped. As a member of the Stasi, he was able to gain some access to things before civilians, but if what he wanted was unavailable, his position did not matter much. He spat on the ground in anger, as if to get rid of the distaste of his situation. The public transit that was available finally reached the destination he had been looking for: a seedier than usual section of East Berlin, still bearing the marks of bombing from the Second World War. Now, however, tendrils of ivy and bushes covered the rubble, lending it an aura of deliberate cultivation. To Hertz, it seemed as obscene a delusion as anything else in East Berlin. However, as tantalizing as it was to ruminate on these feelings, he needed to be focused on the task at hand.

Various individuals with tattered clothes, heavy boots, and wild hair filled the area, yet these were not derelicts but members of the growing counterculture movement of East German youth. The Honecker government was intensely suspicious of this demographic and spent a great deal of time monitoring them. Hertz had spent some time here before being transferred to his department, and he still had contacts among them, one of which he noticed leaning against an old fence pole—a tall fellow with wild, bleached hair and tight-fitting clothes. Approaching him directly was out of the question. Hertz was clearly out of place here, and for him to approach the other person would expose him and jeopardize an extensive network of internal surveillance. Instead Hertz relied on his old signals.

Making eye contact with the person he wanted to speak to, he shook a cigarette from its pack, lit it, and exhaled in the person's direction. The other fellow began to rub his chin. To anyone else, it suggested that he was thinking of something, but Hertz recognized it as the counter sign. Hertz gave the all clear by appearing to watch something off in the distance, though he heard the distinctive shuffle of the other man's approach. If he had walked up deliberately, it meant that he was unable to talk and Hertz would brusquely rebuff him. However, a shuffled approach meant that everything was fine.

"Do you have another one of those?" the man asked, pointing to Hertz's cigarette. Without a word, the Stasi agent offered him one.

"You don't look like you belong here," the man stated, perching it behind his ear.

Hertz shrugged. "I was looking for someone and ended up here," he explained.

"Well, what do they look like?"

Hertz gave a general description of a woman's build and height, while the other man provided details.

"Does she have dark, spiked hair and wear a leather jacket?" he asked, signaling to Hertz what the woman's appearance now consisted of.

Hertz nodded. "Have you seen her?"

"Not lately," the man replied. "However, I know where she sometimes hangs out, and I'll be glad to take you there."

"No thanks," Hertz explained. "I have to be somewhere else, but can you give her a message for me?"

The other man nodded.

"Tell her to meet her brother at our favorite spot on Karl-Marx-Allee at four o'clock. She'll know where that is."

"Stalin's toilet at four o'clock," the man repeated. "Got it."

Hertz said nothing at the derogatory term the man used to refer to the street. When Karl-Marx-Allee had originally been constructed during the Soviet occupation, it was known as Stalinalle and many of the buildings had been fronted with tiles. While this beautification was intended to be a tribute to the Soviet dictator and ensure that the buildings on this avenue did not resemble the tired-looking buildings of the rest of the city, it instead had the effect of resembling public restrooms. As a result, it was sometimes referred to as Stalin's toilet.

Even after the East German government renamed it Karl-Marx-Allee, the name remained and was frequently used by the more antiestablishment elements, of which Hertz now found himself in the midst of.

"Yes, Karl-Marx-Allee," Hertz repeated, emphasizing the proper title to avoid attracting attention of any informants in the crowd. "Tell her to meet me at our favorite place at four o'clock."

The man nodded once more, indicating that he had received the message and the warning.

Without saying anything else, Hertz turned and walked back the way he had come. He didn't bother glancing at his watch. He was hopelessly late for his meeting at the hospital, but he didn't care. His mood was improving as the earlier nucleus of an idea began to take shape. Hertz knew that very soon he would be rid of this annoying burden.

Chapter 33

"When You Close Your Eyes"

When the door opened, Alexi realized that in the darkness he had been sitting with it to his left side. Though muted, the sudden light still took a moment for him to adjust to. He realized his vulnerability and turned to face the sudden opening.

"Do not be alarmed" came the familiar voice. "It is time to go."

"That was quick," Alexi muttered, seething from being caught dealing with his own anxiety.

"Hardly," the man replied. "You do not realize it, but you have been in here over an hour and a half. Secure and comfortable while your apartment was ransacked. I trust you had nothing of any sentimental value there?"

"Certainly not," Alexi replied indignantly, his professional pride returning.

"That is probably just as well," the man said. "It wouldn't be there anymore, anyhow. Here, I have something for you." The man handed Alexi a large paper bag. In it were a complete change of clothes, glasses, a hat, and another small bag.

"You need to change your clothes, yes, even your underclothes," the man explained. "I'm sure that comes as no surprise to you. Nor should the need for urgency."

Alexi nodded and began to remove his shirt. He paused for a moment, glancing at the man.

"I'm also certain it comes as no surprise that we will be ensuring you have no concealed weapons or listening devices."

Slightly chagrined, Alexi continued to disrobe, tossing each item of clothing out into the garage to be retrieved and searched by one of the others. When all of his clothes were removed, he began to put on the ones from the bag.

"Some of them are the correct size, but others will be slightly larger," the man explained. "You are now Vladimir Gagarin, a Russian tourist, originally from Arkhangelsk. You work in the docks, unloading ships. You are a recent widower with no children. Your father was killed in the liberation of Danzig in 1945, and you are here to visit the site of the battle. That is the reason you are here: to visit the location of your father's death and have the comfort of some family connection."

The man waited until Gagarin repeated the legend that he had been given. The other man emphasized the few corrections that Gagarin needed to know and watched as he put on his clothes. The shirt was the correct size but with one arm slightly longer than the other. The trousers were loose fitting. Gagarin buttoned the shirt and attempted to put on his tie, but the collar was too tight.

"Leave the top button undone," the man advised. "Just put on your tie and pull it up as far as you are able."

Gagarin did as he was directed, and when he was finished, the other man handed him a pair of scuffed shoes with worn soles. Gagarin could see that they had been polished and buffed, and inside one or two of the tacks were poking through.

"You are of very modest means," the man explained. "But you still take pride in your appearance, despite the butter stain on your tie from your meal of perogies this evening. Your right arm is slightly smaller, due to an injury that prevents you from working. You have used your few savings to make this trip. Now sit down while we alter your appearance."

Gagarin sat while one of the other men applied a false mustache and small sideburns to his face. As the adhesive was drying, the man brushed Gagarin's hair, parting it from the other side, slicking it down with gel. When he had finished, the man dabbed gray powder onto Gagarin's sideburns and eyebrows, giving him the appearance of being slightly past middle age, an impression complemented by the black-rimmed glasses.

"You will also need these," the man said, handing him the smaller bag. Gagarin knew that it would contain his "litter," which were the items that helped lend credibility to his legend. There were a handful of Polish zlotys, the local currency, as well as a damaged Russian passport with a crease going through part of the photo, which Gagarin suspected aided in its resemblance to him. The passport also had the "propiska" or work-related passport stamp, which as a resident of Arkhangelsk he was required to possess. There was an almost empty pack of Russian cigarettes and a nearly empty matchbook with the name of a local restaurant on it, as well as a piece of paper with the address of a hotel. There were a few Russian and Polish coins, and some lint. The billfold had another Russian ID card, creased and faded photos, and nothing else. The billfold was old and some of the stitching was unraveling.

"Put this on," the man said, handing him a light overcoat, smelling of cigarettes and vodka. Gagarin knew that it was not to fend off the cold or rain, but that it would help to conceal any of the features of his build. As he was fitting into it, the man once more asked him various questions about himself. This time, Gagarin answered all of them correctly.

"When the building was being searched, it appeared that the ones doing the searching became quite worked up at not finding you," the man explained. His voice exhibited the same calm, disinterested tone that he had always shown. "This resulted in a great deal of shouting and checking surrounding apartments. Oddly, their search was confined to your floor and predictably turned up nothing. But it is amazing how something as simple as discovering a side door to the stairs leading to the back entrance being left ajar can divert all attention. They left the premises some time ago; however, you and I both know that there is still likely to be some surveillance on the building. Therefore, we will leave by the garage door and walk to the car that is waiting for us. Please do not attempt to draw any attention to yourself, or us, as I will then be forced to take drastic measures. I'm certain you understand what I mean? Before we leave, please take a drink of this."

Gagarin nodded and took the offered bottle of vodka and then followed the man, discovering that his shoes caused him to limp slightly. He noted, with professional appreciation, the attention to detail they displayed. They made their way up to the main entrance of the building and stepped out into the street. There were few cars and fewer people. As they stepped through the door, Gagarin looked across the street to the alley but noticed no one. They made their way along the sidewalk as the other man carried on a banal conversation, leaving Gagarin ample opportunities for answering yes, or no, or some other noncommittal response. They had been undetected thus far, and Gagarin was daring to hope that they would remain so when he heard footsteps coming up behind them.

"Halt, please" came the command in Polish, not Russian. Gagarin became alert but did as he was told, as did his companion.

"Will you please let me see your identification?" they were ordered, and Gagarin was able to get a close look at who was speaking. There were two men, both in plain clothes, but Gagarin suspected they were part of Poland's secret police, the MBP, and not regular police officers. Both Gagarin and his companion handed over their passports and identification, The first man looked at them and then handed Gagarin's to the other plainclothesman, confirming Gagarin's suspicions.

"Will you please state your business for being out on the streets at this hour?" the plainclothesman demanded.

Gagarin, his feet increasingly uncomfortable in his shoes, shifted from one leg to the other and looked at his companion for a response.

"We're just coming from a friend's house," he explained. "We met at a restaurant and went back to our friend's house for a few drinks."

"Gdansk is a long way from Arkhangelsk," the plainclothesman said to Gagarin, ignoring the other man. "What are you doing here?"

"I came to see where my father died," Gagarin responded. "He was a soldier in the Red Army and died at the battle of Danzig."

"When was that?"

"March 30, 1945," Gagarin answered.

"How does a Russian know a Pole?"

"At the restaurant, I was asking about the battle of Danzig," Gagarin explained. "This man and his friend knew about the battle and we struck up a conversation."

"Our parents lived here under the Nazis, and my father died in a Nazi prison," the other man explained.

"What was the number of the apartment you were visiting?" Gagarin's companion responded.

"There was an incident earlier this evening at the building you left," the plainclothesman explained. "Were you aware of this?"

Both men responded in the negative, insisting he must be mistaken.

"There was no commotion in our building," the man said

The plainclothesman was about to reply when his companion leaned in to whisper something. Gagarin recognized the Russian accent to the second man's Polish but was still able to make out what he was saying; he was explaining that the apartment number they provided was on the ground floor, and the apartments searched were on the second floor. The first man snorted in response and handed the documents back to the other men.

"Where are you staying while you are here?"

While trying to remember the name, Gagarin swayed on his feet in an effort to keep the shoe tacks from poking the soles and then fumbled in his pocket with his left hand for the slip of paper, which he showed to the plainclothesman. As the police officer took it, Gagarin gave a small burp and the smell of vodka greeted his nose.

"I am sorry to have detained you, gentlemen," the man replied, returning their IDs without smiling. "I hope you have a good evening."

As they left, Gagarin heard the officer make a derogatory remark in Polish, but they continued up the street unmolested. At the next corner, they turned down a side street and Gagarin's companion removed a set of keys and unlocked a car near the corner. Gagarin paused to look inside before he opened the door, relieved to see that there was no one inside. The man pulled onto the street and headed into the darkness, driving at a speed that would not attract attention.

"These shoes are killing me," Gagarin muttered, kicking them off.

"Other people have worse problems," the other man said, and that was the only thing he said for the duration of their drive.

Gagarin had numerous questions but had sufficient experience to realize that his companion wouldn't say anything; they were mutually distrustful of each other. The car drove through the dark streets of Gdansk until it reached a stockyard near the docks. There, the driver approached a side gate and was waved through. They wove their way through the alleys between the buildings until they reached one with its doors open and drove in, the doors closing behind them.

"You can change your clothes now," the man said, motioning for Gagarin to follow him. He led him to a small office on the other side of the warehouse, where a mechanic's jumpsuit was waiting for him.

"Empty your pockets and leave everything here," the man said. "Now hurry, you have a plane to catch."

"What about my face?" Gagarin asked.

"It is one only a mother could love," the man replied mirthlessly. "Leave the glasses behind. That will be sufficient to alter your appearance."

Gagarin quickly slipped out of the old clothes, resisting the urge to toss the painful shoes across the room. He quickly put on the jumpsuit and a pair of work boots. They were grimy and filthy, but Gagarin knew that they were also believable and vital, so he forced himself to ignore his reluctance and put them on. The boots were, indeed, more comfortable than the shoes, and as he was tying the last boot, the door opened and his companion impatiently motioned for Gagarin to follow him.

Outside the office, he noticed two other men dressed as he was, though his companion was still wearing the same clothes as before.

"You will go with them," he said, motioning to the two other men. "I wish you good luck."

The other men motioned for Gagarin to follow them and led him outside to a battered van.

"Get in and pull that tarp over you," the man said.

Gagarin climbed into the back of the van and saw a large oilcloth bunched up in the corner. Clearing himself a spot on the floor, he pulled the tarp over him, as directed, and made himself as comfortable as possible. As the van drove off, Gagarin felt each bump and pothole they passed over and grew nauseous from the exhaust fumes that made their way up through the floorboards. He did not know how long they drove, but eventually the bumps became fewer and he suspected that they were now going through the city. Finally, the van drew to a halt and he heard the two in the front mutter to each other. The smell of fresh air suggested that they had opened the window. A guard offered a tired greeting and made disinterested inquiries as to their health and families, to which the two men made equally disinterested replies. The van began to move once more, and Gagarin knew they had gone through some kind of a checkpoint.

Since they were not traveling fast, Gagarin suspected they were in a lot of some kind. The window of the van was still open, and he was grateful for the fresh air. As the van slowed, he heard the whine of an engine and recognized it as one belonging to an airplane. The van stopped, and he heard the door open. Before he could move, the tarp was pulled back and he found himself staring up at one of the workmen who had ridden with them. He was holding a gun.

"Come with us, comrade," he said and smiled.

Chapter 34

"Perfect Strangers"

Cameron knew the look on Kendrick's face; he had seen it many times before in his dealings with her. The only consolation he had was that neither he nor any of their team were the cause of it. However, he did suspect that it came as a result of circumstances surrounding this case, as she had just had a private meeting with Eberhard and had been moody ever since. Cameron wanted to ask her how it went, and wanted to know what directions they had been given and what the focus of their operation would be now, but he knew that to pester her would be a mistake.

Kendrick was a professional; she was methodical, reasonable, and intuitive. He had once made the mistake of playing chess with her and lost, soundly. Afterward he realized that the reason she had won was because she did not take the customary advice of thinking two or three moves ahead. She focused on winning and worked backward from that. If she was considering something, it meant that there was still something to be done.

She'll tell me when she's ready.

"Eberhard says they've lost the target," she muttered as if she had read his thoughts.

"What target?" Cameron asked. "Krug's killer?"

"I wish it were that simple," she sighed. "No, they've lost contact with the secondary target of our operation."

"That kid?"

"He was hurried out of the school where he was being housed a few nights ago, and no one knows where he is," she explained.

"Do you think that it has anything to do with Krug's death?" he wondered.

She nodded. "That is a distinct possibility. It apparently happened the night he died."

"Can we reasonably assume that the mission has been compromised?"

"That is a delightful gray area that no one seems to be able, or willing, to navigate through," she moaned. "I asked the same thing, and apparently, so did Washington, London, Bonn, and nearly all points in between."

"So, what do we do then?"

"As I already said, right now we're to do exactly what we were sent here to do, and that is to play music," she told him, flopping down into a chair.

"But if the kid is gone, there's no point," Cameron protested. "Wasn't that the entire point of us being here?"

"Calm down, cowboy," she replied. "*We're* just here to be a distraction for whatever else the big boys are planning to do. We are playing to our strengths and their suspicions; that is why we've got an American cover band making an appearance in East Berlin, where it is wildly popular with the East German counterculture. As an added incentive, some of Doug's backstory had been resurrected to send out and see if it gets any nibbles, which it seems to be doing. We were never supposed to be the main operation, remember? I'm confident *that* aspect of things hasn't changed."

"Why would they have us go through with it then?"

"To show the East Germans that sometimes a cigar is just a cigar and a band is just a band," she said. "Make them feel foolish for getting worked up over nothing and lull them into a position where the mission could be reattempted later, under more propitious circumstances."

"Do you think that would be possible?"

"I don't know." She shrugged. "But let's face it, the D-Day invasion had a rain date, so anything is possible."

"So I guess just go ahead as planned and just focus on the tour is the best option after all."

"I should think that, in and of itself, would have sufficient reasons for concern for you," she replied. "It certainly does for me."

"Why you?"

"My functions as your manager aren't merely a front," she grumbled. "This is causing me a great deal of headaches as well. Nothing serious, mind you, mostly logistics and handling all of the public relations falderal."

"I never expected to hear you utter the word *falderal*." Cameron laughed. "But you can't get upset with us; the guys have been pretty well behaved this trip!"

"Hardly choir boys, but I concede that you haven't been peeing off balconies and swimming in hotel fountains," she said and smiled. "No, you are not the problem; it is just all of the niggling little details. I had forgotten how involved these tours can be. Add to that all of the various protocols required for being on a foreign tour and it gets worse."

"Toss in a few extracurricular elements for spice and it gets real interesting, doesn't it?"

"That would be a yes." She yawned, leaning back and closing her eyes.

"Well, then give yourself a break from the other stuff and focus on the tour like the rest of us," Cameron suggested.

"Lead me not into temptation," Kendrick warned. "I have to confess, though, that has been my secret fantasy lately."

"Oh, has it now?" Cameron smiled enthusiastically.

"Oh, you seriously think you invented it, don't you." She laughed, rolling her eyes.

Cameron waited a moment before asking the question that had been bothering him.

"Was there ever really a plan B?" he asked.

Kendrick did not respond, but from the drumming of her fingers, he knew she had heard.

"I told you and told you and told you, I suspect there is," she finally replied. "And if there is, it hasn't been shared with anyone at my level. But that is hardly surprising."

"Why?"

"Because we have a leak somewhere," she reminded him impatiently, sitting up and facing him. "Not just a small one, remember, but someone who knows exactly what we are doing and at a very high level. The plans for this were done in highly secure situations, with limited top-echelon personnel involved to prevent this very thing. Well, guess what? Somewhere along the way, someone was listening at a keyhole, it seems."

"I hate to seem like I'm beating a dead horse, but wouldn't it seriously be the wise thing to rethink this?"

"Well, that is what they're doing now," she explained. "And, while they are, the Roadhouse Sons are going to be continuing their tour, convincing anyone that might be watching us that everything is perfectly normal and there's nothing to see here. So please move along, folks, to buy time for the big boys to try to figure out what to do next."

"Well, when are we going to find out what they've decided?" Cameron demanded.

"Quite possibly never," Kendrick said. "Remember, even though you guys have done some things for us in the past, and even though some of you are not unfamiliar with this type of work, none of us has any experience with things on this level, not even me. And don't forget that we have two people who are civilians and not even supposed to be here at all."

"So it really does come back to this," he sighed. "Just shut up and play."

"You learn quickly, grasshopper." She smiled.

"Well, why not then?" he muttered. "I always wanted to go out with my music."

"Let's hope it doesn't come to that point," she replied.

"Why not?"

"Because the rest of us might have envisioned other final plans."

Chapter 35

"Midnight Maniac"

Hertz made his way along the street, looking for the meeting place. He was stepping a bit lighter than he had been this morning. The meeting at the hospital had gone better than expected. Yes, there was some disappointment at not having met at the correct time; however, that was mitigated by the news that they would soon be free of their troublesome patient by the next morning.

Before that could take place, however, Hertz needed to deal with certain logistical issues. The first was finding a place for them to stay. He knew that young Mikhail would test even his parents' party loyalty. Luckily, Fuchs was able to detail an apartment used for visitors that they could use until Mikhail needed to be transported back to the school. The second was meeting his contact.

He knew from the description given to him earlier that she would be sporting dark hair set into spikes with hair gel. Such a person would not be difficult to find in the midst of the more staid East Germans, and he was correct. He spotted her almost a full block away.

Margaret Engels had been a Stasi agent for several years. She had originally been recruited as an informant, but it was quickly realized that she would be invaluable as an agent to help them monitor the rock counterculture. The Stasi took advantage of the movement's desire to distance itself from anything resembling authority to help

Margaret re-create herself as Alina. Funds were allocated for a new wardrobe of cast-off clothing and odds and ends of jewelry and pins, as well as access to hair colors and wigs for her to use, though it was decided that the primary color would be black.

Hertz noticed that she saw him, as she gave the all clear by lighting a cigarette and exhaling straight up into the air. If there had been any difficulty, she would have blown the smoke in the direction of the impediment. To his relief, he did not have to worry about anything.

"Do you have another light?" he asked, indicating that he had not been followed. She offered it to him without saying a word. To the casual observer, her seemingly disinterested looking around was an attempt to ignore him and get him to leave. To the practiced observer, she was continuing her surveillance while he stated his business.

"I suppose you've heard about the upcoming performance by that American band," he said.

She shrugged and then nodded her head.

"They want you to be there," he told her.

"I had planned on it," she muttered, her tone dripping with the customary boredom of rebellious youth. Alina was always so natural in her insouciance that Hertz was never able to tell if it was genuine or affected, and he was always suspicious of it.

"They want me there as well," he told her.

That caught her attention and she turned to face him. "What the hell do they want you there for?" she asked and smiled.

"To coordinate objectives and efforts." He smiled back.

"With who?" she demanded.

"Apparently with the rest of you," he said and laughed. "Fuchs isn't certain of what we're supposed to be looking for, but he is wild that we be looking for it. He wants me to be present at the show and to participate in the function they are planning afterward."

"Why is he rabid about this in the first place, or you being part of this, all of a sudden?"

"He's convinced this is part of something bigger, but he's not certain of what," Hertz muttered. "Or, if he is certain, he isn't telling me. He expects me to figure it out and deal with it."

"So that's why I suddenly get the pleasure of your company then?" she sneered. "Well, if you're going to keep me here, I want one of those American cigarettes of yours."

"I have to save them," he warned, shaking out one for her. "I have to have them on hand to keep the brat quiet."

"No one is without burdens," she sighed disinterestedly, tucking the cigarette behind her ear. "You realize that the Americans are arriving tomorrow and their performance is tomorrow night? That doesn't give us much time for determining objectives, does it now?"

"I am aware of that," he confirmed. "So do you have any ideas about why they might be coming?"

"No, but I think it is entirely propaganda," she replied. "They want to show us how far the armistice has reached, with decadent Western music playing in the Konzerthaus Gendarmenmarkt, in the very capital of East Germany. They make a big fuss, get lots of pictures of East German youth wallowing in their degeneracy, and proclaim it a victory. Then they go home and no more is said about it."

"That's an awful lot of trouble and expense just for a propaganda victory," he teased.

"It is more expense than you think," she said. "You do realize that it isn't *in* the Konzerthaus, correct? They have to play in front of it, in an outdoor performance. You also realize that you can't charge for an outdoor performance? The entire show is a free expression of the arts for the youth of East Germany, courtesy of the East German government. Of course, the East German government isn't paying a mark for this."

"You mean, the Americans are paying for this?" Hertz gasped in disbelief.

"Hardly," Alina replied and laughed. "From what I've been told, they're simply making certain that the Americans don't get paid for it. However, they have made certain that the company promoting this event has paid for the security, the space, and all of the permits, expenses, and everything else connected with it. So, yes, it is going to be a costly propaganda victory for them. Just what our illustrious leadership would be willing to do to make the other side look foolish and get a shitload of hard currency."

Hertz smiled but didn't take the bait. It was too much of a temptation to get people to complain about the government and then inform certain ears that always itched to hear incriminating statements. Hertz had to remind himself that no one was safe.

"You know, I think I wouldn't mind this so much if I didn't have to bring that brat with me," he muttered.

"Why do you have to do that?"

Mikhail's reputation was such that nearly everyone in the Stasi knew about him to some extent. Many of the ones who worked in this particular field were horrified at the thought that they might have to work with him, owing to their activities with his interests. A collective sigh of relief was breathed when Hertz became the chosen one.

"Fuchs thinks that will help me have greater access to things and to better blend in with the crowd, instead of being a single man. That might attract too much attention, he said."

"Perhaps someone should tell Opa that there will be hundreds and hundreds of people there, with and without partners or groups. One man among all that would not even be noticed, without a kid in tow."

"You know, my dear," he warned, leaning in close enough to whisper in her ear, "even though your position and role allows you a certain latitude in criticizing the leadership, I wouldn't carry it too far. You never know when they might change their minds about things."

He gave her a knowing wink, realizing how patronizing that would appear to her and measuring his success by the flash in her eyes.

"You don't need to worry about me," she snapped, stepping back from him. "So you're bringing your little friend, eh?"

"Like I said, I have no choice." He shrugged.

She studied him for a moment and smiled. "That might not be such a bad idea after all, you know."

"Why the abrupt turnabout?"

"Nothing abrupt about it," she teased. "I seriously think that might actually help."

"How?"

"Like I said, I'm fairly confident that this entire performance is only a propaganda ploy," she explained. "We've heard nothing about any intended plans, if they have any. So, if we have as many young teens as we can get there, it would be easier to see how they play their hand."

"Of all the thousands in East Berlin, you think I have to make a special effort to have that one present?"

"He's already in our hands," she pointed out. "He has already been granted special access to American music and contraband. If he wasn't already here, I am willing to wager they would have brought him."

"But how would the Americans know he would be there?"

"They wouldn't," she conceded. "But the boy would know *they* were there, and Fuchs would know *he* was there. Let him hang around them and hear what they have to say or what they might try to do. If he acts up again, like he is certain to do, you can always say it was the Americans who incited him. If he's provocative enough, we can always use it to close the border, leaving this American cultural representation not only embarrassed in front of the entire world but also stranded here while their situation is straightened out. A little time peeing their pants at the border crossing or shitting themselves in a holding cell would be enough for Fuchs to cream himself over because then he would have something to brandish in the press at their expense."

"Your patriotism and concern are moving," Hertz said and smirked.

"They always were," she replied with a toss of her head.

"Is this going to change your previous plans?" asked Hertz. "I mean, I'd hate to have you fill out new reports to turn in."

"We leave bullshit like that for returning defectors," she scoffed. Hertz chuckled.

"You seem surprised," she snapped.

"Not at all," he replied, calmly ignoring her pointed remarks. "I know that we are all too busy doing our jobs to waste time creating new ASAs."

Alina tossed back her head for a lusty laugh at that remark but only because it covered her nervousness. Everyone in the Stasi, in either the foreign or domestic counterintelligence department, knew about the ASA, or American Special Actions Agents, the mythic creation of agents trying to fulfill the unrealistic expectations of their superiors.

Erich Mielke, the Stasi's ever-micromanaging director, placed a great deal of pressure on agents to produce tangible proof of Western attempts to undermine or attack the East German state. Fear of disapproval produced a strong desire to ensure results and created an unhealthy mentality among agents. When combined with the desire of East Germans who had defected to the West and then returned, to regain favor with the East German government, the agents created a viral strain of fantasy about American undercover agents specifically targeting various elements of East German society. This fantasy was embraced, wholeheartedly, because it justified everyone's fears.

It began with one or two isolated reports, then a few more. These reports were taken at face value due to the fact that they supported the theories of Stasi leadership. Once this fact was established, American Special Agent reports, or ASAs, began coming in at an alarming rate. To anyone looking at this situation with an objective eye, there were more red flags than a May Day parade. To Mielke, however, this was validation for his paranoia, and he would constantly boast of his agents' efforts in uncovering nefarious Western plots against the German Socialist utopia.

As Mielke's enthusiasm grew, so did the reports, each one struggling to outdo the other. This disturbing detail perpetually escaped Mielke's notice but not that of the KGB, which was forwarded copies of all of the ASA files. It was when a Soviet analyst sat down and began to give them a close examination that it became evident they were all fairy tales, and poorly constructed ones at that. Thus, the ASA threat to East Germany vanished like the morning mist, leaving a humiliated Mielke in its wake.

To ensure that this never happened again, Mielke instituted strict policies to prevent the advent of any more ASA type reports, and even now it influenced the actions and reports of Stasi agents.

"Then you might be the only one. This situation is going to be too good to be true for the old men," Alina said and chuckled. "Here comes their enemy to beard the lion in its den. They will be looking for anything to make the Americans look bad. Schnitzler has been nearly apoplectic about this show for weeks now. Have you seen him on television?"

"I can only imagine." Hertz shrugged. Like most East Germans, he did not enjoy the official commentary of Karl-Eduard von Schnitzler, host of *The Black Channel*, East Germany's response to West German news. Most people would turn off their televisions or change the station when he came on. Hertz never openly expressed his views on the program, but he suspected that even most of the East German leadership couldn't tolerate the man's openly ass-kissing propaganda.

"So, do you have any exact instructions for us?" asked Alina.

"Like you said, keep your eyes and ears open," Hertz sighed. "At the hint of anything suspicious, I want you to alert headquarters by your usual method."

"How will I get access to a phone in a situation like that? I can see your time with the leadership is having its effect. Your brain is becoming as ossified as theirs!"

Hertz grabbed her by the vest and pulled her close.

"I warned you," he hissed. "You are coming dangerously close to going too far. You have a protocol of contacting Vopo officers in an emergency. That entire plaza will be crawling with them, as we both know. If no one can find me, find one of them and have them get you in contact with the main office. We both know the phones will be manned by anyone and everyone available that night just waiting for something to happen. Am I making myself clear, or do I need to repeat myself?"

Alina sullenly pushed him away from her. "I understand," she snarled.

"Good," he said coldly. "Now, how will I find you there?"

"I'll be sure to wear something bright," she muttered.

"And so will just about everyone else," he snapped. "Do better than that!"

"Fine then!" she said. "Meet me on the steps of the Französischer Dom, the French Church, an hour before the show starts. We can reconnoiter the square together, the two of us and your little friend. Is that more acceptable?"

"Much better." He smiled coldly. "However, I would appreciate it if you arrived a bit earlier and did some looking around yourself first, then show me what you have found. I like that better, don't you?"

"You phrase that like it's an option," she murmured.

"Trust me, it isn't."

Hertz could tell that Alina wanted to say something but was pleased that she decided to keep the remarks to herself.

"Then what time, exactly, do we meet?" she asked.

"What time does the performance begin?"

"It begins at six," she explained. "A local East German band opens for them and performs for a half hour; then there's a brief intermission and the Americans go on. They have to be done by eight o'clock. They are offering a reception for a limited number of invited guests, and they have to be back in West Berlin by nine o'clock."

"Why by then?"

"Because that is only how long the ministry will let them stay. They wouldn't have cared if there wasn't the planned reception afterward."

"Yes, they would want to limit the exposure."

"Exactly," she confirmed. "So the reception is limited to thirty minutes."

"How do you get these tickets?" Hertz asked.

Alina shrugged. "I'm not certain. From what I've been able to find out, some people associated with the band simply go through the crowd and pass them out randomly."

"We need to make certain we get some."

"I've already set my sights on that objective," she replied coyly.

"I had no doubt." He smiled. "Very well then, I will meet you at the French Church at four o'clock tomorrow. I'll expect you to have already gone through there and acquired a view of how the performance is going to be laid out and where we should focus efforts."

"Don't worry, I'll have everything taken care of," she assured him.

Without a word, Hertz went back the way he came, intent on the details of tomorrow evening. Alina watched as he went and then headed off.

Chapter 36

"Layin' It on the Line"

Gagarin looked from the gun to the man's face. He did not recognize him, and the man's smile only made him more menacing.

"I said, please come with us," the man repeated, waving the gun to make Gagarin move. The man stepped back as Gagarin climbed out of the van. Emerging into the garage, he noticed two other men, with guns, who had been standing just out of view from the interior of the van. The driver of the van appeared from around the front, also holding a gun. Gagarin realized he was surrounded and unarmed. Slowly, he raised his hands.

"There is no need for that," the first gunman said. "Simply follow us, please." He pointed his gun in the direction he wanted Gagarin to move, and the gunman who had driven the van led the way.

The group emerged from behind a building, and Gagarin could see they were on a tarmac. In the distance a large cargo jet, bearing the name he recognized as a Swedish company, was being loaded with various crates. As they moved, the group tightened around him, and he felt a gun in the small of his back. He knew that, except for the one in front of him, the other gunmen had their weapons trained on him as well. They were all dressed the same, in the same jumpsuit as him, and it was then that he noticed the logos on their backs. It was the same as the airline.

"Do not cry out or draw attention to yourself in any way," the gunman said. "Simply follow the man in front of you to the plane."

Gagarin did as he was told while the man pressed the gun into his back. When they approached the steps leading up into the plane, a car pulled up from where they had emerged. Gagarin turned his head to see, but the other man nudged him harder in the back with the gun. The car drew alongside them, and the man inside called out to them in Polish. The group stopped and one of the men responded in broken Polish.

"Szwecja (Sweden)," he said. "Nie mówić po polsku (we don't speak Polish)."

The driver of the car made a remark under his breath that Gagarin didn't hear, but judged by the tone, it was not polite.

"Identitetshandlingar," the driver said slowly, in Swedish. "Identification papers."

The man who had spoken nodded and laughed, reaching into the pocket of his jumpsuit and withdrawing several passports and some yellow sheets of paper. Gagarin assumed that the passport he had used earlier was among them. Then he remembered that they had instructed him to alter his appearance. Gagarin knew that had been insurance against any description that anyone who had seen him earlier would provide. He counted the passports and sheets of paper that the man in the car was handling. There were five, the same number as this group. Apparently they had documentation for them all. Gagarin realized that they had not informed him of his new name and briefly wondered how he would exploit that oversight if he were asked his name, and decided against it. The spokesman had already indicated they did not speak very good Polish, so the man would hardly be inclined to conduct an interrogation in fits and starts. The emblem on the side of the car indicated that he was part of the airport security, not any government agency, and therefore would not be overly ambitious regarding security or protocol. Add to that the difficulty presented by the language barrier, and the man would be even more inclined to be on his way. As Gagarin assumed, the driver handed everything back to the spokesman and drove off.

"I appreciate you being quiet," the gunman muttered and gave him a slight shove.

They continued to the steps, where the gunman told Gagarin to pause while one of the men made their way up to the plane. Once there, he turned around and Gagarin could see light reflecting off of his gun barrel.

"As you can see, there is a gun trained on you at the top of the stairs, and three others behind you at the bottom of the stairs. I trust there will be no trouble?"

"None," Gagarin assured him.

Once inside the plane, he could see that it was stripped to the bare bones, save for a small, enclosed area where the seats were located. Gagarin noticed that there were only four seats facing each other. On the opposite wall from where they entered, there was another door that obviously went into the cockpit. The door was closed, and the plane was running, so Gagarin assumed the pilot and copilot were already on board. One thing that Gagarin thought unusual was that there were no windows in this section.

"Please have a seat," the gunman said, motioning to one in the corner. "And do please buckle in; we are in a hurry."

Gagarin did as he was told and was hardly surprised when the gunman and one of his associates sat opposite him. As Gagarin buckled his seat belt, he noticed that the second gunman kept his pistol trained on Gagarin while the first gunman buckled his belt, and then the roles were reversed. When they finished, Gagarin heard the door close. A few moments later, the plane began to move. There were only the three of them in the seating area, and no one spoke as the plane gathered speed. Gagarin felt it lift off and decided to break the silence.

"Is it all right if I talk now?" he asked.

"Of course," the gunman said, "if you'd like to."

"Are you still going to train that gun on me?"

"For the time being." He smiled.

"First, let me say that, while you're very good, you are obviously not KGB." Gagarin smiled.

"No, we're not the KGB," the gunman assured him. "Nor are we CIA or MI6."

"Who are you then?" Gagarin asked, suddenly more concerned than ever.

"Let's just say that we're a private firm that was contracted to make a delivery."

"Namely me?"

"That is correct."

"Where are we going?"

"We determined a long time ago that it was best to operate on a need-to-know basis. At this point in time, there is no need for you to know that. Now try to make yourself comfortable. I'm afraid there are neither refreshments nor movies on this flight, but the trip won't be that long."

They continued their flight in silence, the monotonous sound of the engine being the only sound and the flight itself uneventful save for the occasional turbulence. All that time both men kept their guns trained on him but said nothing. Finally, a voice came over the intercom and spoke in Swedish. The gunmen smiled.

"We have just left Polish air space," the first gunman said but did not put down his gun.

"I can assume that we are not heading to Russia," Gagarin said.

"No, we are not heading to the Soviet Union," the gunman assured him.

"Then where are we going?"

"I told you, all things are on a need-to-know basis," the gunman replied. "Informing you that you are not going to Russia has exhausted that mandate as far as you are concerned."

Gagarin noticed that neither gun moved, and so the flight continued on in silence.

Chapter 37

"Authority Song"

Cameron savored the quiet moments before they let the fans into the after-party. He was still riding the euphoria of the performance and was quite jealous of sharing it with anyone. He grabbed one of the tequilas that Doug and Casey ensured would be waiting for them and sipped it as he thought back to the high and low points of the evening.

The crowd was one of the best they had encountered on the tour, joining in with their favorite songs and interacting with the band's performance. Cameron was able to initiate impromptu competitions with different sections of the audience, as to who could sing which chorus loudest, or getting them to stand up and dance. The entire auditorium was a mass of gyrating bodies cheering, singing, shouting, and clapping their approval of everything the band did. It was the type of magic that he lived for, that justified all of the bad paydays, the canceled gigs, the broken-down band trucks, the flea-infested band houses, and the bologna sandwiches heated on the dash of a car.

Yet, while he enjoyed the magic, the shadow of the other reason for this tour still loomed menacingly on the horizon—the anxiety of it even greater now than before. They still had not received any direction regarding their activities. Yes, Cameron fully realized that the Roadhouse Sons had no direct part in it, but it was still obvious that something had gone terribly wrong, something with dire consequences, and something they were directly involved in.

The Roadhouse Sons were riding a roller coaster of a mission, and he had been informed that the brakes were gone. Where was this going to end up? As of showtime, Kendrick had not received any notifications about changing, nor had she disappeared during the performance. The last that Cameron had seen of her, she was conferring with Elsa regarding interviews with the guests. Wessel had been his usual omnipresent self, the flash of his camera blending in with the pulsating lights on stage.

If they're still around, then there's nothing new to report.

It occurred to Cameron that Wessel had never once blinded him with his flash during the show as sometimes occurred with photographers. He wondered if Wessel had perfected a method of synchronizing his shots with the lights? Pain in the ass that he might be, the man did great work, so Cameron was not going to worry too much about it.

Besides, it sounds like they've opened the gates.

Soon various people began streaming into the lounge the band had reserved. At first, it was just a few, and then it began to be more and more. Some of the other band members were outside with the people who were waiting, while Cameron was inside. They divided the duties in shifts: two would be working the crowd, and two would have a chance to relax during the brief down period. Cameron usually chose to relax in the lounge when it was his turn. Evan had gone back to the dressing room to change out of his sweaty clothes from the show. Ed and Rich made their way through the crowds to sign autographs and pose for pictures. Now, it was all hands on deck, and Cameron positioned himself in the middle of the floor and spread his arms wide.

"*Hallo, meine freunde!*" he cried, with a big smile. With smiles, laughs, and applause, the guests responded in kind, some in German, some in English. And so the party began. Cameron made his way through the crowd, accepting congratulations on the performance and politely declining drinks by holding up the bottle he already had.

Too easy to drink something I shouldn't otherwise.

As he did so, he quietly took notice of which of the team was, and was not, there. He saw Kendrick by the door, talking to the manager of the theater. Rich and Collier were each teamed up with a small knot of fans. Evan had reappeared and was accepting a gift of drumsticks from one of the guests. Out of the corner of his eye, Cameron saw Elsa in a corner with a group of girls, all talking excitedly to her as she made various notes in her notebook. Everyone was present and accounted for, except for the roadies and Wessel. Cameron could understand Doug and Casey being absent; they were taking care of the equipment that the band used instead of the house equipment, as well as the guitars. Wessel, on the other hand, was supposed to be working these events.

Well, he has gotten a lot of these shots already. Maybe he's doing a spread on the roadies. Still, Cameron made a mental note to talk to him about his absence later.

As the event wore on, the day's activities began to take their toll on Cameron and he looked for a place to sit down. The room did not have many tables, and the ones it did have were full. This started to put him in an ill humor until he noticed Doug and Casey at a table in the corner, with some open seats. They weren't being bothered too much by the guests, which Cameron had to chuckle at. It had been his experience in the past that the roadies were the first ones the fans gravitated to, in hopes of being able to meet the band. Now, with the special arrangements provided by the access passes, they did not enjoy as much attention.

Yeah, but you guys are the ones who pass out the passes.

"Is this seat taken?" Cameron asked, pulling out one of the chairs.

"It is now." Doug laughed, turning back to Casey, and resumed his conversation, complete with shadow punching and grimacing.

"Oh shit, don't tell me you're talking wrestling again?" Cameron moaned good-naturedly.

"No, we're talking wrestling *still*," Casey corrected, with mock disdain. "I can't help it. I'm a huge wrestling fan and love hearing these stories! Collier has been keeping me entertained by some of his exploits, too!"

"You know, I always thought that Doug here was just a fan of wrestling," Cameron said. "He was always buying those magazines and watching it on TV whenever he got the chance. I never knew that he had actually done it."

"I have another confession to make," Doug sheepishly informed him. "When I was reading those magazines and watching the matches, I was actually checking the classifieds, so to speak."

"Really?" Casey exclaimed. "You mean they advertise for wrestlers in those things? Wow! I wondered how you guys got hired."

"It isn't like the want ads that you're thinking of," Doug corrected him. "The magazines talk about who is running what shows and where, who they are using, and which one of my friends was getting the big push someplace. The stories are a little … well, let's just say the promoters let the writers have fun with them. But the match results and the territories they cover were what I was interested in."

"So you were going to bug out on us?" Cameron demanded, with a smile.

Doug gave him a smile and a shrug.

"Sometimes musicians develop more feuds than wrestlers," he said and laughed. "I had to make certain that I could find another job if you guys went south!"

"Well, here's to that not having been necessary," Cameron said, holding his glass.

"You know, I think I remember seeing you, or at least hearing about you," Casey said, studying Doug.

"You've heard of the Crimson Mask?" Cameron laughed. "Hey, Dougie, you better give him an autograph! You found a fan way over here!"

"No, he wasn't the Mask then," Casey replied, studying Doug carefully. "Didn't you also wrestle as, oh crap, I can't think of the name."

Cameron noticed that Doug simply sipped his beer, not even looking at his assistant.

"I've got it now," Casey exclaimed. "How could I have been so stupid? You wrestled under your own name, Doug Courtland!"

Doug gave a slight nod and raised his glass in salute.

"When did you come up with the other name?" Cameron asked.

"I didn't; that was suggested to me by Paul Vachon when I worked my way across the country," Doug explained. "Working under a mask lets you work twice on a show—once with it, once without it. *Crimson mask* refers to when a wrestler gets his head cut open and the blood covers his face. That would usually happen to me, so Paul thought it would be a good gimmick to have in the bag, as they say."

"Yes, I saw him wrestle without it." Casey laughed. "Let's see, it was 1975, in Montreal, over at the old Expo grounds, I think. I don't remember who you wrestled though."

"To be honest, I don't either," Doug said. "That was when I was breaking into the business and was often used to help fill out a card. But it was a lot of fun working for Grand Prix, I'll tell you that."

"So, if you were working in Montreal for Grand Prix, then you were working for the Lion, Yvonne Robert. Wessel has been filling me in about Montreal wrestling."

Doug didn't say anything at first, but Cameron noticed that he was studying Casey very closely as he sipped his beer. He knew from Doug's silence that something had not set right with him, but he was not ready to say something.

"I know you really are a wrestling fan," Doug said, "but I didn't know Wessel was, too."

"Yeah, I like it." Casey shrugged. "I can't say about Wessel though. But here he is; you can ask him yourself."

"I'm sorry I wasn't here," the photographer said, out of breath. "I was called away during the show."

"Anything serious?" Cameron asked.

"No," Wessel assured him. "Just something that needed to be taken care of. Do you mind if I sit down?" Before Cameron could answer, the photographer pulled out the last empty seat at the table, sat down and crossed his legs.

"Have I missed anything?" he said, smiling.

Cameron noticed that he seemed slightly nervous, lightly bouncing his foot. "Only a room full of guests waiting to get their pictures taken," he grumbled.

"Yeah, about that. Elsa thought we had enough photos of guests, so she said I could let that slide for a couple of shows," he insisted.

"Well, you know what you're hired for better than I do," Cameron said.

"Okay, out with it!" Doug demanded with a smile, lightly slamming his glass down on the table. "What was she like?"

"Excuse me," stammered the photographer. "I don't know what you're talking about!"

"Don't try to pull that on me, man," Doug teased. "You've got all the signs; you were missing when you were supposed to be working, you're out of breath, your hair is more of a rat's nest than usual, and your shoes look like they were laced up by a drunken two-year-old. So what was she like?"

Cameron, intrigued by Doug's observations, looked at Wessel's shoes and saw that Doug was correct. Rather than being laced in a proper way, they skipped holes on one side and crossed over each other, bearing a closer resemblance to a circuit board than to a laced shoe. To anyone else, it would indeed look like he had laced them in a hurry. However, Cameron instantly recognized them as a signal that Wessel had something important to tell him. He gave Wessel a stern look.

"I can explain," the photographer pleaded.

Cameron held up his hand. "Save it. You can come with me and tell it to Kendrick as well! I think she'd be interested to hear what you have to say, too. After all, she hired you, didn't she? She might as well know what you've been doing on company time."

Before Wessel could say anything, Cameron rose and took him by the arm, navigating him through the crowd.

"I'm serious," Wessel pleaded. "I can explain!"

"I know you can," Cameron whispered to him. "But you can't do it here."

Cameron spotted Kendrick at her customary place near the door and motioned for her.

"We need to talk," he said as she approached. He still had a grip on Wessel's arm and a stern look of disapproval.

Kendrick caught the little nod he gave her and motioned for them to follow her.

"There's an unused room that I've been using as an office; we can meet in there," she said, leading them out of the crowd. The hallway contained some of the guests who had come out of the reception for a little fresh air and quiet. They all recognized Cameron and shook his hand or asked for an autograph. Not releasing his grip on Wessel, Cameron apologized and said that he would give them one just as soon as he came back. Once inside the room, Cameron released his grip and closed the door.

"What is it?" Kendrick asked.

"Gagarin is in orbit," Wessel told her slowly, almost whispering each word.

Kendrick nodded her understanding. "Then they decided to go through with it," she whispered.

"The launch was a bit messy," Wessel explained. "It seems that others wanted him to go to Mars, while we wanted him to go to the moon. There was a slight delay, but we were able to make a successful launch."

"How messy?" Kendrick asked.

"They were able to launch him just before the others got to the launch pad."

"But how can they do that?" Cameron asked. "The other objective was compromised! Is that back on?"

"Yes," Wessel said. "Because they found the lost lamb."

"Are you certain of this?" Kendrick demanded.

"Yes," assured Wessel. "Word came at the same time they announced the cosmonaut was in orbit. But there's something you need to know."

"I don't think I want to," Cameron muttered.

"We have to develop a new plan to bring the lamb to market,"

Wessel sighed. "And we have to do it immediately. Right now, it looks like it involves all of you."

"You cannot be serious!" exclaimed Kendrick, but Wessel assured her that he was.

"Eberhard needs to talk to you immediately," he informed her. "The target has been located, and a preliminary plan for receiving him is being worked out. Some of this has been shared with Elsa but no details with me. Eberhard is on his way here, now."

"They had all of that worked out," Cameron protested. "There was an entire plan for accomplishing that, and it didn't involve *us*."

"That all went to hell," Wessel said.

And are we going to follow?

"Cameron, we're going to need to wrap up this after-party," Kendrick said.

Cameron saw from her expression that she was already deep in thought, possibly formulating a plan or thinking of the questions she'd need to ask.

"That won't be a problem," he assured her. "It is almost time for us to wrap it up anyhow. Do you want me to go and start gathering the others?"

Kendrick nodded. "I don't need to tell you not to say anything, do I?"

"Hell no." He laughed. "Do you want to meet back at our suite?"

Kendrick nodded but made no further comment.

As Cameron left, he found Doug waiting in the hallway.

"What are you doing out here?" Cameron asked.

"Partly making sure no one was listening at keyholes and partly waiting for you," the roadie explained.

"Listen, man, whatever it is, it's going to have to wait," Cameron said, pushing past him. "We've got some serious shit to deal with."

"It might not be able to wait," Doug whispered, grabbing the musician's arm. "I'm serious."

"What is it then?" Cameron demanded. "And make it quick!"

"It's about Wessel," Doug whispered. "There is something wrong with him."

"What? You mean like he's sick or something?"

"No, I mean like he's making me suspicious."

"Oh, you've got to be kidding me," Cameron whispered harshly. "Look, the Germans have vetted him and brought him in! They have picked him out, and he's on our side. What the hell is making you suspicious of him, anyway?"

"It's the way he's always asking questions about how much I know about what we're doing, like he's trying to get me to second-guess you guys or something," Doug explained.

"Look, maybe you've forgotten the hair trigger that this whole thing is tickling, but none of the rest of us have," Cameron hissed. "He's probably making certain that you've got all this straight. Remember, you're not one of us!"

"You don't need to remind me of that," Doug replied coldly. "But he seems to be trying too hard to make himself my best buddy lately, and that makes me suspicious, too. Like all that wrestling talk Casey was laying on me; he's been researching me and I don't know why!"

"You *always* get suspicious of people, damn it," Cameron growled. "Look, if the big shots who are calling the shots say he's okay, then who's to say he's not, me or you? You better have a good explanation if you want me to keep listening."

"Fine," Doug spat. "But haven't you always touted those stupid rules to me?"

"Keep your voice down!" Cameron hissed. "Yeah, Moscow rules, what about them?"

"One of them is never go against your gut, correct?"

"Yeah, so?"

"Well, he's setting off more bells with me than a fire truck!"

"So does *everyone* with you, for God's sake," Cameron said. "You've been suspicious of just about everyone we've encountered here—Elsa, Casey, now Wessel. Besides, maybe he *was* researching you. You forget one of the reasons you're here? Yeah, that is probably why they've been looking at you, closely, and making sure you are on the level. Now listen, shit is about to get serious around here, and I need to make certain I don't have one more situation to keep my eye on. I want you to just do as you're told and not give us any headaches. Am I making myself clear?"

"Perfectly," Doug said.

Cameron did not miss the icy coldness of his friend's response but right now had too much on his plate to deal with it.

"Then make certain all of our stuff is back at the hotel; we'll be joining you there in a little while."

With that, Cameron hurried off, not looking back at his friend. He returned to the function room and made the announcement that the Roadhouse Sons wished to thank all of their new friends for some wonderful memories, but they had to call it a night. He saw Rich, the center of attention to a group of lovely ladies, give him a dirty look.

"We've got a busy day ahead of us tomorrow," he said into the microphone, looking at the bass player. "We've got to get plenty of rest and drink our orange juice."

From the sudden lack of protest in the bass player's expression, Cameron knew Rich had received the veiled reference conveyed by the color orange, their time-honored code for something important, and would obediently, though reluctantly, comply. The band saw their fans off, getting in one last hug and kiss from the eager young ladies and one last photograph with someone else. Finally, they were alone.

"What's the deal?" Rich asked.

"Not here," Cameron whispered. "Big shit though. Kendrick wants us back at the hotel, pronto. Where's Doug?"

"He and Collier skipped out a few minutes ago," explained Evan. "Doug said he was taking the instruments back to the hotel, and Collier said he'd help him."

"All right then, that's two accounted for," Cameron sighed. "And it looks like the rest of us are here now, so let's go!"

At the hotel, Cameron and the others headed to the room and were surprised that Eberhard had arrived and that Doug was not with Collier. Cameron noticed the solemn expressions on everyone's faces and the soft static from the radio.

"Kendrick sent Doug back to his room," Collier explained. "This is just for, well, us, for lack of a better word."

"What do you mean, us?" Cameron asked.

"I mean, we can't have any civilians here," Collier said. "This is the serious stuff, I'm afraid. We can't even have Rich here."

"Holy shit." The bass player whistled. "I've never been out of the loop on anything before."

"I'm sorry, man," Collier said. "But you've never been up against anything like this before."

"Okay then, I'll see you later," Rich replied, not putting up an argument. "I'll crash in Doug's room if you guys don't send for me."

Kendrick waited for the door to close and then nodded for Collier to lock it.

"I'm afraid I have some news for you guys," she explained. "Cameron already knows, but I need to inform the rest of you that the purpose of our little trip has changed."

"Changed how?" asked Cameron, though he suspected what the answer would be.

"The secondary objective has been located," Kendrick said. "And we are expected to help transfer him to the West."

"What the hell are you talking about?" cried Evan. "From the beginning you guys have spent every waking minute reminding us that we are only ancillary aspects of this mission and not the actual thing. Now, at crunch time, that all changes?"

"Not entirely," said Eberhard. "You are still an ancillary aspect, only now it will be on site, not at a distance."

"That is as clear as mud," remarked Cameron. "I want a straight answer, with no bullshit jargon or any dancing around. What does this have to do with us, and what are we supposed to do?"

"I'm sorry," said Kendrick, "but the integrity of this mission …"

"The integrity of this mission has been blown completely to hell," snapped Cameron. "And you're all running around like Dutch boys trying to stick your finger in the dike to keep everything from collapsing! Double speak and superfluous language might work in helping *you* feel better, but it does jack shit for putting together a Hail Mary."

"Need I remind you …" she began again, this time to be interrupted by Evan.

"It's no use," the drummer said. "I'm in complete agreement with Cameron! If I understand what you're insinuating, then we have the right to have a clear explanation of what we're being asked to do. Our necks are even more on the line than they were previously and are just as much on the line as any of yours. Like Cameron said, out with it, and in plain English."

Kendrick seethed for a few moments but conceded their point.

"Very well," she began. "As I said, the secondary objective has been located. You will recall that he was removed from his previous location to an undisclosed one."

Okay, I guess we do still need to keep things encrypted. There is always the possibility that we're being listened to.

"Yeah," said Evan. "What about it?"

"Our sources have informed us that he has been located," she continued.

"And he must be in East Berlin, or none of this would matter to us," said Cameron.

"You are entirely correct," Kendrick sighed. "And this is where it gets even more personal. They have indicated that he will be at the show."

Shit. Knew it.

"We don't wish to alarm you, too much," Eberhard told them.

"Too bloody late for that," remarked Evan.

Kendrick shot him a warning glance, but, to everyone's surprise, he gave her a defiant glare.

"You are correct that, from the beginning, you were expected to merely be a diversion," Eberhard continued. "We are all fully aware that you lack both the training and expertise to conduct an operation of the type we are contemplating. We are still only expecting the band to perform as originally intended. However, the difference now is that instead of distracting an operation several miles from you, you will be distracting one that is only a few feet from you."

"Was that explanation designed to make us feel any better?" asked Cameron.

"It was the best I could do under the circumstances." Eberhard smiled.

"Okay, so what exactly is the plan, or do we even have one?" Cameron asked again.

"We do, actually," Kendrick assured him. "Basically, it follows the previous one. While you are performing, an operative will make contact with the target and, using a prearranged procedure, will transport the target to agents waiting to conduct them to safety."

"That doesn't sound too complicated," conceded Evan. "Do we know who these agents are?"

"We do, you don't," said Kendrick. "I'm afraid we can't go into too much detail with you at this point."

"Why the hell not?" Cameron demanded.

"Because we have a leak," she explained. "A rather highly placed leak."

"What? You think it's me?" Cameron snapped.

"Of course not," Kendrick snapped back. "If I did, you wouldn't even be here! But, due to the delicacy of the situation, we're keeping the details known only to the ones who are going to be executing the operation, and that doesn't include you."

That word again.

Cameron understood the gravity of the situation and the need for even closer security than before.

"Well, like Evan said, this doesn't sound too complicated," he sighed. "Basically sing, mingle, and smile, while you guys work your magic behind the scenes."

"In a nutshell, yes," Kendrick confirmed, with a wry smile. "We'll be working out the logistical details with Casey, Collier, and Wessel. They've had experience with these types of operations before. The only standing orders you have to worry about are to do whatever they ask you, if they ask you to do anything."

Both Cameron and Evan concurred with that order.

"I do have one question though," Cameron said. "Exactly how are you going to get him to follow whoever it is that you have selected to bring him across?"

"It is best you don't know such details," Eberhard said. "The less you know, the less you are responsible for, and the less you would potentially reveal."

Or maybe you just haven't figured that part out yet?

"I don't mean to add any additional pressure to this situation," Kendrick added. "But there is something else you should know."

"I am aquiver with anticipation," Cameron muttered.

"I heard that," Kendrick snapped, glaring at Cameron as he blushed. "What I was going to say was that we are on a bit of a deadline to accomplish this."

"Exactly how much of a deadline?" Evan asked.

"We have to have this done by nine o'clock tomorrow night," she said.

"You have *got* to be shitting me!" cried Cameron. "Are you serious? You do realize that that's less than twenty-four hours from now?"

"I'm well aware of that," she acknowledged. "So I suggest you get some sleep. We have to get an early start. We have our own deadlines for when to be at the East German border checkpoints and if we are late, they will use that as an excuse to make your lives miserable."

With everything else you laid on us, you think we're going to be worried about being a few minutes late? Shit!

Chapter 38

"Girls with Guns"

Petrovsky's hand trembled as he replaced the receiver on the phone. A white-hot rage came over him as he processed the report he had just been given. Alexi was gone. The agents who had been sent to retrieve him had found his apartment empty but all of his belongings still there, including his coat draped over a chair in the kitchen.

"He was to be monitored at all times!" Petrovsky had screamed into the phone.

"I assure you, he was," insisted the man on the other end of the line. "The building had twenty-four-hour surveillance! He was never seen leaving that building."

"A man cannot simply disappear into thin air," Petrovsky wheezed, his chest beginning to tighten. "Somehow he must have slipped past you!"

"We continued to monitor the building for several hours afterward," the other man insisted. "No one was seen leaving the building except for two drunk men later on."

"What? And you didn't detain them?"

"They were stopped for questioning, comrade, I assure you," the man protested. "However, while one of them did hold a Soviet passport, neither he nor the other man matched the description of Ustimovitch, and they were released."

Petrovsky nearly dropped the phone at this admission of incompetence.

"That was him, you fool! Do you mean to tell me that no one even suspected he might wear a disguise? What of Alexandrovich? Why didn't he detain him as directed?"

Petrovsky had given orders to the KGB agent assigned to the trade delegation to take Alexi into custody. However, Petrovsky realized what others overlooked: that Alexi was a highly trained agent, one of Petrovsky's brightest protégés, and would be aware of any overt attempts and would thus be able to take measures to avoid them. The only way to deal with him was to catch him off guard. The plan had been to inform him that word had been sent for his return to Moscow. That would let him know that he was being reevaluated, but he would have no idea as to how. Would it be favorable or unfavorable? Then, before he could formulate a plan, they would keep him off guard by celebrating. Yes, Alexi would still be wary, as anyone in their right mind would be, but the fact that he was not being loaded onto a plane bound for Moscow at that very moment would suggest the possibility that he might have been rehabilitated in the eyes of the chief directorate.

"I'm afraid Comrade Alexandrovich became intoxicated in the course of the evening," the other man replied nervously. Suddenly, it all became clear to Petrovsky what had happened, and each breath burned in his lungs as the scenario unfolded in his mind. Alexandrovich had, as directed, informed Alexi of his impending transfer and taken him out to celebrate, as directed. However, Alexi was obviously not as unaware of what was happening as they had hoped. He had, in fact, caught on to what was transpiring, possibly from the beginning. Alexandrovich, either through overconfidence, carelessness, or sheer stupidity, had not monitored the vodka that Alexi drank or that he had consumed. As a result, Alexi remained sober and alert while Alexandrovich became drunk and incapacitated, allowing Alexi to slip away.

"Then Alexi must still have been in that building when you

arrived," Petrovsky sputtered, struggling to catch his breath. "Was the building searched? Answer me!"

"Yes sir, the building was thoroughly searched," the man assured him.

"The entire building?" Petrovsky demanded.

"No sir, the search was limited to that floor," the man explained. "We went in through the front of the building, up the main stairs, and also up the fire escape," the other man protested. "We even had the rear entrance of the building watched! We were at the building only a few minutes after he had returned home. It is impossible that he could have gotten away!"

"And yet, you're telling me that he did," Petrovsky seethed. "Was there a back stairway or a garage to the building?"

"There was a back stairway, yes," the man confirmed. "We had someone watching the stairwell and no one came up or down, other than our own agents searching for him. There is a garage, but it belongs to the building next door, and there is no entrance to it from Ustimovitch's building."

"What of his apartment then?" Petrovsky demanded. "Did you search every inch of that?"

"Of course," the man assured him, nervously. "We nearly destroyed it. There was no place that he could have hidden. It was even obvious that he had just barely been there."

"It was obvious," roared Petrovsky. "How? Did he leave a time card?"

"No sir," the man insisted. "But there had been a light rain that night, almost a mist, and his coat was still slightly damp."

"Who else lives on that floor?"

"There is an elderly Polish couple, a young woman who works in one of the local stores, and an abandoned apartment across the hall from him."

"And you checked all of those thoroughly?"

"Yes sir, we did," the man assured him. "The elderly couple and the girl said he never talked or interacted with anyone. MSW agents, as well as the Polish police, searched both of their apartments. They found nothing. The abandoned apartment had not been used for some time, and the dust had not been disturbed."

Petrovsky heard what the man was telling him, analyzing the situation as he would have handled it and as he would have taught Alexi to handle it, as well. He came to one horrifying conclusion.

"They helped him then," he muttered.

"What did you say?"

"I said they helped him," Petrovsky replied, choking out his response. "The people helped him to escape!"

"Who could have helped him? The Americans?"

Petrovsky felt his head throb at the stupidity of the man he was talking to.

"The Americans, the British, the Germans, the French, probably even the goddamned Vatican for all the difference it makes!" Petrovsky screamed. "The fact is he could not have prepared for this contingency alone, or on the spur of the moment. He had been developing this plan under your very noses all along!"

"How can you be so certain of that?" protested the other man.

"Because Ustimovitch is not the intellectual pygmy that the rest of you are," shouted Petrovsky as he slammed down the receiver. He stood leaning against his desk, the tightness in his chest lessening.

Alexi was gone. The spy too valuable to kill and too precious to lose was gone. Where? Where else? It was obvious that he had gone to the West, that the fears Petrovsky had harbored and his superiors dismissed were entirely justified and were now an undeniable reality. The stupidity and closed-mindedness of his colleagues had probably just cost them a valuable agent, if not the war. Like a small leak that grows bigger, Petrovsky saw all of the networks, the spies, and the plans that Alexi had been involved with suddenly unraveling. There was no way to estimate the damage that this defection would cause. Petrovsky had hidden him away in an obscure trade delegation in an effort to keep him out of sight of the enemy, fearing that they had been searching for him in Russia. Now it seemed that very plan had been the boon the enemy had waited for. Petrovsky realized that the head of the KGB needed to be alerted right away.

He picked up the receiver and began to dial, but it slipped out of his hand and fell to the floor. As he bent to pick it up, a sharp pain shot up his left arm and he dropped to the floor beside the buzzing receiver. And so it was that Victor Chebrikov, the chief of the KGB, would never learn about this devastating breach of intelligence until long after it was too late.

Chapter 39

"So You Ran"

Cameron had picked at his breakfast and only absently sipped his coffee. He was thinking about not only the mission but also the upcoming night's performance and even the trip itself. From Hamburg, they would be making their way to East Berlin. When he was younger, he had always assumed that the border of East and West Germany was the same as the border of East and West Berlin. As he became better at geography, he found that this was not the case. He never worried about it until now. Now he realized that it was nearly a three-hour trip.

"It is not quite that long, Mr. Walsh, I assure you," Eberhard said and laughed. "It might be three hours by American standards. But there is something you are forgetting; we Germans have the autobahn and no speed limits on much of it. It won't be quite so bad, I promise you."

Still, to Cameron, it was a potentially three-hour trip through what could basically be considered enemy territory. In all of the briefings they had been given, not much had been devoted to that aspect of the tour, aside from mentioning that the East Germans look for anything and everything to find wrong and give you a hard time about it.

Big help.

Kendrick and Casey had both advised him to go through his pockets and remove anything that might be considered contraband.

As an agent, Cameron did not do any drugs and knew that neither did Evan. He was confident that neither Rich nor Doug had been using any on this trip, and that they would not have to worry about any of that being found. Prior to leaving the United States, Kendrick had instructed them to remove anything that could be construed as political from their luggage. Anything that had camouflage or the American flag on it was frowned upon, so they all had dutifully removed such items. Rich and Doug had even taken the added precautions of getting rid of some olive-colored T-shirts they both had, for fear of them being mistaken for fatigues. Finally, their assembled wardrobes consisted of just about anything you would find in a thrift store.

Or in a musician's closet.

"The West Germans aren't going to care one way or another," Kendrick had explained. "However, the East Germans always look for something to harass you for, so get rid of those things."

Cameron had been told they would be required to exchange their currency from West German to East German marks when they initially crossed into East Berlin.

"What's the exchange rate?" Rich had asked.

"It doesn't matter," Wessel explained. "It is worth practically nothing in the East and absolutely nothing in the West."

That reminds me of a lot of gigs I've played. Finally! Something I can relate to.

There weren't too many people around for him to chat with since everyone else was doing the same thing, making sure there was nothing that anyone could have a problem with. Kendrick was with Eberhard going over all of the permits and paperwork required for crossing the border. Cameron had no idea where Wessel could be and wasn't really interested. Elsa had not been with them the past two days, but Cameron had been assured that she did have a press pass to be with them in East Berlin. Ironically, while everyone else was getting rid of anything considered contraband, Casey and Doug had been dispatched to buy cartons of American cigarettes for the band to bring over.

"Those items are almost as good as currency," Eberhard had explained the previous evening. "The East German border guards don't mind them, and they can be conveniently offered without appearing to be bribing someone. Remember that. It might come in handy in the future."

Cameron wandered out to where the band truck was parked. There, he was alarmed to see the back of it opened and someone inside. Hurrying over, he noticed that it was Casey. The roadie had one of the older, more beat-up BH800 speakers opened and seemed to be lining it with some shiny material.

"I thought you were off with Doug," Cameron said. The roadie was startled by the interruption and gave Cameron a dirty look but continued working.

"It doesn't take two people to buy cigarettes," Casey muttered. "So I decided to stick around and patch up this old speaker for us. Tonight's gig will be an outdoor show, and we might need to use some extra speakers for increased sound."

"Have you ever been there?"

"Where, East Berlin?" Casey asked. "Nope, why?"

"Just wondering." Cameron shrugged. "I've never been either and wondered exactly what it was like."

"Well, I can tell you it's not like anything you've ever experienced before."

"In a good or a bad way?" Cameron laughed.

"Either way you want it, I guess," Casey joked. "But one thing that is a little hard to get used to is that on the map, it looks like West Berlin is surrounded in East Germany. But, from what everyone tells me, once you get there, it's kind of like East Germany is surrounded by West Berlin."

"I really don't need to be getting my mind around any philosophical shit right now, you know," Cameron teased.

Casey shrugged, with a toothy grin, and got back to his work. Cameron, too, resumed his wanderings about the parking lot surrounding their hotel. He came to a small cafe and decided to order a coffee and enjoy a few quiet moments before returning to the hotel.

Today is going to be crazy; savor the moment, you dumb bastard, and don't think about shit.

Soon there was no putting off any longer that it was time for them all to regroup and get their last-minute instructions before heading off, so Cameron returned to the hotel. He remembered that Kendrick had also wanted to have a final inspection to make certain their appearances conformed to their guidelines, and so he quickened his pace. As he passed the band truck, he heard the sound of someone in the back.

"How the hell long does it take to work on one of those things?" He laughed, sticking his head around the corner. To his surprise, it was not Casey working on the speaker but Doug.

"What the hell are you talking about?" the roadie asked. "I've only been here a few minutes! Where have you been?"

"Sorry, man, I thought you were Casey," Cameron apologized. "He was doing what you're doing when I went for a walk."

"Well, if you think I look like Casey, you need to lay off the hard shit this early in the morning," Doug snapped. "You better get your stuff and get out here; they want to get going pretty quick."

Cameron nodded and hurried off to gather his belongings.

Gathered outside, the Roadhouse Sons certainly appeared a motley crew, and that did not provide Cameron with any additional confidence in this assignment. Wessel had once again reappeared and was dressed in a flannel shirt, khaki pants with ample pockets for his film, and a pair of beat-up sneakers. Evan wore his usual trademark ensemble—the untucked, buttoned shirt with jeans and loafers. Collier wore a red T-shirt bearing the remains of a faded Coca-Cola logo, faded jeans, and beat-up sneakers. Doug was unmistakable in his usual black trucker cap, black leather vest, denims, work boots, and faded brown shirt, which always helped him to blend into the background. Casey seemed to always be the contrast to Doug, dressing in sneakers, blue jeans, a denim vest, and faded orange shirt. Rich wore his customary faded black T-shirt and blue denims, giving the aura of the Old West, and reminding Cameron of a movie that he enjoyed as a kid.

Well, counting Kendrick, I suppose we are *the* Magnificent Seven, *with Wessel as one of the villagers who brings us in, maybe? Hopefully no gunfire or bull fights.*

"All right, I think we'd better be on our way," said Kendrick.

Initially they had planned to take three vehicles so could be more comfortable. However, with the sudden change in the dynamics of the mission, that plan was scrapped in favor of limiting it to two vehicles.

"Yes, it might not be as comfortable," Kendrick explained, "however, two vehicles are easier to keep track of than three."

Cameron agreed to travel in the band truck, while the others made themselves comfortable in the car. Wessel, having traveled in the East before, drove the car and led the way for the rest of them. Doug, driving the truck, was clearly enjoying himself once he learned the route they were traveling was on the Bundesautobahn 2.

"An open road and no posted limits," he said and giggled. "I love this country! Hey, Casey, how difficult would it be to move here?"

"Don't ask me, man." Casey laughed. "I sort of got moved here. I didn't have much to say about it. One thing I do know, however, is that sometimes they do post speed limits, especially if conditions aren't entirely safe, so be careful. Just follow the other car; Wessel will know how fast to go."

"Okay, let's get something straight right now, Dougie boy," Cameron snapped. "Maybe there aren't any posted limits on the highway, but there are still the laws of physics! So don't get crazy."

"Have I yet?" Doug asked. "Listen, don't worry. You're just a little edgy about going into the Commie zone. Relax, everything is going to be fine. We're just going to do this show and head to the next one."

"Life is never as simple as that," Cameron muttered. "Besides, how do you know this is what's bothering me? Are you a psychologist all of a sudden?"

"You've been getting moodier the closer we've gotten to this date." Doug smiled. "I don't need no college degree to figure out why. Look, we're going to be okay; I'm sure of it."

I'm glad one of us is.

"Besides," Doug continued, "it's too late for us to do anything about it anyhow."

Cameron glared at his roadie as Casey tried to find a good station on the radio.

"While we're still in the West, we should be able to get some good music," he said, trying not to smile at Doug's remark.

"Don't they have music on the radio in East Germany?" Cameron asked.

"Nothing you're going to want to listen to," Casey assured him.

"Do they jam the American stations or something?" Doug asked.

Casey shrugged. "For a long time, they took the transmitters out of radios that could pick it up, but that got stopped," he explained. "The transmitters just got sold on the black market. Now they try to broadcast over it, or jam it, or scramble it. I think it is more successful closer to Poland, but here by the border and close to West Berlin, they have a problem."

"Will we get into any hassle for listening to American stations or anything?" Doug asked.

"Well, I doubt any American stations broadcast over here." Casey laughed. "But, if you're talking about Western stations, then, yeah, they might give you a hard time while you're in East Germany or East Berlin."

"Shit, just what we need," Cameron muttered, but made no complaint as Casey finally found a good station for them to listen to. The musician had determined to enjoy as much as he could as long as he could, and tried not to think that this might actually be the last time he enjoyed this freedom. Cameron upbraided himself for feeling this way. He was a professional, both as a musician and a special agent. He was not doing anything but playing his music in a band. As far as covert activities, he did not have a direct involvement with them and did not know what was going to be done. There was no way that anyone could expect him to have any responsibility for it.

You need to calm the hell down, man.

To lighten his mood, he began a discussion about the different clubs in Germany that Casey had worked for or been in. He encouraged Doug to tell wrestling stories, and for his part, Cameron regaled them with road stories of his own. This had a tremendous calming effect on him, and before he knew it, they were approaching the border.

Wessel's car had already pulled over for the border guards to inspect it while the passengers got out. Kendrick motioned for Doug to pull alongside them as the East German guards took their positions to inspect the truck. When Doug parked, each of the passengers of the band truck emerged and stood along the side of the truck. Cameron thought of baseball, barbecue, and anything else he could think of in order to *not* think about how much this resembled a lineup or a firing squad. He wondered if anyone else was doing the same.

Wessel accompanied Kendrick and one of the border guards, who inspected the papers associated with the truck and double-checked the passports that each of them held. Casey's passport gave some trouble, as it did not have specific dates of entry, but rather had renewed extended-stay visas. To the East Germans, this seemed to be suspicious.

Or you are just tickled pink to have something to bust our balls about.

Kendrick and Wessel explained about Casey being stranded by the war, his inability to repatriate right away, and his decision to just stay in Germany and work.

"It is a situation that has been totally approved by both our government and the West German government," Kendrick insisted.

The border guard made a remark in a nasty tone and handed the paperwork back to Kendrick. Cameron wondered what the man had said, but judging from the way Wessel rolled his eyes, he figured he was better off not knowing.

"This is just the warm-up for the real search," Kendrick informed them. "Right now, we are just at the part for the currency exchange. Hand over everything; no American dollars or West German marks are allowed in. Only East German money is permitted."

Cameron went with the others to the office where they were

required to declare how much Western currency they had on them, and to hand over the currency to a representative of the East German border patrol. Then it was exchanged for the correct amount of East German marks, and the agent gave them sharp instructions, which Wessel dutifully translated.

"He is reminding you to observe all instructions issued with your passport stamps and also reminding you that you must spend as much of this money in the East as you can," the photographer said.

"How the hell are we supposed to do that?" Rich asked. "We're not going anywhere or even leaving the concert location. Don't they realize that?"

"Probably not," Wessel explained. "If they did, they don't care. Look, just buy a couple rounds of drinks or something after the show. Let them see you spent something, and they won't give you a hard time about it."

After what seemed an inordinate amount of time exchanging their money and repeatedly inspecting their papers, the band made its way to the next stop, where the contents of the vehicles were inspected. That required Doug and Casey to pull out all of the various speakers, monitors, and other items that had been carefully packed in. Cameron could see that Doug was becoming increasingly irritated at having people impatiently gesture and shout at him in German, but to Cameron's relief and the roadie's credit, Doug said nothing. Finally, they were permitted to go on.

After carefully, but quickly, repacking the truck, they continued on their way. Neither Cameron nor Doug were prepared for the stark contrast between the eastern and western parts of the country. The cars were not as plentiful, or as nice, as they had been in the West, and the general atmosphere of everything seemed to be equally as drawn and fatigued. In some cases, it reminded him of driving through the very rural parts of America, where communities had been far removed from more urban and commercial centers. This made it even more striking, as these were not separated from western markets by anything other than ideology. The people, too, did not seem to be as friendly as on the other side of the border. There were the occasional waves, mostly from younger people, but for the most part, anyone they had passed would watch them move on, without much notice or interest.

This is what it would be like if we had lost, Cameron thought. Then he realized that the war was still technically going on and that things could still change.

Oh shit, could they change!

"You two are pretty quiet," Casey said. "Didn't expect things to be quite so different, did you?"

"No, I didn't," muttered Doug. "To be honest, I wasn't sure what to expect, really."

"I kept thinking of *The Spy Who Came in from the Cold* if you want to know the truth," Cameron admitted. "The movie made life here seem so bleak and dreary. In the back of my mind, I always told myself that was just how the movie was made, in black and white. But, now ..."

"But now you think there's some truth to it?" Casey asked.

"It does seem a bit like it," Cameron admitted.

"Well, their economy here is pure shit, all centrally planned and mostly state owned," Casey muttered. "Add to that the fact that the Russians were never about to let the Germans escape war reparations, even if they were a Soviet satellite, and you realize the East Germans have never had a moment when someone wasn't standing on their throat since Hitler took power."

"Is that why the bootleg music seems to be doing so well over here?" Cameron asked him.

Casey nodded.

"Yes, and that is also why Honecker and his Stasi buddies hate it so much and keep a close eye on it and are going to be keeping a close eye on you," he said. "Even closer than they have already."

"What do you mean by 'already'?" Doug asked him.

"Man, if you think that the arrival of an American band, one that is popular among the East German underground by the way, would go unnoticed by old Markus Wolf and his lackeys, you are sadly mistaken," Casey explained. "I know, for a fact, that you have been watched."

"How do you know that?" Doug asked.

"Because you're *here*." Casey smiled. "That's all it takes. Old Wolf has more people working over on the other side of the wall than he does working here."

"Shit," Doug exhaled.

Cameron could tell by the look in his friend's eyes that, for the first time, the enormity of what they were dealing with had finally occurred to him. For a moment, Cameron thought that Doug might be having a flashback to the night in Seattle when their old world had come to a violent end. Doug remained quiet for a little while, but Cameron saw him relax, and that made Cameron relax. He knew that some measure of nervousness was inevitable, even if it were simply the anxiety caused by being in a new location. There was just no way around that. However, as Cameron had learned so long ago, there is also the anxiety that paralyzes, like a deer in the headlights. What they had experienced in Seattle could, conceivably, produce that kind of fear. So many people around them had died, and Doug was nearly in that number.

Fortunately, he had long ago steeled himself to doing what they were expected to do, and Cameron was pleased to see the anxiety in his friend's face be replaced with determination, then confusion. Cameron followed his friend's gaze and saw Wessel's car pulled over to the side of the road.

"You better pull over as well," Cameron advised.

As Doug pulled up behind the photographer's car, Cameron could see another car parked in front of Wessel's from which two men emerged. They approached Wessel's car from each side, and Cameron suspected they were security officers. One of them rapped on Wessel's window and was handed some of the paperwork they had been required to produce at the border.

Are they going to watch us shit, too?

The men returned the papers to Wessel after examining them

and made their way back to the truck. As they approached, Doug rolled down his window.

"Please present us with your travel documents," the man said in perfect English, but with a heavy German accent. Doug handed them over as directed. The man examined them carefully, saying nothing, but grunting in acknowledgment of whatever it was that he was looking for.

"You will follow the car in front of you," the man directed. "They will be following us. We are going to take you to the location of your performance. Please do not try to deviate from that route, and try not to fall behind. There will be an unmarked car following you to ensure your compliance with these directions."

With that, the man handed the paperwork back to Doug and returned to his car. Watching the other two vehicles pull back onto the road, Doug fell in behind Wessel's car. Looking in the side-view mirror, Cameron noticed several cars following them.

"I wonder which car is the one with the security detail in it?" he asked.

"Probably all of them, if you want to know the truth," Casey muttered.

"Are you shitting me?" Doug asked, looking in the mirror.

"No, not really." Casey shrugged. "The East German security forces are probably the largest employer in the country, if half of what I hear is true."

As the small caravan made its way through the East German countryside, Cameron and the other two rode mostly in silence. There was nothing on the radio but German-speaking stations and some classical music, none of which appealed to them. From time to time, one of them would make an observation about something they saw. That would elicit a short conversation from the others but would soon run its course, reducing them to silence once more. Doug, intent on not missing any turns or directions from the lead cars, did not contribute more than a few remarks here and there, leaving the bulk of the conversations to Casey and Cameron.

As they drew closer to East Berlin, Cameron noticed that things seemed to be even more worn and dreary. Even the buildings that had some paint on them bore signs that they had been painted long ago. The colors, once vibrant, had a washed appearance. Inside East Berlin, Cameron saw open lots and piles of old bricks and rubble, as well as scaffolding. However, there was little active construction. Chunks were missing from the sidewalk, and the street was dotted with potholes.

"Just like driving on a road in Vermont during mud season," Doug grumbled. "I thought these guys had such great roads. What the hell is up with this?"

"They've got great roads on the autobahn," Casey informed him. "They use that to transport what goods they can import and to move the military around. Here in the city? Well, as you can see, they are doing a lot of reconstruction from the war and that poses some problems."

"I thought Berlin had been agreed upon as an open city?" Cameron asked. "Did it get blasted early on or something?"

"I'm talking about the Second World War," Casey explained. "See, during the war, the Russians got the brunt of the Nazi war machine. More people died in Russia than anywhere else. So, when the Russians invaded, they made certain that the Germans were going to pay for what they had done. Since they couldn't exert much, if any, influence over the parts of Germany that fell under Allied control, they had to content themselves with squeezing retribution out of the sections that were under Soviet control."

"And I take it, they did?" Cameron asked.

Casey nodded. "Oh, shit yeah." He whistled. "Or rather, they are. If anything had any value, it went back to Russia—industrial equipment, resources, you name it. The Russians figured if it was useful, it was too good for a German. They then set up a Communist government here to make certain Germany could never be a thorn in Russia's side ever again, and the East Germans have been trying to be more Communist than Moscow ever since. Part of doing that is by pretending the Russians aren't still the de facto landlords here."

"What does that have to do with it?" Doug muttered, trying to wend his way through the outskirts of the city.

"Well, pretty much if the Russians ask the East Germans if they can do something, it is really just a polite way of telling them what they are going to do—build military sites, help manage their industries, that sort of thing."

"Are you telling me that they don't even let the East Germans run their own shit?" gasped Cameron.

"Man, I'll let you in on something," Casey said. "As long as there is a hammer and sickle flying over the Kremlin, the Germans will be paying for the blitzkrieg, either covertly or overtly. There is no way around that."

As they talked, Cameron noticed that things seemed to be a little better the more they got into the city. At first, it wasn't as perceptible, but gradually he noticed that the streets were cleaner and it did not appear to be so run down in parts.

"Over there, you can see Saint Walter's tower," Casey said, pointing to a large structure mounted by a silver ball.

"What the hell is that?" Doug asked.

"That is the best example of East German lack of planning ever." Casey laughed. "Back in the sixties, the East German government wanted to build a television antenna, and they decided to make it bigger than any of the churches in Berlin to show the triumph of Communism over religion. They had this big, freaking contest for architects to design it and finally decided to have it look like Sputnik. You know, that Russian satellite?"

"Oh yeah, I have heard of that," Doug remembered. "Didn't that cause a big stink when they did that?"

"It had people all over the world shitting their pants because now the Soviets could launch something into space," Cameron explained. "They figured the next thing would be a missile that could hit Washington, London, Peoria, or anyplace that Moscow wanted. That lit the fire under us to get moving on our space program."

"Exactly," said Casey, resuming his narrative. "Anyhow, they got all set to dedicate the whole thing and had it all draped with a big cloth so no one could get a view of it beforehand. Walter Ulbricht, the East German leader at the time, and a whole bunch of Communist dignitaries were there, and everyone was making speeches about that damn thing being the highest point in Berlin and how it symbolized the triumph of Communism over the West and science over religion, blah, blah, blah. Then they dropped the cloth covering it for everyone to see and discovered a big, huge, freaking mistake."

"What was it?" Doug asked.

Cameron tried not to laugh at the roadie's enthusiasm. Casey pointed to the tower again.

"The way it was designed, when the sun hits it, the reflection forms a big-ass old cross!"

Cameron looked again and realized that Casey was right. There, shining on the reflective tiles, was a large, white cross.

"I bet that went over well." Cameron chuckled.

"Ulbricht was pissed!" Casey laughed. "Everyone started calling it the Pope's Revenge or Saint Walter's tower, after Walter Ulbricht."

Cameron took that as a sign. Not that he was religious in any way. His mom stopped making him go to Sunday school when he was eight, and he hadn't been back in a church since. However, thinking about how the Communists wanted to score some big victory and having it turn against them made them all seem a little less omnipotent, and made him feel a little more hopeful.

Finally, the caravan pulled into a large, open square in front of an imposing building. On either side of the central building were two more equally imposing buildings, surrounded by scaffolding. Doug was directed to park between the large building and the scaffolded building to the north of the square.

"Where are we?" Doug asked.

Cameron noticed how quiet the roadie's voice was, as if he didn't want anyone else to hear him.

Shit, he's nervous again. Great, that is just great.

"That building there is called the Konzerthaus, or concert hall," Casey explained calmly. "The big space we're in is called the

Gendarmenmarkt because way back some cavalry regiment was here. Those two big buildings, I'm not sure. I think they might be museums or something."

"You know a lot about East Berlin," Cameron remarked. "I thought you said you'd never been here."

Casey shrugged. "Man, I've been in Germany how long? I've asked some of my, um, *friends* what Konzerthaus and the square were like to get an idea about the layout and how to handle it, and they gave me the whole lowdown on the place, simple as that. That story about the tower? Shit, that's the biggest joke in Germany since the damn thing got unveiled!"

Cameron shrugged and looked around, trying not to be embarrassed for once again forgetting Casey was an agent, as well.

There was a large stage being constructed in front of the steps to the Konzerthaus. From where he stood, Cameron could see it was intended to provide the large crowd with maximum visibility of the band. Cameron felt a bit of relief that they expected so many people to be there.

Maybe I've just been overreacting?

At the back of the truck, Doug and Casey were standing off to the side, presenting their papers to yet another security guard. Kendrick was speaking to one of the officers and motioned to Cameron to present the man with his documentation. Amid various orders, issued in German and translated into English, each piece of luggage was inspected. The discovery of several cartons of cigarettes in their suitcases did cause a bit of a stir, until Kendrick produced the guidelines that showed they were permitted.

"The guys smoke them and sometimes share," she said, through Wessel's dutiful translation. This apparently pleased the guards, who pointed to themselves. Each took a carton. Cameron wanted to protest but knew that to do anything but smile would cause monumental problems.

After the inspection of the luggage came the inspection of the guitar cases. As the guards each grabbed an instrument, Cameron writhed inside. One of them was incredibly clumsy and was not careful about handling the instruments. Another guard opened the case that carried Cameron's favorite guitar, the one the used the most. The thought of anyone, even a fellow musician, handling his instruments made him uncomfortable. There was always the risk that something could happen and you would be unable to play, thus putting you out of a job. Now, with non-musicians, and unsympathetic ones at that, he was even more concerned. To his horror, the guard removed it from its case, slung it over his shoulder, and pretended to play. Visions of the entire concert being canceled due to the ineptitude of an East German inspector flashed before his eyes.

If he does anything to that guitar, the war resumes right here!

Then, to Cameron's amazement, the guard gently lifted the guitar and moved his hand along the frets, nodding in appreciation to the smoothness of them against the guitar's neck. He held it as if he was playing the instrument and softly strummed it. The guard smiled and said something to Wessel, who pointed to Cameron. For one brief and horrifying moment, Cameron was afraid the guard was going to ask him for it.

"Das ist nett," the guard said, removing the guitar from around his neck and carefully handing it back to Cameron.

"He said that is nice," Wessel translated.

"Vielen dank," Cameron replied, taking the guitar.

The guard smiled and began speaking in German.

"Tell him that's all I know." Cameron smiled at Wessel, who dutifully relayed the information. The guard laughed and nodded.

"He was asking how long you have played," Wessel explained.

Cameron was about to answer the question, but the other guards, discouraging any attempt at friendly interaction, barked at the one talking to Cameron, and they all resumed their inspection as the truck was unloaded.

Doug and Casey each brought a piece of equipment down the ramp, one at a time, while the guards examined them against the manifest they had. All of the luggage was replaced in the car while this went on. As the equipment was being unloaded, Kendrick had Wessel ask the guards if it would be possible for one of the roadies to transport the inspected equipment to the stage to be set up, while the other one unloaded. After debating the issue for what the guards felt was sufficient time to establish their authority, they consented to her request.

"We need to get this stuff set up as fast as we can for the sound checks," Kendrick grumbled to Casey. "They're probably going to want to check the system once we've set it up, too."

"It will go a lot faster if I've got help moving it and had someone up there hooking it up," Casey told her, looking at the musicians.

"I can work with you setting up," Rich volunteered.

Collier agreed to help move the equipment, and Evan said he would work with Doug.

"That just leaves me, I guess," said Cameron. "I'll help set everything up and start the sound checks."

The system worked out well, he thought. They were able to get the speakers and monitors in place while Kendrick and Wessel sorted things out at the truck. Though he couldn't hear what was going on from where he stood, he could watch. Occasionally, Doug and Evan would bring things off the truck too fast for the guards, who angrily ordered an item returned. Finally, once the drum kit had been moved and set up, it was time to do the sound check. Cameron went back to the car to get his guitar cases and bumped into Casey going through the trunk.

"What are you looking for in there?" Cameron asked suspiciously.

The roadies kept their bags in the truck with them, and therefore, Casey had no reason to be in the trunk. To Cameron's surprise, it wasn't Casey but Collier.

"Oh, I snagged my shirt on something during load-in and had to change," he explained.

Cameron noticed that Collier had, in fact, changed from his red T-shirt and now wore an orange one. That, combined with the denim vest and his physical resemblance to the second roadie, was what had led to Cameron's confusion.

"Why are you wearing a vest?" Cameron demanded.

"Hey, this is my last clean shirt," Collier protested. "I don't know what I snagged my other one on, and I don't have anything else to change into if this gets torn."

Cameron saw no reason to argue with his decision, and the two men returned to the stage where, as assumed, additional security checks were being done on the sound equipment. With the musicians assembled, the elaborate dance of questioning, examining, and explaining resumed under the watchful eye of Kendrick and the contributions of Wessel. Finally, the moment arrived when all of the microphones, monitors, and speakers had been set to the proper volume and settings for each instrument and musician. The sound system was checked and approved, and the lighting was set up.

The show was still a little ways off, but at last they were ready to begin. Standing on the stage, Cameron noticed the sea of people that had been gathering in the square while everything was happening. Looking over the crowd, he noticed how many there were already, and he wondered how many of the people watching him knew who he was or had listened to bootleg versions of his records.

I also wonder how many of you little bastards are agents!

Chapter 40

"Red Sector A"

Hertz pushed his way through the gathering crowd on the street, Mikhail close behind him. To his credit, the boy was so thrilled at being at a concert that he had given Hertz little trouble, aside from the expected annoyances brought on by adolescent enthusiasm. Even now, he peppered Hertz with questions and requests but did not stop talking long enough to notice that Hertz was not listening.

"My God, this thing doesn't start for another hour and look at all these people," Hertz snapped, trying to make his way to the building known as the French Church, which loomed before him but seemed to ever remain just out of reach. "I can just imagine what it will be like in the square!"

"I hope its wall-to-wall people," Mikhail enthused. "Can we get close to the stage? I want to get as close as possible. I've never been to one of these before!"

"They aren't all they're made out to be," Hertz assured him. "It is a lot of propaganda hype to get people to fall for the American tales. It will be over before you know it, and you'll realize you went to all this trouble to hear something you could have listened to at home on your stereo."

"Will they have records or tapes here?" Mikhail asked, ignoring Hertz's dampening remarks. "Can I get one? I don't have anything by these guys. I'd like to have a real American album."

"What are the ones they give you?" Hertz demanded. "Aren't they American? What is wrong with them?"

"It isn't the same," Mikhail protested. "I didn't get them myself, so I don't know where they are from! I want a real American record, and I want them to sign it, too! Can we get them to sign it?"

"I don't know if I can even get you to see them," Hertz snapped. "Can't you see all of these people here? They all want the same thing as you! They've all bought into the Western propaganda as well. Now shut up and let me concentrate. I'm trying to find someone!"

They pushed through, and Hertz at last saw the steps of the building, but they were empty. Checking his watch, he saw that he was on time and at first became angry at her delay. Then he remembered there were more than one set of steps to the building. Making their way around the corner, he spotted her.

Alina was at the top of the steps, leaning against the pedestal of one of the pillars. She was dressed similarly to how he had seen her before, with one glaring difference: her hair was orange. She was languidly blowing smoke rings into the air, indicating it was safe to talk, and at first appeared not to notice him. However, as he approached, she stretched and began to descend the stairs and met him halfway down.

"I didn't think you wanted to be too visible," she explained, sitting down.

"That was wise." He smiled. "Alina, this is Mikhail, my charge. Mikhail, this is my friend Alina. If you are hoping to be able to get access to this performance, she is the one who would best be able to help you."

The boy became excited at this news and began to pepper the girl with questions and requests, until Hertz cut him off.

"How do things look?" Hertz asked.

"I think this will be a big event," she said. "As you can see, there is the stage. The Americans have already set up their equipment and are elsewhere right now. The people you see there now are from the German band that will be performing first, though the man in the black cap was on the stage with the Americans' equipment, so I think he might be attached to them. I haven't gotten close enough to be certain."

"The German band will suck," Mikhail declared.

Alina rolled her eyes but otherwise made no remark. Hertz simply ignored him.

"Have you met any of the performers yet?" Hertz asked.

Alina shook her head. "Not yet. They were quite busy with their preparations for the show; however, I did get some smiles from some of them, so it is likely I can capitalize on that later."

"You met the band?" Mikhail gasped. "Can I go with you then?"

"Shut up," snapped Hertz. "If we can arrange for you to meet them, we will. If we can't, you'll shut your damn mouth."

"Over there, beside the stage, you can see a curtained-off area," Alina pointed out, ignoring their exchange. "That's where the band is staying until it is time for them to go on stage, and that is also where they will be having their reception afterward."

"How do you get into that reception area?" Hertz wondered.

"They have a limited number of special passes that they hand out in the crowds, from what I've been told," she explained. "The ones that get them are able to get backstage."

"Do you know how to get them?" Mikhail asked eagerly.

Hertz was about to reprimand him once more but then cast a knowing smile to Alina. From the smile she returned, it was evident that she had the same thought.

"I think I know how," she replied coyly. "I have certain charms that might make that possible."

Mikhail was barely able to contain his enthusiasm, and Hertz had to rebuke him, harshly. The boy adopted a resentful silence but cast a grateful smile at Alina. As they were speaking, the square began to fill up with even more people than before.

"I think we were wise to meet here," she said. "We actually have the best seat in the house to watch the performance."

"We're not here to watch them," Hertz reminded her. "We need to be hearing what they are saying."

"I listened to the sound system," she replied. "You'll hear every whisper, believe me. Besides, do you really think they'd be foolish enough to do anything that obvious during the performance?"

"No, my dear, I do not." He smiled. "That is why I am counting on those various charms you referenced to get us tickets to the reception. If they are going to say, or do, anything subversive, they will be doing it then."

"My thoughts exactly." She smiled, lighting a cigarette.

"Can I have one of those?" Mikhail asked sheepishly.

The girl looked to Hertz for direction.

"What the hell, give him one," he said.

The three watched as the square continued to fill. Outdoor lighting helped illumine the growing, teeming sea of humanity before them. Soon floodlights began sweeping the sky and the square, adding to the sense of excitement that even Hertz could feel building. As he watched, he thought of the number of agents and plainclothes police officers that were also in that crowd, and he began to relax. If the Americans were going to try anything, it would be easy to detect. As he turned to speak to Alina, the floodlights swept the stairs and her hair seemed to glow even brighter.

"I suppose it's a good thing you colored your hair that color," he said. "It will be easy to spot you in this crowd!"

"That was precisely why I did it." She smiled. "I knew I would have a hard time being found, so I thought I'd make it easy."

"You are a clever girl," he said and smiled back as the master of ceremonies came out onto the stage.

To thunderous applause, the man announced the evening's show and lineup, giving initial credit to the Ministry of Culture and the East German government to loud but comparatively tepid applause, as they acknowledged the cooperation with the Americans and the West Germans. At this point, he reminded the crowd to comply with appropriate behavior, without defining what that was, and then he announced the opening band.

★★★

Cameron nursed his tequila. He knew he had to keep it cool but decided to have just one drink before going on stage. The warmth of the liquor, combined with the sounds of the band onstage, helped make him feel more relaxed.

"They really aren't bad," said Rich.

Cameron was a little startled—he hadn't heard the bass player coming up behind him—but smiled instead of getting upset.

"No, I guess they are pretty good." He laughed. "But you can tell they learned all their songs on the radio and are singing phonetically. The inflections and emphases are a little awkward."

"But the crowd is eating it up," said Rich. "That's always the main thing!"

"Do you think we'll do as well out there?" Cameron wondered.

Rich shrugged. "I honestly have no idea. We could be the greatest thing since Bismarck or be booed off the stage as soon as we get on."

"I was thinking that same thing." Cameron chuckled.

"Man, I'm still trying to get my head around being here in the first place." Rich smiled. "We've come a long way from that shit hole in Rutland, wouldn't you agree?"

"Oh, hell yes!" Cameron exclaimed. "Headlining an international tour. We're finally rock stars!"

He checked his watch and realized that the opening band would soon be halfway through their set.

"A few more songs and we need to be on deck," he told the others. "Any questions?"

They discussed the opening set and how they would handle their break.

"Remember, back here for ten minutes only," Kendrick repeated. "For security purposes, the Ministry of Culture wants fraternization limited to the reception exclusively. Understood?"

No one argued; they were all perfectly willing to comply. They had no intrinsic desire to cause trouble, and even if they did, the Ministry of Culture had posted a few policemen in the back to ensure that all regulations were complied with. The policemen's uniforms were field gray, with military-style field caps, and Cameron and the others had initially mistaken them for soldiers.

"Vopo," Wessel had called them. From the first time Cameron had heard that word, he thought it was an insult until someone explained that it was the abbreviation for Volkspolizei, or German People's Police.

"They're the cops you guys mentioned?" Cameron gasped. "They look like soldiers to me."

"Well, they are structured a bit on paramilitary lines," Wessel agreed. "But they are the police."

Even more incentive to be a good boy.

Cameron counted the songs the band was playing. The opening band's set list indicated they would be playing twelve songs, and this was number seven.

"Okay, guys, let's get it together," Cameron called out. "They'll be done in a few minutes. Let's get ready to make an entrance!"

Cameron and the others gathered their instruments, except for Evan who already had his drumsticks in his back pocket. Cameron was calculating the time that would be required to get the other band off and have the roadies haul off their equipment.

It shouldn't take too long; their equipment was in front of ours. Haul it off and we go on. They only had a few monitors and no speakers. Ten minutes, fifteen tops.

Cameron finished his drink and gathered with the others near the stairs leading to the stage. While he was waiting, he had Doug double-check the refreshments that were set aside for the other band, to make certain they were out.

A courtesy from one group to the other.

He counted the twelfth song and then moved into position. The song ended to loud and wild applause, and then, to Cameron's amazement, the band started another song.

"Did I miscount?" he asked Rich. The bass player shook his head.

"If you did, then so did I," he replied.

"Maybe it's an encore?" Collier proposed.

The band agreed that it might be.

"I'm not going to begrudge them that on their home turf." Cameron smiled. "I just hope they don't get carried away with it!"

Kendrick moved to the bottom of the stairs and checked her watch. There was no mistaking the concern on her face.

"We've got a tight schedule," she said testily. "We *have* to be at the border by nine o'clock. We can't afford any delays."

"Don't look at us, sweetheart," advised Cameron. "We're all in our places with bright, shiny faces. Go tell the other guys to get a wiggle on."

Cameron did not need her to remind him of their deadlines; he had them firmly planted in his mind. The set list was planned out, to the minute, to accommodate the performance, the after-party, and the exit.

If anything else is being done during that time, I hope it goes off without a hitch.

To the band's amazement, the other band broke into a second song. This caused a great deal of irritation and commentary, but Cameron did not know what to do about it.

We can't cut off their power or their mics; that will ruin the whole evening.

To his relief, Kendrick motioned for Wessel and whispered something in his ear. The photographer nodded and hurried up the stairs.

"I had him tell the band they needed to hurry; they were disrupting the ministry's schedule."

"Are they?" Cameron smiled.

Kendrick shrugged.

"Bands need ministry permission to perform in East Germany. The ministry was not keen on this entire event to begin with; to cause complications is not going to make things easy for the offending party in the future. They're not stupid; they'll wrap it up."

Kendrick's ploy worked because at the end of that song the lead singer made some remarks in German, which were received with more applause but no further performance.

One by one, the other musicians made their way to the backstage area and were greeted by the Roadhouse Sons with smiles and handshakes. Cameron asked Doug and Casey to go onstage and help remove the other band's equipment but were stopped by Wessel.

"They said they were sorry to have delayed you, and they would get their equipment when you removed yours to prevent further inconvenience," he explained.

Cameron was not thrilled with that, knowing how easy it would be for one bit of equipment to become confused with another and one band could easily have something that belonged to the other.

"But there's nothing I can do about that now," he muttered and turned to his bandmates. "Okay, guys, listen up! We cut off two songs from the first set list; that should bring us back on schedule."

"Better make it three, considering our intro and entrance," suggested Evan.

"Which three?" Collier asked.

"The last three," Cameron said as they started up the stairs.

They paused just behind the curtain, as the master of ceremonies was speaking. The Roadhouse Sons couldn't understand everything the announcer was saying, but they did hear "America" and "rock and roll" and could hear the speaker's voice as he built up to a climax. They emerged from the curtain when he said, "Roadhouse Sons" and felt the tremor of excitement as the stage lit up and the crowd erupted into wild applause.

Is this how David Bowie feels?

Cameron was so overwhelmed, he almost knocked over his microphone stand.

"Hallo, Berlin!" he shouted, spreading his arms.

The other band members let out a rebel yell and pumped the air with their fists, a gesture enthusiastically echoed by the crowd. As Cameron looked out from the stage, the surging mass of humanity raised its collective voice in applause and cheers.

Holy crap, they're out of their minds and we haven't done anything yet!

He tried not to think that this was a reaction orchestrated by the Ministry of Culture, though he suspected that if it was going to instruct the crowd to do anything, it would be to sit on their hands. No, this was a genuine welcome.

And, by God, we'll let you know it is appreciated!

Cameron nodded to Evan, who began an enthusiastic, rhythmic beating of his drums, each of the band members nodding their heads in unison with the lights and the drummer's cadence, before striking the cords on their guitars. The lights then erupted into a flurry of multicolored flashes, and the crowd began to roar. Cameron was grateful for the guitar parts, as they allowed him a moment to reflect on exactly what was happening. He was playing not only in a foreign country but, at least nominally, in a hostile one as well. He was playing for a crowd that had only heard them on bootleg records and illegal broadcasts. Now the Roadhouse Sons were live and in person.

The guitar piece ended and the drum piece resumed, the lights keeping up with the change in the music. Through either a trick of the light, or perhaps in actuality, the crowd seemed to be moving their heads in time with the music, getting into the song before they even played it. To Cameron, this was a dream come true, a validation for his years as a musician. His heart swelled as he began the song.

"Out on the road for forty days," he began, and the crowd drowned him out with their cheers.

They know this song! He laughed to himself as he continued the lyrics. There were claps and cheers and people vying for the band's attention. Cameron could not remember when he had heard the band play like this before.

That's stupid, we've always done great. However, even he had to admit that the circumstances they were playing under made the entire experience seem even more moving. A fact brought home when he began the chorus.

"We're an American band," he sang out, and the crowd sang along. "We're an American band! We're coming to your town, we'll help you party it down, we're an American band!"

Cameron paused in his singing while the crowd went wild. In the sweep of the lights, he thought he noticed a flash of color.

Don't be ridiculous; there's a ton of stuff to focus on.

Yet, when he began the next verse, his eyes were drawn to the front of the crowd.

"Four young chiquitas in Omaha," he sang, and his eyes rested on a line of young women in the front, one of them with orange hair. The verse continued with enthusiastic response from the audience.

"Now, these fine ladies," Cameron sang, pointing to the front row. "They had a plan; they was out to meet the boys in the band." He gave the ladies in the front row a thumbs-up, and each one responded as if he had said it just to them.

This time the crowd sang along with the chorus, giving it more emphasis and gusto each time it was repeated. Undoubtedly, there was a desire to take advantage of the anonymity provided by a crowd and use the lyrics as a veiled protest against a government that did not permit open protests. Yet, just as arguably, there was the simple joy and enthusiasm of the moment and having a good time.

When the song finished to thunderous applause, Cameron was relieved not to see any of the Vopo officers standing at the top of the stairs, ready to cart them off as they went into their next song. Cameron smiled as he watched the dancing and swaying to "Some Kind of Wonderful" and "Statesboro Blues." When they began to sing "All Night Long," Cameron truly wished that this could go on all night long.

★★★

Casey made his way among the gyrating crowd as he had done every performance of the tour. People would bump against him and then give him room. His clearly marked backstage pass indicated that he was a member of the band and afforded him an element of deference from the fans. He had been to enough shows in his life to know that people who worked for the band were a reflection of it, and so he always tried to be polite and smile when they spoke to him. Casey did not like getting caught in conversations because that usually led to someone concluding they now had an intimate connection with the band and would try to use that to their advantage. To help prevent that here, Casey merely had to pretend he did not speak German, though of course he did. However, no one needed to be made aware of that.

Working his way through the crowd, he spotted the person he had been looking for. He had seen her earlier in the crowd: a young woman, apparently alone, dressed in the tattered costume of the underground movement and sporting orange hair. It was difficult to miss her. When the floodlights swept through the crowd, they lit up her hair like a neon sign.

Approaching her, he was about to tap her on the shoulder when she turned and saw him. As chance would have it, at that moment the light swept through the crowd and shone on him, revealing his orange shirt. Casey pointed at his shirt and her hair and began to laugh. He held up his pass, indicating he was with the band. At that, she began to smile as well.

Casey reached into his vest pocket and withdrew another backstage pass and held it up. He pointed to her and held it out. With a confused look on her face, she took it and examined it. Then a smile broke out as she understood what it was. She gave him a hug and a kiss and thanked him profusely in German. He nodded and turned to walk off when she grabbed his arm. She said something to him as he turned to face her, but between the band and the crowd, it was impossible to hear what it was she said. He shook his head and touched his ear to indicate that he had not heard.

"*Mein kleiner bruder,*" she said, leaning into him. Casey tried to figure out what it as she said, a fact she clearly understood from the confused look on his face. She repeated the word *bruder* louder and held her hand out, indicating a height.

"Oh, your brother!" he said, finally understanding that she wanted another pass for her brother. With a smile, he handed over another one and once more turned to leave. Again she put her hand on his shoulder to stop him. When he turned back, she tapped her temple and smiled at him, then pointed to his head. This time Casey had no trouble understanding what she wanted. He had a cigarette behind his ear. Before handing it over, he lit it for her. She accepted it with a smile and took a drag, exhaling it straight into the air. She gave him a wink and a smile and then turned back to watch the band. Casey resumed his mission of going through the crowd, passing out invitations to the after-party.

★★★

Gagarin shifted uncomfortably in his seat. The pressure was becoming unbearable. The two gunmen still sat opposite him, their guns still trained on him.

"Can I please use the bathroom?" he asked. He refused to beg or plead. No matter what else, he would keep his dignity.

"You may," the first gunman said. At that, the second gunman rose and stepped back, gesturing for Gagarin to rise. Both men still kept their guns trained on him in case he tried anything. They pointed to a small door.

"The restroom is there," the first man said. "You may use it, but the door will remain open so we may watch you. I assure you, our interests are solely ones of security, nothing else."

Gagarin bristled at this but realized the only alternative was to soil himself. Reluctantly, he agreed. Mercifully, he did not need to sit down, so he was spared that indignity. When he finished, he was directed to resume his seat.

Shortly after he did so, he felt the plane begin to descend, and a voice instructed them to make certain they were buckled in safely. Gagarin wanted to laugh at the absurdity of conducting this like a commercial flight but saw the wisdom in remaining silent. They had not been airborne long, and he was trying to determine where they could be landing. Without a watch to tell him how long they had been aloft, that was impossible. He heard the wing flaps alter the flow of the air outside and knew that they were preparing to land. Not long after, the sound of the rushing of the airstream indicated they were approaching ground, and at last came the anticipated bump and squeal of the landing gear against the tarmac. The plane slowed down and taxied for a time before coming to a complete stop.

"How long are we going to remain here?" he asked his captors.

"Until we receive word on what to do with you," the first gunman replied.

"When will that be?" Gagarin asked.

They made no reply.

★★★

Hertz watched the crowd from his vantage point at the top of the stairs, looking for the flash of Alina's orange hair. The night was a kaleidoscope of colors and looking for that flash of orange was nearly impossible.

"Where is she?" Mikhail pestered. "Do you see her? Is she coming?"

"If I saw her, I would tell you," he snapped. "And if you bother me one more time, you'll regret it."

"I'm just asking a question," Mikhail snapped. "Why won't you let me go down there to be closer? I can't hear the band from up here!"

"If you can't hear them from up here, then you are deaf and there is no reason for you to be here at all," Hertz warned. "Now stop being a little ass and try to enjoy yourself."

"How can I?" Mikhail demanded. "I want to be down there where I can really enjoy myself."

"You'll just get into trouble," Hertz replied wearily.

"Forgive me for wanting to enjoy my childhood!"

Hertz leaned into the petulant boy's pouting face. "If you give me any more trouble, you will never enjoy another thing in your life."

Mikhail's eyes widened in fear as he leaned back.

"Do you know who I am?" the boy warned. "I'll report you! I'll have your job for this!"

"Do you know who *I* am?" Hertz smiled. "I'm the last person they could find who would put up with you. Your days as the golden boy are running out, you little puke. You have pushed too many buttons for anyone to give a damn about you anymore. If you

350

ruin things for yourself here, it is back to Russia with you. Do you understand me?"

Mikhail looked at him with wild incredulity but didn't say anything.

"I asked if you understood me?" Hertz repeated, leaning in closer.

Finally, Mikhail nodded.

"Good." The man smiled. "Now stop being a pain in my ass." He glanced at the boy out of the corner of his eye and saw that the young man wanted to say something but wisely chose not to, at first.

"I see her!" he cried, pointing.

Hertz, too, saw the mop of orange hair wending its way through the crowd to where they were. As she came up the stairs, Hertz noticed the look of satisfaction on her face and knew that she had been successful.

"Did you get them?" he asked to confirm his suspicion.

"I did," she assured him. "However, I only got two. They are apparently limited to how many they give out per person."

"That will do," Hertz assured her. "I think that it would be just as well for you to take him as me. Seeing you apparently unattached will help you get to know them better. I doubt even they will mistake this one for your boyfriend."

Mikhail sneered in response.

"I already told them I needed the second one for my younger brother," she said. "They were only too happy to oblige."

"Excellent then." Hertz smiled. "I'll wait here for you."

"I'm afraid not," she warned him. "I overheard the security details complaining about how hard it will be to clear the square following the performance. No one is allowed to remain here to discourage fraternizing. However, I do have an idea."

"Let's here it then," he grumbled.

Alina smiled at his frustration. Hertz traditionally disliked anything he felt was beneath him upsetting his plans. Since he was working undercover as the boy's guardian, there was no opportunity for him to overrule the Vopo's directives without drawing undo attention to himself. Now, having to form a plan at the last minute and subject it to revisions as he was doing so, was clearly an irritant.

"There is really no reason for you to remain here, anyway," she explained, moving him away from the boy to avoid being overheard. "We are not planning any activities other than observation. I can mingle with the band, and you can meet me where I parked my friend's car."

"What if something happens?" Hertz demanded. "How will you respond to that situation?"

"There will be Vopo on duty," she assured him. "I'll hardly be alone. If I notice something that needs attention, I can always scream and tear my clothes, indicating some type of assault. That will bring everything to a halt and bring in the authorities."

"As good as that sounds, I'm hoping it won't come to that," Hertz sighed. "Having too many people involved will be pointless."

"Agreed," said Alina. "So the reception is only for thirty minutes, by order of the ministry. My meeting point for my ride was roughly a fifteen-minute walk from here, but that was due to the crowd coming into the square and the redirected traffic. I doubt it will be that long going out, but, allowing additional time in case of delay, let's say that he and I will reconnect with you one hour from the end of the performance."

"That sounds reasonable," Hertz agreed. "I'll stay here until the performance ends, in case there is some incident. I'll leave with the crowd and meet you there."

Alina gave him the directions to the meeting point, as well as the description of her friend's car.

"Very well," he muttered. "I suggest you take the little shit down toward the stage, so he doesn't feel any more deprived of this experience then he is claiming. That will help control him better."

"I have no doubt I can handle him," she assured Hertz. Whispering in the boy's ear, she indicated they were heading down to the stage, and as she had predicted, he was quite eager to cooperate.

Hertz watched them make their way through the crowd once

more. The bob of the orange hair moved through a sea of humanity until it became lost in the dazzle of the lights.

★★★

"Okay, grab some water and rest your fingers a bit," sighed Kendrick. "This is going to be a short break, and I do mean *short*."

"What's going on?" Rich moaned. "I'm beat and hoping for at least a few minutes."

"The police are giving the other band a hard time about leaving their equipment on stage with ours. They're afraid something might happen and things will get mixed up. They are pressuring them to get moving, and they can't get anything off of the stage until we're finished."

"So how long do we have then?" Collier asked her.

"You've got five minutes," she replied. Her response was greeted with a flurry of protests, to which she nodded in acknowledgment.

"I know," she assured them. "I know, believe me, I know! But there is absolutely nothing we can do about it. Grab some water, grab some beer; hell, take a pull from a bottle of tequila if it will make you feel better! But, when you're done, you need to get back on stage and finish the last set. When you're done with that, you've got thirty minutes for an after-party. The roadies are going to have to be ready on the spot to start tearing down, so walk off with your instruments and hand them over when you get offstage."

Cameron had hoped to have some time to check the strings on his guitar. He had changed them before the last show but admitted that he had played pretty hard both that night and tonight. Realizing he would no longer have that opportunity, he went to the car to swap for his other guitar. There, he was accosted by one of the Vopo, who angrily ordered him away from the vehicle. Wessel, attracted by the noise, came over to help diffuse the situation. Cameron explained to him what he was trying to do, and the photographer translated it for him. Cameron wasn't certain what Wessel had told the guard, but the man's response was accompanied by emphatic head shaking.

"I'm sorry, man," Wessel apologized. "But you can't touch the vehicles until you leave. They were supposed to have explained that to you before the show."

"No one explained shit to us, and you know it, because you would have been the one who would have had to do the explaining!" Cameron snapped.

The photographer simply shrugged and gave him a sympathetic look.

Sympathy—a word found in the dictionary between shit and syphilis.

Calming himself, Cameron regrouped with the others and returned to the stage.

"Let's shake things up a bit," Cameron said as they took their places. "Collier, 'Kashmir'!" The other guitarist smiled and struck the cords on his guitar.

In time with the beat, all of the musicians but Evan slowly advanced toward the edge of the stage. Cameron could not help but visualize a ticking clock inexorably moving to the magic moment of nine o'clock, when they would be at the border checkpoint to make their passage into West Berlin. Would they have any difficulty leaving East Berlin? Were there any surprises waiting for them? The general consensus was that they would keep as low a profile as possible while in East Berlin. No activities not previously approved by the Ministry of Culture, no interviews, and only the limited number of guests in the backstage area.

Slow and steady will win the race.

Collier was able to hit all of the notes to the song, and when Cameron closed his eyes, he felt himself transported back to Montreal on that cold February day when he had heard Jimmy Page perform the guitar parts that Cameron's own fingers were now performing and Robert Plant sing the words his friend was now singing. Was it really only nine years ago? It seemed like an entirely different world, which, in reality, it was. A world where the two biggest kids on the block had not yet gone to war. Cameron smiled, remembering the reason he and his buddies had made that trip. They were all struggling musicians, who wondered if they would ever get a chance to make it big and decided to at least make the trip to hear their favorite band. They had originally had tickets for Led Zeppelin's Boston show, but when that was canceled, they decided to make the trek to Montreal. At the time, Cameron wondered if that might not be the high water mark of his musical career.

Now I wonder if this will be my swan song?

As the last notes of "Kashmir" died out, they began the introduction to AC/DC's "High Voltage," and Evan amazed the crowd with his vocal similarity to AC/DC'S Bon Scott. So much so that the Roadhouse Sons decided to break with their established set list and move right into "TNT," where, as Cameron had suspected, the crowd eagerly participated in Angus Young's famously ad-libbed "oi" chant. Out of the corner of his eye, Cameron noticed a flash of orange. At first, he thought it was Collier's shirt, but then he noticed that Casey was once more working the crowd and had once again encountered the girl with the orange hair.

Have fun now, man. We're going to be busting our asses when teardown comes. Then he noticed that she was introducing him to another young man.

Ouch, shot down.

★★★

Casey spotted her before she had spotted him. As she had indicated, she had her younger brother with her. Casey could tell by the expression on the young man's face that he was enjoying the show.

Spotting Casey by his shirt, she wended her way through the mass of people and came alongside him. They each smiled and nodded to one another, in the manner that people who don't know what to say to one another are wont to do. Combined with this was the language barrier that Casey had no idea if, or how, he should cross.

"Do you speak English?" he said, leaning close to her ear so he would not have to shout too loudly. She paused for a moment, as if she had not heard correctly. He was about to repeat it when she suddenly understood and shrugged.

"*Sehr wenig*," she said. "A little bit."

Casey gave her a thumbs-up.

"I speak little English," the boy said. "I am Mikhail. I like this music."

"That's good," Casey shouted above the sound. "Would you two like to come backstage?"

Alina gave him a puzzled expression, looking to Mikhail for direction. He translated the request into German, and she nodded emphatically.

"*Ja!*" she said and smiled as Casey led them to the site of the reception.

"You can wait here until the party," he explained to Mikhail. "The band is almost done. When they are done, you will be able to meet them here."

"That is good; that is good!" Mikhail enthused. "Do you have records? Do you have tapes?"

The boy's heavy accent, combined with the volume of the speakers, made it difficult for Casey to understand at first. Then, as Mikhail repeated his question slowly, making motions suggestive of a record album, Casey was able to understand.

"We have tapes," he said into Mikhail's ear, nodding emphatically. "Would you like one?"

Now it was the boy's turn to nod enthusiastically. Casey motioned for him to wait and ducked behind the curtain divider; he returned momentarily with two plastic cassette cases. Mikhail was nearly beside himself when Casey handed them over, showing them to Alina and babbling in a mixture of German and Russian. Alina smiled and winked at Casey, who returned the gesture.

"Wait here," he said, pointing to the ground where they stood. "I will be back soon."

Alina nodded, but Mikhail gave no indication that he had heard anything Casey said. With another wink and nod, Casey went back into the crowd while Alina watched him go, avoiding any direct eye contact with the Vopo who ogled her.

★★★

Gagarin shifted in his seat. The boredom was becoming oppressive. The two gunmen sat opposite him as still as statues. Gagarin was reminded of elderly Buddhist monks that he had met in the Far East, their placid expressions unchanged as they meditated for great periods of time.

"How much longer?" Gagarin demanded.

"I assure you that, one way or another, you will not have too much longer to wait," the first gunman assured him.

"What is that supposed to mean?" Gagarin exclaimed.

"There is a deadline that defines the length of time we are to detain you," the gunman said. "When that deadline has been reached, you are to be released."

"You mean, you are to let me go?" the Russian asked.

"That depends upon the circumstances that reveal themselves when that moment arrives," the man explained.

"You mean, there is a chance I will not get out of here alive?"

"As I explained to you already, information is need to know only." He smiled.

★★★

The final notes of the last song were beginning to fade into the night. As was their custom, the Roadhouse Sons ended with a song that enabled Evan to do the drum solo from Led Zeppelin's "Moby Dick," with the guitarists holding their fists in the air, their heads bowed. Out of the corner of his eye, Cameron saw Doug and Casey, with the other roadies, waiting just off stage to begin tearing down.

Looks like we're even more pressed for time than I thought!

The Roadhouse Sons lined up along the edge of the stage and acknowledged the cheers and applause of the crowd with smiles, waves, and a bow. Then they left the stage. The applause and cries for "encore" were overwhelming and, just for a moment, they considered completely disobeying orders and going on for one more song. However, they all knew what was hanging in the balance and what important factors were going to be determined by their behavior. Yet, at the same time, the cries of the audience could not be ignored.

"One more curtain call," said Cameron, leading the way. The band stepped around the roadies who were hastily disconnecting the cords to the microphones and powering down the monitors. The applause grew louder as Cameron and the others returned to the edge of the stage, holding out their hands in an expansive gesture, blowing kisses to the crowd, and each giving an individual nod and bow to the audience. Looking out over the square, Cameron saw them waving scarves and hats, as if he were a famous politician or a rock star.

Wait a minute, I am a rock star!

Laughing to himself, he reached into his pocket for his extra guitar picks and began tossing them to the crowd. The other members followed suit, except for Evan, who only had his drumsticks. After a few moments, they had tossed out all the picks they had. Casey and Doug were supposed to have been working the crowd earlier, passing out copies of their cassettes in anticipation of not being able to have too many people at the after-party, so Cameron hoped that at least some of the crowd was not disappointed. At last, it was time for them to surrender the stage to the road hands, who were even now hastily removing the equipment.

At the bottom of the stairs, a small group of fans with a different ticket had been allowed to gather for autographs, which the Sons dutifully signed, with genuine smiles, as they posed for photographs and then hurried on to the next person in line. They all enjoyed the flurry of hugs and kisses as they made their way to the roped-off reception area. Once there, Cameron grabbed a bottle of water. Kendrick had them all on limited beverages.

"You'll need your wits about you," she had warned. "No more than two alcoholic drinks each at the show." As they protested this puritanical imposition, she offered them a slight concession.

"If it is any consolation, I will be doing the same thing," she said. "However, once I get to West Berlin, I intend to rectify that, and you're all welcome to as well!"

Wessel introduced Cameron and the others to the guests. Cameron was delighted to see that some of the guests did, in fact, speak English, so he would not be entirely dependent upon the photographer to help him interact with them. Out of the corner of his eye, he saw the girl with the orange hair talking to Casey. They seemed to be having an intense conversation with lots of laughing. Cameron was about to remind the roadie of the pressing schedule they were on, when he realized it wasn't Casey after all. It was Collier, whose features and attire had confused Cameron once more. As if on cue, Casey passed by him wheeling a stack of monitors, which he deposited by the truck, and hurriedly returned to the stage to get the rest.

The girl in the orange hair spotted Casey and waved. A young man who had been standing with her went over and patted Casey on the back. Just then, another enthusiastic fan gave him a hug and began excitedly chattering away in German.

★★★

Hertz made one stop before he left the square. Finding one of the Vopo officers, he had produced his credentials and made arrangements for a patrol car to be waiting for him at the location Alina had provided. She was, indeed, one of their best and most capable undercover operatives, but it never was a good idea to assume that any agent could be responsible for all things. In the event that something would go wrong, Hertz wanted to have the means to respond. He looked at his watch and noted that it was seven fifty-five. The show would be ending by now.

Alina told him that the after-party was limited to thirty minutes. She had asked for extra time, in case she was delayed by the crowd. It had taken him barely ten minutes to get to the location without hindrance. He did not anticipate that it would take her longer, as the number of guests attending the band's reception was limited to only a select few. Even given the possibility of people waiting behind for a chance to meet the Americans, it should not take her longer than that. The Vopo officer he had spoken to informed him that they were under orders to begin dispersing the crowd as soon as the band finished.

"People will not be allowed to remain in the square, Herr Hertz," the officer explained. "Individuals who remain past the allotted time are to be charged with unlawful assembly and disturbing the peace. This announcement will be made throughout the evening."

The ticket holders were to be instructed where to wait, and all other individuals were to be removed from the square. The reception was to end at precisely eight thirty, and all persons were to leave at that time. Given that timetable, Hertz decided that if Alina and Mikhail had not returned to this location by eight fifty, he would respond accordingly.

★★★

Mikhail recognized the roadie who had given him the cassette and eagerly went over to thank him again.

"This is my first time at a concert ever," he gushed to the man, patting him on the back. "This is great and incredible!"

Casey smiled as the boy searched to find the words to express himself. To the roadie's relief, the boy did not go on for long.

"Do you have a cigarette?" the boy asked.

Casey hesitated before answering.

"Are you allowed to smoke?" the man asked. "I don't want to get into any trouble."

"Yes, I can," Mikhail insisted. "There is no trouble."

Reluctantly, Casey shook out a cigarette, which the boy grabbed eagerly. Casey offered him a light and smiled.

"You know, if you want to be on the safe side, you can hide in one of these," he suggested, patting one of the speakers. "I do it all the time when I want to grab a nap and not be found."

"The safe side?" Mikhail asked, confused by the expression. "Hide? I do not know what you mean."

Casey opened the back of the speaker to reveal an inside that could accommodate a person if the person did not mind being a little cramped. He then got inside to demonstrate how he would use it to hide out when he wanted to be alone. As he emerged, he pointed to Mikhail and then to the speaker. The boy understood the hand signals better than he had Casey's question and, with a laugh, climbed inside. Casey carefully closed the speaker but did not latch it. He patted the top of the speaker to let Mikhail know that he was still there and hadn't abandoned the boy.

"What are you doing?" Wessel cried. The photographer, seeing someone being induced into climbing into the speaker, hurried through the crowd.

"Relax," said Casey, laughing, as he opened the speaker again. "The kid just wanted to see the inside of it. He's fine, don't worry!"

"That is reckless and irresponsible," the photographer cried, his voice rising. "Someone could think that you are trying to smuggle someone out of the country that way by locking them inside a speaker!"

Heads turned as Wessel shouted, but Casey could not tell if they understood what he had said or simply were responding to the noise.

"Or they could think that because of your overreaction," snapped Casey as he helped Mikhail onto his feet.

As the boy emerged from the speaker, he dropped the scarf he was wearing. Out of the corner of his eye, the roadie saw several of the guards watching them and noticed Kendrick approaching with a disapproving scowl. Just then, there was a loud clatter that caught everyone's attention. Doug, assisting one of the other roadies, had slipped on something and fell into the table that held the liquor and refreshments the band was offering, sending bottles and glasses scattering amid shouts and screams. Doug quickly jumped up, but from the way he began hopping back toward the stage, it was clear that he had hurt his ankle.

This confusion distracted Kendrick and Wessel long enough for Casey to blend back into the crowd to avoid their attention, but not before secretly picking up the scarf and suggesting to Mikhail he go back to the girl with the orange hair. When Kendrick and Wessel turned back around, everyone was gone.

★★★

Cameron made his way through the small crowd of people gathered in the VIP section that had been established for them. He did not think it was as much fun as some of the other places they had been on the tour, and that was not based solely on his discomfort in being behind the Berlin Wall. The space was both the reception area and the path that the two bands needed to take to load their equipment. It reminded him of movie scenes set in a Middle Eastern bazaar: a teeming mass of people, and lots of shouting and yelling by the various roadies, convinced that a misplaced piece of equipment had been purloined by the other crew. Added to this were lovely ladies competing for attention from one or more of the band members and the company responsible for dismantling the stage. When Cameron considered the Vopo milling about the edges of the scene in their paramilitary uniforms, he felt as if he were in a scene from *Raiders of the Lost Ark*.

Well, that Indiana Jones guy got away from those Germans all right. Maybe I should have Doug try to find me a bullwhip and a fedora?

Cameron stopped and tried to chat with some of the guests; a few of them spoke some English but not as many as in the western part of the country, he noted. Many of them approached him and told him, in practiced English, that they enjoyed the show. Cameron and the others got lots of enthusiastic thumbs-up signs and pats on the back; however, the constant din of activity kept him from getting to interact with people too much. He realized that might have been the intention all along. Despite all of this, the guests were enjoying the wine and beer, and his eyes were dazzled by the flash of bulbs as everyone took or posed for pictures. That was when Cameron realized what had been nagging at him all day.

Where was Elsa?

Cameron began looking for Kendrick to ask her where the

reporter was. At that moment, there was a loud crash behind him, and he turned to see Doug falling backward into the table that held the refreshments. Some of the liquor spilled and splashed, and people jumped backward to avoid the mess, some of them shouting German expletives as they did so. Before Cameron could reach him, Doug was up and hopping over to the stage framework to lean against it.

"Are you all right, man?" Cameron demanded.

Doug nodded. "Yeah, I'm okay," he panted. "I guess I was running too fast and got light-headed and fell. I'm okay."

"What was that hopping?" Cameron pressed. "Did you hurt your ankle?"

"I gave it a little twist," the roadie admitted. "I just didn't want to put any weight on it until I was certain I hadn't sprained it or anything."

"Well, how is it?"

Doug stepped cautiously and was relieved to find his leg didn't give out underneath him.

"Guess I'm not too banged up." He shrugged and glanced over at the mess he had left. "Should I go clean that up?"

"I wouldn't bother with it," Cameron sighed, glancing at his watch. "I'm sure they've got people to take care of that. Besides, it is damn near time to get moving. Do you need me to help get those speakers into the truck?"

"Nah," Doug assured him. "I'm okay, and I can use the dolly to get those things in. But, if you see Casey, tell him I'm going to need him for some other stuff."

"Got it," said Cameron, turning to where he had last seen the other roadie. Casey wasn't there.

★★★

Mikhail hurried over to Alina, who had been watching the young man without his knowledge. She had seen him climb into the large speaker at the man's suggestion and had begun to head over there when the photographer began shouting, in English of all things.

However, a loud noise interrupted the buffoon, and Mikhail had emerged and headed back toward her.

"I saw you with that crew member," she confronted him. "What were you doing over there?"

"He gave me a cigarette and was telling me about where he sometimes sneaks off to smoke if he wants to be alone." Mikhail laughed, offering her what was left of his cigarette. She waved it off.

"Does that hold a person?" she asked. "I mean, comfortably?"

"It didn't seem too comfortable to me." He laughed. "But I could make myself fit in it if I wanted to. I think he can because he is smaller than me."

"That is very interesting," she said thoughtfully and then smiled. "Listen, the party is about to clear out any moment. Head back to the stairs and wait for me there; I have something I need to do before we leave. I won't be long."

"What if I don't want to?" Mikhail protested.

"Then I will have no choice but to rip off your willy and feed it to the pigs," she warned. "Listen, if what I have planned works out, you will have more of an experience than just getting a cheap cassette!"

"Really?" he gasped. "What are you going to do?"

"Never mind." She smiled wickedly. Just do what I said and don't give me a hard time. If this gets ruined, you'll have no one but yourself to blame!"

With a conspiratorial smile, Mikhail hurried off to do as she asked. Alina waited for him to disappear into the crowd and went in search of the man she had been talking to. She did not worry about Mikhail wandering off. She knew she had left enough mystery that he would not let her out of his sight. If she had looked back, she would have seen that she was right.

Mikhail watched her make her way through the crowd. He suspected that she was going to try to find the man he had been talking to, and he was right. Over by the truck, he saw the familiar orange shirt. He watched as she approached him. They talked for a few minutes, and then he saw her lean in to him. The man leaned back, a big smile on his face, and leaned into her. He could hardly believe what he had seen. To Mikhail's amazement, she leaned into the man once more. As she made her way back through the crowd, she turned to the man once more and waved. He returned the gesture and finished loading the truck.

"I thought I told you to wait for me on the stairs," she snapped, finding him still in the crowd.

"I was afraid we'd get separated," he responded, suspecting correctly that she didn't believe him. With an annoyed expression, she grabbed his arm and dragged him through the vacating crowd.

"Did you kiss him?" Mikhail asked, unable to contain his curiosity any longer.

Alina smiled.

"Would you like to keep this evening going a little longer?" she asked.

"Is that what you were talking about earlier?" he demanded.

She smiled and shrugged. "Possibly," she replied. "Or it could be something better. In any event, would you like to have a little more fun or not?"

"Of course," he exclaimed. "Who wouldn't?"

"All right then," she said, grabbing his arm. "Follow me!"

To Mikhail's surprise, they did not go in the direction of the French Church's steps, where they had been. Instead Alina took him in the opposite direction. She stayed close to the French Church, following along the edge of the building so as not to arouse the suspicions of the Vopo. Ducking into the shadows, she removed her orange wig and tossed it on a pile of construction debris.

"What did you do that for?" Mikhail gasped.

Alina smiled at his assumption that it had been her natural hair.

"What I am about to do, I do not want to attract too much attention." She giggled.

Passing around the Konzerthaus, they reconnected with Jagerstrasse where it emerged from the square. They went for two blocks before she paused and checked to make certain they had not been followed and was relieved to discover the street was empty.

"Are you thirsty?" she asked him, removing a hip flask from her jacket pocket.

"Is that booze?" he asked.

"A little something to take the chill off," she said, touching it to her lips. Then she offered it to him. "Here, you try some."

Mikhail eagerly took it from her and, as she suspected he would do, ignored her admonition to drink it slowly. The harsh liquid burned his throat, and he coughed as it went down.

"What is that?"

"That is some American whiskey." She laughed. "I managed to get it from that roadie. I also managed to get something else."

"What?"

"The address of where they are going to be staying," she said and smiled. "Would you like to go to a *real* party?"

"Where?"

"West Berlin." She smiled.

★★★

Cameron found Kendrick supervising the departure of the last of guests and crew. From the looks of it, she was as eager to get out of there as he was.

"Hey, where was Elsa during all this?" he asked. "I figured this would be the big story for her, wouldn't it?"

"One would have thought," Kendrick replied brusquely. "Do you have everything packed and ready to go?"

"Oh yeah, I did that before this party thing got underway," he assured her, wondering at her response.

"What about everyone else?"

"Same thing all the way down the line, boss lady." He smiled, knowing how much she hated that expression.

As if in confirmation of his suspicions regarding her desire to leave, she ignored his remark.

Shit, this is serious.

"All right then," she said. "There is no reason to hang around then. Get everyone rounded up and let's go."

Cameron looked at his watch; it read eight thirty-five.

Twenty-five minutes to reach the border.

Would that be enough? He had no idea. Rather than think about that, Cameron found the others and informed them that it was time to leave.

"Not a moment too soon." Doug yawned.

"Are you all right to drive?" Cameron asked. "What about your foot? Are you sure you're not too tired?"

"My foot is fine." Doug smiled, doing a little jig, but then he limped a bit. "And I'm not that tired, just ready to be on my way."

"Well, I see then; let's not keep you," said Cameron.

The band returned to the vehicles they had arrived in. This was decided upon beforehand, as they had no way of knowing if the border patrol would make note of who had originally been in which one. Wessel's car was led by an unmarked police car once again, and Doug followed in the band truck, trailed by another unmarked car. They pulled onto Jagerstrasse and drove for one block before turning south onto Friedrichstrasse.

"This should be easy," Doug muttered, breaking the uneasy silence of the cab.

"Why?" Cameron asked.

"Because from here it's a straight line to Checkpoint Charlie," Casey explained. "That is the only checkpoint for foreigners and our only route home."

And the perfect spot for something to go wrong.

★★★

Hertz studied the people who straggled past him, listening to their chatter about the show. In his seemingly disinterested eavesdropping, he did not detect anything that would have given him grounds for alarm. There was no reference to any derogatory remarks about the East German government, the Soviet Union, or Communism and no cause for concern. At least not as far as he was concerned. It would be up to other people if concertgoers were to be censured for enjoying the event too much.

Hertz glanced at his watch as the crowd thinned to a few stragglers. It was eight forty-five. Some of the people had been talking about the party, so he knew that they had been there. Therefore, if they were already reaching this point after having left the show, there was no reason that Alina should not be there as well, even if the boy had given her trouble. Hertz suddenly became suspicious.

Ordering the officer into the car, they made their way back to the square, retracing the very route that Alina had instructed him to take. Once there, Hertz's suspicions were confirmed. Save for the cleanup crew removing the last of the staging and sweeping the square clean of any reference to a concert, the square was empty.

"Something must have happened to them," the officer remarked.

Hertz ignored the man's overly obvious statement.

"I need you to contact the border checkpoints," Hertz ordered, giving a description of both Alina and Mikhail. "I will also need your car."

"But, comrade, I am responsible for this vehicle!" cried the officer.

Hertz shook his head. "It is being commandeered for the purposes of state security," he snapped. "There are two checkpoints within immediate proximity, one at Grenzübergangsstelle and one at Invalidenstrasse. If we separate, we can check them both."

"Grenzübergangsstelle is only for foreigners," the officer protested. "Why would they be there?"

"If they were trying to sneak out of the country, who would be transporting vehicles large enough to attempt such an action? The Americans who just left here!" Hertz barked. "You need to check the crossing at Invalidenstrasse; that is the other nearest one."

"But what about the railway crossings?"

"If they try those, there will be the description of them to alert the guards, once you stop arguing and phone it in," Hertz explained. "If we receive word that anyone matching that description has been detained there, we can investigate. In the meantime, we are wasting valuable time arguing!"

With that, he pushed the officer out of the way, got behind the wheel of the car, and hurried off, leaving the dumbfounded officer to watch him go.

★★★

Mikhail stumbled on the curb as he followed Alina down the darkened street. She wished she had not let him have that second drink from the flask.

"It's not much farther," she assured him. "I have a car parked down here."

"Can I have some more of that?" he asked.

"I don't have much," she explained. "You've had three already. Let's save it until we get to the party!"

Once they arrived at the car, Alina tossed her punk vest into a dark alley. Opening the trunk, she removed another jacket, less conspicuous than her vest. She produced a coat and handed it to Mikhail.

"You spilled booze on yourself," she said, wrinkling her nose. "Change into this; it won't attract so much attention."

"But I like this coat," he whined. "It is an American denim jacket!"

"You're everyone's golden boy," she assured him. "You can get another one."

Mikhail was not persuaded and refused to remove it.

"What if I tried to get you one of the band's jackets?" she said and smiled. "I think I might be able to do that."

Mikhail enthusiastically embraced this suggestion and tossed his coat into the alley with hers. The jacket she gave him was a dark windbreaker. Reaching inside one of the pockets, she produced a Greek fisherman's cap and put it on him.

"That makes you look older," she said. "Less likely for the border guards to question why you are out this late."

Mikhail nodded dumbly, with a smile on his face.

"On second thought, here," she said, handing him the flask. "Maybe just one more drink before we go, for luck!"

Mikhail took the flask and toasted her, then took another sip.

"Not all of it," she snapped. "Save some for later!"

Mikhail smiled and wiped the corners of his mouth as he handed it back.

"You've got something on your lip," she said. "No, wait, let me get it!"

Removing a handkerchief from her pocket, she delicately wiped it over Mikhail's upper lip, presumably to wipe something off, but in actuality she was applying a faint hint of makeup to give the appearance of someone who had just shaved his mustache.

"There, that's much better." She smiled, noting how it made him look different. Helping him into the car, she pulled onto the street and headed for the checkpoint at Invalidenstrasse.

★★★

Cameron noticed the lights in the distance. He could not determine if they were the lights of the checkpoint or just the lights of the city. As the light never seemed to change the closer they got, he determined that it was just the vanishing point on the horizon, and that did nothing to make him feel any better. He wanted to be through the checkpoint and on safe ground.

Getting in here wasn't so bad, I guess. Hopefully getting out won't be any worse.

Cameron saw the brake lights of Wessel's car light up, as they had done so many times already when he slowed or stopped at an intersection. This time, however, it was different. They had arrived at the border of East Berlin.

He had seen these border checkpoints so many times in the movies: sparse and bare buildings, surrounded by barbed wire, sniper nests, and sandbags. To see it now seemed almost anticlimactic. There were no sniper nests, or sandbags; however, the buildings were still squat and spare. At a designated spot, the car came to a halt. However, Cameron noticed the unmarked cars turn around and drive off into the night.

Is that good or bad?

"What do I do?" Doug asked.

"Stop the truck and don't do anything until you are told," Cameron advised him.

"Don't shut it off though," Casey warned. "They might want you to move it."

Doug put the truck in neutral and applied the parking break. They could see the others getting out of the car and presenting the guard with their travel papers and passports. To Cameron's alarm, all of them were ordered to stand by the building. Another security guard motioned for Cameron and the occupants of the truck to get out of the vehicle.

When all of them were together, the guards began asking them questions in German, and Wessel translated them into English.

"What was the purpose of your visit?"

"Did you stay in any establishment not approved by the GDR?"

"Are you in possession of any contraband or anything that you need to declare?"

At the guard's instructions, the trunk of the car was opened and the contents removed. As before, the guitar cases were opened and Cameron once again feared that the instruments would be damaged. However, this time they were not removed from their cases, and Cameron began to relax. He checked his watch and saw that it was nearly nine o'clock.

Just made it.

"You need to exchange your currency," Wessel told them. "No East German marks are permitted to leave the country."

They lined up at the counter and one by one handed over their money. That was when the trouble began. The guard noted the amounts on their receipts and noted the amounts they were exchanging and became angry.

"What is the issue?" Kendrick demanded.

Wessel shrugged his shoulders and gave his typical sheepish response.

"You were supposed to spend a certain amount of money in the GDR, and you didn't spend any," he explained. "They are not happy about that, not at all!"

"What were we supposed to do?" Kendrick wanted to know. "We didn't have the opportunity to go anywhere or do anything. How were we supposed to spend any money?"

"I'm just telling you what the rules are," he pleaded. "I have no control over this situation."

"Well then, what do they propose to do about it?" she wondered.

"They will be keeping what you were supposed to have spent," he muttered.

"What the hell, man?" Rich shouted. "How can they do that?"

"They can do whatever they want," Kendrick warned. "It is their ball field."

"Besides, it isn't like it's worth anything, anyhow," whispered Casey.

This attracted the attention of the guards, who erupted into a new stream of shouting.

"They want no talking while in line," Wessel said, motioning for everyone to keep quiet.

Cameron's anxiety returned. He looked at each of his bandmates and tried to go back to the feeling they'd had at the end of the show, that feeling of accomplishment and optimism that made everything so worthwhile. However, it was hard. He saw the same concern and frustration in their faces that he felt. He, too, was afraid that there would be some type of issue that might keep them there. To add to his anxiety, he could see out the window to the street and knew that just a few feet away was safety from all of this.

So near, yet so far was the cliché that kept repeating itself in his mind.

The guard at the counter angrily counted out the few Deutsche marks they were permitted to keep. When Cameron received his, he realized that he would be lucky if he could buy a beer with it.

Once they had exchanged their currency, they were directed to go back outside. As they were doing so, Cameron heard the phone ring. They were assembled outside when the guards who had accompanied them were called back inside.

While he waited, Cameron looked off in the distance and saw the border crossing that he had always heard referred to as Checkpoint Charlie. Next to it was a large white sign with black block letters telling all those who approached that they were coming to the American sector. It also reminded military personnel that carrying weapons while off duty was prohibited, and urged people to obey the traffic laws. These admonitions were written not only in English but also in French, German, and Russian. Cameron could see the American flag gently waving in the slight breeze and smiled at the comfort he took from that little flash of red, white, and blue.

As he was standing along the side of the building, a car suddenly came to an abrupt halt. Cameron recognized it as a police car, but the man who emerged from the driver's side did not appear to be a policeman. Or, if he were, he was a plainclothesman. The stranger rushed into the building, giving the assembled crew a dirty look as he passed them. Angry words were exchanged, but Cameron, unable to speak the language, could not understand what they were saying. He was about to ask Wessel when he noticed the photographer become very nervous.

Oh shit, this can't be good.

The young man and the guards came out of the building, and Cameron noticed that they all deferred to the newly arrived individual. They shouted for Wessel to come and talk with them and gave him a flurry of instructions, to which he tried to respond but was constantly interrupted. The younger man's demeanor was plainly menacing, and Cameron suspected that one German might treat another differently from the way they would treat a foreign national. Wessel must have come to the same realization because he suddenly began pleading with them, which made the younger man disgusted. He finally barked an order to Wessel and pointed to the others, to which the photographer responded with a submissive nod.

"I have bad news," he explained. "Some people have been reported missing."

"What does that have to do with us?" Kendrick demanded.

"They were last seen with the band at the concert," Wessel explained. "They think you have them."

★★★

Alina made her way along the darkened streets. She was careful to hurry but not so much as to draw attention to herself. That was the last thing she wanted. She did not have a watch but suspected that, by now, Hertz would have realized she was not returning and would have sounded an alarm. Her plan would be risky enough without have to deal with a traffic stop.

She reached into her jacket pocket and withdrew the two passports and press credentials she had secreted there earlier. Both appeared to have been issued by the West German government, though both were forged. They listed her as Margaret Gehlen and him as Mikhail Dobrynin, each assigned as press liaisons for the East German Ministry of Culture's international exchange program. Such a legend would explain their departure at such a late hour from East Berlin, as they were required to be present at the concert put on by the ministry.

A photograph of Mikhail in a Russian newspaper had provided them the opportunity to locate someone of a similar build to pose for a passport photo. To help ensure that the deception would be successful, the subject had worn a small mustache when the photo was taken. By smudging makeup on Mikhail's lip, it was hoped that it would give the impression that he had just shaved it off. Under the harsh light of day, there would be no mistaking that it was makeup. However, under the partial glow of the streetlights, aided by the fisherman's cap, it had a greater possibility of success.

After helping Mikhail into the car, Alina had removed the dark plaid skirt she had worn to conceal the plain black one she sported now. Mikhail was enough under the influence of the drugged alcohol that he had not noticed the change, which hopefully meant he would not mention it later. Occasionally, Alina had noticed lights in her rearview mirror and would make a turn down a side street to see if she were being followed. She was not. Realistically, she doubted that it would be possible for her to be followed, as there could not be any description of the car she was driving. However, tonight was no time to take chances.

"Give me the flask," Mikhail slurred.

"What?"

"Give me the flask," he repeated. "I want some more."

"You can't drink it now," she insisted. "We'll be at the border crossing in a minute, and that will cause trouble."

"I don't care," the boy shouted. "I want a drink! I want it now!"

"Will it keep you quiet?" she snapped.

"I can't make any noise if I drink." He laughed.

Reluctantly, Alina handed him the flask. Permitting him to imbibe too much was a dangerous risk. What would he say, or do, under the influence? He was trouble enough when he was sober. Eliminating his inhibitions was asking for serious trouble, but it had been a calculated risk she decided to take to get him across the border. However, it was clear that if his demands were not met, he would make trouble and potentially ruin everything. Mikhail giggled as he tipped the flask. She was convinced that he simply liked the thought of holding it, as what little alcohol had been in it was no doubt long consumed.

"Be sure to put that away when we come to the border," she admonished him, to which he simply laughed louder.

"Are we really going to a party?" he asked.

"What? You don't believe me?"

"What kind of a party?" he asked, ignoring her question.

Alina was repelled by his narcissism, and also alarmed. What would this little idiot do when they reached the border?

"I'm not entirely certain," she told him. "However, I'm sure it will be more fun than back at the square."

"Will they have more stuff to drink?" he whispered.

"I think you've had enough for right now," she warned, to which he became sulky and resentful.

"You're as bad as Hertz," he snapped. "You never let me do what I want!"

"I didn't say you couldn't," she shouted. "I simply said I think you've had enough for right now. Once we get to where we're going, I don't care what you do!"

"Seriously?" he asked suspiciously, ignoring the vocalized rejection in favor of focusing on his own pleasure.

"Trust me," she seethed. "I never meant anything more in my life. Now put that flask in your pocket and let me do all the talking!"

She slowed the car as they approached the checkpoint and rolled down her window. She handed over the credentials that they had and waited as the guard inspected them. Mikhail, too, was quiet, but the subdued giggling made her nervous.

"Your entry was stamped at the Chausseestrasse crossing," the guard informed her. "Why are you here then?"

"We were reporting on the concert arranged by the ministry," she explained. "My colleague here had too much to drink, and I wanted to get him back to our hotel as soon as possible."

"So why cross here?" the guard demanded. "You should have gone back to the other checkpoint!"

"We crossed there earlier because we had business in that part of the city," she explained as Mikhail began to giggle louder. "Our hotel is not far from here. We're assigned to travel with the band while they are in Berlin."

Mikhail's giggling became even louder, and he started to pound on the dashboard.

"Enough with this," he shouted. "We need to get going; we'll miss the party!"

The guard looked from the boy to Alina, with a disapproving look on his face. At that moment, a police car pulled up behind them. The driver, a Vopo officer, exited his car and approached theirs, shining a flashlight inside to examine who was there.

"Please step out of the vehicle," he growled.

Alina gave Mikhail a warning look and repeated the guard's instructions.

"I want to get going," he protested angrily. "I don't want to get out of the damned car!"

"If you want to get to the party, then do as you're told," she snapped. "You don't have an option."

She got out of the car and watched as Mikhail struggled to stand up and then leaned unsteadily against the car. She went to help him, but the guard held up his hand, ordering her to stay where she was. Her heart beat faster as Mikhail crossed his arms and began mumbling.

The two guards conferred with one another, but she could not hear what they said, though they each looked over at her quite often. The border guard handed the police officer the passport and letter that she had produced, pointing out the suspicious entry visa stamp. They huddled together, examining everything once more. She became anxious as their whisperings and body language became more animated. Finally, the police officer approached her, holding her documents.

"We've had reports of two people who might be attempting to cross the border," the man said, quietly studying their credentials again. "They are a young man and a young woman. Isn't it a coincidence that a young man and a young woman suddenly show up here not fifteen minutes after the border guards received that call?"

"I told them why we're here," she insisted. "We're press liaisons for the Ministry of Culture, assigned to follow the Americans as part of the cultural exchange. We're here heading back to the hotel we're assigned to. You have not only my credentials but also a letter of reference from the ministry. Call that number if you don't believe me!"

"We both know that there is no one at the ministry at this hour," the guard snapped. He then turned to the police officer. "What were the descriptions of the people we were to be on the lookout for?"

The second guard approached and studied the two young people carefully.

"Neither of them match the description," he said, and Alina caught the note of disappointment in his voice. "And your report said nothing about a car. The report said they were on foot. If that's the case, they won't show up here; it's too far. They'll hit the railway stations and go by rail. Those locations are the ones nearer to the Konzerthaus."

The first guard was hardly pleased with what his friend had told him but realized that he was probably right. He took the passports into the guardhouse to be stamped. Just then Mikhail fumbled in his coat and dropped a pack of Marlboros on the ground.

"Damn it," the boy muttered, bending over in a clumsy attempt to retrieve them before the guard saw them, but it was too late.

"What do we have here?" The guard reached out and grabbed them.

"You can't have them," Mikhail shouted. "They gave them to me!"

With a sadistic smile, the guard held the pack out of Mikhail's reach. The commotion attracted the attention of the other guards. Alina realized that this was endangering their chances to get across the border.

"Let the guard have them," Alina told the boy. "You can get more later."

Mikhail looked at her, and she could tell he was suspicious.

"Just let him have them," she insisted. "It's not worth the trouble."

Reluctantly, Mikhail stopped struggling. With a triumphant smile, the guard put them in his own pocket. He muttered some remark that Alina did not hear, but the boy did. Mikhail let out a cry of rage and lunged at the guard, but he stumbled over his own feet and landed on his face, scratching his nose and cheek.

"That's enough!" cried Alina. She helped him up and began to put him back in the car.

"Get him out of here," the guard snapped, handing over the passports and motioning for the barrier to be raised.

Without further remark, Alina shut Mikhail's door and returned to her side of the car, retrieving their papers. As she drove through the checkpoint, Mikhail began to sob.

"I'm bleeding," he cried, touching his abrasions with his hands and showing her the blood on his fingers.

"Be grateful that is all that happened," she sighed as they approached the opposite checkpoint. Alina could see a guard waiting for them in the spotlight. Suddenly, two other men appeared next to him. They were wearing suits, not uniforms. Her breath caught as she stopped the car in the no-man's-land between the two points.

"Mikhail, I want you to listen to me," she insisted, turning to him. "I have to tell you something, and it is very important. Do you understand me?"

"What?" Mikhail sobbed, his nose running.

Alina struggled with how she could word what she was about to say because at this very moment she realized there was no option left to her if she was to successfully carry out this assignment. There was no going back for her. She knew that the promise of a party and a chance to rebel against the people who were watching him was enough to get him to come with her across the border, but would that be sufficient inducement to get him to go along with the rest? Looking in the rearview mirror, she saw the East German guards gathering at the barrier and knew that it was still possible for them to realize their mistake and shoot. She began to shake as she waited for the boy's answer. The wrong answer could ruin everything.

"Mikhail, I am never going back there again. I am going to stay in the West."

Mikhail nodded in understanding but said nothing. The euphoria brought on by his excitement had vanished, along with his self-induced intoxication. Taking its place was a horrified expression as the realization that, for all intents and purposes, his life as he had known it was over. Alina continued moving toward the checkpoint.

"You lied to me!" he suddenly cried. "You said we were going to a party! You never said anything about defecting. What will I do now?" He began to sob.

"I didn't mean to lie," she said. "That is all I can tell you now."

"Why?"

"Because that is all I know," she said as she rolled down her window.

When she arrived at the opposite barrier, the young solider, accompanied by a man in a suit, approached her.

"My name is Margaret Engels," she said. "I am an agent with the Ministry for State Security, and I am requesting political asylum."

"Wonderful," the man said, smiling warmly. "We've been expecting you." His British accent relieved a great deal of tension as he motioned for the barrier to be raised and for her to move forward.

"What about me?" demanded Mikhail, his voice breaking as he struggled with his limited English.

"Don't worry, son," the man said and smiled. "We've been expecting you, as well."

★★★

Cameron could not believe what he was hearing. As he repeated it to himself, it became even more unbelievable.

"Do they seriously think we're helping someone escape from this fucking country?" he demanded.

Wessel nodded dumbly. "I'm afraid so," the photographer muttered.

Cameron was infuriated at Wessel's disinterested tone. "They want to inspect the vehicles, the luggage, everything," he informed him.

"Everything?" the musician exclaimed, but he knew that protests would be useless.

As they were speaking, the guards from the station, under the direction of the man who had just arrived, were searching under the band truck with flashlights and barking orders, in German, to Doug and Casey. Cameron knew that his roadie could become very frustrated very easily and feared that a flare-up of Doug's temper could land him, if not all of them, in an East German jail. Casey was trying to explain things to the German guard but with little success. Looking about, Cameron noticed Kendrick engaged in a serious conversation with the young man, who apparently spoke English, and knew that she was unaware of the danger that was brewing behind her.

"You better get over there and help Doug and Casey," Cameron grumbled to Wessel. "It could get ugly."

"What the hell is going on?" demanded Rich.

"It appears we are suspected of helping someone try to slip out of the country," he grimaced. "So everything and everyone get searched."

"You've got to be shitting me," the bass player gasped.

Cameron shook his head and pointed to the band truck. The back door was open, and the roadies were removing all of the equipment, one piece at a time. In an obscene mockery of the roadie's load-in procedure, Casey removed the equipment as Doug brought it to the back of the truck. Microphone stands and cases holding cables and power cords were all emptied and searched under the watchful eye of the newly arrived individual. Casey was trying to put everything back into the cases while the guards barked orders at him. As Wessel tried to translate the guards' orders to Doug, Casey went to get something out of the front of the truck.

"Why don't I go over to see if I can give them a hand?" Collier suggested.

Before anyone could say anything, he had taken Casey's place and was unloading the equipment that Doug had brought to the back of the truck.

As Cameron watched, it seemed as if Wessel and the man were in a bit more of an intense conversation than if Wessel were simply translating for them. Kendrick came and stood beside Cameron and watched this display with a sudden interest.

"Doug, they want to see that big speaker, the one with the stickers on it," Wessel told him. "You need to bring it down for them to inspect."

"We're bringing everything down," Doug informed him. "I'll get that when I clear the rest of this stuff out of the way."

"No, they want to see it now," Wessel insisted. "They want to see it right now!"

"Well, they are just going to have to wait," Doug snapped. "There's too much shit in the way for me to get it out, so they're going to have to wait till I move some!"

"What seems to be the problem?" asked Cameron as he hurried over to the truck. The guards, seeing his rapid movement, held up their hands and one of them pointed a gun at him.

"Oh, you're going to need to stand over there," Wessel said, apologetically. "They want to keep this restricted to just the road crew."

Cameron held up his hands and slowly walked back, letting them carefully observe him and not pointing out that Collier was there as well. As he was moving back, Cameron noticed Doug light a cigarette and lean against the large speaker they wanted to see. When Cameron had returned to where the others stood against the building, the guards turned their attention back to the truck. Noticing that Doug was no longer bringing stuff to the back, they became agitated and started shouting at him again.

"What do you want me to do now?" Doug asked.

"Doug, you need to bring that down here so they can inspect it," Wessel shouted, impatiently. "You need to do it right now!"

"If they want to inspect it right *now*, they can get in *here* and do it," Doug snapped. "I can't get it around this stuff!"

Wessel translated Doug's response to the man, who then began barking more orders to the guards. One of them returned to the guardhouse, while Casey and Collier climbed into the back of the truck and started moving things around to accommodate Doug and the heavier equipment. Doug, for his part, continued to lean against the speaker, smoking a cigarette. Just then, one of the guards emerged from the guardhouse, carrying a handheld device that Cameron recognized as something used to detect body heat. The guard climbed into the back of the band truck and gestured for Doug to step out of the way.

The roadie tossed up his hands, as if in surrender, and dropped his cigarette.

"Doug, he wants you to step away," Wessel assured him.

"In case you hadn't noticed, I figured that out," Doug replied, backing into the far corner.

Wessel then began speaking to the guard in German, motioning to the large speaker that Doug had been leaning against. The guard moved the heat sensor over it and shouted something. The other man became angry and started shouting and pointing from Doug to the speaker.

"He wants you to open it up," Wessel said triumphantly. "You had better do what he says, too."

Muttering under his breath, Doug removed the strap that held the old speaker together and pulled off the back panel to reveal the empty interior. From where Cameron stood, all that was visible was the speaker's silver foil lining. The guard spun around and shouted at Wessel, and then pointed to the empty speaker. Wessel, his eyes wide, shrugged his shoulders apologetically and shouted replies. Then he began shouting at Doug.

"How can that be empty?" Wessel demanded. "I saw Casey putting someone in it at the show, and it registered the presence of body heat."

"Maybe it registered body heat because I was *leaning* on it while waiting for you guys to figure out what you wanted me to do," Doug barked. "And also because I dropped my cigarette next to it. As far as seeing Casey put someone in here, maybe you are full of shit and didn't see any such thing."

The guard waited for the translation of Doug's response and then began shouting at Wessel again. Casey, in the meantime, began to put the equipment on the ground back into the truck. To Cameron's amazement, this went unnoticed by Wessel and the guards. Collier shouted something to Doug that Cameron did not understand, but Doug obviously did, as he nodded and replaced the panel. The guard was too busy watching Wessel and the other man shouting at each other to notice that Doug had slid the speaker back into place and removed the cloth that covered the second speaker. The guard turned around and saw the speaker and started shouting again, gesturing angrily at Doug.

"They didn't want you to replace it," Wessel explained. "They want to look at the inside closely. You need to reopen it."

Doug gave a loud sigh and pulled the second speaker out of the corner. He removed the back panel just as he had done for the first, revealing that this, too, was covered in silver foil and was totally empty. The young man jumped into the truck and shone his flashlight over it and around the inside. He knelt down and began rapping against the sides; then he climbed down and confronted Wessel, clearly angry. The photographer stepped backward, trying to avoid the man, and began pointing wildly at Casey and Collier. To Cameron, it looked like he was trying to make an excuse for a mistake. Wessel spun around and confronted Collier.

"I saw you put someone in that speaker," Wessel shouted. "I saw you do it at the concert. It was a young man!"

"You didn't see me, man," Collier insisted. "I was on stage the entire time; you must have seen Casey!"

Dumbfounded, Wessel looked at the musician and realized he had confused him with the roadie. The man, standing behind Wessel, noticed the change in the photographer and said something in German. Once more, Wessel looked as if he were apologizing, and to Cameron the photographer's behavior was looking more and more suspicious.

"Casey, did you or did you not put someone inside that speaker?" demanded Wessel. Casey shook his head.

"No, man, that would have been stupid," Casey explained. "I was showing some kid at the show where I sneak off for a private smoke break, but that was it. He didn't like my hiding place because it was too uncomfortable."

"What did he look like?" Wessel insisted.

Cameron smiled to himself as Casey gave a generic description of someone who could have been the young man in question, Charlie Chaplin, or a million other people.

"Did he speak Russian or German?" Wessel demanded.

"Oh, man, I'm not sure," said Casey, a look of deep concentration on his face. "Neither, come to think of it. He spoke a little bit of rough English and we talked that way."

Wessel hesitated to respond as the other man asked questions for the photographer to translate.

"Did the kid have an accent of any kind?" Wessel asked.

"Oh, come on," Casey shouted. "All of you bastards have accents!"

Cameron smiled, as Wessel seemed to be on the verge of tears. The other man was not happy about Casey's response and began gesturing with his arm to indicate everyone there. Once more, Wessel gave a weak, submissive nod and came over to talk to them.

"Someone very important is missing," he explained. "That man is convinced that the person I saw was the one he was looking for, and he thinks you are hiding him."

"They have searched the entire truck and all of our equipment," Kendrick protested. "They didn't find anything, they have no reason to detain us, and I demand that they let us go immediately. We are guests of the East German government, and I will file a complaint with our embassy if we are delayed for any reason!"

"You might not want to antagonize him," the photographer whispered. "He is a very important person, and it might not go so well."

"Is he with Chairman Honecker's office?" Kendrick demanded, unimpressed by Wessel's compliance with the situation. "Because that is the aegis we are operating under, and that is the office that will be notified of any complications."

"Please," Wessel begged, "just let them look a little more; that will satisfy them."

"They've looked over every inch of that truck, even under it," Kendrick pointed out. "The only place they haven't searched is your car. Perhaps they should look there?"

Wessel became clearly agitated by this.

"There is no reason to search my car," he insisted, emphatically shaking his head. "I had nothing to do with this."

"Do with what?" Kendrick demanded. "No one has done anything!"

The plainclothesman, who had been watching this exchange, whispered something in the photographer's ear and pointed to the car. Wessel meekly obeyed the command and went to unlock the trunk. Casey had been standing by the car, and when the photographer opened the trunk, he began removing the luggage and the guitar cases, setting them on the ground. The plainclothesman searched the trunk with his flashlight while two of the other guards searched inside the car. The plainclothesman stood up, holding a scarf. He balled it up into his fist and began shaking it at Wessel, who by now was fully panicked. The two exchanged words in German, and Wessel gestured wildly. Cameron was not certain what was being said but ascertained by the photographer's behavior that he was begging.

"This isn't looking good," Cameron whispered to Kendrick.

"Not for him anyway," she conceded.

"What about us?" he asked, to which Kendrick merely shrugged.

Cameron looked back to Checkpoint Charlie. He remembered one of his uncles telling about when he was stationed in Berlin during the early sixties. He had been in one of the armored personnel carriers during the standoff with Russian tanks.

He told me the West Berliners showed their support of the Americans by putting bottles of booze on their tanks. He remembered downing a whole bottle of cognac and not getting drunk; that's how scared he was. Man, I could go for some cognac myself, right now!

"I demand to contact the United States Embassy," Kendrick shouted, losing all patience. "We are American citizens, guests of your government, and have done nothing wrong. We are being illegally prevented from leaving this country, and I will not stand for it any longer!"

Cameron saw the young man's jaw clench, but he soon regained his composure and gave a wicked smile. He said something to Wessel, poking him in the chest. Wessel nodded and turned to the others.

"You don't understand," he pleaded. "This is serious. They found evidence of a missing person in your vehicles ..."

"Correction," said Kendrick. "They found evidence in *your* vehicle! The only thing that belongs to us is the band truck, and that has no evidence that anyone was in it; therefore, they have no grounds on which to detain us any longer."

"But … but … I'm working for you," Wessel insisted. "Therefore, by extension, my vehicle is yours as well."

"Is it registered in our name?" Kendrick pressed. "No, it is in yours, and yours alone."

"But I saw him climb into the speaker," the photographer insisted. "He was in the band truck!"

"Did you find anyone there?" Cameron asked. "No, you didn't! Apparently, that scarf is something of interest to them, and it was found with you! I think you're the one who has to worry."

The other man had been standing behind Wessel and had said nothing up to this point, but he addressed Kendrick.

"My apologies, madam," he said. "You are correct that I cannot detain you here, and I will not do so any longer."

"Wow, you speak pretty good English," muttered Cameron.

"Danke schön," he said and smiled. Then he gave orders to the guards to open the barrier. Without hesitating, they loaded their belongings and got into their vehicles.

"I'd love to be a fly on the wall in that car," muttered Doug.

"If I know her, you won't need to be," Cameron said. "The conversation will still be going on when we get out!"

As they approached the American side, Cameron noticed Eberhard standing in the guardhouse. For the first time since arriving at the checkpoint, he began to relax. The guard came out and motioned for them to park their vehicles. As they did so, Eberhard approached them.

"Good evening," he said pleasantly. "We have transportation to take you to your next destination. I'm afraid time is of the essence."

"Where are we going?" Wessel asked him.

In response, Eberhard removed a pistol from his coat.

"You are not going with them," he explained. "You are under

arrest for betraying the security of the state as well as for the murders of Hagan Krug and Elsa Scholl."

"He killed Elsa?" gasped Cameron.

"In her hotel in Hannover," Eberhard replied. "When she was going through the photos of the after-parties that she had not attended, she noticed some of Wessel's personal guests were known Stasi agents. At first, she put it down to mere coincidence. But in her reports she told us that they only appeared to be present when she wasn't. She stole the photos to send to us. Wessel apparently discovered that and killed her in an attempt to prevent her from doing so. However, he was too late."

"Oh, man, I would hate to be you." Casey smiled at the photographer. "You burned your bridges with the West Germans, and now the East Germans think you betrayed them, thanks to a well-placed scarf, so you have no value to them either. You are up shit creek, my friend."

"Yeah, what was that business with the scarf?" Cameron asked.

"They told us the Russian kid would be at the concert," Casey explained. "Once they found that out, the West Germans had a double agent working in the East make contact with him and make certain he got a ticket to the party. During the concert, he wandered backstage to check things out, and I showed him the big speakers. Doug and I had lined them with heat-reflective materials in case we did need to hide someone in them. It would have prevented their body heat from registering. That was why we had two speakers: in case we had to hide him in one, we could use the other as a decoy. However, if we did that, there would be accusations of kidnapping that would be hard to disprove. So she had a plan. We had Wessel see the kid get into one of the speakers as a diversion."

"I am certain this is fascinating, but you need to be going," Eberhard insisted. "That van will take you where you need to go. Never mind your things—just hurry!"

"Like hell," snapped Doug. Hurrying to the back of the truck, he slid open the door sufficiently for him to remove the guitar cases. "These things go with us!"

Once a roadie, always a roadie. Cameron smiled.

They quickly boarded the waiting van and sped off into the night.

"Okay, back to what we were discussing," Cameron said to Casey. "Why did you do that stuff to the speakers?"

"It was part of a really elaborate shell game." Casey smiled. "You know, like the ones I played at the hotels? To see if you could guess where the marble was? Well, the way I kept you from noticing things was to wiggle my fingers and snap my knuckles, right? That was what we did here. Doug was the first part; the speakers were the second."

"What did Doug have to do with this?"

"I was bait, remember?" Doug said.

Cameron noticed the lack of anger in his voice, but there was still the resentment. "That whole dinner with Stoughton was him laying out his plan. My connection with Gus and the *Mustang* was supposed to attract their attention, just like calling Kendall 'Ed Collier'."

"By doing that, we hoped that the East Germans would pay all sorts of attention to you guys and not notice anything else," Casey said. "The fact that Doug had a wrestling connection with Montreal was key. That was where the KGB agent who tried to recruit Doug and Kalbe would go and report. We were right, and that was where they made their mistake and tipped Doug off. When Doug became suspicious of Wessel, we checked him out and noticed some suspicious activity that revealed him to be a double agent."

"You went along with this?" Cameron asked Doug, clearly resentful of his friend's cooperative attitude. "You would always get super pissed at us in the past for wondering about that! Now it wasn't an issue?"

"When you guys did it, I always had to prove my innocence," Doug calmly reminded him. "Stoughton didn't think twice about me being innocent and let me decide if I wanted to do it or not. I was free to walk away any time before we boarded the plane to come here, no questions asked. When a person is appreciated, they are willing to go the distance."

"So, to make certain we would be able to keep tabs on the

East Germans and legally be able to handle any action that might be needed, they brought me in." Casey laughed. "Did you think my resemblance to Kendall was just a coincidence? It was designed to see if we could keep people off guard. In case we needed to extricate the target, we could use one of us as a decoy while the other performed the mission. We found out that it had the added benefit of confusing Wessel because, on more than one occasion, he would ask me questions that he intended for Kendall, whom he knew as Collier."

"It seems that whoever gave me the name Collier did it deliberately," Kendall explained. "That was the name of a Soviet agent who was trying to defect in Seattle, where I guess you guys were working at the time."

"I'd really prefer not talking about that," Cameron muttered, his hand aching. He flexed it nervously as Kendall resumed his explanation.

"We were certain that the Soviets only knew that the real Collier was dead," Kendall continued. "We don't suspect they knew he was trying to turn on them. Wessel would try to get me to talk about Seattle and how long I had known you guys, but he always ended up revealing more about their plans by the questions he asked."

"No shit." Cameron whistled. "So what happened with the target?"

"We have no idea," Kendrick confided.

★★★

The first gunman looked at his watch and noticed that it was nine twenty-five. They had five minutes before they decided whether or not Gagarin would remain alive. Just then, an announcement came over the intercom.

"The package has been received," the voice said.

"What does that mean?" Gagarin asked.

"It means we don't shoot you—yet," the gunman replied.

★★★

The van arrived at Templehof Airport through a secured gate that bypassed the terminal. There, a jet was waiting for them. As they emerged from the van, another car that had been waiting on the tarmac opened its doors. Two men in suits emerged, accompanying a rather subdued young man. They approached Kendrick, introduced themselves, and waited while Kendrick made the introductions to the band.

"Guys, permit me to introduce Christopher Harrington and Mark Clarkson. They are our British counterparts. Gentlemen, I would like you to meet Special Agents Cameron Walsh and Evan Dixon, Major John Kendall, Special Agent Ryan Casey, Rich Webster, and Doug Courtland. I will permit you to introduce your guest."

"Good evening, gentlemen," Harrington smiled. "I will be delighted to make the introductions, but we will have to do it on the plane. I'm afraid we are a bit pressed for time. If you will follow me, please."

Before anyone could say anything, Kendrick and the British agents hurried toward the plane, with the band following after them.

"You take these; I'll carry the rest," Doug said to Casey.

"Hey, man, this gig is over," Casey said and laughed, brushing off Doug's remark. The roadie glared at him and shoved the guitar cases into him.

"Until we get to wherever we are going, you are still a roadie and I am still your boss," Doug snarled. "Now do your job, or I'll demonstrate some of those wrestling moves I've told you about!"

"I'd do as he says, if I were you." Evan laughed, hurrying past them. "He means it!"

With a stunned expression, Casey did as he was told and hurried to catch up with the others. Once on board, Cameron watched as he helped Doug secure them in the first-class cabin and went to find a seat. There were many to choose from, as they were the only passengers on board. Even the flight crew was minimal. That was

391

when Cameron got a good look at the young man. He watched everything from his seat, with both interest and concern.

Looks as scared as a rabbit.

"Gentlemen, if you will please buckle in, we must be on our way," Harrington told them. As he was speaking, the door was secured and the stairs wheeled away. The stewardess rapped on the door to the cockpit and barely had time to sit down before the plane began moving.

Shit, they are in a hurry!

The entire plane was silent, save for the occasional whisper among some of the guys. It was not until they were airborne and the pilot informed them they were able to move about the cabin that anyone spoke.

"Gentlemen," said Harrington, standing up so he could be seen, "I would like to introduce you to Mikhail Nikolaevich Sechenov. He is the son of the man you have heard referred to as Gagarin. We have explained to him that his father wishes to work for our side now but did not want to cross the Iron Curtain without him. He has agreed to accompany us and to be reunited with his father. I understand from my conversations with him that he was present at your performance this evening. Perhaps that might be a topic of conversation with him, to help put him at ease."

Casey was the first to get up to talk with him, and Cameron thought that was the wise choice, as they did have a previous bond.

Well, if you can call trying to stuff him in a speaker a "bond."

The boy was reluctant to talk at first but gradually opened up as the trip progressed. Cameron wasn't certain if it was the language barrier or the fact that the boy was obviously scared.

Probably both, I bet.

Gradually, however, the boy did begin responding to them. He became very interested, and much more animated, when he learned that Doug and Kendall had been professional wrestlers. This was no doubt aided by the fact that they had convinced him they were secretly putting Jack Daniels in his Coke when they would go to the galley for drinks. Mikhail had missed the quick wink they gave to

McIntyre when they said it to him, indicating they were doing no such thing.

★★★

Gagarin was startled by the movement of the plane and the announcement that came over the intercom.

"The package is en route."

"What does that mean?" Gagarin asked.

"It means you live." The gunman smiled, putting his pistol away.

★★★

When Cameron asked where they were going, the only responses he received were smiles. Judging from the way they were traveling, he suspected they were heading west. They were obviously not staying in Germany, and the plane was not that big, so he was certain they were not going to America.

Okay, that leaves only the rest of western Europe.

However, the atmosphere was more relaxed than he expected it would be, and even McIntyre joined in the laughter as Doug and Kendall attempted to demonstrate wrestling holds to Mikhail as they regaled him with wrestling stories. Finally, they were told to return to their seats and prepare for landing. As they did so, Cameron looked out the window and noticed the lit-up face of Big Ben.

London. I should have known.

The plane touched down and taxied along the runway, past the terminal, and to an isolated spot. There, they remained.

"We are awaiting the arrival of the boy's father," Harrington explained. "I suspect that there are already accusations of kidnapping being leveled against us, which will be mitigated by reuniting the family as quickly as possible. I have no idea how long the wait will be for the other plane, unfortunately. They were supposed to have left when we did and had roughly the same distance to travel. However, as you may be aware, there are always delays. You are free to move about the cabin until then, if you wish."

Before they could do that, however, another plane taxied into sight. Soon Cameron saw two different crews moving two different stairways to the respective planes.

"Is there any particular order to how we get off?" he asked as the hatchway was opened.

"I will defer that question to our British hosts." McIntyre smiled at Harrington.

"We will accompany young Mr. Sechenov off before the rest of you and reunite him with his father," Harrington said. "After that, whatever order you decide upon is your own business, but I certainly hope our American cousins remember—ladies first."

They all waited as the British agents, and the boy, exited the plane. For courtesy's sake, they chose to wait a few minutes for father and son to have some type of reunion. McIntyre was watching from the window for the signal from Harrington that it was suitable for them to leave.

"Okay, boys," she said. "Let's go home!"

As they descended the stairs, Cameron looked over and saw a man wearing mechanic's overalls standing with Harrington and the others. He thought that it was odd for a mechanic to be there and then realized it must have been a disguise used by the KGB agent. As each one reached the bottom of the stairs, they were called over to meet the former Soviet agent so he could thank them personally for helping reunite him with his son. Cameron, being the last off the plane, was the last in line. In the odd lighting, it was hard for him to get a good look at the man, though he thought there was something familiar about him. However, he brushed that idea off as ridiculous.

He probably just reminds me of someone I know.

However, the feeling didn't leave him as he got closer. When it came time for him to shake the man's hand, the feeling was even stronger. McIntyre was about to make the introductions when the man interrupted her.

"Mr. Walsh," he exclaimed with a smile that chilled Cameron with sudden recognition. "You have hardly changed a bit since I last saw you in Seattle! How is your hand?"